GOLDEN
WITCHBREED

GOLDEN WITCHBREED

MARY GENTLE

WILLIAM MORROW AND COMPANY, INC.
New York

For my Grandfather

CLAUDE WILLIAM LAURENCE CHAMPION

who was, among other

things, a story-teller

Contents

viii   CONTENTS

Principal Characters

Lynne de Lisle Christie, envoy
Sam Huxton, marine biologist, head of the Dominion xeno-team:
Timothy Eliot, xeno-biology
Audrey Eliot, xeno-ecology (land)
John Lalkaka, geologist
Margery Huxton, xeno-ecology (sea)
Elspeth Huxton, her daughter
John Barratt, demographer
Dr K. Adair, medical research
Carrie Thomas, xeno-sociology
Maurie Venner, assistant sociologist
David Meredith, envoy

Dalzielle Kerys-Andrethe, *T'An Suthai-Telestre,* Crown of the South-
    land, also called Suthafiori, Flower of the South
Evalen Kerys-Andrethe, her daughter
Katra Hellel Hanathra, First Minister of Ymir
Katra Sadri Hanathra, his sister, *s'an telestre*
Sadri Geren Hanathra, her son, shipmaster

amari Ruric Orhlandis, *T'An* Commander of the Southland army
Ruric Rodion Orhlandis, her *ashiren,* called Halfgold

Sulis n'ri n'suth SuBannasen, *T'An* Melkathi
Hana Oreyn Orhlandis, First Minister of Melkathi
Nelum Santhil Rimnith, Portmaster of Ales-Kadareth

Telvelis Koltyn Talkul, *T'An* Roehmonde
Verek Howice Talkul, his son
Verek Sethin Talkul, his daughter
Sethin Falkyr Talkul, Sethin's son
Asshe, commander of the northern garrison

Jacan Thu'ell Sethur, *T'An* Rimon
Zannil Emberen n'ri n'suth Telerion, Seamarshal of Morvren Freeport
Arlyn Bethan n'ri n'suth Ivris, *T'An* Kyre

Talmar Halten n'ri n'suth Beth'ru-elen, A Crown Messenger
Achil Maric Salathiel, *l'ri-an* to the envoy
Aluys Blaize n'ri n'suth Meduenin, a mercenary

Kanta Andrethe, the Andrethe of Peir-Dadeni
Eilen Brodin n'ri n'suth Charain, an intelligencer
Cethelen Khassiye Reihalyn, a minister in Shiriya-Shenin

Tirzael, an Earthspeaker
Branic, a Wellkeeper at Terison
Rhiawn, a Wellkeeper at Terison
Theluk n'ri n'suth Edris, an Earthspeaker
Arad, a Wellkeeper at Corbek

Dannor bel-Kurick, Emperor-in-Exile
Kurick bel-Olinyi, ambassador from Kel Harantish

Gur'an Alahamu-te O'he-Oramu-te, a barbarian woman
Speaker-for-the-People, a fenborn of the Lesser Fens

the Hexenmeister of Kasabaarde
Tethmet, a fenborn of the Brown Tower
Havoth-jair, a sailor
Orinc, of the Order House Su'niar

PART
ONE

Carrick V

A ramshackle collection of white plastic and steel buildings stood at the edge of the concrete landing strip. Beyond the trade station grey rocks stretched out to a startling blue sea. A fine dust sifted down.

I walked away from the ship's ramp and stood on the hot concrete, the pale sun burning down on my head. The light off the sea was harshly brilliant, dazzling; Carrick's Star is nearer white than Earth-standard yellow.

Behind me there was the bustle of the shuttle-ship unloading. I was the only passenger disembarking on Carrick V. On the FTL starship, now in orbit, I'd been busy with hypno-tapes of the languages and customs of the world. Orthe was the native name, or so the first expedition reported. Orthe, fifth world of Carrick's Star, a sun on the edge of the galaxy's heart.

I shouldered my packs and went across to the station. Shadows on Earth are grey. At their darkest they have a tinge of blue. Orthe's shadows are black and so sharp-edged that they fool the eye; while I walked I had to stop myself avoiding shadow-holes in the concrete.

A moss-like plant clung to the rocky soil, and from its dense blue clusters sprang small crimson flowers on waist-high stems. A hot wind blew off the water. There were whitecaps. The arch of the sky was cloudless, the horizon amber-hazed.

Pin-pricks of white light starred the sky.

I took a deep breath and stood still. The mark of a world on the edge of the core of the galaxy, these were Orthe's daystars. For a second everything—sea, wind, rock, sunlight—stood out shockingly alien.

A man walked out of the trade station, waved a careless hand, and headed towards me. He wore shirt, britches, high boots—and a sword belted at his hip. He was not human. An Orthean.

'Your pardon, *t'an,* you are the envoy?'

I recognized the speech of Ymir.

'Ah—yes.' I realized I was staring. 'Pleased to meet you.'

For my part, I prefer aliens that look alien. Then when they ritually eat their first-born, or turn arthropod halfway through their life-cycle, it isn't so much of a shock. You expect it. Humanoid aliens, they're trouble.

'And so am I pleased to meet with you.' He bowed slightly. The speech inflection was formal. 'I am Sadri Geren Hanathra of Ymir.'

His papers authorized him as escort for the Dominion envoy: they were made out and signed by the head of the xeno-team, and countersigned by someone I took to be an Orthean official: one Talmar Haltern n'ri n'suth Beth'ru-elen. Like everything else on this mission, it had the air of being a haphazard arrangement.

'Lynne de Lisle Christie.' It being customary to give country of origin, I added 'Of the British Isles, and the Dominion of Earth.'

He stood well under six feet, about my height. His yellow hair was short, the hairline somewhat higher than I expected. As he glanced back, I saw that it was rooted down his neck, vanishing under his collar. Either the custom was to go clean-shaven or the Ortheans had little body-hair. There was none of that fine down that marks a human skin; his—as he held up his hand in greeting—I saw to be smooth, slick-looking, with almost a hint of a scalepattern.

He was young, with a cheerfully open expression, but with the air of a man accustomed to lead rather than follow.

'Christie. Not a Southland name—but of course not.' He gestured. 'Come this way, I've a ship waiting off North Point.'

Drawn up on the rocky shore was a dinghy, attended by two Orthean natives. The older one took my packs and stored them at the prow. Geren scrambled in and sat at the stern. I followed, less agile. No one offered help. The two Orthean males pushed us offshore, climbed in, and began rowing.

'There is my ship,' Geren turned to me, pointing. 'The *Hanathra,* named for my *telestre.* A good vessel, but not as fartravelled as yours, I think.'

A *telestre* was something between estate and family and commune, I thought. I wasn't sure of the details. Hypno-tapes always give you that feeling at first: that what you're hearing is never exactly what the other person is saying, and that you can never find the right words yourself. It wears off with use.

A sailing ship lay anchored offshore, the kind of craft the Ortheans call *jath*. It was no larger than a galleon, though not square-rigged: triangular lateen sails gave it the rakish look of a clipper.

'Have we far to go?' I asked.

'A week's journey, perhaps, if the wind favours. More if not. We're bound for Tathcaer, for the court there.' Geren's smile faded. 'You must realize, *t'an*, you'll be the centre of some attention. You should beware intrigue.'

The word he used was not precisely intrigue, or conspiracy, or politics; it is an untranslatable expression that includes the Orthean term for challenges and games.

'Thank you for warning me. It's kind.'

'If I mean what I say?' He laughed. 'I do. I've no love for the court. I'd sooner sail the *Hanathra*. But don't believe me just because I say so. Take no one at their word.'

It was a taste of that same intrigue. I was certain he did it deliberately and I liked him for it, but it emphasized how much of an unknown quality Carrick V was, and what a series of locked doors I would have to open.

Coming out from the shelter of the point, the dinghy began to rock. The water was clear: the pale green of spring leaves. A fan of spray went up, polychromatic in the white sunlight. We crawled through the troughs of the waves toward the ship.

There was a pause while they tossed a rope-ladder down the hull, then Geren went up it like an acrobat. I looked at the wet, dark timber, and the rushing gap between the ship and the rocking dinghy. The rope-ladder jounced from the rail, rungs rattling against the hull.

The boat rose on a wave crest and I grabbed at the ladder and went up it, swinging dizzily, missing my footing and barking my knuckles. Acres of canvas gleamed and swung overhead. Feeling sick, I got two hands to the rail and heaved myself onto the deck.

A barefoot Orthean woman in shirt and britches leaned over the rail, neatly caught my packs and set them on deck. She and another woman swung out davits, the two men came up the rope-ladder as if it were a staircase, and all four of them began hauling the ship's boat onboard.

The distant island rose and fell gently. I had a last sight of the starship's shuttle towering over the trade station.

'This way!' Another woman shouted and beckoned.

I followed. The deck was crowded with men and women furiously working; I kept dodging out of one person's way only to find myself in someone else's. Masts towered. Canvas blocked the sun, shaken out to snap on the wind.

A door below the poop deck led, by a dark, narrow passage, to small cabins.

'Yours.' The Orthean female opened a door. She wore a corded sleeveless jacket, and her thick black mane was done up in a single braid. Her skin was faintly patterned, and there were webs of lines round her eyes.

In the dim light her eyes seemed to film over as she watched me, and then clear again. The Ortheans have a 'third eyelid', a nictitating membrane like a cat's eye. And something else. I looked at her calloused hands.

Put them side by side with mine and they would be no wider, but she had five slender strong fingers beside her thumb. And thick nails, kept filed down on all but the little finger, which sported a hooked claw.

'Afraid you're sharing,' she said, 'but I'm mostly nightwatch so we shouldn't get in each other's way.'

'Thanks. I'll try not to cause you bother.'

'You think I didn't fight for the privilege?' She had a surprisingly human grin. 'I want something to tell my children about the famous Otherworld envoy.'

'Surilyn!'

The woman's head jerked up. I recognized Geren's voice.

'I'd best get to the helm.' She turned. 'The shipmaster's cabin is there, call *t'an* Geren if anything's too unfamiliar.'

I went into the cabin. It was narrow; bunk bed one side, sea-chest the other. A square, iron-framed port with inch-thick bolts let in green-gold light. I had to stoop. The ceiling—the underside of the poop deck —showed beams a foot thick. There was the constant creak of timber and the lap of waves against the hull.

I sat down suddenly. The ship shook throughout its length, quivered, and settled into a steady pushing rhythm, driving ahead. It was an uneasy motion.

Sitting there, with the blankets rough under my hands and the sunlight sliding up and down the wood, I had a moment of stillness. This was not a starship, not even a sea-going ship on an Earth ocean; the voyage would not end at London or Liverpool or the Tyne. Sadri Geren Hanathra and the woman Surilyn, they were not conceived, born, or brought up on Earth.

I began to accept the fact that here, on this world, I was the alien.

The *Hanathra*, under intermittent wind and plagued by cloud and squalls, sailed on into the Inner Sea. At the end of the first nineday week Geren told me the season was famous for fogs and summer calms. I spent time below decks, talking to whoever was off duty; and every day I stayed a little longer in the intense sunlight, getting acclimatized.

Zu'Ritchie, the youngest of the crew, had what I took to be a birthmark covering most of his face. He was unusually pale-skinned, and the mark took the form of grey dapples, like fern-patterns on the skin, that extended from his forehead down over his cheek to his shoulder.

'That?' Surilyn said. I questioned her when the boy wasn't around. 'That's marshflower. It only means his *telestre* borders the Fens.'

I had to be content with that. Later, in warmer waters, some of the crew stripped to the waist and I saw that the 'marshflower' extended over his torso. The pattern grew larger and darker, almost black in places. Natural markings, I realized. Zu'Ritchie was not the only one with it, though his was most pronounced; and he was a little teased because of it.

The second shock—and it was only a shock because it was so like and yet *unlike* humanity—came when I saw the rudimentary second pair of nipples that both sexes carried low on the ribs. Most of the women were small-breasted compared to the Earth-norm, their bronze-brown nipples as small as the males'. I suspected that in times past, if not now, the Ortheans had littered a larger number of children at one birth than we ever did.

I watched Surilyn coiling a rope, the muscles moving smoothly under her brown skin. Her black mane was unbraided, and I saw that it rooted down her spine to a point well below the shoulderblades.

My own hackles raised at the thought. Almost us, and yet not us.

I wondered what other, less visible, differences there might be between our two species.

A thin line grew out of the haze and became solid. Surilyn, leaning beside me on the rail, pointed.

'Those are the Melkathi Flats . . . see those hills on the horizon? That's the beginning of Ymir.'

We were not close in to the coast, I noted. No passenger was going to jump ship and slip away . . . Not that I would; at the moment I needed to act through official channels.

'How long until Tathcaer?'

'We'll be in on the noon tide, if the wind holds.'

Carrick V has no satellite and therefore only solar tides, low at dawn and sunset, high at midnight and midday.

'I'm going below,' Surilyn yawned. She squinted at the dawn haze, which showed no sign of clearing. 'Noon. *If* the wind holds.'

'Christie,' Zu'Ritchie called, *t'an* Geren wants to see you in his cabin.'

'I'll be right down, tell him. Sounds like my holiday's over,' I observed.

'I'm sorry,' the black-maned woman said. 'All you've told us, about the Otherworlds, they were fine stories.'

'But did you believe them?'

She grinned. 'Can't say that I did. But I'll be sure and tell my children.'

'You're going home after this voyage?'

She shrugged. 'The ship's due for refitting, I'll stay aboard. Likely Suan will bring them down from my *telestre*, they're old enough. She's their milk-mother.'

I had no time to press the point.

'Till I see you, Surilyn.'

'Till we meet, Christie.'

I went below and found Geren in his cabin. He straightened up from the map-table as I entered.

'Drink?'

'Thanks.' I smelled the spicy odour of herb-tea brewing. I crossed the swaying cabin to look at the charts.

The first was a single-hemisphere map. There was no indication of what the survey satellite showed in the other hemisphere: a myriad islands, none with civilization above the stone age level. This was a map of the oikumene, civilized Orthe.

It had the look of all old cartography, ornate and inaccurate. There were two continents joined by a long island-archipelago. Most of the northernmost continent was left blank, but its southern coast was filled in with what I assumed were cities, kingdoms, ports—and was annotated *Suthai-Telestre*, the Southland, and so must be our destination.

The southern continent seemed only to be occupied round the coasts. The centre of the land mass had hieroglyphics I couldn't decipher.

'We sailed from here,' Geren said, putting his finger on a group of islands far out on the edge of the map. 'The Eastern Isles, here, and then we—' he drew his finger across and up to the southern coast of the Southland '—sailed so across the Inner Sea, to Tathcaer.'

Tathcaer was marked at a river mouth midway along the coast. A good central base for an investigative xeno-team, I thought—but not if, like the one I was going to meet, you couldn't leave it.

Geren handed me a bowl of herb-tea. He didn't smile when he spoke. 'I hope you'll forgive my calling you in like that, but I wanted to talk to you before we dock in Tathcaer.'

'Geren—'

I thought, would it be better to wait until I reached the officials at Tathcaer before beginning discussions? Geren Hanathra was little more than a messenger.

'No, wait. I must say this.' He sat on the table, oblivious to the swinging lamps and the shifting pale light. 'I don't press advice, usually, but . . .'

'But now you're going to?'

'It's perhaps not wise. You're the envoy, after all.'

I leaned against the table. 'I'd like to hear it, Geren.'

'This, then. I am of the party that supported contact with your Otherworld. I have even met—though not to speak to—those of your people who are present in Tathcaer.'

'And?'

He rubbed six-fingered hands through his yellow mane, then looked sharply at me. His eyes veiled. 'And so I likely know as much about you as any here, though that is little. But I know how you, envoy, will seem to those at court.'

'Yes?' I had to prompt him again. He stood, pacing in that confined space. I wondered whether all Ortheans had that grace.

His eyes clouded again. He had the marshflower also, I saw, faint as a watermark.

'It is not good. *T'an*, they will look at you and say: here is a loose-haired and swordless woman, with a child-face and eyes like stone—'

I laughed, choked on the herb-tea, and coughed myself into sobriety. 'Geren, I'm sorry.'

'I say only how you seem to us. And much of it is custom only.' He faced me. 'I suppose strangeness of dress is to be expected, and hair neither cropped as in Ymir nor in Peir-Dadeni braids—and that you never blink, and lack the witch-finger; well I dare say we look as strange to you. And in a priest's skirt, too, and you are no priest . . . and, Christie, you are young.'

'Twenty-six. Less for Orthe, your years are longer than ours. As for youth,' I said, 'time cures that soon enough.'

He chuckled reluctantly. 'You're not offended?'

'I've come here as envoy,' I said. 'I must be awkward, I must deal with your people as I would with mine. I'll make mistakes, yes, that's not to be avoided, but it doesn't matter. Watching me, you'll see the truth of Earth. I can't bring books or pictures to show you what we're like, all I can do is be. I've come to see—and be seen.'

After a moment he nodded. 'Yes. Of course. *T'an,* it was foolish of me to think that you would not know your trade.'

'I'm no expert.' It was true enough. My two previous appointments had been with established embassies, this was the first time I'd worked alone.

I looked down again at the maps, marked with the imprints of the *Hanathra*'s many voyages. So much I didn't know about Orthe, so much data lost, or mislaid in the rush to get someone—anyone—here. But under the circumstances, that was inevitable.

'But you must promise me you will at least bear a *harur* blade. It is the one thing that will tell against you.'

I was silent. It was not a promise I was prepared to make.

'Christie, I'm thinking only of your safety.'

'I know. I'm not offended.'

'No,' he said, exasperated, 'I believe you're not.'

I left him. The dawn mist hung in pearls on the rail and deck, glistening and cold. Restless, I went below again. I lit the oil-lamp in my cabin, shuttering it in its thick glass casing. The air was damp. Surilyn was asleep. I didn't disturb her.

On the sea-chest lay the traditional paired Southland blades: the *harur-nilgiri,* too short to be a sword, and the *harur-nazari,* too long to be a knife. I picked up the longer of the pair, the rapier-like *nilgiri,* gripping the cord-wrapped hilt. I flourished it, remembering old pirate fantasies, childhood games. The weight was unfamiliar on my wrist. I did not know how to carry it, wear it, or use it. I put it back.

Sadri Geren was wrong. Even if etiquette demanded it I had no business carrying a *harur* blade. That required a lifetime's training, and a lifetime on Carrick V, not Earth.

By noon the haze had thickened into fog, and the wind dropped.

From the deck, the masthead was invisible. The sails vanished into grey moisture. Zu'Ritchie descended from the crow's-nest wringing wet, and reported no thinning of the fog at that height.

'Drop anchor,' Geren ordered.

'How long?' I asked.

'Summer fogs don't generally last above a day or so in these waters.'

'Can't we go ahead anyhow?'

'You're not a seawoman, are you? Despite your British Isles. We can anchor here safely. Further west and we'd come to the mouth of the Oranon River and be drifted south. And there are the Sisters Islands not far south of here.'

When he spoke of the sea you could tell where his heart was. Then he was not thinking of the court at Tathcaer, or the ship and crew, but only of rocks and islands, tides and currents, and the prevailing winds of the Inner Sea. Some care more for inanimate things than for people. Geren was like that.

'You must guest at my *telestre*,' he said, his face animated again. 'If they ever let you outside Tathcaer, come to Hanathra. If you had the time I'd take you voyaging down to Quarth, Kel Harantish, even the Rainbow Cities—an envoy should know the sea-routes. The Southland isn't all of Orthe, no matter what they say in Tathcaer.'

'I will if I can. How far is it?'

It was unlikely I'd have time for contacts other than the strictly official, at least to begin with. Still. . . .

'A good-weather voyage to Quarth and Kel Harantish? Perhaps six or seven weeks. A half-year to Saberon, first of the Rainbow Cities, and further to Cuthanc.' He looked up and was suddenly serious. 'Christie, remember I make you that offer in all honesty. If you should need to leave Tathcaer, come to me.'

It was cold on deck, despite the coat I had on over jeans and tunic. I shivered.

'All right, Geren. If I need to.'

By night the fog had dispersed, and for the first time I saw the Orthean summer stars. Carrick's Star lies on the edge of the galactic core. The sky holds thirty times as many stars as Earth's; I stood on the deck of the *Hanathra* and the starlight was brighter than Earth's full moon.

And before the next morning's mist had burned away, the ship came to the estuary of the Oranon River.

2

Tathcaer

Sails flapped wetly as the ship tacked to come about. The light of Orthe's white sun on the water was blinding. I went forward out of the way, and looked ahead.

To the east mudflats gleamed. Spider-thin shapes flew up from the reedbeds, wide wings beating; their metallic cries came loudly across the water. *Rashaku*—lizardbirds. They triggered a flood of associations. Long-horned beasts grazed the blue-grey watermeadows—*marhaz? skurrai?* No clear visualization came with the terms. Beyond them, chalk headlands retreated down the coast into a distant haze.

There is always some degree of haze on Orthe. Not weather, specifically, but a quality of the planet's atmosphere; the same quality that makes radio transmissions impossibly distorted.

With radio, I thought, I'd've been talking to the xeno-team in Tathcaer by now. No, with radio, I probably wouldn't be here at all . . .

If my predecessor as First Contact envoy had had radio, he might have had the benefit of satellite weather transmissions; might not have died when the Eastern Isles ship was caught in a storm.

'Christie,' Zu'Ritchie paused briefly as he passed me. 'Look—Tathcaer!'

The vast estuary was choppy, and wide enough still to be mistaken for open sea. The ship wallowed. The wind dropped, caught, the sails snapped out—hills and a crag loomed up, and we were driving straight for a harbour.

Two spurs rose up, and the harbour lay in the crescent between them. The early sun shone on the buildings rising behind it, packed closely together. I gripped the rail, dampened by spray, as we came under the shadow of the fortress-crowned eastern spur. Rivers flowed into the harbour from the far side of each spur; the same river, it came to me. The Oranon split some dozen miles upstream to enclose the island that was Tathcaer. An island-city. And the land to the east was Ymir, and the land to the west, Rimon.

The ship glided in between other anchored ships in a forest of bare-masted *jath* and a multitude of smaller craft. Some boats threw ropes and guided the *Hanathra*'s bulk into the anchorage under Easthill. The nearer river was shallow with many bridges while the other outlet of the Oranon by Westhill was wide and deep. I watched the bustling activity.

I have seen cities (not only on Earth) that stretched as far as the eye could see, horizon to horizon; cities it would take a week to drive across. So I could understand why the xeno-team's tapes referred to Tathcaer as a 'native settlement'. Settlement? I tasted the word in my mind, looking at the myriad buildings cupped between low whaleback hills, at the sprawling confusion of white and sand-coloured low build-ings. And the bulk of Westhill just clearing the haze way across the harbour, crowned with another squat brown fort pocked with the black shadows of windows. Shouts and cries came from the moored boats, and from the docks beyond.

It came to me that there was more of this city over the saddleback between Easthill and Westhill. And that, call it settlement if you like, Tathcaer is nonetheless a city.

Geren came across the deck.

I picked up my packs. 'You coming ashore yet?'

'No, I've to see the *Hanathra* safely docked, then report to the court. I may see you there.' He squinted at the quay. Half his mind was on the ship still. 'They're sending a boat. There'll be court officials to find you a place, staff; show you the city.'

The first thing they could show me was a bank, I decided, then I could change the money-drafts that our respective governments had decided were valid. The shipboard holiday was finished, it was back to routine—but a new world is never routine.

I said goodbye to Surilyn, Zu'Ritchie, some of the crew, and Sadri Geren himself. Then I climbed down into a ferry, the rowers bent to the oars, and we glided away from the *Hanathra*. I saw her furled sails and the line of her hull sweet against the river, then faced front as we went into the confusion of the city.

The quay was stacked with crates and cloth-covered bales, and crowded with Ortheans. Back against the buildings (I supposed they were ware-houses) stood canvas-sheltered food booths; the smells of cooking were unfamiliar, pungent. Shouts, the squeals of pulleys, the ever-present creak and sway of the ships' masts . . . Dung and other unidentifiable odours came from the harbour. Longtailed scavenger *rashaku* yammered over the dirty water. A gang of young children tumbled past. There were children underfoot everywhere; on the foodstalls, in the warehouses, on the moored ships.

I stood on stone paving, between bare masts and high buildings. They were flat-roofed with many-angled walls and, as far as I could see, windowless. I looked round to spot anyone who might be there to meet me. My balance was a little off. That must be the sea: Carrick V's gravity is only an imperceptible fraction less than Earth-standard.

I knew the xeno-team must be in Tathcaer, if only because my first priority was to get them travel permits from the Crown. But I was beginning to wonder if I'd have to find them on my own, when I caught sight of a middle-aged Orthean obviously heading towards me.

'Envoy?' At my nod, he bowed. 'I'm Haltern n'ri n'suth Beth'ru-elen, of the Peir-Dadeni *telestres.*'

The same Haltern that countersigned the travel permit? One of the minor official contacts the xeno-team must have with the authorities, I guessed.

'Lynne de Lisle Christie, British Isles.'

'The Crown sent me to meet you.' He used that informal term for the ruler of the Southland, the *T'An Suthai-Telestre.* 'When you're settled in, we can arrange for an audience. End of the week, perhaps?'

This was said all in one breath. He had a cropped blond mane brushed forward, disguising its retreat into a mere crest, and watery aquamarine eyes. That whiteless stare was forever alien, Orthean. Over the shirt and britches that were common Ymirian dress he wore a loose tunic, green and a little threadbare, with a gold feathercrest on the breast. *Harur* blades hung on worn belts. He had a vague, harassed look about him. If Geren had anyone in mind when he warned me about intrigue, I thought, this is just the type.

'No audience before the end of the week?' I queried.

'There's a residence to be found. Staff. Wardrobe. *Marhaz* and *skurrai. L'ri-an.* The Crown would not wish you to come to court before you feel ready.'

Before you've learned not to make a fool of yourself, I translated bleakly.

'After all,' Haltern added reflectively, 'when God made time, She made enough of it to go round, don't you agree?'

The *skurrai-jasin* slowed on the steep hill. The sky above the narrow twisting passage—you couldn't call it a road—was a star-dotted strip. Featureless walls intensified the heat. *Kekri* flies clustered on open drainage channels. They rose as we passed: long-bodied, thick as my thumb, wings flashing like mirrors as they hummed on a low-pitched note. Some of the walls supported vines, but their fist-sized blue flowers couldn't prevail against the stink.

Haltern, leaning forward, spoke to the driver. The *jasin*-carriage swung left up an even steeper hill, into an even narrower and more convoluted alley.

'Can they manage?' I indicated the beasts.

'Surely. They're strong.' For the first time he used the informal inflection to me. 'They're *skurrai* from Dadeni Heath; that breed could pull twice our weight up a worse slope than this. You see their quarters, that's where their strength is—'

He broke off and glanced apologetically at me. 'I could be a bore about *skurrai*. Beth'ru-elen *telestre* lies close on the Heath, we breed similar stock.'

'They're beautiful,' I said, and he seemed vaguely pleased by the implied compliment.

The *skurrai* were yoked double: reptilian animals with cleft feet and paired double horns, cropped and capped with metal. White sunlight shone on pelts the colour of new copper wire as they plodded up the hill, ruminatively uncomplaining. They stood about waist-high, and they still looked too small to me to be that strong. The *jasin* rattled and jolted on.

I'd seen two or three places that might do as present Liaison Office and future consulate or embassy, but for now I was content to be carried round Tathcaer. It was a large city and I wouldn't cover it in one afternoon, but I wanted to see as much as I could.

'There's one here.' Haltern stopped the *skurrai-jasin*. 'I thought it might prove suitable, though Easthill's far from the Citadel; but you may prefer it that way.'

I dismounted, stiff-legged, not really sorry to be out of the springless carriage. Haltern was unlocking the gate of a blank-walled, two-storey building. The gate opened into a tunnel leading to a central courtyard, but instead of walking through he stopped and unlocked a door to the house.

He wasn't as stupid as he managed to look, I thought. The post of liaison officer and envoy was separate from the xeno-team's first contact agreement, and while it wasn't an important post in itself it might pave the way for full diplomatic contact, and eventually for the opening up of Carrick V to the Dominion of Earth. Therefore I couldn't be seen to favour one faction over another. And to be situated in an obscure part of the city was a fair way to start. Haltern would bear closer acquaintance.

'You're at court?' I asked him, as the heavy wooden door swung open. We entered the mosaic-floored hall. It was cool, smelling of dust and spices.

'In the Crown Messengers. I was in the Peir-Dadeni *tha'adur,'* he used a Dadeni term, 'but the *t'an* Turi Andrethe seems to have loaned me permanently to the Crown.' He smiled. It was a young smile, deceptive. 'Hence my being sent to you.'

The place was smallish: a kitchen and two rooms on the ground floor, three rooms on the first floor, the whole surrounding a tiny courtyard with stables. It was surprisingly light, for all its blank exterior—many windows opened on to the courtyard. Haltern took me round the beam-ceilinged rooms. Old, warped a little here and there, but sound. Thick, flawed glass was leaded into the window. The plumbing was as primitive as reports had led me to expect.

A flight of stairs from the courtyard brought us out onto the flat roof. The heat struck down hard: Carrick's Star is strong in the ultraviolet. The wind up above the city was like warm water. Sweat ran down my back.

Gravelled tar was tacky underfoot. Tubs spilled emerald blossoms, and a lemon-sharp tang cut the air. I walked to the low guard wall.

'I don't think I'll find anything better than this.'

'I'm glad you like it.' Haltern was at my shoulder. 'The others of your people—and there were only eight of them—have laid claim to five separate buildings.'

I could almost fathom his wonder. Buildings seem rarely to be put up singly in Tathcaer—the norm is a sprawling complex centred on a courtyard with a cistern or well. They are used either by members of the same *telestre* or of the same Guild (which, as they say, is a trade-*telestre).*

In front of us the city was laid out like a map. To me it looked congested. There are no streets in Tathcaer. No streets as such, I should say; there are paved and unpaved ways that twist between the various *telestre*-houses, but these are not named. The one exception is Crown Way.

The top of Easthill was behind us, and Westhill was visible across the harbour. In the hollow of the island plaster-walled buildings were yellow and white and pink under the intense sun. Old stone buildings jutted up at intervals, their architecture oddly curved and unfamiliar. The rivers were distant threads, marking the city limits, spanned by bridges and crossed by roads that led away to blue-grey hills. But over the spurs and slopes of the city, past gardens and domes, at six or seven miles distance, a rocky plateau jutted out of the haze. Stone buildings topped the sheer cliff. Beyond that the land went down into northern distances, and daystars shone in a powder-blue sky.

'The Citadel,' Haltern pointed, 'at the end of the island. And see there, below, the House of the Goddess; and the prison, and there—'

He pointed out landmarks: markets, companion-houses and theocratic houses, the Guild Ring, and The Hill—that rich district of the city that houses the *T'Ans* of each province of the Southland: Ymir, Rimon, and Melkathi; Roehmonde, Morvren Freeport, Peir-Dadeni, and the Kyre. I couldn't take it all in at once. At last he was quiet. When I turned to see why, he had the worried expression that seemed part of his face.

'What's it like,' he said, 'out there?'

He was the first Orthean to ask. Perhaps Geren and his crew hadn't truly credited I was alien. Haltern did.

'Some worlds are very like this. Some are very different.' I shrugged. 'What can I tell you? There are so many worlds.'

He shook his head. 'Incredible.'

'Earth—' I stopped. He wasn't the one I should talk to about that. And I couldn't discuss population and famine and taxes and urban decay on an afternoon like this. 'Earth's different again.'

He nodded. 'I'll give orders, have this place furnished tomorrow. One of your countrymen—Eliot, is that the name?'

'Probably.' There was a Timothy Eliot with the xeno-team.

'Eliot has extended an invitation for you to guest with his *telestre*. With his household,' Haltern corrected himself. 'I'll take you there.'

'I thought *telestre* was land?'

'Land, people; people, land—the same thing.' He made his way towards the steps, then hesitated. 'I don't mean to correct you, *t'an.*'

'I'm ignorant of many of your customs. How am I to learn if no one corrects me?'

I saw that pleased him.

'I'll arrange for *l'ri-an* too,' he said. 'Meanwhile, if you'd like to take a late meal, my *telestre*-house is not far from here.'

At first light there was a discordant clamour of bells. I lay half asleep in bed, listening to the varying chimes: near and far, low and high. Tathcaer keeps natural hours, dawn to sunset. Given a choice, I don't.

When I began to wake up properly I took a look at the room. I hadn't noticed much arriving at Eliot's place the night before. Eliot had been out, and his wife Audrey had been hospitable enough to let me go straight to bed. I was still a long way from being acclimatized to Orthe's 27 standard-hour day.

The room was plain: pale plaster walls, the beams boxed in, long drapes to hide the windows and a plain-woven carpet on the floor. All chosen to be as un-Orthean as possible. Xeno-teams are notoriously odd in their methods of adjustment.

I dressed and went downstairs. Voices came from the kitchen. There I found Timothy Eliot at the table, and Audrey Eliot at an iron cooker brewing (by the smell) genuine Earth coffee.

'Ms Christie—'

'Lynne, please.'

'Lynne.' Eliot grinned. He was a solid man in his late thirties, hair thinning on top, wearing a bright shirt over faded jeans. 'I'm Tim. You met Aude last night? Good. Sorry I couldn't be here to welcome you.'

'The rest of the team are down the road.' Audrey brought over a china jug of coffee and a plate of toast. She was younger than Eliot, a bright nervous woman. 'I'll take you round later and introduce you.'

'Thanks.' I found it a relief to be speaking English again. We talked over breakfast. They were a husband and wife team, xeno-biologist and xeno-ecologist, paired with the rest of the team for six years.

'Ten months of it in this hole,' Eliot observed, squinting against the brilliant sunlight flooding the kitchen. Most of the furniture was in plain style again, not like the flamboyant carving and ornamentation I'd seen in Haltern's *telestre*-house.

'Tim,' Audrey said warningly, 'don't prejudice the guest.'

'Oh well . . .' He waved a hand carelessly. 'Lynne's working on our behalf. Isn't that right, Lynne?'

'Not entirely. As the government's representative, I've a duty to be impartial.'

I can never say things like that without sounding pompous, and I could hear myself doing it again.

'But nevertheless, a duty to plead our case to the Crown?'

'Yes, of course.'

'Hopefully you can get us travel permits. *We* can't get them. Damn it, why agree to a contact team if you're going to keep them cooped up in one settlement all the time?'

There was long-term indignation in his voice. It would be harder for them—the sociological half of the xeno-team could at least study in Tathcaer.

I tried tact. 'I think that they don't worry too much about time.'

'That's true enough.' Eliot turned to Audrey. 'One day, and she's seen it; that's the way these aborigines are.'

'You've been on many worlds, Lynne, I expect?' Audrey left the stove to sit down at table. She was wearing a robe with pleats and short hem, something that would have been fashionable about three years ago. I'd brought few clothes: one formal skirt-and-jacket, and jeans and shirts. It's less costly to buy on-world than pay the weight penalty on FTL ships. But xeno-teams are allowed leeway there.

'I was on Beruine, the water-world.' But not for long, I silently gave thanks. 'And then with the embassy on Hakataku.'

'Ah. One doesn't seem to see many women in the diplomatic side of the Extraterrestrial department, somehow.' Eliot smiled, it was meant to be pacifying. 'But I'm sure they wouldn't have sent you if you weren't capable.'

'I'm sure too, Mr Eliot.'

There was an awkward pause. Then Audrey Eliot said, 'What's the news from Earth?'

'The usual, I guess. Squabbles between the PanIndian Federation and post-communist China. I've nothing very recent.' Even with FTL, the trip to Carrick V takes over three months.

'More recent than us—'

There was a rap at the window, and a man walked through the back door. He was in his thirties, dark, and wearing an Ymirian tunic over jeans.

'Hello, Tim, Aude. Heard we had a visitor.'

'John Lalkaka, Lynne Christie.' Eliot served introductions like tennis balls.

'Are you going to get us travel permits, Ms Christie?' Lalkaka leaned against the doorframe.

'Hard to say. I haven't seen the authorities yet.'

'Lord! I hope you can. I'm the last man to criticize ET civilizations—'

I intercepted long-suffering glances between Tim and Audrey.

'—but ten months standard in one settlement! You wait, Ms Christie. Until you've been clanged awake by dawn bells every day for ten months solid; ten months of lousy food and worse plumbing—'

'John.' Eliot grinned and shook his head. 'Give it a rest.'

'*I* miss civilization,' Lalkaka said, not at all offended, 'and when I get back from this mission I intend to spend the next ten months in a rest centre—not at home, but somewhere you can get all the comforts. TV, pre-packed dinners, stereo-tapes . . . Bombay, maybe, or Hyderabad.' He laughed, teeth white against his brown skin. 'You wait. A month here, and you'll have your own list to add to mine.'

'I don't doubt it,' I agreed.

'Oh well.' Lalkaka slouched in, sat down, and helped himself to coffee. 'What's the news from home?'

The focus of the world has long since shifted east: Asia holds the twenty-first century's future. Nothing of real importance happens in the declining West. Still, I felt it from Lalkaka and both the Eliots: what interested them was the British Isles. Home.

'Not again!' Audrey intervened. 'Lynne, how about this evening— Tim, you remember what I said?'

He nodded and turned to me. 'We're having a gathering tonight. The team, and a few people from the city. If you come along you'll stand less chance of having to repeat yourself so much.'

'Sure. I'll be over at my office for most of the day, moving in, but the evening's fine.'

'You're up on Easthill, aren't you?' Eliot gave me a look that said, smugly, that information travelled fast. 'I'll send a carriage at sunset-bell. You might not find your way otherwise.'

3

T'An Suthai-Telestre

When I found my way back to the Easthill Malk'ys household, there was a young Orthean waiting for me. He introduced himself as Tasil Rannas n'ri n'suth Methris, cook and housekeeper, and said he would deal with all my supply problems. His *telestre* was a few miles upriver and he apparently had some connection with Haltern's own staff.

The furnishings arrived. Rannas and I spent an hour or two re-arranging things, the two downstair rooms being made up as office and reception, and the first floor as my own quarters. Then Rannas went out to the streetbooths and returned with a second (and, by Orthean standards, extremely late) breakfast: bread, fruit, the pale, bitter herb-tea, and whitemeat from the fishmarket—which I suppose, strictly speaking, isn't 'fish': Orthean seabeasts are almost all mammalian.

I retired upstairs to unpack, leaving Rannas to settle the kitchen. His thick accent was all but incomprehensible to me, and I suspected my Ymirian wasn't very good. We communicated in gestures where words failed.

There was little to unpack. Some polyplastic crumple-free clothes; personal effects; the micro-recorder, and the sonic stunner that was one of the few weapons allowed on Pre-tech worlds. It was keyed to my sweat and fingerprint pattern: quite simply, it would not function for anyone else. The department provided it ostensibly as a protection against wildlife. Other uses have been known.

I had also a locked case with credentials, bank drafts, and similar papers; keyed again to my own bio-patterns.

Rannas opened the door. 'One from the court to see you, *t'an.*'

'I'll be right down.' Bells sounded as I left the room, the single chimes for midmorning.

I found Haltern in the office, staring out of the window and humming tunelessly. There was a boy with him.

'*T'an.*' He inclined his head. 'Is all well here?'

'You're most efficient, I compliment you.'

Again, the bow. It took the place of a handshake, here where that custom was not common.

'The Crown gifts this household to your office for as long as you need it.' Haltern beckoned the boy forward. 'I've brought you your *l'ri-an,* Christie, *ke* is Achil Maric Salathiel.'

The Ortheans have two neutral pronouns, one for the inanimate and *ke* for the animate. Animals are *ke,* and sometimes the Goddess is, and so are children, though I didn't know why. *L'ri-an* I was more sure of, that was a personal assistant; the word has its roots in the term for apprentice.

He was thin, brown skinned, with a short-cropped black mane. He looked at me sullenly, and then nodded. '*T'an* Christie.'

'Yes. Right. Ah—you'd better go and find Rannas in the kitchen, he'll look after you until we get settled down.' Personal staff were the rule here, and though I was paying a silver piece a day for the privilege I still wasn't happy about it.

'I could have found you an experienced *l'ri-an,*' Haltern said. 'But, Christie, as you're not used to the custom I thought it would be better for you to train *kir* yourself. Fewer disagreements.'

'Isn't he a little young?' But he would be older, Earth-standard, than he appeared.

'*Ke* is *ashiren,* a child, under fourteen. You'll have to stand as foster *telestre,* but that's a formality.' He added, 'The *telestre* is Salathiel, they keep the Westbank ferry. While *ke* is with you, you stand as *s'an telestre.*'

That clicked into place. Geren had said 'landholder', *s'an telestre,* the ruler of an estate. In loco parentis. Custom is custom, I thought.

'I need to find a bank,' I reminded Haltern.

He steepled his sharp-nailed fingers. 'You'll want the Guild house at Singing Gold. I'd also suggest you visit the market, you'll want riderbeasts. Maric is capable of tacking up and stabling them, by the way. And—'

'And the court,' I said.

He gave me a wary look. 'I could perhaps arrange a private audience for the beginning of next week.'

'I'd prefer it sooner.'

'Well, I suppose . . .' He shifted uneasily.

'I can't insist, of course. But I'd like to show willing.'

He hesitated, calculating. 'There's the open audience this afternoon, but that's the Fiveday common audience in the Long Hall. It's not a special reception. There won't be any of the *takshiriye*, the important *t'ans* of the court, there; at least, not the influential ones.'

We looked at each other. He smiled.

'I'll call a *skurrai-jasin*. What was the last bell, midmorning? Then there's time for dinner at my *telestre*-house.'

'I'll get my papers.' I fetched the document case and rejoined him.

'You're wise,' he said as we went out, 'to see the *T'An Suthai-Telestre* without other influence. Tell me, *t'an*, are all Otherworlders as hasty as you?'

'It pays off sometimes.'

The carriage waited in brilliant sunlight. We jolted off over the paving-stones.

'*T'an,*' he said. 'No, what is your Otherworld custom—Ms Christie—'

'I think you'd better settle for Christie.' I'd got used to that on the *Hanathra*. And I could see that Haltern, being the kind of man who makes character judgements, had made one, and I was curious.

'Christie,' he said with that mixture of honesty and formality that is peculiar to Ortheans, 'be wary. When I heard of another Otherworld envoy, I thought—no, never mind, I was wrong. But there will be those among the *takshiriye* who are no friends to you or your world. They can be dangerous. I admit you seem able to handle the job—'

'And why not?' I was too sharp. Eliot's earlier remarks had touched me on a sore point.

'I meant no offence.' He spread his hands. 'How was I to know your court would not send some lordling or hanger-on, or woman who cared for nothing but her own ambition? We've had such from Quarth and Saberon and Cuthanc. Remember, we know nothing of the Earth court.'

Haltern took me at face value, whatever the department's view of my appointment might be. And that, I realized, might be similar to Maric: a young person to be shaped by events rather than be a shaper.

'We don't have a court,' I said, 'we have a parliament. At least, we do have a Queen—Elizabeth III—but she doesn't have the authority that your Crown does.'

'A Crown without authority?' Haltern was incredulous, and more than a little shocked.

I spent the rest of the carriage-ride to the city trying to explain the

India-China power axis, the isolated Western enclaves, and the workings of British parliamentary democracy.

His *telestre*-house was not far from the Guild Ring. The *l'ri-an,* a taciturn old Orthean male, served a light meal of salads and herb-tea, in a bright room that faced out into a walled garden. A slender treefern trailed thick purple flowers. Petals littered the flagstones. Haltern and I sat by the open window.

'I use rooms in this place in summer,' he said, in the course of conversation. 'While the court's in residence in Tathcaer. In winter they move to Peir-Dadeni, lock, stock, barrel—and Crown Messengers. Inconvenient, but traditional. And no one is going to argue with the Andrethe.'

'Andrethe? I thought the Crown ruled.'

'In theory.' He sipped the bowl of herb-tea and set it back on the table. 'In practice, no *T'An Suthai-Telestre* would cross the Andrethes of Peir-Dadeni; that I say though it is my own province. It's the only province that swears equal alliance, rather than allegiance.'

'And the rest?'

If Haltern was talking, I was sure there was a good reason.

'From your point of view?' He nodded sharply. 'Peir-Dadeni and Ymir are pro-Earth. Rimon over the river . . . uncertain. Roehmonde's never supported any contact with your Otherworld, nor has Melkathi; but then, nothing good ever came out of Melkathi. Morvren Freeport would trade with the Golden Witchbreed themselves. As for the Kyre, they'll be as remote from you as they are from us.'

'And Tathcaer?'

'Oh, they call it the eighth province sometimes, as being purely the Crown's island. That's why you Otherworlders must stay here in the city.' He shrugged. 'But it's the heart of the Southland, without it the Hundred Thousand would fall apart.'

I didn't recognize the term. 'The Hundred Thousand?'

'The *Ai-Telestre.* Traditionally, the hundred thousand separate *telestres* of the Southland. The provinces are nothing, the cities come and go, but the *telestres* are forever. Goddess grant.' Unselfconscious, he signed himself with a circle over the breast. 'But you must know, Christie. You have an Otherworld *telestre* of your own.'

'No. I'm not a landowner.'

'*Own* land? Goddess forbid! I am not landholder, but still—!' He was scandalized. Then the outrage faded. He said carefully, 'But matters are different, doubtless, on Earth?'

'Yes.' I left it at that. He had the courage to admit that other cultures might be different from his own. At the moment, I didn't want to trouble him with just how different.

'Now the Crown has you here, there will not be much attention called to you.' He was subdued. He hesitated, then said, 'I imagine that's why I was sent to you, rather than one of the *takshiriye*. Choosing one would offend the others. If you did but know, it's something of an insult. Had you been, say, ambassador from the Rainbow Cities, there'd have been a delegation to meet you, perhaps with Turi Andrethe or Ruric Orhlandis with them.'

He sat back, fair mane ruffled. His tunic was rubbed bare in places and his boots were scuffed, he was overweight for an Orthean, and approaching the middle forties. It would be easy, I thought, to dismiss him as one more native court official. Easy and quite wrong.

'I'm not that important,' I said. It was true. If nothing useful came out of my time as envoy, the Dominion would wait a few years and send someone else. 'It's also very difficult to make me feel insulted.'

The membrane blurred his eyes briefly, and the corners of his mouth twitched. He chuckled. Outside, bells sounded in the heat.

'Noon,' he said. 'If you're still determined on this audience, we'll go up to the Citadel.'

Crown Way—that one named, paved road that runs from the docks clear up to the Citadel—was crowded. We drove down into the centre of the island where it was noisy, and the road was blocked with *skurrai-jasin* and heavier carts. But going up out of that we came among older buildings and quieter districts, passing under fronds of *lapuur* that were never still, even in that wind-sheltered place. From time to time Haltern indicated landmarks: the theocratic houses of learning, the Wellhouses . . . You needed landmarks in this trackless, signless city.

Shadows dappled the white flagstones as we drove into a square the size of a parade ground. Barracks and prison and the House of the Goddess formed three sides; the fourth was cliffwall.

The crag reared up fifty feet—not a great height, but sheer, grey rock webbed over with blue vines. A zig-zag walk was cut into the cliff face, the single entrance of which we now approached. Solid rock had been carved into a gateway, and a heavy iron grill hung ready to be lowered. I stared up the cliff, seeing a similar gate at the top.

'There's no way but on foot,' Haltern said, dismissing the *skurrai-jasin*. 'We'll go up if the audience is over. Hei, Kyar!'

One of the soldiers at the gateway came over. They were in green and gold uniforms, two pikemen, four with what looked like crossbows. These were the èlite, the Crown Guard.

This soldier, with the *harur* blade of an officer, was a woman. She said, 'May I aid you, Haltern of Beth'ru-elen?'

'Is the Fiveday audience open?'

'Yes: pass on.' She stared at me. I suppose I returned the compliment; I wasn't entirely sure hers wasn't only a ceremonial position.

'My thanks. Christie?'

I followed Haltern, nervous now that it came to it. Any offworlder has that responsibility, that he or she will be taken as the measure of their world. And a lot depended on how this meeting went.

It was a long hot walk up the path. We were in a constant stream of Ortheans, in the dress of every trade and province. Haltern paused once, and I with him, looking back across the arrowhead-shape of the island below. A fresh wind came from the sea, taking the edge off the heat.

We passed through the upper gateway into gardens. Paved walks led to the Citadel itself, looming behind feather-leaved *lapuur* trees. A huge and sprawling complex of buildings—or perhaps one building; with Ortheans you can't be sure. Carved, painted stonework; rounded towers and secretive windowless walls.

Inside was chill. High ceilings echoed to passing footsteps, galleries hissed with quiet conversations. We came to a hall, a long abruptly-angled flight of steps, and then were suddenly in a long stone-paved room.

'Here,' Haltern said quietly, 'this way.'

Two fireplaces held braziers, coals glowing against the stone's chill. A line of Crown Guard stood down each side of the Long Hall. Sunlight came whitely in through slit windows, falling on tapestries, and on the bright robes of male and female Ortheans.

Haltern led me past conversing groups. Some stared at me: my formal skirt and jacket bore no resemblance to anything Orthean. But I'm not so different, I thought, looking round. Skins varied from satin-black through brown and tan, but there were many as pale as I. Likewise brown-blonde hair, green eyes; these were common; and I was pretty much of average height.

I felt as if I had walked into a room full of half-animals, crop-maned and six-fingered. It comes at some point in every visit to an alien world. Half animal and half human: it was the whiteless eyes, the blurring that might have been a trick of the light and wasn't, that gave the curious subtlety to the Orthean face.

'How long?' I stifled nervousness.

'A little while.' The inevitable Orthean answer.

Banners hung at the end of the hall, crimson and gold, blue and emerald; and over them all the green and gold firecrest of the Crown. The Ortheans, as they came closer to the far end of the hall, took advantage of the benches there to sit and talk. As each one's turn came, they went to stand before the Crown.

I sat in silence beside Haltern, mentally rehearsing Ymirian speech inflections. Then, seeing that he also seemed worried, I hazarded a guess why.

'Haltern, would you call yourself one of the pro-Earth party?'

'Why, yes, I suppose I would.' He looked at me sharply, and then nodded as if confirming an impression. 'You're right, Christie. I was concerned. There are a number of us who've backed this policy against all odds.'

'So have we.'

'Yes . . . yes, of course.'

I could see him calculating. He was given to evaluating people accurately, I guessed. And his support might influence others in favour of Earth.

'After this one,' he said. 'Just walk up and give your name.'

The present speaker was a broad-faced Orthean female in the sash of the metalworkers' Guild. She stood with her arms folded, speaking a language—Rimon, I think—that I didn't comprehend. I missed the sense of the Crown's answer, but the voice was husky, tenor, and—when I could see—younger-sounding than its owner.

The *T'An Suthai-Telestre* was a small woman of about fifty, lean and tough-looking. Her skin was sand-coloured. Her blue eyes and fair lashes gave her the wind-blasted squinting look that professional soldiers acquire. Her braided mane was a shade darker than her skin, and was retreating slightly at brow and temples.

She wore boots, britches, and loose tunic, all in green and thickly encrusted with gems and gold embroidery. The tunic had a quilted look, slashed to show a shirt woven of some iridescent cloth. The same fabric, *chirith-goyen,* lined a cloak that fastened at the throat. This I assumed to be against the Citadel's chill, but it gave her a half-suffocated appearance. As she talked she sat back with her legs extended, the *harur-nilgiri* blade lying across her lap. She fingered the hilt compulsively. Her voice was even and controlled, and the woman metalworker nodded now and again as if perfectly satisfied.

A final word and that audience was over.

It was barbaric, anachronistic and alien; and it intimidated me. I took the few steps that put me in front of her.

'Your excellence.' I managed the bow that custom demands. 'My name is Lynne de Lisle Christie. May I present the respectful greetings and felicitations of the government of the British Isles, and of the united governing bodies of the Dominion of Earth.'

The Orthean woman sat up a little. Her eyes were suddenly bright.

'We are most pleased to receive the envoy.' She gestured, without looking behind her. One of the Guard placed a stool in front of her. 'Come, be seated.'

I obeyed. It was a favour, I could tell by the whispers behind me. Most of the nervousness was wearing off.

She enquired as to my health, the quarters I had in the city, any aid I might need and any difficulties I might be having. I answered as well as I could, remembering to mention Haltern n'ri n'suth Beth'ru-elen; thanking her also for anything else I could think of.

And, both of us having got the formal rubbish over and done with: 'I had not thought to see you here so soon,' she said, in the less formal mode.

'I wanted to present myself to your excellence as soon as possible, so as not to appear impolite.'

'And so you come to the open audience. I like that.' She smiled. 'You understand it was my decision that your people should come here. And my decision that they should have a representative of their own Crown here.'

I agreed, wondering if there might be an opening for a fully established consulate soon.

'I hope,' the *T'An Suthai-Telestre* continued, 'that you will visit more of the Southland. I'm sure you'll receive many invitations. Don't let your duties here keep you from travelling.'

It took me a second to realize what she'd said. Then, very carefully, I said, 'With your excellence's permission, I'll accept. Does this invitation extend to my people who are already here?'

'Unfortunately, no. Not yet.' She hooded her eyes. 'Lynne Christie, you will undoubtedly receive invitations from people it would be safer not to visit. My Hundred Thousand are not all willing to befriend Otherworlders. I think it is necessary that they witness what they would condemn. Travel where you will. I'll write you free passes for the *telestres.*'

'So that Earth may witness what she would befriend?'

She chuckled richly. 'Oh, indeed, indeed. So it must always be. Go out and see my people, Christie.'

'The *T'An Suthai-Telestre* is most kind.'

She was apparently satisfied. Then she frowned. 'I permitted a weapon to be brought here. Do you have it?'

I took the stunner from the clip under my jacket.

'Show me.' She held out her hand. A sonic stunner is not impressive, only a grey oval casing with a flat stud on one edge.

She handed it back distastefully. 'It kills?'

'No, your excellence, merely renders unconscious.'

She shook her head. 'Show it as little as possible, there are places it would be taken for rank Witchcraft. Better: find another weapon.'

'Your excellence commands.'

She sat back again, interlocking her claw-nailed fingers, gazing at me.

'You could almost be a woman of Ymir or Rimon,' she said at last. 'It will be hard to keep in mind that you are not, and that you bring such weapons. I am not sure if I should not have preferred you to be a recognizable stranger, at least.'

'Our people aren't so different.' I've sometimes wondered if the department's policy of preferring empaths for diplomatic service is right; it does mean that we identify with aliens, sometimes overmuch so.

'Are they not? We shall discover the truth of that, perhaps. But I think we will not speak of it now.' In that crowded hall she asked no questions about Earth. 'I thank you and your world for your greetings. We shall speak again, Christie, you have much of interest to tell me; the audiences must continue, however. I wish you good speed, and the Mother's blessing.'

I backed off, my place was taken by somebody else; and then I felt Haltern take my arm.

'This way. Suthafiori favours you,' he observed as we passed down the hall. 'It won't affect her policy, but I envy you her good will.'

'Suthafiori?'

'The Crown: Dalzielle Kerys-Andrethe. They call her Suthafiori, the Flower of the South; she was beautiful—'

'Haltern. *T'an.*'

I stopped in the doorway to see who'd interrupted. It was a woman. Haltern eyed her with wariness and distaste.

'I introduce myself. I am Sulis n'ri n'suth SuBannasen, *T'An* Melkathi.'

Her accent was one I didn't recognize. She wore a sari-like blue garment, and over that a leather cloak fastened with a silver chain. Her skin was translucently pale, her features fine and hard, and her sleek cropped mane was white. She looked to be at least seventy.

'Lynne de Lisle Christie.'

'The envoy. I hope you like our land, *t'an*. It must be very different from your own.'

'I haven't been here long enough to draw conclusions, *T'An* Sulis.'

When she moved, I saw that she supported herself with a silver-topped cane.

'A pity you may not leave Tathcaer. My own province of Melkathi is worth visiting.'

'Perhaps I will, then, *T'An*.'

Her eyes flicked up. Age had whitened the nictitating membrane and it was semi-retracted, giving her a hooded, hawkish aspect.

'Will you so? Then I will gladly receive you in Ales-Kadareth.'

'The envoy has much to do,' Haltern said urbanely.

'So, yes, of course.' As she looked at him, her smile vanished. 'And she is so young, and so like us. It is unfounded rumour, then, Haltern, that makes these Outworlders out to be some Witchbreed spawn grown cunning with disguise?'

'Your pardon, *T'An* Sulis.' Haltern bowed fractionally. 'Your knowledge of the Golden Witchbreed is doubtless far superior to mine.'

She gave him an unfathomable stare, and turned back to me. 'Perhaps you may visit me yet. *T'an*, I wish you well.'

Once out of the Citadel, the white-hot glare of the sun was a shock. I felt as if I'd spent days underground. An instinctive deep breath brought the unfamiliar faint mineral taste of the wind. Haltern was frowning.

'What's the matter?'

'Nothing. Only that I did not know Melkathi's ruler was at court, nor do I know why she should be at the Fiveday audience.' He sucked his teeth thoughtfully. 'I'd hazard it was chance, but it served her well. Christie, that SuBannasen has no love for Earth.'

'No,' I said. 'Haltern, what about the Golden Witchbreed?'

The scent of *sidemaat* fire-roses and flowering *lapuur* trees followed us down the cliff-walk.

'They were a cruel people,' Haltern said at last, 'and long gone now, though some half-blooded remnants of the race remain far to the south of here, over the Inner Sea, in the city Kel Harantish. They claim the pure blood there, but I doubt it. They need no excuse for their familiarity with treachery except practice. As for Sulis—and I should not slander her or her *telestre*—she is like all of us Southlanders. Prone to see Witchbreed in anything new and anything new as Witchbreed trickery.'

The Golden Empire fell some two thousand Orthean years ago, after a five-thousand-year reign; and the Golden Witchbreed have since attracted all evil legend and conjectured abominations into their history. How much was true, the hypno-tapes couldn't say.

'You'll be suspect, for some,' Haltern added as we came down into the square. 'But you have the advantage that you bear none of their features.'

'Which are?'

'A pale skin that has a shade of gold in it,' he said, 'whitemaned and with yellow eyes. They were tall and thin-boned; for the rest, I know not.'

We waited in the shadow of the cliff for a *skurrai-jasin*.

'I was given to understand that the Golden Witchbreed no longer existed.'

'Nor do they, except perhaps for Kel Harantish.' He shrugged. 'That's where you'll have your name coupled, when any doubt you.'

'Do you doubt me?'

'No,' he said. I believed him.

The bells rang for mid-afternoon as our *jasin* carriage came. I remembered I was due at Eliot's house that evening. The *T'An Suthai-Telestre* had put me in one hell of an awkward position.

I wondered how I was going to break it to the xeno-team that I had travel permits and they didn't.

4

A Dinner at
Eastharbour-Salmeth

The *skurrai-jasin* jolted through narrow passages. Hooves clopped a muffled rhythm. There was the scent of *kazsis*-nightflower and dung, a curious sweet-acid mix. The driver, a greymaned old Orthean female, leaned and spat chewed *ataile* leaves onto the rutted earth. I saw her eyes for a moment as she turned. The membranes were drawn back, the pupils swelled to velvet-black holes.

She had brought a message from Eliot: the dinner was now being held at one of the team's other residences. I missed telephones and a postal service.

The carriage clattered under an archway and into the courtyard of Eastharbour-Salmeth, an hour after the rapid sunset. I climbed down and paid the driver, and stood for a moment by the fountain.

The alien city was hot and quiet, the natives gone home behind shuttered windows and barred gates. Night winds blew. The immense stars of the Core blazed overhead, casting a pale light on the fountain. Roofs stood black against the brilliant sky, fringed with stars so numerous that they merged into clouds of light.

I heard a rising hum of conversation as the door opened.

'Good,' Eliot said, 'you're early. Come in and meet everybody. This is our host, by the way, Sam Huxton.'

'Ms Christie, come in. Please, let me take your coat.' Huxton was about forty, tall and burly and dark-haired. His hospitality was overwhelming. 'This is Margery, my wife—Marge, here's company for you. This is John Barratt.'

Barratt was a sharp young man, who shook hands lightly and then showed a marked disinclination to let go.

'And Adair, and I think that's Carrie over there and—'

'We've met.' Lalkaka grinned at me.

'And Maurie . . . Well, that's all of our team. It won't take us long to get to know each other.'

'Or to get thoroughly tired of each other.' Barratt gave me a smile that made me doubt his sobriety. 'I don't mean to be offensive. Social activities here are—limited. We all know each other very well indeed.'

It was a long room, lit by oil-lamps, shuttered against the brilliance of the night. By now there were Ortheans arriving. Groups split up and reformed, talking, and drinking a pale Ymirian wine. Standard formal reception, I thought.

'Adair,' said a neat and fussy-looking man beside me. He was in his sixties, old for field-work. 'I'm medic here. There are a few shots I've developed that you ought to have, Ms Christie. Can you call on me tomorrow? I'm down at Eastharbour-Kumiel. You're not prone to hayfever, by the way?'

'Not so far.'

'That's good.' He nodded at one of the younger team members, whose name I couldn't remember. She appeared to have a streaming cold. 'This planet is hell for anyone prone to histamine reaction.'

'We'll be out of date at the department,' I said, thinking aloud, 'with the time-lapse. I'll need to catch up.'

'I've done you a faxsheet,' Adair said. 'The usual run of allergies. As they say, don't drink the water. Mind you, the natives are tough, they seem to survive any infection. Don't bank on doing the same. Stay out of sick-rooms. Oh yes, there's a list of foods you should avoid—they don't eat eggs but I'm not sure if that's a taboo or not. You'll have to see the expert, Barratt. Not now.'

The Ortheans stood together, their dark eyes flicking nervously round the room. When they moved, bright fabrics flashed, jewels shone, and *harur* blades clashed on belts and chains. They seemed unused to the Huxtons' idea of a reception, and stood holding drinks and looking lost.

'You probably didn't catch my name,' a middle-aged woman said. I took a second look: she was from Earth, though what she was wearing was mostly Orthean. 'I'm Carrie Thomas, xeno-sociology. Come over here and have a drink. I promise not to say a word—you must be sick of us by now.'

I accepted a glass of the pale wine, feeling like the proverbial bone in a dog-kennel. 'Mrs Thomas—'

'It'd better be Carrie, love, we're all going to get to know each other very well. Too well, if they don't let us out of here.' Frustration appeared on her face. 'Here I am, with the first socially mobile pretech world on record—no caste-system, nothing—and can I get a look at a working *telestre*? Can I, hell!'

She broke off and laughed. 'Oh lord, and I promised I wouldn't bend your ear! There I go. It's the lure of a new face, none of us can resist it. I can see John and Maurie hovering like vultures, waiting to get at you after I've finished.'

I chuckled. 'I'll keep them waiting for a bit, then. Mrs Thomas, Carrie, I mean—you're the first one I've met who seems to have some sympathy for the Ortheans themselves.'

'Ah, you've been staying with the Eliots. And Lalkaka and the Huxtons are the same. Don't blame them. They were keen, a while ago. It's having no opportunity to work. Now me and Adair and Maurie—' here she pointed to the woman with the streaming eyes '—we're not so badly off.'

'Speak for yourself,' Adair said, reappearing. 'For a culture with practically no privacy taboos, they're damned hard to examine physically.'

'Addie would like some nice dead specimens to play with,' Thomas said caustically. 'Fortunately, or unfortunately, the Ortheans cremate their dead. It's the live ones that bother me. I'll give you an example: Why is it that the young are called "it" until they're adult? This *ke* pronoun . . . It may be that there's a rite of passage, that they have to earn the social right to gender, but it doesn't ring true. All societies do some division of labour according to sex—all but this one.'

'They tend toward triple and quadruple births,' Adair said, vaguely pursuing his own line of thought. 'I did get a look at one adult male specimen. You've noticed the second pair of nipples? Well, this one—and it may just have been a throwback, I don't know—it had what I suspect is a vestigial marsupial pouch.'

'A *what?*' I said.

'A thick fold of skin here—' he drew his thumb across his belly '—about three inches wide and one and a half deep. I can only assume that at some point the male Ortheans cared for the young.'

'Yes, but listen, Addie—'

While Carrie Thomas was arguing with him, I slipped off to refill my glass. A small child in a night-robe appeared at the far door and wailed on a low key. Margery Huxton rushed over to pick her up. They were close by me so I couldn't very well ignore them.

'What's your name?' I asked the child. She was about four, dark-haired, strikingly like her mother. She stared at me in silence.

'Oh, she won't say anything.' The woman set her down and said confidentially, 'It worries me sometimes, but it would be worse if we couldn't bring her with us. But sometimes I think she doesn't remember much English at all.'

'What's your name, *ashiren-te?*' This time I asked in Ymirian.

'Elspeth Huxton, of the British Isles.' Her accent was unfamiliar. I realized she'd learned her Ymirian by hearing it, not from tapes. 'Goddess give you good day.'

'And to your mother's daughter.' It was the traditional return.

'One of the ladies up on The Hill has Elspeth tutored with her own children. Well, you can't isolate a child, she needs others to play with.' Margery Huxton sighed. I had her placed now, she was a xeno-ecologist and her husband was a marine biologist. She said, 'But I do worry about what she might pick up.'

I felt sorry for her, trying to hold the tide of Orthe back from her door. Then I wondered if it wasn't Elspeth I should be sorry for—she'd have to adapt back to Earth.

The girl wriggled out of her mother's embrace and ran to the door. A late guest bent down and took her hand, exchanging a few words with the child.

This guest was striking: darker than the usual run of Ymirians, with skin the colour of flaked coal, a cropped black mane and a narrow, merry face. I judged her to be in her early thirties. She wore a padded, sleeveless leather jerkin over shirt and britches, marking her as a soldier. As she let go of the child's hand I saw that one shirt-sleeve was empty, neatly folded up and pinned. It was the right arm and her *harur-nilgiri* was slung for left-hand use.

She caught me staring and gave a broad white-toothed grin. The child swung on her arm, and she lifted her up and gave her back to Margery.

'Ruric,' she said to me, inclining her head casually. 'You're the envoy, Huxton tells me.'

'That's right, the name's Christie.' I checked an impulse to shake hands, and then couldn't think what to say. At last I said, 'You like children?'

'The *ashiren?* Other people's, and part time.' Another flash of white teeth. 'Elspeth comes to my household to learn with the others there. It's something to meet a child from another world, after all.'

At that point we were called in to dinner—to the great relief of the

Ortheans present—and I found myself between Lalkaka on the one side and Ruric on the other.

The Ortheans' talk was soft and swift. The cutlery laid for dinner seemed to confuse them. They fingered the eating-knives that hung at their belts and eventually tried (with varying degrees of success) to handle forks. Only the dark woman used her own knife. This, with its split point, she used both as knife and fork, eating nimbly with her single hand.

'You're from Tathcaer?' I asked. Her accent was faint, not immediately identifiable.

'I'm from more or less anywhere. Melkathi, the Skulls garrison, Peir-Dadeni . . . I've just come back from Medued-in-Rimon.' She put down her knife to raise her glass. 'Have you been here long?'

'A few days.' I remembered that, as well as the *T'An* households, The Hill was also the location of the barracks. The crippled woman would be a soldier, then, perhaps a retired soldier.

'What do you think? Or isn't that a fair question?'

'It isn't, but yes, I like the city.'

'You're one of the few, then.' She looked round the table, and turned back to me. It was only then, seeing her full-face, that I noticed her eyes. The membrane retracted, leaving them clear, and the whiteless irises were yellow. As yellow as buttercups, as yellow as ospreys' eyes. Sunny and friendly eyes; I felt drawn to her.

'You must come to my household—'

'You must visit Easthill Malk'ys—'

We broke off, having spoken simultaneously, and laughed.

'Ms Christie.'

I made the mental effort and switched from Ymirian back to English. 'Yes, Mr Huxton?'

'Call me Sam. Maurie was just asking about travel permits.'

I nodded. 'I saw the *T'An Suthai-Telestre* this afternoon.'

'And is she willing to raise the ban?'

'She's sending me out of the city,' I was careful in my phrasing. 'I rather think that when she gets reports back, she'll be willing to let all of us travel more freely. It shouldn't take too long now, Mr Huxton.'

'Sod that!' Barratt was explosive. 'More delays, and meanwhile you go buggering about all over the country—'

Carrie Thomas hushed him. I saw the dark woman, Ruric, glance at me with amusement. She must understand some English, I thought.

'It's more of a concession than we ever managed to get,' Adair said. 'I feel it's encouraging.'

Audrey Eliot agreed, sharp and nervous. She said, 'But what about Earth? We only have the three-monthly dispatches. What's the news?'

So I had no further chance of speaking to the Ortheans, I had instead to drag out every item of home news that I could remember. All of them, even Barratt in his half-stupor, sat there like hungry children taking it all in. It made me wonder, empath or not, what my opinion on Carrick V would be in a year or so.

And the Orthean guests, with that singular urbanity that etiquette demands from them, talked quietly of ships due and harvest prospects and affairs back at their *telestres*.

Saryl-Kabriz

In the false dawn the stars fade and the east is dim. Ortheans call it the first twilight. Then comes the pale blaze of sunrise, too white, too brilliant for Earth, searing through the river-mists, opening the day.

The sky was clear, cloudless, the daystars no more than burrs round the horizon.

'It'll rain later, *t'an*,' Maric said, coming in with hot herb-tea in a blue glazed bowl.

'Mmmrghph?'

'Before the noon bell. The wind's south-westerly.'

I muttered something incoherent, and when he'd gone, dragged myself up to a sitting position in bed. The Orthean day was too long. When I woke, I never felt as if I'd had enough sleep.

I rose and dressed slowly, aware that since I should have to keep what clothes I did have for formal occasions, the sooner I bought Orthean clothes the better it would be.

It rained after sunrise.

The report I'd begun the day before looked fatuous in the light of morning. I wiped it off the micro-recorder, deciding to leave reporting until I had a better idea of what I was talking about.

There were numerous messages brought in by the *l'ri-an* of various households, mostly in the form of a couple of lines of script inviting me to dinners and functions, and mostly from households interested in trade. It was too early to have a policy on that—Carrick V not being classified as restricted or unrestricted access, as yet—but I accepted them, to be on the safe side.

About mid-morning, when the rain was clearing, Haltern appeared.

'There you are.' He handed his cloak to Maric, after removing a paper from a lining-pocket. 'Yesterday's weekly broadsheet. The part that will interest you is towards the end.'

The paper was grainy, probably reed-based. The printing was sophisticated for this level of culture, something of the order of Caxton or Gutenburg. It was one sheet, dated Merrum Sevenweek Fiveday, and it was mostly incomprehensible to me, gossip about people and places I didn't know. But squeezed in at the end was a notice of the *Hanathra*'s return.

' "We announce the arrival of still another Offworlder," ' Haltern read aloud over my shoulder. ' "And also draw our readers' attention to the ship's route, which is: passing the Inner Sea close to the Desert Coast, and close also to the city Kel Harantish." '

'Meaning?'

'Meaning Witchbreed. The slur is nothing, but it shows prevailing opinion.'

There wasn't anything I could do about it. I said, 'This broadsheet, this is just in the city, is it?'

'Yes. The church often passes these things for use inside Tathcaer's walls.' His eyes veiled. 'They like to see their effect, before they loose them in the Hundred Thousand.'

'The same applying, of course, to dubious Offworld visitors.'

'I—ah—couldn't say.'

I rubbed the rough paper between thumb and forefinger. It told me things purely by existing. For example, the Ortheans were highly literate. That didn't fit with a culture at this level either.

'You've had invitations, I see.' Haltern hesitated. 'Has there been one from SuBannasen?'

I shuffled through them, there was nothing from the *T'An* Melkathi. 'Not so far.'

'Well . . . Remember what I said. Nothing good ever came out of Melkathi.'

'And if she doesn't remember it,' a voice said, 'I will.'

It was the dark woman from the Huxtons' reception. She'd obviously come in as the doors were left open.

'*T'An.*' Haltern made a low bow. 'I didn't mean—'

'Don't be a fool, Hal.' She grinned and slapped him on the shoulder, left-handed. His pale eyes were veiled with embarrassment. 'I didn't realize Dalzielle had sent him to you, Christie.'

I must have looked as puzzled as I felt. Ruric gave a great shout of laughter. 'Sorry, Christie, I should have introduced myself last night.'

'The *T'An* Ruric Orhlandis of Melkathi,' Haltern said uncomfortably. *'T'An* Commander of the Southland's army.'

'Also called Onehand and Yelloweyes, and a number of things I won't repeat outside the barracks for fear of Hal's modesty.' She turned to me. 'Now you've found out my secret, does that mean I'm not welcome?'

'Good grief, no.' I saw she was joking. Army Commander, I thought; and she calls the Crown Dalzielle. Here's another *t'an* come to get a look at the Outworlder.

'I must go,' Haltern said, 'I've business elsewhere. Christie, good day to you. And to you, *T'An.*'

'Come to noon-meal tomorrow?' she called after him, and he nodded.

'He's a good man,' she said. 'Don't trust him.'

Ortheans are capable of that kind of contradictory advice. She approved of Haltern, that much was obvious.

'What can I do for you?' I asked.

'Do?' She walked back and forth across the room, studying it, and gazing out of the window at the courtyard. 'Nothing, that I know of. I came to see if I could be of use to you.'

'Yes?'

She hitched herself up to sit on the arm of the great carved chair, and grinned at me. 'Yes, and to satisfy curiosity, I own to that.'

She was honest. I grinned back. 'I'll try.'

'Coming to the point, you'll be travelling, by what you said last night. And since there's no *skurrai jasin* outside Tathcaer you'll need riderbeasts, and so—are you a rider?' she interrupted herself.

'I've done some riding.' That was horses. I didn't know what I might be called on to ride here.

'Good. If you haven't yet seen to it, I wondered if I could be of any help to you?'

'Yes, I—'

'Only I don't know your customs. If I offend, say so.'

'You don't, and I could use some help.' Probably I could have arranged it through Haltern, but I wasn't about to refuse the woman's offer.

'Good.' She stood, energetic. 'If you're not busy now, there's a beastmarket down at Beriah's Bridge.'

Outside, the paving stones were slick with moisture. There were no *jasin* carriages in sight. We began walking down the hill towards the east river.

The rain had passed. The tops of buildings were swathed in mist, rolling in from the harbour. When it swirled aside, pale sunlight washed over the white walls of the city. Shadows were blurred, and blue. The muggy air and shifting light seemed to muffle the calls of the street-traders and the rumble of cartwheels. And there was, as there always is, the smell of the sea.

'You must have wanderer's blood,' Ruric said, 'to come so far from your land.'

'Itchy feet, I guess.'

'Yes, I know another like that. My—' here she used a term I didn't catch '—he's a wanderer before all else. I'll travel when necessary. But you, to come so far. . . .'

'I suppose it's—a hunger to breathe a different air?' I wasn't certain myself.

'If I had to leave—' she stopped mid-sentence, and her shoulders went back. 'I love Tathcaer. Out of all the Southland, I love the White City.'

Her cropped mane fell in a raven's-wing over her forehead. When she was serious, as now, I could see the thin lines worn into her snake-smooth skin.

'Is it strange to you?' she demanded. 'You, offworlder, do you have cities on your world that you love?'

'Yes, of course.'

'Ah, we are not too different, then.' She was alert, mercurial, and I had the feeling that deeper thoughts were going on under her stream of speculation.

'Will you guest with me?' she asked. 'When you are done with this travelling.'

'Yes,' I nodded. 'I'd like to.'

We went down the hill. The *telestre*-houses, fronting passages with blank walls and barred gates, made me feel again the essential secrecy of the alien city. Having an entry, all these things were open to me, but a stranger could be left to wander the narrow ways, alone and lost.

We passed Guild Ring, that collection of trade *telestres* that has spread and grown until at the very least forty buildings stand connected by bridges, walkways, and steps between their upper floors. All trades are there: goldsmiths, booksellers, cartwrights, saddlers, ship's chandlers, *chirith-goyen* merchants (where we detoured to place orders for clothes), and a multitude of others quite incomprehensible to an alien. The elected Guild Council live there, watching the ebb and flow of trade as keenly as the shipmasters watch the tides.

From Easthill Malk'ys to Beriah's Bridge is perhaps two *seri,* something over two-and-a-third miles. We reached the embankment a little before noon.

The Beastmarket is close by the bridge, an ancient high-walled enclosure. Grim stone echoed to the bellowing and trumpeting of driven beasts, and as we entered I heard the bars of the pens rattle in their sockets.

'They are the *marhaz,*' Ruric said, 'and there are *skurrai* down there. If you take my advice, there's a man who supplies the army's mounts. He's less likely to cheat you if he sees me.'

'Suits me.' The beast-smell was pungent here.

She smiled widely. 'I ought to learn your customs. How do you bargain in your Otherworld?'

'In my part of it, we mostly don't.'

Her eyes clouded in surprise, the subtle flick of membrane that passes in Orthean for much body-language.

'Grief of the Goddess, you're Freeporters! Then perhaps I should do it, or you'll pay more.'

'You're the expert, *T'An.*'

'Oh, *T'An,* is it?' Amusement flickered. 'At any rate, I know the *marhaz* traders.'

The *marhaz* were tall and bulky, but moved lightly in their pens in that roofless hall. White sunlight gleamed on their pelts: plush black, cropped white, shaggy bronze. Their lizard eyes were dark and brilliant. The pelt appears similar to hair or fur, but like that of most large Orthean landbeasts is actually composed of thread-thin fibres, very tough and flexible, which resemble feathers in structure. Great tufts feathered their cloven hooves, dung-spattered in the close confinement. Broad bony quarters and deep chests—they were first cousins to the *skurrai,* I thought. Long thick necks tapered to broad-jawed heads, deep-socketed eyes, and feathered ears. And on the forehead, just below the ears, the first pair of horns jutted out. Straight, as long as my forearm, with a spiral grain. Under them was a second pair, no longer than a finger, but equally straight—and sharp. The *marhaz* looked dangerous, heavy beasts.

Ruric chatted to a trader, and I leaned on the pen bars. Close by, a black *marhaz* mare with jet horns rolled its eyes. A grey stood still, coat twitching now and then as it shivered. And there was a striped white and bronze beast, its horns cropped and capped with metal.

'Christie, come down this way.'

I joined Ruric. 'Found anything?'

'Says he has a *marhaz* gelding, *ke's* quiet.' She eyed me. 'I thought you'd prefer that?'

'You thought right.'

'There,' the trader said. An *ashiren* led a grey crop-horned beast out of one pen. Ruric scratched its pelt, chucking under her breath, and studied its eyes.

'*Ke's* from Medued,' the man said. 'Two years old.'

The dark woman stepped closer, gripped the pelt in her single hand and pulled herself lightly up, stomach-down over its back and then swinging her leg astride and coming upright. It rolled slit eyes, shifted and stepped back, then stood at the pressure of her knee and heel.

'Medued,' she said. 'Kerveis always was a good trainer.'

She didn't dismount the normal way but lifted one booted foot over the *marhaz* gelding's neck and slid to the ground.

'Well?' She looked questioningly at me.

'If it'll put up with that, I expect it'll put up with me.'

She laughed. 'That's wise. Well, don't tell him yes or no now. You'll need packbeasts, let him show some of the *skurrai* before you talk money.'

The *skurrai* were the breed I'd seen pulling *jasin* in the city. All had their horns cropped and capped.

'*Marhaz* will fight with you, if trained,' Ruric observed. 'A *skurrai* —*ke* hasn't the sense for it.'

By mid-afternoon when we left, I had closed orders for the grey *marhaz*, a black *marhaz* mare as a re-mount, and two *skurrai* mares as baggage carriers. I made a mental note to tell Maric.

'There's tack,' Ruric said, 'but your *l'ri-an* can probably cope with that.'

'I hope so.' At times like these I wonder if one jeep or land rover would violate the no-technology rule that much. 'You're not working on commission, are you?'

When we had that satisfactorily translated, the Orthean woman hooted with laughter.

'Come up for noon-meal tomorrow,' she said as we parted, 'up at the barracks, at Hill-Damarie.'

'Get dressed,' Adair said, 'you're all right. If those shots give you a reaction, come back and see me again.'

I tucked my shirt into my britches. In the Ymirian fashion, every-thing laced together rather than buttoned; even the soft leather half-boots laced at the ankle. But I was beginning to feel comfortable in Orthean dress.

Eastharbour-Kumiel overlooked the boatbuilders' yards. From this window I looked across warehouse roofs through the clear afternoon to the ribbed hulls of unfinished ships.

'If you're going up-country you'd better take a medical kit.' Adair sighed. 'Young woman, I hope you're prepared to be uncomfortable. Because you will be.'

'I realize that.' I heard the jealousy in his voice.

He turned away, clearing up instruments.

'To be honest,' I said, 'I've wondered why you didn't apply to the department to open negotiations with one of the other nations on this planet.'

'We considered it. It seems this is the biggest political unity on the planet —' he turned, '—and naturally it's the one your people want contact with. So I suppose we don't try the others until things break down irrevocably here.'

Barratt rapped perfunctorily on the door as he came in.

'Something may break down,' he said darkly. 'I don't give the Dominion itself more than twenty years. At the outside.'

He grinned at me, picking me to pieces with his eyes.

'War?'

'Nothing so simple. We've come too far, too fast. And we haven't adapted.'

Adair watched him, worried. Absently, he said, 'It's not that I can't see your point—'

Barratt swung round on me. 'You know yourself how overloaded the ET department is. That goes for all the member-nations. People are being sent out half-trained, too young, too inexperienced—'

I ignored the implicit slur. Adair took his arm, but Barratt shook him off.

'And for why? Maybe a hundred million stars in this galaxy. Maybe a hundred thousand planets capable of supporting life we'd recognize as life. And—when we do at last, at long last, get the light-drive—how many do we find inhabited?'

No one spoke. We knew the answer. I wondered how long Barratt had been drinking. He was flushed a dull red, almost purple colour.

'All of them,' he said in threnody, '*all* of them. So we go out exploring, trading, forming links and alliances—'

'John, for God's sake shut up,' Adair said.

'—but there's too many worlds and too few of us. It's a strain on resources now. In twenty years it'll fall apart. I'm telling you, it'll be sheer bloody chaos.'

As he went past me I caught the stink of alcohol and sweat.

'Can't you do anything for him?' I asked when he'd gone.

Adair shook his head. 'We need to go home. He needs to. That's all. He's been away too long, with too much time to think.'

I went back to Easthill Malk'ys.

It was almost dark at noon the next day, and the bell chimes came muffled through the pelting rain. I had the hood of a thick cloak pulled up, and still the sea wind drove damp cold into my bones. Below the knee, rain dampened the legs of my britches. The great cold body of the *marhaz* gelding shifted uneasily, hooves thudding on the paved way. Maric trailed behind on the *skurrai* mare.

In common with other buildings, the barracks showed blank walls and barred gates to the outside world. Maric spoke to the guards and the gates were opened. Inside it was like a small village, everything—stables, smithy, kitchens, dormitories—opening into the paved ground in the centre.

Hill-Damarie was at the far end, a fortress within a fortress, stone walls streaming with moisture and vanishing up into lowering grey clouds. Maric leaned up from the *skurrai's* back and heaved on a bell-rope. Ruric herself unbarred the gate.

'Come,' she said, not with a bow but with that rare Orthean hand-clasp. 'We have guests, as you will see. It's good that you come so: none outside these walls will have recognized you.'

Maric led the riderbeasts off to be stabled, and I followed Ruric through the high archway into Hill-Damarie.

An old *l'ri-an* took my cloak, and Ruric waited while I dried the rain from me with a cloth. The rooms were high-roofed here, stone groins left undecorated. Thick embroidered *chirith-goyen* hangings cloaked the walls. The floor was paved with a veined stone and covered with pelts. Despite it being midday, the elaborate brass oil-lamps were lit against the rain-twilight.

The Orthean woman opened a door into a small chamber. A fire burned in the hearth, and a table was laid before it. Three or four people who stood by the flames turned as we came in. I was met by Haltern's bow, and a joyful handclasp from a richly dressed young Orthean male. It was a moment before I recognized him.

'Christie, it's good to see you.'

I'd last seen him barefoot, shirtless, shouting curses at the harbour pilot. Now he wore blue *chirith-goyen* cloth, soft boots, and *harur* blades with sheaths embroidered in gold thread.

'Good to see you too, Geren.' He was the same as ever: yellow-maned and open-faced.

'You know Haltern, of course,' Ruric continued. 'This is Eilen Brodin n'ri n'suth Charain, of Peir-Dadeni.'

Brodin was a hawk-faced and sardonic Orthean male in his early forties, with the dark skin of south Peir-Dadeni. His brown mane was braided down to mid-spine, he wore the slit-backed robe common in that western province, and the nails of his right hand were uncut.

'*T'an* Christie.' He gave a very offhand bow.

Ruric excused herself and left. When Geren began talking to Brodin, Haltern came over to me.

'I've heard SuBannasen is leaving the city,' he said thoughtfully.

'So?'

'Carrying news of your intention to travel . . . Well, there was no way to prevent that news spreading, even if you wanted to.'

Ruric re-entered with two more people. One was a cloaked woman. When she put her hood back she was instantly recognizable.

'*T'An Suthai-Telestre.*' Haltern bowed, and Brodin and Geren followed suit.

'Dalzielle will serve as my name, if there are foreign ears,' the Crown said.

An old man stood with her, barefoot, clad in a length of brown cloth that wrapped round his waist and continued up over his shoulder as a cloak. The outline of muscles and tendons showed plain under his snake-textured skin.

There was no taking this one for human: the paired nipples showed bronze against his brown skin, and his shaved mane came down in a black vee-shape between his shoulder-blades. His mud-splashed feet were high-arched, six-toed, claw-nailed.

'Lynne de Lisle Christie.' His voice was resonant. One sharp-nailed hand touched my arm. He gave me a stare like cold water.

'This is the Earthspeaker Tirzael,' Ruric said soberly.

There are two titles given by the church: Wellkeepers, who are the custodians of the theocratic houses, and Earthspeakers—who are wanderers, advisors, students, mystics, a multitude of things of which we as yet have no more than a superficial understanding.

'We are safe, I think,' Suthafiori said, and took a seat at the table close by the fire. She undid her cloak and laid it over the back of the carved chair. 'Christie, sit with me. Ruric, do we all starve?'

'No, *T'An.*' She and the same old man who had taken my cloak served the meal. Then I knew she must have sent the rest of the *l'ri-an* away.

There was an almost tangible air of cabal. Crown, Army Commander, Crown Messenger, representatives of Peir-Dadeni and the church, and one of the most wealthy shipmasters . . . This, I thought, is the nucleus of the original pro-Earth party.

'Does it seem overly dramatic to you?' Suthafiori smiled at me. 'To me, also. But it doesn't always pay for the *T'An Suthai-Telestre* to be seen in certain matters.'

'Am I to speak of this, then?' Brodin leaned forward. He had the expression of a man smelling something distasteful.

'Not in so many words, but if my cousin in Shiriya-Shenin were to hear this hinted at, then well and good.' She added quietly to me, 'Brodin holds the same position for Kanta Andrethe at her court as Haltern does in mine, which is to say, eyes and ears where they are most needed.'

The fire sputtered in the grate, and the smell of rain came in through a partly open window. This was a meal in the Orthean style, where great dishes were set on the table and it was up to the individual to serve themselves, using their own eating-knives. It's not as easy as you might think, eating with only a knife, but I'd thought it wise to practise, and didn't disgrace myself. Conversation was desultory while we ate, but after that when wine and herb-tea were served, I found out what kind of inquisition I faced.

First there was questioning by Tirzael and Suthafiori, seemingly with the intention of discovering everything they could about Earth and the Dominion. They must have gained some facts from the xeno-team, I knew, and would be double checking; so I kept my answers as simple as possible.

Suthafiori leaned back, cradling a glass goblet in her six-fingered hands.

'You understand,' she said at last, 'I cannot support you as far as I would wish. I have to look to the interests of all the *telestres.* And besides, if I go against the desires of the Hundred Thousand they are likely to name a new Crown, and one less friendly to your world. I find myself convinced of my policy, therefore I let you travel—but you must do your own reasoning with them.'

I wondered how many were open to reason. 'Yes, *T'An.*'

Ruric shook her head, taking her gaze from the fire. 'Dalzielle, I'm your reluctant ally, as you know. I say, take the measure of these people very carefully before we admit them to our lands.'

This was the *T'An* Commander speaking, and not the woman. Her yellow eyes met mine.

'Christie's honest, I grant you, but can we judge by one?' She shrugged. 'I've known good men even in Quarth, and how many sea-raids has that city mounted on our coasts?'

'This is old business. We have to deal with the present.' The Crown turned. 'Haltern?'

He was serious, the mask of vagueness dropping from him. 'Since the first contact and the arrival of the Otherworld team, every intelligencer in the Southland has come to Tathcaer seeking news. I say, end rumours, send the truth out. Christie should travel to as many *telestres* as possible. Better we discover the facts, then let these others—Kasabaarde and the like—come to us for news.'

'Oh, I doubt Kasabaarde must come to us for information.' Suthafiori and the Earthspeaker seemed to share private amusement. Then she sobered. 'Brodin, what word from the Andrethe?'

'That she would welcome Otherworld visitors at the court. Truth told, she's tired of Tathcaer and the Kerys-Andrethe *telestre*—forgive me, *T'An*—keeping this new thing to themselves.' There was no noticeable apology in the man's abrasive tone. 'She will consider your further plans, but does not guarantee support. But I add this myself, *T'An*, there are as many foreign ears in Shiriya-Shenin, being a river port, as there doubtless are in seaport Tathcaer.'

'We hope to make contact with all of Orthe, in time,' I said to Suthafiori. 'From our point of view it's a good thing if they're prepared beforehand, if only by rumours.'

'That depends on what they prepare for.' Again there was a glint in Suthafiori's eyes. 'Geren, how say you on that?'

'There are rumours in the near Rainbow Cities of Otherworld visitors.' He linked his hands, staring at the claw-nails, then looking up. 'As to Kel Harantish. . . .'

There was an almost imperceptible stir. I saw Ruric lean forward, and Brodin frown.

'I docked there before sailing to the Eastern Isles, as your messenger directed me.' By his expression, he hadn't liked being sent on the Crown's errands. 'The so-called Emperor-in-Exile took care to question me himself. They have a close interest in the matter. I answered as little to the point as I could, and took care not to outstay my welcome.'

A ripple of amusement went round the table, breaking the tension.

The Crown signalled for more wine, and the old *l'ri-an* refilled the goblets.

Seeing Ruric and Geren, I noticed their hands lay close together on the table as they talked. One pale and dappled, claw-nails white; the other velvet black with tawny nails. Many-fingered, like great spiders. My *arykei,* she had said. In the informal inflection that was bed-friend, lover. A wanderer before all else. It was plain in the way their hands touched: Ruric Orhlandis and Sadri Geren Hanathra.

'And you,' Suthafiori turned to me, 'what do your people say?'

'At some point the Dominion has to classify this world, as to the amount of contact that will go on between you and us. Which may be much, or very little, taking into account your wishes and our capabilities.'

The Dominion has a complex structure of classification according to the technological level of a civilization, but I wasn't about to suggest to the Ortheans that they were low-level.

Suthafiori nodded slowly. 'That is our policy with outsiders. It's not our business what is done in, say, Kel Harantish or the Rainbow Cities. Unless it comes within our borders—then we are ruthless, root it out.'

'I have spoken with your kin of "war",' Ruric added. 'Your ways are strange to us. But do you know, if you attack us, you have not one enemy but a hundred thousand. That is our strength in war, and our failing in peace. We have no unity among the *telestres.*'

'There's no need to talk of fighting.' Suthafiori was reproachful. 'But trade, now, that's another matter.'

'It must come through us.' The voice was Tirzael's, cold, and with no deference in it.

'There are medicines and suchlike, things that may aid us.' She was mild but determined. 'If it's to our advantage, it's foolish to prevent it.'

'There are no quick nor easy answers.'

'No. No, there are not.'

After a pause Tirzael said, 'I passed through Medued-in-Rimon on my way here. The talk is all of Witchbreed—meaning yourself, *t'an* Christie, and your kin here. The Wellkeeper there speaks of rumours that the Crown is seduced away from good policy by Witchbreed cunning. If you would stop this talk, then you must be open.'

'The church supports me in this?' Suthafiori pounced.

'Neither supports nor opposes you as yet, *T'An Suthai-Telestre.* Go slowly. Better spend years, even generations, to come to the true judgement than do in haste what cannot be mended. Here is a thing we have not faced before, to open our borders to those from the stars. Yet the

stars are the Sunmother's Daughters. *T'an* Christie, your people must
be *n'ri n'suth* to us at the least.'

'That is decided, then,' Suthafiori stated. 'It remains only to decide
which *telestre* you visit first, Christie.'

'Agreed. Ah, now, wait.' Ruric gave an order to the *l'ri-an*. *'T'An*, I
have an Otherworld drink you must try, Christie's kin the Eliots sent it
to me. Let's wait, and decide the rest afterwards.'

There was some talk of various destinations. Then the *l'ri-an* returned with glazed drinking bowls and a great jug. The acrid smell of
coffee flooded the room. Good for Aude Eliot, I thought. Coffee was
one of the things I was going to miss on Orthe.

'Try it first,' Ruric invited me, 'give your opinion on how correctly
it's been made.'

It was hot, and bitter. I took a sip and waited for it to cool.

'What about Shiriya-Shenin?' Brodin asked. 'You take the court
there in Torvern, and it is near the end of Merrum now: should the *t'an*
Christie travel with you?'

'My cousin is my supporter,' Suthafiori said. 'It's my enemies I
would convince.'

'There's the Melkathi faction,' Haltern observed.

I stood to pour out the coffee. Another mouthful was less scalding. I
blinked. The bitter taste increased, there was a sudden flood of saliva in
my mouth.

'Christie!' Ruric shouted.

A faint ringing or humming seemed to come from the air. I must
have moved. Then the stone floor swung out from under me, and I put
out my hands to stop it smashing up. Distantly, I heard the bowl splin-
ter as I dropped it. The floor was solid under my hand, but I was sliding
down into a pit.

'Don't touch it!'

Geren's voice.

I felt my hands scrape the cold stone. Someone's arm was tight
round my shoulders. The whole of my vision filled with yellow sparkles,
until I was drowned and dizzy.

'Christie—'

Firm hands clamped round my jaw, forcing my mouth open, and
someone thrust blunt fingers down my throat. I spasmed like a hooked
fish, bent forward, and vomited copiously.

As my eyesight cleared, and the confusion subsided, a goblet of
water was put in my hand. I drank it and was able to stand up. The pain
subsided to strands of hot wire in my stomach.

I was between Geren and Haltern, both supporting me. Their fingers
burned on my skin. I was hot and cold by turns.

'Are you well?' Geren demanded.

'I—think so.'

'In my household!' Ruric's grip on my arm was surprisingly strong.
Her face ran with tears. 'Goddess! in my household—Christie, forgive
me.'

Brodin stood holding the jug. His nostrils flared.

'*Saryl-Kabriz,*' he said. 'The odour is unmistakable. *T'an,* I do not
know why you are not dead.'

I was able to stand unaided now. Haltern called the *l'ri-an,* and the
mess was cleared up. It was only then that I realized someone had tried
to poison me.

Someone had tried to poison me: it was only the infinitesimal difference between human and Orthean biology that kept me alive.

I found I was shaking, and took hold of Ruric's arm again.

'Why me? Or was it for me?'

All eyes went to Suthafiori. She smiled grimly.

'There is no one here who does not have enemies. And we are all
players in the game. But no, even a fool could guess you'd be asked to
taste it, Christie. It was meant for you.'

My head swam. It was not just reaction to the poison. Someone had
tried to kill me. And they were taking it so calmly. I met their veiled
eyes, aware that these were aliens. Not human. And maybe dangerous.

'In my house,' Ruric repeated. 'Well, I am your supporter, Dalzielle.
I suppose to have the envoy die in my house might please your enemies,
as well as mine.'

'The *T'An* Melkathi,' Haltern suggested.

'It has SuBannasen's style. And she and I are not friends,' Ruric
said. 'But my *l'ri-an* are loyal, I'd have sworn to it!'

'It appears you were wrong,' Suthafiori said gently. 'But let's end
this now. Ruric, find an escort for *t'an* Christie back to Easthill
Malk'ys, and a physician.'

'Geren and I will go,' she said. 'Dalzielle, you'd better take an escort
too.'

'No, I have my own ways of returning to the Citadel.'

With Ruric still apologizing, we moved out towards the stables. I
was still dizzy. No one had ever hated me badly enough to want to kill
me. I'd been hurt and I didn't understand why.

But I was coming to understand that Carrick V was dangerous.

Puddles covered the yard. The sky brightened, the wind was cool.

Clouds were breaking up, going north on a swift wind. As we entered the yard Maric rode out on the *marhaz* gelding with the *skurrai* on a leading rein.

He saw me and his eyes widened, doubt and shock written across his face. He yanked at the reins but Ruric ran forward and caught his heel and tipped him over. The *marhaz* skittered sideways. The boy hit the paved yard, sprawling heavily.

'What?' I said, bewildered.

'You saw *kir* face,' Geren said. '*Ke* never expected to see you walk out of here alive. Ruric, bring *kir* here!'

She thrust the boy at us. Suthafiori stood back beside Tirzael, her hood drawn up. Haltern held the boy's arms.

'You were in the kitchen,' Ruric said calmly. 'All *l'ri-an* go there, why should you be suspect, you were waiting for the *t'an.*'

'Yes.' His voice broke.

'Let me.' Tirzael came forward and spoke quietly. The conversation was inaudible, and the boy was crying.

'To use children, *ashiren—!*' Ruric swore.

'*Ke* says,' Tirzael came back to us, 'that *ke* was approached and threatened by two men, then given a substance—*ke* doesn't know what, only *ke* is sure it wasn't poison—and told to put it in the *t'an* Christie's drink. *Ke* saw the foreign drink prepared in the kitchen and put it in that, thinking perhaps one of the *t'an's* friends was playing a joke on her.'

The yard was quiet except for the boy's crying. It tears me up to see kids cry.

'Of course that's not all of it.' Ruric bristled with hostility. 'No doubt *ke* was bribed as well as threatened, and *ke* knew very well that it was poison.'

Suddenly she pulled the boy's head up and struck him across the face. 'She is *s'an telestre* to you—what were you thinking of!'

'They were going to kill me!'

'I doubt we'd find the men,' Haltern said, 'certainly we'd never trace who hired them.'

Suthafiori touched my shoulder, saying quietly, 'If it were me, I would take that journey that we spoke of.'

'I can't go yet, I've made appointments.' I watched the boy. 'What are—what happens to him now?'

'That's for you to say, you still stand as *kir s'an.*' Ruric's answer was disinterested. 'You could let the city Watch have *kir*, there may be things *ke* hasn't told us. Or send *kir* back to Salathiel *telestre* and they'll punish *kir.*'

'Oh lord.' I couldn't think straight. 'Look, kid—*ashiren-te*—if anyone else comes to you, you come and tell me. All right?'

He stared blankly at me.

'How much were they going to pay you?'

'Five gold pieces,' he said. Ruric made a hissing noise under her breath.

'Right, you work for me till you've paid off twice that, we'll call it done with. Yes?'

Brodin looked the boy up and down. 'You're a fool, *t'an,* you'll have your throat cut inside a week.'

'No,' Maric said, 'she won't.'

He gave me that sullen look that I was used to. You couldn't blame him for being intimidated.

'All right, I know. Go and get the riderbeasts, will you?'

He crossed the yard, making soft noises to call the frightened *marhaz* gelding.

I said, 'I don't propose to blame a child for what's happened here. You find me the man or woman responsible, and then I'll put a complaint before the authorities.'

Ruric sighed and scratched her head. 'You're right. I've got a short temper, I'd have had *kir* whipped raw.'

'You must travel outside Tathcaer,' Suthafiori said, 'and soon.'

'I'm sorry, *T'An,* if I'm going to be any kind of an envoy, I've got to keep the appointments I made for next week.'

'I've to go to Roehmonde next week or the week after,' Ruric said thoughtfully. 'Suppose she comes with me to Corbek, and begins with the *telestres* there?'

'Is that agreeable to you?' the Crown asked me.

I was suddenly tired, and could only agree. My mind was blurred, but it didn't sound a bad plan.

'Then I say goodbye,' Suthafiori said, '*t'an* Christie, we'll meet again on happier occasions.'

I rode home to Easthill Malk'ys between Ruric and Geren, through the rain-washed alleys. The air was cold and the sun too bright, there was the subliminal awareness—now brought into sharp relief—that this was not Earth. We rode without speaking, and Maric came behind on the *skurrai* mare.

Fourteen days later I left Tathcaer.

PART
TWO

6

The Road North

Corbek in Roehmonde is five hundred *seri* from Tathcaer, a good six hundred standard miles through semi-civilized country, riding the *marhaz* on dirt-track roads. And travelling in the last weeks of Merrum and on into Stathern, that season where summer gives way to autumn.

'Given good roads, good riderbeasts and good weather, I'd call it twenty days.' Ruric stood with Adair and myself under the archway of Hill-Damarie. 'For us, not on forced march, and allowing for storms. . . . Say twenty-five days. The end of Stathern should see us in Corbek.'

She went out into the yard. It was full with men, women, *marhaz* and *skurrai.* The riderbeasts threw their heads back and bugled fiercely. Chains rattled on the carts, Ortheans shouted, somewhere a child bawled. Dirt skirled on the wind. The confusion was illusory. Stable *l'rian* were hard at work, and the troopers had long since got themselves ready, and were now in the relaxed attitudes any soldier assumes at a moment's notice.

I saw Ruric in close conversation with a commander, Kem, a young redmaned male. He strode off shouting orders for the placement of the baggage cart.

'I'll say goodbye now.' Adair shook my hand. 'If you do find out anything new, I'd be grateful if you'd send me duplicate tapes of the reports. How we can be here this long without pinning down the species' life-cycle, I don't know. You may see things outside the settlement that we don't here.'

'OK, doc. Keep an eye on the shop for me, will you?'

He nodded and left. I'd been to all the diplomatic functions requiring my presence in Tathcaer and there were no more duties for me in the city.

It was a blustery day, clouds travelling fast on a southerly wind, a haze on the horizon. Hill-Damarie's stone walls reflected back the early heat.

'The *skurrai* are going with the cart,' Maric announced, appearing out of the chaos. *'T'an,* may I ride Oru?'

I wouldn't be needing the black *marhaz* as a remount on this kind of journey, and he might as well ride it as ride on the cart. He was astonishingly competent, for a kid.

'Sure, why not. Is Gher ready?'

'Yes. Thank you!' He grinned, and went to get the grey *marhaz* gelding.

Gher was placid because he was stupid. I was becoming attached to the riderbeast but having ridden him round Tathcaer, getting some of the stiffness out of my muscles, I was still dubious about riding him for days at a time.

I was checking the straps of the baggage roll behind the high-backed saddle when Haltern came by. I had the micro-recorder and the sonic stunner in that pack and I was taking good care of it.

'Be wary,' he advised. 'The Roehmonde *telestres* are strange country.'

I might have dismissed him as a fussy old woman, but it had taken me six days to recover from the *saryl-kabriz* poisoning and I still had a high temperature and a throat like sandpaper.

'You think there'll be trouble?'

He shrugged, then looked up sharply. 'The physician, Adair, he spoke to you of that?'

'No, he just came to see me off.'

I hadn't mentioned the poisoning attempt, though naturally it would go in the report to the department. But that would take over three months to reach Earth. All my decisions would have to be reached unaided and I didn't want the xeno-team butting in. I'd warned them to be careful but I hadn't been specific.

('What happened?' Adair asked when he examined me for my supposed allergy. 'Eat something that disagreed with you?')

Haltern said obliquely, 'At least you're in no greater danger in the provinces than you are in Tathcaer.'

'Under the circumstances, that's not as reassuring as it might be.'

'Come back safe, Christie, and soon. The sooner they let your kin loose on the Southland—' he left the sentence unfinished. The sooner they stop trying to scare off Lynne Christie? I wondered. I should be

used to that kind of pressure, having been trained as envoy. Maybe
there was some basis for Barratt's gibe about undertrained personnel.

'Goddess give you a clear road,' Haltern said. He raised his hand
and waved and was swallowed in the crowd. I realized I was going to
miss him and his knowledge and his half-pretence of timidity. I knew he
would be about his curious unobtrusive business, eyes and ears in the
right places to gather information.

'I think they're ready, *t'an.*' Maric came back leading Oru. He
swung himself up into the saddle. I hauled myself up Gher's cold flank.

I was almost beginning to regret the kid. I had to give him coppers,
or else he'd be tempted into stealing from me, and he'd be with me until
he worked off his fine and his debt—a long time. And now he had
started talking to me, I was hearing more about west-bank Salathiel and
the *telestre's* chain-ferry than I really wanted to know. But he was
tireless and enthusiastic, and I couldn't dislike him.

Ruric walked back with two children clutching at her legs. She
handed the dark-skinned pair over to her *l'ri-an.*

'Grief of the Goddess!' she swore good-naturedly. 'Terai, look after
the *ashiren.* Christie, we're ready. She's their milk-mother,' she added,
seeing me glance at the young woman *l'ri-an.*

A sudden pause produced a moment's hush: one *marhaz* pawed the
flagstones, I heard a child crying somewhere outside the walls.

The troopers mounted *marhaz.* Most carried cloaks rolled up and
strapped behind the saddles. They wore mail-coats that came down as
far as the thigh, and dun surcoats belted over the polished links. They
mainly favoured curved *harur* blades, and a few carried winch-bows.
There seemed to be no standard uniform except for the firecrest of the
T'An Suthai-Telestre and the metal rank-badges carried on their belts.
They shouted at each other, laughing and exchanging insults, and I
found it difficult to picture these men and women fighting.

Ruric kissed the children, then mounted a dark striped *marhaz* and
rode up beside me. She nodded to Kem. A small drum-frame was
beaten, an atonal pipe wailed and the troop formed up with magical
swiftness in ranks of three: baggage carts in the middle of the troop with
the *skurrai* packbeasts behind. They moved off behind Ruric and Kem
and I.

There's something about cavalry on the move. The hollow multiple
sound of hooves on stone, echoing between high walls; jingling of harness, creak of leather, the hissing of the *marhaz:* there's a rhythm to it. I
glanced behind at the bobbing heads and wondered what it would be
like to face them at full gallop. They'd cut through a crowd like butter,

I thought, as we came off Crown Way and down into the city; and I had some intimation of how deadly they could be.

'I'll miss the old city,' Ruric said affectionately. She rode heel to heel beside me.

'And your *ashiren?*'

'Yes, of course—but they're not Orhlandis *telestre,*' she said. 'Herluathis and Iric are being fostered with me from Vincor *telestre.* And my Rodion is being fostered in Peir-Dadeni.'

Down through the narrow passages, just wide enough for the baggage carts, between high blank walls. Past alleys that stank. Past the fishmarkets and the beastmarkets, odorous and noisy. Then out onto the embankment, riding under the shadow of the city wall—twenty feet high and a dozen thick—down to the Sandferry Gate.

'We'll ride ahead when we get out of the city,' Ruric said. 'The troopmaster knows the route I've planned.'

Sandferry is an old stone bridge, with carved piles. The river runs crystal over orange gravel. A fine lace-like yellow weed floats just under the surface.

Ruric reined in to let the troop pass. Gher sidestepped, and skittered in a circle before I could bring him round.

The air was colder, blowing up from the estuary. Downstream, Beriah's Bridge began the south-eastern Melkathi road. Upstream, the city walls followed the bends in the river, and I could see four more bridges. There were fewer people here. It was peaceful to sit and look out over the lush water meadows to the hills of Ymir.

We followed the troop out of the shadow of the wall, into the fierce sunlight, across the bridge.

I turned in the saddle. The city's white walls flashed back the early diamond light. I heard bells, and saw the full sails of a *jath* ship in the estuary, and the pennants flying from the grim Citadel.

I would have ridden a gallop back to the docks, begged a shipmaster to sail me to the Eastern Isles and stayed on that desolate rock until the next ship came from Earth—if I'd been able to foresee what was going to happen to me before I entered Tathcaer again.

'It'll be easy riding this first day,' Ruric said. 'The Hanathra *telestre* lies about twenty-five *seri* east of here, they'll guest us for one night.'

The troop rode behind and below us as we climbed the track into the hills. They were making good speed, considering that the baggage carts must slow them down.

'Should we wait for them?'

'No. Crown law holds pretty well in these parts.' She managed the striped *marhaz* one-handed, reins looped up on the saddle, controlling it with pressure of heels and knees. Gamble, she called it; a lively sharp-horned beast. 'When we get into rough country the troopmaster will send scouts ahead. But you were thinking someone would try and follow up that poison?'

'It had crossed my mind.'

'I can't say it won't happen.' Her grave eyes met mine. 'There's no knowing the truth of it. Haltern names SuBannasen—though she's gone back to Ales-Kadareth now—and I believe him. But there'll always be such things. We're all players of the game.'

'What reasons do you have for suspecting SuBannasen?'

'My own,' she said shortly.

We rode on in silence for a time, with the heat shimmering over the blue-grey mossgrass, and the lizardbirds calling their metallic notes. It was difficult to tell where dust-starred hill ended and star-dusted sky began.

'Sorry,' she said at last. 'That was a hard year, the uprising in Melkathi, and it's with me still. Sulis n'ri n'suth SuBannasen has her own reasons for hating me and for striking at me through you. And since you're an Offworlder she may prove your enemy too.'

'I was wondering where I came in.' Some of the black resentment in me spilled over. 'I suppose at least I'm having some effect here—no one ever tried to kill me on any other world.'

'No one ever—' she cut off. 'Christie, you must come from a strange world. You bear no *harur* blade, and I've heard you called coward but I don't believe that's true. You have your own weapons. And yet it's so different.'

Gher balked at a slope, and I brought him round and thumped my heels heavily into his ribs. He turned his head and glared reproachfully from wide-set eyes.

The Orthean woman said, 'When I was your age, I'd birthed a child and fought in four uprisings.'

There was a challenge there. Even allowing for the difference between Orthean and standard years she was barely a decade older than me. I grinned. 'Sounds dangerous. I prefer travelling—light years from Earth—and seeing new worlds. Of which, by the way, I've set foot on three so far.'

'Hei! You sound like Geren. He'd sooner sail than fight.'

The track wound on into the hills, chalk dust going up from under the *marhaz* split hooves and whitening boots and britches. The moss-grass made a tight blue-grey carpet. It was high, empty country.

'I'm the same as you,' Ruric said, 'a small piece in a large game. There'll be other *T'An* Commanders after me, and other envoys after you. Which is good. We can't judge a world by you. And you can't judge the Southland by a Roehmonder priest or a Dadeni rider—or even a Melkathi woman.'

The day wore on, and the dust the troop kicked up hung in the heavy air. There was no wind in the hills. It was hot.

Ruric leaned back in the saddle, hooding her eyes and staring directly at the sun. The Ortheans can look on the face of their Goddess, their mysteries are mysteries of the light and not the dark.

'Nearly noon,' she said, with the radiant shadow of the sun still in her eyes. 'We're making good time.'

As we crested the next rise I saw we had only come up over a spur of the hills, and not crossed the hills themselves. They swung away into the north-east, ranging into the distance, hullbacks sharp against the sky. Above them rode the scatter of daystars that Southlanders call *siriye* after the starmoth. They dotted the sky like flour.

We crept across the landscape like flies. Six hundred miles, I thought. And I could drive that comfortably in three days.

The feathery *lapuur* grew up to the foot of the downs like a sea. In the stillness of that day-starred noon, they were a slight but ceaseless movement. As we rode down under the trailing ash-pale ribbons, they shrank back. Thermosensitive. I put up a hand to brush them aside, and the fronds that slid from the *marhaz's* cool flanks for a moment curled and clung to my skin. An automatic reaction to body-temperature: but I shivered. It's never far, that tension endemic to being on alien soil.

I saw clearings and the smoke of settlements, and fields of grain further off. In some areas they were burning off stubble, but when we came down off the hills the grain was standing heavy and amber beside the road. Ruric leaned down from the *marhaz* to pick a stalk, offering me one of the double-headed ears, and we rode on chewing the bitter kernels and spitting out the husks.

We dropped back after the midday stop for food, and rode with the troop. They were in a straggling line, talking and singing.

'Ceremonial visits are easy duty,' Ruric commented, 'even if it does mean riding to such Goddess-forsaken outposts as the Skulls Garrison. They're alert enough when there's need for it.'

Whoever compiled the xeno-team's language tapes hadn't spent their time round the Hill-Damarie barracks. Their slang dialect was unintelligible, though from the looks I got I gathered the Outworlder was being discussed. I made a mental note to question Maric later.

About mid-afternoon it began to cloud up, a wind coming from the west. Before long it was raining. A few drops spattered down through the *lapuur* fronds, there was the hiss of a wood in a rainstorm, and visibility shrank to a grey circle. I hastily unstrapped my cloak and put it on, pulling the hood up.

Rain seeped through to thighs and shoulders. I could feel water down my back, and see it dripping off the rim of my hood. The troop closed up, centring round the carts; hoods up and heads down, riding with the rain at their backs. Ruric rode down the column to consult the troopmaster.

The Southland's word for road is the same as their word for boundary. In the main we were following tracks that marked the borders of *telestres*. I watched for a markstone with the Hanathra insignia. The afternoon passed in the curious yellow light of a rainstorm.

My legs were aching and I had a sore backside and I was as wet as I'd have been in a river. Gher ambled disconsolately on after Ruric's *marhaz*. I kept quiet, knowing my temper was filthy. I didn't even want to think how I was going to feel once I dismounted. But God knows you can't enthuse about the wonders of primitive societies and then scream for a jeep when you have to ride a *marhaz* in a downpour. The wind blew gustily. We plodded on. Somewhere behind me, a trooper cursed and spat. I thought about hot food, hot drinks and hot baths.

'How far now?'

Ruric gave the crook-shouldered shrug that was her trademark. 'Two or three *seri*. Not far.'

'Will Geren be there?'

'He's still in the city. Sadri is *s'an telestre*, you'll meet her.'

Not long afterwards we came to a fork in the road, with the Hanathra sign on the markstone. By the time we had ridden across the *telestre* the rain was down to a drizzle. Ruric rode with Kem, and I fell back beside Maric and the troopers.

We topped a rise and I saw the household spotlit by the low sun, against a background of purple rainclouds. At first I thought it was a village, and a sizable one at that; then I saw that each building was interconnected, the main polygonal stone building throwing out wings and offshoots and outbuildings covering several acres of ground. We rode round past storage sheds and beastpens, and under an archway to a courtyard the size of a field. The pale yellow stone, lit by the level westering sun, glowed golden. An antique coping in the centre marked the well.

A crowd of *ashiren* came running up, chattering and screeching, and squat, red-pelted beasts hissed at the *marhaz* heels as they splashed through the spreading puddles. Kem called an order, the troop dismounted and began leading the riderbeasts towards the stables. By now there were adults with the *ashiren,* some helping the troopers, some coming to greet Ruric.

There was a certain respect in the way they spoke to her. She was all ease on the surface, but it was obvious she was known and had a reputation.

'Christie,' she called, coming over.

I threw one leg over Gher's quarters, slid to the ground, and would have fallen flat if the Orthean woman hadn't shot out a hand to catch me.

'Jesus wept!' I bent double, rubbing knotted thigh and calf muscles.

'That was the easy day. You wait until tomorrow.'

I tried my recollection of Ymirian curses. She laughed, pushed me one-handed at the main doors, and then we were out of the rain and in a flagstoned hall. Water pooled round my boots. I straightened, winced.

'We must go round and check their quarters afterwards,' Ruric said, and then bawled at a short stocky woman. 'Sadri! Sadri, is there any hot water in this *telestre?*'

A squat iron boiler radiated heat. Piped through to the bathhouse next door, hot water filled a tank that looked to have been carved from a single granite block. There was the headachy smell of *lapuur,* that fierce-burning firewood.

I sat on one of the underwater ledges, relaxing in water almost too hot to bear. It was bliss. Ruric sat on a ledge opposite, her cropped black mane floating like seaweed. She ducked her head, blinked the water out of her veiled eyes, and massaged the stump of her right arm. It had been taken off midway between elbow and shoulder, a nub of smooth skin and lumpy flesh that was not ugly, only wrong.

'Aches in wet weather,' she said, ducking her head again, and coming up blowing water. 'That I also owe to Melkathi, and Ales-Kadareth.'

'What about Melkathi?' I said. 'I ought to know.'

'The whole business? Yes, you did. Perhaps this wouldn't have started so soon, if it wasn't for that.'

I occupied myself with the gritty soap. Every fibre of me ached.

When I looked up, Ruric said, 'I can't explain it without telling you something of my *telestre,* so bear with me.'

'You don't have to.'

After a silence she said, 'I've spoken to your kin. Is it true that on your world people of the same household live apart, in different lands, with no disgrace?'

'Yes, it's true.' I saw she still looked unconvinced. 'Me, for example, I've lived in several parts of the British Isles. In the south, when my parents were alive—they died when I was thirteen—and then in London with the de Lisle half of the family.' Without thinking, I added, 'They never exactly approved of the Christies, but they couldn't refuse to take me in.'

'But they were your *telestre.'* She was watching me narrowly.

'My mother's side of the family. The Christies were never quite good enough for the de Lisles. I suppose I decided to use them, they're an old diplomatic family; but I'm not sure that they didn't use me, turning me into another career diplomat.' I stopped. I was tired, liable to run on.

'What would we be if we weren't driven?' Ruric said dreamily. 'Me, not a soldier; you, not the envoy. This was your birth-mother's kin, was it; or your milk-mother or foster-mother?'

'Birth-mother.' Orthean relations are complex. 'Never mind: tell me about Melkathi.'

Her dark face, seen through wisps of steam, was serious and open. It was the turning point (rarely recognized) when she became a person to me.

'You've got the look,' she said, 'I've got it too, I know. That's what it is about you Otherworlders. You're *amari,* motherless. Landless, too.'

'I can see how it would look that way.'

'And my *telestre . . .'* she nodded, making comparisons. 'If we'd had an Earthspeaker to put us right, it would have been different; but the church has always been weak in Melkathi. And Orhlandis is a poor *telestre,* it won't support more than a score living there. So, like you, I think I was one too many. And yellow-eyed, too.

'How it was: my father was a wanderer, shipped out from Ales-Kadareth one spring, came home seven years later with nothing but the clothes on his back and the babe he carried: that was me. He knew it would overstrain the *telestre* if he stayed, so he and his brother and his brother's sons went to Ales-Kadareth to earn silver. That was the summer of the White Plague. It killed him. It spared them.'

She sat up, rippling the water, soaping her scarred ribs.

'So half my kin were in Ales-Kadareth as *l'ri-an* for the *T'Anfó Melkathi*, who at that time also was from SuBannasen *telestre*. I didn't know or care about that. As soon as I was no longer *ashiren* I came to Tathcaer and joined the army. I should have gone back. But what can you do?'

'Nothing,' I said, remembering.

'The uprising started in Ales-Kadareth. They always do. It's a rebellious city. The Melkathi *telestres* are all dirt-poor. If it was me, I'd change the boundaries, move half the people out, and let the land support the rest—but there's no going against the church.' She sighed, then continued. 'Four years back. I went in with the army, established lines of supply and laid siege to the city. Sure enough the *telestres* began to withdraw support. But 'Kadareth held out. It was bad, four seasons before the siege broke. In the end I wasn't sure if they'd starve before we were wiped out by plague —it was a blazing hot summer, and every disease you can name went through us. I used winch-guns to drop our dead inside the city walls. That opened them up. There was some close fighting before the SuBannasen surrendered—that was when I took a cut in the arm and it turned poisonous. Then I had to judge 'Kadareth by Crown law.'

There was no apology in her tone. Looking at her, I believed she'd done all she said: planned, executed, killed.

'Three of the chief rebels were Orhlandis *telestre*. What could I do? If I spared them, it was injustice. But I hated them. Goddess, how I hated all my kin! And how can you deal with someone justly when you'd like to gut them like a fish? They pleaded. Then they accused me of using Crown law to be revenged on them.'

'What did you do?' I asked.

'What could I do? They were guilty. I hung them on the walls of Ales-Kadareth. And I still don't know if they were right in what they said.'

'Sometimes there is no right thing to do.'

She was quiet, then said, 'But the point of this is, I also had executed the *T'An* Melkathi, who was Sulis's brother. She was *s'an* at that time, but since became *T'An* Melkathi herself. Naturally she'd like to see me dead. This is what you've been dragged into.'

'It would have happened sooner or later. I'm a stranger here.'

'But she'll leave it, you having gone beyond her reach for a time.' She sluiced off the soap, stood up, and climbed unself-consciously out of the bath to get a towel. Unlike most Ymirian clothes, Ruric's had button and loop fastenings so that she could manage one-handed.

I climbed out and towelled my dripping hair, wiped my face, and found Ruric staring at me. She looked me up and down. I felt myself getting hot behind the ears.

'Not one,' she said. 'Not one scar, not anywhere.'

I almost exploded with laughter.

'Let's go and find Sadri,' she said, and glanced at me again. 'Yours must be a very strange world. I wonder what I'd make of it?'

Hanathra *telestre's* main hall was full of people. Besides the household, which seemed to extend family relationships at least as far as sixth cousins, and the *l'ri-an* and the *ashiren* being fostered, there were also the soldiers of Kem's troop.

Oil lamps stood on ledges round the stone walls, and firelight gave some clarity of view beside the six great hearths. It was low-ceilinged, a large hall where pale yellow stone arches held soft shadows. Tables and long benches were set between the pillars. The great crowd that there had been at the beginning of the meal had divided into groups round the hearths, some talking, some singing—Ortheans sing anywhere, given half a chance—or passing gossip and getting city news from the troopers. Kids sat round on soft *wirazu* pelts, pummelling the guardbeasts or fighting or falling asleep. You could see from the colours of the stone that the walls had been rebuilt once or twice, at intervals of several centuries. Where I sat, on a bench inside the hearth-nook that was as big as a small room, the stone was grey veined with blue, old and worn smooth with use.

Maric sat curled up on the furs, staring sleepily into the fire. He was dazed: it was his first time out of the city. Ruric and Sadri sat beside me, talking.

I leaned back, aching, savouring the feel of clean dry clothes and staring up the chimney-shaft at the stars, shimmering in the fire's smokeless heat. It was that point in a journey that brings mild depression, when you look back and feel every inch of the journey, every increasing mile between what's familiar and what's strange. I was the first of my kind to travel into this unknown country. The thought of that—sensed far off down the years, at idealistic fourteen or fifteen—had once fired me to begin a career in the ET department. The reality was at once more frightening and more satisfying.

Ruric shifted beside me, moving the stump of her arm into the fire's heat.

'Does it still pain you?' Sadri was concerned.

'No.'

'You were the best,' she said. There was an expression between them that meant they'd had this conversation before. She turned to me. 'She was the best with the *harur* blades that ever lived in the Southland.'

Ruric's answer was that crook-shouldered shrug. It must hurt her to have that said, I thought, not yet used to the Orthean habit of washing dirty linen in public.

'I don't know about that. You can't make comparison with the dead masters who're gone, or with those who're not yet born—but yes, I grant you, I was the best in my generation.'

There was no pride or pity in her voice. She made it a statement of fact.

'I have still the *harur-nilgiri*,' she added, and her lips quirked into a smile at Sadri. 'Whether my balance is gone or not, you wouldn't like to challenge me.'

'I would not,' Sadri agreed.

The fire crackled restfully, and she eased a log back into the embers with the toe of her boot. The sound of singing came from the distant end of the hall.

Katra Sadri Hanathra was a small woman, no more than four feet ten or eleven inches tall, with a squat round figure. Her skin was fishpale, and lightly marked with marshflower dapples. Her grizzled red mane was cropped short. She had a wrinkled moonface, lined forehead, and wideset eyes in bags of flesh. There was no telling her age, it could have been anything between fifty and seventy. She should have been strikingly ugly—and indeed, with the nictitating membrane over her eyes she sometimes resembled a comatose reptile—but she had the same open expression that Geren had, and the same gift of making you feel welcome.

'How's Geren?' she asked Ruric.

'Refitting ships.' There was humour in her voice. 'I think he's got the idea of the Western Voyage again—convinced that if the *Hanathra* can sail direct west for fifty days, he'll find land.'

'He'll be gone a while and come back with nothing, I know him. You,' Sadri said, with her hand on Ruric's shoulder, 'you're his *arykei*. When are you going to become *n'ri n'suth* Hanathra?'

'If we were one *telestre* it wouldn't keep me in Ymir, or him on dry land.'

'I don't ask you for that reason. You've got good friends here. I'd like to see you come home here, instead of to soldier's quarters in some garrison. Don't you agree?' she appealed to me suddenly.

I felt inclined to pretend I knew nothing about it, but that kind of tact has no place there. As Ruric said later, in the entire Southland, there isn't enough tact to fill a bucket.

'It wouldn't work on my world, or at least, not the part where I was born,' I said. 'Perhaps it would, here. You're used to having milk-mothers and foster-children and—I don't know—you seem to hold your children and relatives in common, don't you? It's much narrower on Earth. Either you belong or you don't.'

'It's the land,' Ruric said. 'I'm Orhlandis-bred, if not born there.'

'The land wouldn't matter so much for us,' I said, and was momentarily alone, faced by alien eyes.

'You never root the land out of you,' Sadri contradicted.

'Where you grew up as *ashiren,*' Ruric said, 'the first fields and paths and coastline that you ever saw. The household. You remember your house,' she challenged, 'and the rooms, and what was in them, and where you slept?'

'Yes, of course.'

'And the hills,' Sadri picked up the thread, 'and the way the light fell, and the winds, and the river, and the paths through the trees?'

'Yes—'

There wasn't too much like that where I was born. No, but I remember the street and the old bombsites the kids used to claim as their territory; all of it mixed up with life before my mother and father were killed. If I had ever got into adolescence while they were alive, quarrelled and cut free, it would be easier. As it is, I have a child's memories. A child who doesn't remember the faults, only the good times.

'They feel it too,' Ruric said, and I saw her and Sadri watching me.

'Still, you weren't meant for that *telestre.*' Sadri returned to her argument. 'Any Earthspeaker would have told you so. It's no disgrace to be born in the wrong *telestre,* and it's the Goddess's will that you go where you can live best.'

'I wasn't born in a *telestre.*' Something of steel flashed in Ruric's voice. 'As I was constantly reminded. I'm *amari,* motherless, born outside the land.'

'It doesn't matter to us.'

'I *am* Orhlandis,' Ruric said, almost brutally, 'I am of Melkathi, I am a Southlander. What would you have me do, Sadri?'

'I've touched scars. I'm sorry.'

Dusk turned to darkness, and rain drummed on the small-paned windows.

'Maybe one day—' Ruric interrupted herself. 'Yes, Kem?'

'Only a rumour, *T'An.*' His eyes flicked nervously over me, and he looked away. 'The *ashiren* say there was a man here earlier, asking if the Commander's troop were coming here; and as they did not know when we were coming, they could tell him nothing. He rode off, but they can't say by which road.'

I saw Sadri's glance at Ruric.

'Now is that one of Suthafiori's messengers,' Ruric thought aloud, 'or is that SuBannasen or some other *t'an* having us followed?'

7

The House at Terison

Maric woke me after first twilight, bringing a basin and a jug of hot water. He knew better than to expect sensible conversation from me at that hour and so left me to dress, having told me that the *T'An* Ruric and everyone else were already up.

Every time I moved, I winced. The inner muscles of my thighs seized up, and for a while I seriously thought I'd done permanent damage. I tried to sit on the edge of the bed, yelped, and collapsed back across it. There was no way I could bend. Dressing was a slow process, mostly horizontal.

The other beds in the room—it was more of a dormitory—still bore the warm imprint of bodies. I washed perfunctorily. Unlike the city households, this had a primitive system of flush plumbing. Somehow I'd expected to find the city more sophisticated.

Before I repacked my baggage I took the sonic stunner out and strapped on the belt-holster. The laced tunic concealed it. I didn't want to analyse my motives for wearing it, but it was comforting.

I limped through half a dozen empty rooms, looking for stairs. There were no corridors, room opened directly into room. Grey clouds were shifting outside and a pale light filtered in. The place smelled of dust and old cooking.

Opening one door, I came into a bare room whose walls were covered in old maps. An enormous iron and glass structure stood under a skylight. It was a primitive telescope. The lenses were visibly flawed but it was still beyond anything I'd expected to see on Carrick V. This world might, I thought, be on the verge of some technological revolution. I studied the star-charts: complex for summer, less so for the Orthean winter sky, empty only by comparison.

A spiral staircase went down from one corner of the room and I went down and found myself at one end of the great hall. Ruric sat with Kem and his Second, poring over a map spread among the ruins of breakfast.

'—through Meremoth and up to Brinor.' She saw me. 'Christie, I didn't think you'd be walking this morning!'

'My legs may let me down yet.' I eased gently onto the bench.

They continued their discussion, while I made inroads on the meal. Meat broth, bread, hot herb-tea; then a fruit with what seemed like sour milk on it—but there are very few Orthean land mammals—and finally *rukshi,* land arthropods.

'It wouldn't be a Crown Messenger,' said Kem's Second, a broad-bellied woman called Ho-Telerit. 'He'd have waited, or given word to the *s'an telestre* here.'

'Someone's got their eyes on us,' Ruric agreed.

'*T'An* Commander,' Kem said, 'you don't imagine someone's going to ambush a troop of the Crown's army? We're not thirty *seri* from Tathcaer!'

'If it were to be done, that would be the way to do it. Where least expected. But no, I don't think that.' Her satin-black finger traced a line across the map. 'I think Sadri can tell any inquirers that we've gone the way I planned: Meremoth, Brinor, and Salmar. Meanwhile, let's see if we can take our follower east a ways, and lay hands on him. I'd like some answers.'

'There's a companion-house near Sherahtha,' Kem suggested.

'Right. Let's move.' She stood. 'Who are your best scouts?'

'Perik and Vail,' Ho-Telerit said.

'See if they can pick up our follower.'

Not long after that we left, Sadri riding with us as far as the border of the *telestre.* It was a bright, starry morning, the road muddy with the previous day's rain but passable. Warm vapour curled up from the earth, and with it came the acrid smell of mossgrass and the sweetness of *ziku.*

'The *telestre* is open to you any time if you come back this way.' Sadri sat astride her black *marhaz.* She squinted at me in the early light. 'And remember Hanathra when there are voyages to your Otherworld —if I can't come, then Geren certainly will.'

We crossed another spur of the hills, coming down about mid-morning into wooded valleys. The slender *lapuur* gave way to taller, broad-leaved *ziku* trees. Bronze-red foliage shaded us from the sun as we followed a winding track.

Indigo shadows came up from the darkness of the wood. Then the sun blazed out again, and we were suddenly riding through sapphire light. Under the bronze trunks of the *ziku* grew a darker blue species of the mossgrass. The hooves of the *marhaz* sank inches deep into it, muffling their tread. The depths of the wood were azure, bright as the sea, and over that blue thousandflowermoss blazed the red fire of the *ziku.* Even the troop rode silent, the pace increasingly slightly, a tension obvious in their faces. No *rashaku* sang.

'Before the *telestres,* it was called the old Commonwood,' Ruric said as we came out into sun and farmland again. 'Some say it once marched from the Fens to the sea.'

Maric made casts with a sling as we travelled and brought down a lizardbird that Ho-Telerit commandeered for the noon meal. It was the first time I'd studied one at close hand. Brown plumage flecked the wings and back but the body was scaled. A thin, wedge-shaped head bore serrated jaws. It had four clawed feet.

'*Rashaku-dya,*' Maric said. 'I used to snare them in their treeholes under the Rimon downs. They're good eating, *t'an.*'

It was a long day, and well into the second twilight before we came to Sherahtha. It was a companion-house on the border where three *telestres* met, run by each in turn; a low and sprawling cobwalled building.

'He's been here before us,' Ruric said, coming round to where I was seeing to Gher's stabling.

'The one that's following us?'

'One man can move faster than a troop. And make a good guess as to what road we're on.' She frowned. 'We'll keep in the hills tomorrow, where he'll have to come close to get a look at us, and see if Ho-Telerit's scouts have any better luck.'

We sat by the courtyard window of another shabby companion-house. Outside, the evening was hot and still. Heat soaked up out of the dry earth, shimmered over the fields of stubble where hay stood in small, egg-shaped stacks. They resembled fields of squat standing men. Hills blocked the western horizon. We'd been riding north-east for two days after leaving Sherahtha.

'Whoever he is, he knows his business. And he's lucky,' Ruric added as an afterthought.

'They lost him in the woods towards Torfael, *T'An* Commander.' Ho-Telerit had just taken the reports from her scouts, trailing dispiritedly into the yard.

'How far from here?' Ruric asked.

'Four *seri*. Perhaps five.'

'Mmm . . . Yes, all right, Ho-Telerit.' She watched the woman stump off. 'I don't like being trailed if I can help it, Christie.'

'So?' I prompted.

She spread the map on the window-ledge. 'We're here on the northern edge of the hills. Corbek's way up here in Roehmonde . . . you see the direct route's still north through Brinor.'

'That's where he'll expect us to go.' He had taken up a shadowy reality in my mind, though no one had been able to give us an accurate description.

'There's a chance Ho-Telerit's scouts have driven him off our track today. We'll go due east, cut across the heathland.' Her wide-spreading fingers left the map, and it coiled up into a scroll. She scratched at her black mane. 'There's a theocratic house at Terison, we can stop over there and go north the day after.'

I didn't feel half-crippled by a day's riding as I had done at the beginning, but I was tired and dirty and suffering mild stomach trouble from the unfamiliar food.

'How far to Corbek?' I asked.

'Two weeks, maybe twenty days. Which reminds me,' she said, 'how's your Roehmonde dialect?'

'Almost non-existent.' The Southland boasted at least seven distinct languages not on the hypno-tapes. That didn't count dialects—to some degree, each *telestre* has its own individual dialect; the provinces reflect language divisions more than political boundaries.

'I was up there about eight years back, doing garrison duty at the Skulls Pass. I'll teach you if you like,' she offered, 'and if you don't mind speaking it with a Melkathi accent.'

'I don't mind if they don't.'

'They're odd people, the Roehmonders,' she said. 'It'll be interesting to see how things have changed since I was there last.'

Off the hills, the ground was soft peat covered with the low scrub they call bird's-wing for the feathery striations on its yellow leaves. The carts made poor time on the wet track.

'There,' Ruric said, as the sun sent our shadows jogging east ahead of us. 'Terison.'

The terrain was becoming drier and there were stands of silverbarked trees. A speck that I had thought was a copse resolved itself into buildings.

'Goddess,' Maric whispered beside me, 'look at that!'

I shared his wonder: it was different from anything I'd seen in Ymir so far. There were two or three structures clustered together. No wall had an angle in it. Above the ground-floor slit windows the walls bellied out to join with their neighbours and make a single upper storey. The roofs rose into onion-domes. As we came closer, I saw the last sunlight give a gold tinge to the brown brickwork.

'It's an old place, they tell me, but it has a good reputation.' Ruric clapped heels to the *marhaz's* barrel-ribs and rode ahead. The dust that was dark on me was grey on her. I saw her reach the outer wall and stop, speaking with someone, and then dismount.

Maric stayed close to me, even when the *marhaz* were taken for stabling. He had his sullen look again. It masked what was almost a superstitious awe of the ancient structure.

It was dark inside the curved entrance arch: brown brick walls and grey stone flags. I stood with Ruric and Kem, accustoming my eyes to the gloom. Several *ashiren* came in while we were there. They wore *chirith-goyen* smocks, with a length of cloth wrapped apron-like round their waists. As they came in they went to the shallow troughs in the stone floor, stood in the water there and washed the dirt from their bare legs and feet. The cloth-apron was used to dry them and thrown into a stone basin. The children gave us bird-bright glances but didn't speak. Ruric seemed content to wait.

The curved arch framed an enamel-blue sky. Palmate leaves the size of dinner plates hung on a vine there, and tiny crimson grapes in fist-sized bunches rested against the bricks. Between us and the smooth arc of the outer wall were strips of cultivated land. A bell began to toll somewhere in the building—comfortingly familiar, after Tathcaer—and a dozen or so older *ashiren* came in. With them came a tall woman and a stocky man.

Ruric stepped forward and bowed. 'Goddess give you good day. Is it possible to claim guest-right for myself and my people?'

'Our house is open,' the man replied. He wore a priest's skirt. 'I'm Rhiawn. This is Branic.'

Ruric gave our names and set Kem to looking after the troop, and we entered the Wellhouse at Terison.

The passages curved and re-curved, the roof was a round arch, even the stone floor was worn concave by use. There were no lamps here, but we passed *ashiren* lighting torches in wall-brackets. There was a smoky tang to the air.

'We've many guests now, at harvest time,' Branic said. She was a

head taller than any of us, and had a permanant half-stoop from the
nearness of the ceiling. 'Some of you may have to sleep in priest's cells,
the guest rooms are full.'

'The roof of the Goddess over us is comfort enough.' Ruric used the
formal inflection for that politeness. Obviously there was no preferential
treatment here, even for the *T'An* Commander. I was too tired to worry
about what they'd make of me.

We came into a round well-lit room filled with tables and benches.
The noise warned me before I got to the door: thirty or so *ashiren*
yelling and chattering. There were stares when we entered but they
soon lost interest. Other Ortheans there looked to be from farming
telestres.

'You're just in time for evening meal,' Branic remarked, and she and
Rhiawn left us to find seats on the crowded benches. The food was
served by them, with help from the older *ashiren.*

Perhaps it was tiredness: as I ate, I seemed again to be among the
half-animal humanoids that the Ortheans at first resembled—especially
the light-boned children with their slender many-fingered hands, and
their blurring eyes. A failure of empathy. It was easier with adults, I
thought. The harsh-faced Branic, she could have been human. And that
woman beyond her, the one so obviously pregnant. And that man—

The man I was looking at turned. His face was horrifically scarred.
Maric, who'd followed my gaze, said, 'Goddess! that's an ugly one,
t'an.'

I hushed him. The Orthean male was fair skinned and yellowmaned,
broadshouldered and tall. It looked as though he'd been burned—all
one side of his face was a red-and-white patchwork. By some miracle he
still had the eye, bright in its nest of ruined flesh. Where the burn
vanished into the hairline, his mane had grown back silver.

I thought about plastic surgery and, as an extension of that thought,
Ruric's missing arm; and it brought home to me the fact that Orthe
needed us. Culture shock or not. You have to be practical.

The meal finished, the benches and tables were shoved back against
the walls and a brazier was lit in the centre of the room. The *ashiren*
settled on the floor in groups, talking, some playing a variant of the
Southland game called *ochmir.* I saw Rhiawn putting two benches together, and a folded blanket over them, and the pregnant woman lay
down there close by the fire. The party with her were bawdy, boisterous.

'Is she all right?' I asked Branic.

'She's come to the Wellhouse for the birth,' the Orthean woman
said, as if that explained everything. 'The Goddess keeps an open door.

For them, too,' she said as one of the *ashiren* brought wine. 'Runaways, most of them.'

'But don't you send them back home?'

'You can't take a child from its mother,' she said, with the inflection that turned 'mother' into 'Goddess'. 'The land's poor here. We work harder than most of the surrounding *telestres*. A lazy one knows running here won't help. The other *ashiren* must have their reasons.'

But they're children! I wanted to protest, and didn't. The young of the species weren't childlike.

A little later I went with Maric and Ruric to oversee the transfer of baggage to our rooms. These were separate small cells with hard beds, buckets for washing, and a pisspot under the bed. All the residents of the house shared the same discomfort. It was simple, primitive, and (I thought, looking at the worn stone floor) perhaps because of that, it had survived for a good long time.

'I must have a word with Kem before tomorrow,' Ruric said, and we went with her back to the round hall—and walked into chaos.

Most of the people there had given up their various occupations of talking and drinking and *ochmir,* and were paying close attention to the woman on the benches. She cried out once, then grunted, breathing hard. They called encouragement, crowding round. Those closest to her were breathing in her rhythm.

'Jesus, isn't there *anything* they keep private?'

Ruric's head turned. I realized I'd spoken aloud.

'Nothing's private in the one *telestre,*' she said, sweetly reasonable. 'And we're all one *telestre* in the Goddess's house.'

'But they haven't even sent the kids out!'

She looked at me as if I was mad and I shut up. If I was shocked, it was culture shock, or maybe species shock.

'Hold her up—'

'Ready!'

'—be careful—'

The woman didn't scream, but she grunted as if she were being kicked. I saw her head tilt back. A dark-skinned male was gripping both her hands. Branic, kneeling at the foot of the bench, threw blood-stained cloths into a basin.

The woman yelled. The younger woman squatting beside her stood up, cradling a bloody mass. I bit my lip. It was a child, and it was covered in a thick membrane.

The young woman, with a practised gesture, hooked her sixth finger and slit the membrane with her claw. The baby choked and then gave a thin squawl. My throat constricted. It was tiny: much smaller than a human baby.

By the time the woman had washed it—she must be a midwife, I decided—the second and third were born, and free of their membranous cases. I felt sick. It was a shame Adair wasn't there, I thought, he would have appreciated it.

'A three-birth,' Rhiawn said beside me, and pointed at the younger woman. 'Kyar will nurse them until Gabrit's milk comes in.'

Adair had said milk was always late with Orthean females. I had a glimpse of how that bound them in interdependence: there must be large family units, there must be milk-mothers and foster-mothers.

I fully expected the mother to be put to bed, but within a short time she was sitting by the fire, wrapped in blankets. She and the father and the milk-mother were each holding one of the babies, swapping them round occasionally. Branic came back with more wine, and everyone present gave some wish for the future, and before long it had turned into a party.

'Are you all right?' Ruric said to me impatiently.

They were an appallingly tough and hardy species, I thought. I nodded, and took the next mug of wine that passed.

The window was visible only as a dark grey slit. Darkness filled the room. I lay awake wondering how long it was to the dawn bell. The bed was hard. I still wasn't used to that. I'd be glad to get to Roehmonde, I thought. Travel here was dirty and insect-ridden and uncomfortable.

Wood creaked.

Several seconds passed. Simultaneously with my realization that, as the floor was stone, it must be the door, came another noise. A harsh slithering hiss.

I held my breath and willed the blood to stop pounding in my ears. The noise had been the drawing of a *harur* blade from its sheath.

Silence.

Could I be wrong? Of course: nothing could possibly happen here.

The stunner was in its holster, flung down on my bags in the far corner of the room. My belt-knife was there too. And I couldn't pretend, now, that I heard nothing. There was someone in the room.

I sensed movement. Then the window was obscured. All in one convulsive movement I slid out of bed, hurled the rough blanket in the direction of the window, and ran. Something caught me a crack across the shins. I stumbled, grazing my hands on the stone floor, and something whipped past my head and thunked into the doorpost.

I reached up and a red-hot iron bar slammed into my palm. I snatched my hand back, yelling. Silence was my enemy now. I heard distant shouts: I was cold with fear, hatred, relief. And I'd marked myself as a target.

Footsteps.

Definite, slow, shuffling; a little to the left of me. I held my breath and crabbed sideways until my shoulder touched the bed. Flat to the floor, I did a half-roll and reached up to touch the slats of the wooden frame. Safe, safe, safe! If I could keep quiet. Absolutely quiet. Whoever it was didn't have a torch. They expected to find me asleep. Something tickled the length of my forearm. I shrunk down.

'Christie!'

A yell down the corridor. In the room the footsteps went back and forth, then the door creaked, then there was silence. I didn't move. A flickering yellow dazzle appeared in my vision. I wondered if I was going to pass out. Then the edge of the door and the brickwork became visible, shadows jumped, and I realized that someone was running down the corridor with a torch.

'Christie?' Ruric shouted.

I crawled out from under the bed, dust clinging to my shirt, bare-legged and feeling vulnerable.

'There—I think there was someone in here.'

'Think? Don't you know?' She jammed the torch in the wall-bracket and came across, grabbing my hand. I yelled. Bright drops spattered.

'I didn't see.' The blood fascinated me. It had run down my arm to my elbow—that had been the tickling sensation. My hand felt as if it had been hit with a hammer. There was a deep slash across the palm. I must have put it up and run it into the *harur* blade.

Ruric abruptly left the cell. There were more torches: Branic, Rhiawn, Maric, and Ho-Telerit appeared. Time disjointed. I sat down while Rhiawn bathed and bandaged my hand, and breathed deeply, and steadied myself against rising hysteria.

My hand was a raw sharp mass of pain.

'You're lucky,' he said, 'it hasn't touched the tendons. You'll keep the use of it.'

He let go of my hand reluctantly, staring curiously at it. Hadn't he seen the difference before? I thought, and laughed shakily. It was my right hand.

'Ruric—' I said. She came back into the cell.

'You've no idea who it was? Were they heavy or light, quick or clumsy? Was it *harur-nilgiri, harur-nazari?*'

'I'm sorry, I—it was too dark—I don't know.'

Branic stormed back in. I hadn't seen her go. She towered over Ruric, furious.

'Your soldiers refuse to let me outside! There are drawn swords everywhere. In the house of the Goddess!'

'Theocratic house or not, it's under martial law.' Ruric was cool. 'I've directed my commander to put guards on all doors, at the stables, and on the outer gate. I want no one leaving here. Ho-Telerit, wake anyone who isn't already awake and get them assembled in the hall.'

Rhiawn left with Branic. I sat on the bed, just beginning to take in what had happened. Ruric seated herself beside me.

'Have you any ideas?' Her hand was on her swordhilt. I saw where her gaze went.

'I don't believe it was the kid.'

Maric looked up, scared. 'It wasn't, *t'an.*'

Ruric didn't look convinced. 'Come along to the hall, Christie, there might be something that triggers your memory. You might recognize someone. No, the *ashiren* too. *Ke* walks in front of me.'

I laced my britches, not bothering to put boots on, and followed Ruric back through the winding passages. Kem met her outside the hall.

It was while they were talking that I remembered the medical kit. It was in the cell. So was the stunner. I wanted the use of both, and I should have remembered before. I was slipping: that annoyed and scared me.

I left Ruric there, going quietly back down the corridor. It wouldn't take a minute, I thought.

I walked into the room and onto the point of a blade.

Assassin

I went down as if I'd been dropped, already rolling, and caught him across the shins. The unfinished thrust took him forward. He fell, twisting. We came up facing each other. It was the man with the scarred face. He had his back to the door, *harur-nilgiri* still in his hand. Unarmed, I fell automatically into the ready position, as if this were a practice bout.

He cut. Incredibly fast. I swayed, let it slide past me. Balance. Too slow. The sleeve of my shirt snagged, the cloth turning red like blotting paper soaking up ink. Adrenalin pounding. Watch the eyes, the eyes and not the blade!

Grey light. Stars. No chance to turn and grab the stunner lying in the cell's far corner. Silver light sliding on metal. The cautious sighting for a skewering thrust. He's angry. I'm unarmed. I've dodged his cuts and slashes: yes, he's angry. Good. And I move right—

Metal skids across brickwork. Panic: no! but it's all I can do to back off safely. Out of reach. How long before I'm cornered: not long. Now: the feint, the circling, eye and eye. The ferocity of the dance.

And thrust.

I can't get close and throw him. No chance, not one-handed. (Concentrate: ignore the raw pain there.) He's stronger than I am, can't hold him.

And the razor-edged thrust—

Caught between two walls, cornered. And if I knock his arm aside, the return cut will take me just between the ribs, blunt and hollow-sounding as a butcher's cleaver; and I can't hold him.

Not fear: certainty. You fucked it up, Christie.

Coming for me quick, no place to move to, can't move; taking me high in the chest, is it, or the throat, or—

So I came forward and saw the surprise on his face. Left-handed, not blocking the thrust but catching his wrist, pulling him forward. The blade slid over my shoulder.

Still gripping his wrist, and the point slammed into the wall. There was a sharp sound clear in the air that—except for hurried breathing—was silent. Ugly: a snapping sound. His hand still tangled in the grip. A moment of numb stillness, neither of us believes this.

He shook his hand free of the guard, dropped the blade, and slammed through the door. Anger took over: utter, cold, and certain. Total: destroying all training and thought. So that I had the door open and was running down the passage, yelling, no, *screaming* with hate; the stunner in my hand and no recollection of picking it up. Running and firing left-handed, but the corridors twisted: I couldn't get a line on him.

He kicked another door shut in my face, and I swung it open—a dead-end room, trapped him. But someone hung on to my arm and shouted, then I was freed and someone caught me a tremendous clout across the head.

'Christie, stop! *Stop!*'

I stood still, shaking, frightened at myself. I hadn't expected to tap such reserves of fear and fury. Careless, I thought. Jesus Christ, use your brains, can't you!

Fear and fury: the time I was beaten up when I was a kid, the time I was followed home by a gang of youths, hugging the street-lit centre of a dark road. The child's fear, and the woman's. And the same snarling reflex: you touch me and I'll fucking kill you!

'He's claimed sanctuary!'

'Ruric?' When I wiped my face, it was wet. Things focussed. The dark woman gripped my arm.

The door opened on a domed room, white plaster walls reflecting star light from a skylight in the roof. The man knelt beside a low circular rim of stone. Light reflected from the well water onto his twisted face. He cradled his swelling wrist. Broken: I saw the jutting edge of bone under taut white skin. His eyes watched me with blank hatred. I raised the stunner.

'You can't kill him, he's under the Goddess's care,' Ruric insisted.

'I'm not going to kill him. Just knock him out.'

'You can't touch him!'

'Don't tell me what I can't do.'

'*T'An* Commander—' Kem came running up and stopped, taking in the situation. I heard others coming. It must have taken a very short time, that clash: the razor-edge of circling metal, and the fear.

It was almost like a practice session back on Earth, unarmed combat against the blows of a wooden staff. There, a mistake meant bruises. And here . . . the shirt-sleeve stuck to my arm, where the hairline cut was already dry. I couldn't seriously believe someone had tried to use a length of sharp metal to kill me.

'He's under the Goddess's protection,' Ruric repeated. Rhiawn and Branic came up, others following them. Kem and Ho-Telerit kept them back.

'You mean to say that because he's standing there—in that room—you won't touch him?'

'In a Wellhouse? I can't. I've gone far enough as it is. Even as *T'An* Commander I'd be in trouble if I did more.' She glanced over her shoulder. Rhiawn and Branic glared at her, stiff-faced. 'Suthafiori would back me, but she doesn't need me making trouble between her and the church. She had enough of that bringing you here. No, I think I've got to leave this one.'

The palm of my hand ached bone-deep. I was afraid. Wounds turn septic. Ruric had had an arm amputated for something not much more serious in its beginning.

'I'm not bound by your laws. I won't kill him. But I'll bring him out.'

She didn't let go of my arm. 'If you use Witchbreed weapons in the house of the Goddess—'

'It's nothing to do with the Golden Witchbreed, it's a coherent sound amplifier!'

'I know that. But anyone between the Wall and the Inner Sea will call you a liar. It's a pity you can't handle the *harur* blades.' There was acid mockery in her tone.

'I have no intention of walking in there with half a yard of butcher's knife and you know it.' And it occurred to me that if he'd had time to draw *harur-nazari* as well as *harur-nilgiri* when I surprised him, I might not be having this argument.

'Unwise, in any case: if you upset the church it won't please your government or mine. The man isn't stupid,' she said, loosing her grip on me, 'It was only bad luck that he didn't kill you the first time.'

'*Bad* luck?'

She abandoned her temper. 'His. And our good fortune.'

'I'm glad you think so.'

She looked at the man, who gave no sign that he heard us. 'I'll leave

Ho-Telerit and her people here, keep him penned in. He'll either give in or attempt escape, in which case she can bring him along after us.'

'He might get away. At least find out who he is, who sent him.'

She shrugged, but stood in the doorway and asked questions. He never moved or answered. She came away, signalling to Kem, who placed guards at the door.

'I'd say he's a hired sword, Ymir or Rimon by his clothes—that style of *harur-nilgiri* is south-Rimon. Picked up in Tathcaer and set to trail us, hoping for a surprise kill.'

Now it was finished I was experiencing a tight knot of tension in my stomach.

'Whoever it was, SuBannasen or another, won't try that again,' Ruric continued. 'Not with us ready for it. And we'll have their name out of him soon.'

'So we carry on to Roehmonde?' I couldn't see any advantage in returning to Tathcaer.

'We do. We're formidable enemies, when we're ready.' She smiled at me, not maliciously. 'Even you, *S'aranth.*'

It was an epithet I'd heard the troopers use, but after Terison it had a different tone. Maric translated it as 'swordless' (with the implication it held of being *ashiren*). I remembered what Geren had said, a long time ago: it's the one thing that might tell against you. All Southlanders acquire use-names. Ruric was Yelloweyes. From then on I was Christie *S'aranth.*

I carried the pain of my hand while it healed, but I was disturbed by the violence of the response it had called out of me.

The sedatives could take the pain away, but nothing could make me sleep the rest of the night. After a while, when it became apparent that there was no use trying, I lay and watched the patch of sky visible through the window: the moving stars, the dulling to first twilight, and the gradual unstoppable lightening of dawn.

I felt . . . not afraid, not angry, not shocked or excited: but as if I had been woken up to the degree where sleep was no longer a human necessity. The effects of shock are the same, I think, whether its origins are good or bad.

Terison was lost in the early morning haze. The mist pulled back from the arch of the blue sky. We rode over peaty heathland among bird's-wing scrub and thousandflower-moss. Light flashed off *siriye* webs white with dew. There was a cool wind, a smell of damp earth, and the harsh calling of *rashaku*. The morning was painfully bright, lack of sleep beginning to make itself felt.

'According to the map we can pick up one of the Old Roads north of here. That should speed up the pace.' Ruric's heels dug into Gamble's hide and the *marhaz* edged closer to Gher. In a low exasperated tone she said, 'Sunmother's tits! What's the matter with you? You're acting like a woman after her first fight.'

'I—well, yes, I suppose it was.'

'You're seriously telling me—'

'That was the first time I ever put combat training into practice. Somehow I never expected to have to.' Gher hissed, reluctant to pick his way through boggy ground, and I reached forward and scratched between his horns. 'I don't know how I feel about it. Your people treat me differently. . . .'

'You've to expect that.' She was shrewd. 'Up until now they've taken you and your kin for overgrown *ashiren*. Now they know you're the same as us, it's just your methods that are different.'

The man's scarred face stayed with me. That, and the noise that bone makes when it snaps.

'I'm not a violent person.'

'Nor I,' said the Orthean woman, 'and never when it isn't necessary.'

'That's what the *T'An* Commander says?'

She laughed sourly. 'I'm no bloody-sword barbarian. I play the game to keep us out of wars. But when I have to, I can finish one in my favour faster than anyone alive. That's why Suthafiori made me *T'An* Commander.'

We lost some time before noon when the cart bogged down in wet ground, but after that we made a good pace and came about midafternoon to stands of *lapuur* trees and level ground. Ruric called a meal break.

'There,' she said as we walked out from under the yellow-green fronds of *lapuur*. 'The Old South Road.'

At first I thought it was only flat land, and then I saw that it ran straight as a ruler towards the low ridges of the north. South, it vanished under the wet earth. A strip of hard ground some thirty feet wide, it made a cutting through the distant ridges.

'The 'Breed made roads where it suited them, and not where it suited the land,' Ruric said. 'Kem won't like travelling on that but I want to make up time.'

I walked over for a closer look. Digging down with a belt-knife, I found some six or eight inches of soil and then rock. When I had cleared enough for a good look, I found a smooth, flat surface of blue-grey stone; a stone that I couldn't begin to scratch with the knife. There was a line too straight to be a crack. Two stones butted together that couldn't be pried apart: this was a paved road.

'Have you finished grubbing about in the dirt?' Ruric asked, strolling back from her meal. 'We're ready to go.'

'Yes. No. How long has this been here?'

She shook her head. 'Legends say since Sandor's time, the last Emperor. I don't know. Way before the fall of the Golden Empire.'

Three, maybe four thousand years. I stood up and brushed the mud off my knees, appalled at antiquity.

'If we—' she stopped, staring back across the heath. 'Ho-Telerit. That was quick. Slow down, woman, you'll have your *marhaz* in a pothole! Wait a minute—only six riders?'

She ran back towards the carts. When I got there, the troopers were dismounting, and Ho-Telerit stood with an unhappy look on her broad face.

'You're swift,' Ruric commented.

'We left only a short time after you,' she admitted. 'We lost him, *T'An* Commander.'

'How?'

'He was missing after the mid-morning bell. My people say he never passed them. I believe them. There's more than one way out of a Well-house, *T'An*, especially if you've a priest's aid.'

'Branic,' Ruric said, hand hooked in her swordbelt. 'That flare-tempered, landless woman Branic!'

Ho-Telerit nodded. I said, 'You mean she let him go?'

'Let him? She likely gave him a *marhaz* to go on. And she knows I can't lodge a complaint, things are touchy enough as it is with the church.' She frowned, then shook her head. 'All right, Ho-Telerit. Kem, I want us moving, right now.'

'Was Branic paid?' I was getting as paranoid as an Orthean.

'No, I don't think so.' She whistled Gamble. Maric came over with Gher. 'That was to let me know they don't like *harur* law in a theocratic house. And there's nothing I can do about it. Let's move. The further away I get from these southern conspiracies, the happier I'll be.'

The Old Road took us north for two days, almost eighty *seri* through desolate moorland. On the third day we crossed the Tulkor river where it joins the river Turi. We came into low hills and flame-red *ziku* forests, and turned north-east to follow the Turi up into northern Ymir.

It was strange country to ride through, almost deserted. If it hadn't been for a few cultivated fields I could have believed it uninhabited. We travelled many *seri* before coming across one of the castle-warren-like *telestres,* and long intervals before we passed any others.

I got into the rhythm of the journey: rising at first twilight and riding until the stars rose, with a break at noon to eat. Sometimes we had guest-right and slept in a *telestre,* sometimes in one of the infrequent companion-houses. But as we went further north the troopers often made open camp, setting up tents and lighting fires like born nomads. If there were no *telestres* for supplies, the scouts did more hunting than scouting.

On Stathern Firstweek Fiveday we arrived at Salmar, usually admitted to be the northernmost of the Ymirian-speaking *telestres.* It was the fourteenth day since leaving Tathcaer.

'I like to break a journey,' Ruric observed, as we walked through the fields of Salmar. Hives stood in rows under the sheltering bird's-wing scrub: hives of the *chirith-goyen* clothworm—or at least, two or three of the several hundred varieties of that species. A lot of the northern *telestres* are *chirith-goyen* harvesters and weavers. And if not the clothworm, then the *becamil* webweaver-beetles.

'But I'd not have done it if I'd known. Mother!' She chuckled. 'A five-birth and a three-birth within days of each other—no wonder they're busy right now!'

I pictured the total breakdown that would have produced in any family I knew. But the Salmar community, a *telestre* of nearly two hundred people, was managing nicely.

'It's all right for you,' I said, 'having your kids in quads and quintuplets. We have ours one at a time!'

She was thoughtful. 'I had a single-birth.'

The intense sun shone on the *chirith-goyen* webs. We walked across the mossgrass, back towards the stables.

'How many births, then, would you have in a life?' Ruric sounded startled.

'Without preventive methods? It's been a long time, but . . . my great-great-grandmother was the ninth child of a family of eighteen.'

She stared. 'I wondered how there got to be so many of you.'

'And you?'

'Two births,' she said, 'perhaps three; or sometimes only one. Not all will live.'

That confirmed what Adair had told me. Allowing for accident, disease, and primitive medical standards, I doubted Orthe would ever have a population problem. I made a mental note to add quarantine restrictions to the suggestions in my report.

'I saw Elmet's three,' I said, 'they looked healthy. But three girls at once, that's a handful.'

'There's the father and the milk-mothers to help. She'll probably stand as milk-mother herself to some of the five-birth.' As we came into the stable yard she stopped and faced me. 'What do you mean, girls?'

'They were, weren't they?'

'They're *ashiren*. How can you tell what sex *ke* will be until *ke* are adult?'

That simple. Standing there in the sunlight, with the hissing of *marhaz* and the burning odour of the smithy: I thought, *Adair, you only had to ask. . . .*

'You mean your young are born sexed?' Ruric was incredulous. 'Born adult?'

'You mean yours aren't?'

There was one of those silences that ensued whenever we tripped over species differences. Maric passed us, leading Oru, and waved to me cheerfully.

'He—'

'*Ke's* about a year off change,' Ruric said. 'The *ashiren* usually develop into adults around fourteen, that's why they're prone to sickness about that time. Christie—if your *ashiren* are born sexed, how can you tell when they're adult?'

'There are changes. Nothing that drastic.' I studied Maric, where he stood holding Oru's head while the smith lifted a back hoof. Something in the mouth, the eyes . . . yes, I could see him as a girl. But my first impression of him as male contradicted that.

I could see Maric as boy or girl, but I couldn't do what the Ortheans do, see *ke* as neuter. It was either/or. And, realizing that, I knew why the xeno-team hadn't seen it. It was not a view one ever questioned. Either/or.

Nothing is private in the one *telestre*. And somehow I seemed to have become part of the Southland, while Adair and Eliot and the others remained isolated in Tathcaer.

How can you bring up a child if you don't know what sex it is? Some reactionary part of my mind protested. But I realized the question was nearly as meaningless to me as it would be to Ruric, and I let the subject drop.

After Salmar we left the hills behind. The land was flat and fertile, broken by winding streams, and there were many of the tri-vaned windmills that the Roehmonders use. We rode winding tracks between grain fields now harvested to stubble and stacks. This part of Stathern was fine, but the nights were getting chill. Still going north, we crossed tawny grassland where double-horned *skurrai* grazed, and were two days travelling between amber mossgrass and eggshell-blue sky with only the hissing bellow of the beasts for company. The *telestres* were large, the Ortheans more reserved—or perhaps it was just that my Roehmonde was worse than my Ymirian—but they granted guest-right to the *T'An* Commander of the Southland.

Hills broke the horizon again as we came to the beginning of the Roehmonde forest *telestres*. The *tukinna* are tall and spindly, greygreen, with crooked branches and rosettes of tightly-rolled leaves. Nothing grows under them but mossgrass and gold-enfern. The *telestres* depend either on timber or hunting for survival. We made camp in clearings, and kept fires burning at night. The silence of the brilliant starlight was broken by snarls and cries, and the metallic whooping of *rashaku,* but we were too large a party to be attacked.

The slash across my palm healed. I rubbed salve in to make it flexible, and took painkillers when necessary. Perik, one of the scouts, offered me *ataile* leaves to chew. I refused, not being sure of the effect on human metabolism. She and I often rode together, and Maric and another scout named Vail rode with us. There was some discussion about unarmed combat, which I demonstrated, and the finer points of *harur* swordcraft, which she attempted to teach me. We were neither of us good pupils.

Markstones were infrequent but we managed to keep to the right track. Ruric was determined to press on in the good weather. Six days brought us through thick forest to Remoth, where gaunt hills went up towards the east, and we skirted west of them through steep rivergorges. The next night brought us to a companion-house at Temethu beside the river Beruth.

'Look,' Maric said. 'Too far for bow-shot, but I suppose we don't need to hunt now.'

Down between the *tukinna* trees I saw first curving backs, then raised heads, and then—in the instant before flight—grave, spindly beasts as large as *skurrai*. Their back fur was rich brown. They rose on strong haunches, tiny front legs drawn up to their scaled chests; they were almost black against the sunlit gold-enfern. I saw them bound away under the trees.

'What are they?'

He touched the brown pelt on Oru's saddle. *'Wirazu.'*

The path curved closer to the river and there was no use talking, the thundering water made it impossible. High, forested gorge walls rose on either side of us, and the daystars were bright in the narrow strip of sky. A fine spray hung over the rocks.

I rode up beside Ruric, Maric following me. He was smart in clean tunic and polished boots. The troop hadn't left Temethu until noon, being occupied with cleaning gear and grooming *marhaz*, and putting on the long-saved last clean change of clothes. Ruric wore a brown *becamil* cloak embroidered with gold thread, and all her rank-badges gleamed on her belt. I'd had to compromise, you can't ride a *marhaz* in a formal skirt. I settled for formal Earth jacket and Ymirian britches.

We crossed the river by a broad stone bridge, riding down a track that was paved where the gorge widened. Clumps of blue thousand-flower rooted in the shale. *Tukinna* furred the high slopes, rising out of the damp shadow. The river ran quietly.

I rode, hearing that wine-glass reverberation: wind in the scrolled leaves of the *tukinna*. There was a disturbing metallic taste in the air.

Smell is the keenest way to memory. I paused, and what came flooding back was the heat of summer streets before I was five years old. To recall that warmth, then to open eyes on the pale northern shadows . . .

. . . and realize that river dampness was bringing me the previously-unnoticed odour of *tukinna*, and that the smell of this alien vegetation was identical to the road-tar that melted in yellow Earth summers, and ran in the gutters of childhood.

Even the most basic certainties can change, form again into something strangely new.

The road made a sharp turn north.

It was Stathern Secondweek Nineday, twenty six days since we left Tathcaer, the fastday before the autumn solstice. I rode over the bridge where the Berufal meets the Beruth and entered Corbek.

PART
THREE

9

Hospitality of
T'An Roehmonde

'Christie?'

'I'm out here.'

Ruric appeared beside me on the balcony. She was wearing one of the long sleeveless Roehmonder coats, unbuckled and showing the rich *zilmei* pelt lining. It was a chill morning, even in the room behind me where the brazier's embers glowed.

'I thought I'd tell you, I'm leaving after the solstice feast tonight. Going up to Path-of-Skulls in the morning.'

'I didn't think you'd go so soon.'

'I want to talk to the garrison commander, Asshe. He's an old friend of mine.' She leaned on the wrought iron balustrade, gazing out over Corbek. 'I want to know what he makes of all this . . . of course, the garrison gets its supplies from the *telestres* north of here, but he comes down to Corbek on occasion. And I've got to make the official visit in any case—the Barrens are quiet, and he thinks the barbarians are planning another series of raids.'

'And Corbek?' That was the crux of it.

'You saw it when we came in! There was always a problem here, even eight years back when I last saw the place, but never—*never*—this bad.'

Corbek lay spread beneath us, its clusters of towers and domes in pale grey stone. Frost whitened the wrought-iron gates and balconies. Carts jolted through unpaved lanes. From here it was just possible to see over gentle slopes to the watermills along the Berufal, and the barges on the Beruth. Thick early morning haze hung over both rivers like cotton wool, the horizon was grey, and it was only at the roof of the sky that I saw pale stars and sunlight. Hidden—but not forgotten, sharp in my mind—were the wooden shacks and mud-rutted slums where the rivers met.

'There are always a few landless men and women,' the Orthean woman admitted, 'and it's inevitable that they drift into cities, I suppose. But so many—and with *ashiren!* What's the Wellkeeper thinking of?'

'What could a Wellkeeper do?'

She swung round, her back to the sheer drop. 'Send Earthspeakers to find out why they left their *telestres!* Find new *telestres* that they could become *n'ri n'suth* to. Apprentice them as *l'ri-an* in the city! What else are Wellhouses for?'

She paced the stone tiled floor, apparently oblivious that she was barefoot to the cold. Her single hand sought and rested on the hilt of her *harur* blade. When she looked at me again her opaque eyes had cleared, and she relaxed.

'Sorry. Why shout at you, after all? But I don't like to see this, and I wish you didn't have to either.'

'I haven't seen real poverty on Orthe before, no. But I was bound to meet it eventually.'

'Is it so inevitable, then, for you?'

'Yes, I think it is. And I can remember when there were no beggars on the streets of London. Corbek's slums, for all their dirt-poverty, at least function.'

The line of sunlight crept down the face of the bluff, brightening the windows and balconies of the rooms built into the cliff. Our shadows fell sharp and black against the half-circle arch that opened into the room.

'How long will you be away?' I asked.

'Say, eight or nine days riding north, and I'll have to stop over a few days. . . . Expect me early in Torvern Forthweek, if the weather's good.' Her preoccupied expression returned. 'I'll send one of the troopers south now, let Suthafiori know how things stand here. Not that she can do much.'

'Maybe I'll ride back to Tathcaer with you,' I suggested as we went into the low-ceilinged room. 'I should have finished here in three weeks' time.'

'Yes, why not,' she agreed.

I never made that ride with her.

The Roehmonders ring their day bells in chimes. The cascade of the sunset bells died away across the city. I finished brushing my hair quickly, standing before the full length mirror of beaten silver. I couldn't help smiling: the deceptive light of Carrick's Star had tanned my uncovered arms and face, but the rest of me was pale. I was piebald. The snake-texture of the Orthean skin doesn't tan.

Formal dress again: dark skirt and jacket, the price for coming to a civilized city. But I was glad to be there, glad not to be on the open road with dirt and bugs and no hot water.

I went down the flights of stairs that honeycombed the cliff, inside and out, to where Maric waited with Gher and Oru. We rode along the muddy lanes to the end of the bluff. It was a *seri* or more to the *T'An* Roehmonde's household. Our breath steamed on the air. Semi-circles of light shone from the arches above us. The last of the season's *siriye* floated in the chill. Ruric rode up on Gamble, coming from the river side of the city, not inclined to talk much.

The descending line of the cliff face merged imperceptibly into the walls of the *T'An* Roehmonde's household, and we turned and rode through a tunnel hacked out of the rock. Coming out of the low arch, we were in the natural amphitheatre formed at the side of the bluff, in a vast courtyard surrounded by domed buildings and round towers. The main doors of the hall were open, spilling light out into the ornamental pools and fountains; and when I looked up past the carved facade of the hall I could just make out the dome of the Wellhouse that crowned the bluff.

'Maric,' Ruric said quietly, as we dismounted, 'you're *l'ri-an* for the envoy tonight in the hall. Just keep your ears open in the kitchens, will you?'

He nodded, taking Gamble's rein and leading the other *marhaz* away.

'What do you think he's going to hear?' I was curious.

'If I knew, I wouldn't ask.' Then she grinned. 'All right. He'll hear whatever won't be said within earshot of the envoy, the *T'An* Commander, or the *T'An* Roehmonde. Which might be useful.'

The game again, I thought. The omnipresent game of intrigue played within the *telestre,* or between *telestres,* or between cities—and perhaps between worlds, now.

'*T'An* Commander.' A plump Orthean male met us, bowing. '*T'An* envoy. Please, come this way.'

He led us through an antechamber and into the main hall. I recognized him from the reception committee of the day before: he was middle-aged, and unusually overweight for an Orthean, with a dark mane receding into a crest. The Roehmonder dress—long tunic, loose trousers tucked into short boots—was topped in his case by a *wirazu* pelt, and a belt studded with gems the size of hazelnuts. His six-fingered hands were clumsy with rings, a beaten silver chain hung round his neck, even the hilts of the *harur-nilgiri* and *harur-nazari* were thickly ornamented. The name surfaced after some digging in my memory: Verek Howice Talkul. Talkul was currently the ruling *telestre* in Corbek.

'Ruric!' An elderly man came forward and gripped her hand, looking her up and down.

'*T'An* Koltyn.'

'Ah, you sober southerners,' he remarked, taking in her plain dress. Her only ornaments were the rank-badges on her belt. 'I give you greeting. You also, envoy. Come: sit with me.'

He leaned on Howice's arm as he walked. Telvelis Koltyn Talkul, *T'An* Roehmonde, was the oldest Orthean I'd seen. His mane was white and sparse, his eyes half-veiled, and the flesh seemed to have shrunk onto his bones. Narrow chin and broad forehead: the Orthean face was not very human, studied in that condition.

'Sit' was a misleading term—the Roehmonders ate reclining on low couches. We made our way between them. Knowing Ymirian, Roehmonder had not been too hard to pick up. Koltyn's pace was slow, he stopped often to introduce other members of the *telestre*. Names filed themselves in my memory. There were over a hundred people in the hall, from *ashiren* to the old. And all one family: brothers, sisters, uncles, mothers, cousins, *n'ri n'suth:* the linkage of a *telestre* is inclusive and complex.

A great firepit was sunk in the middle of the hall, and *l'ri-an* walked on a level below us, turning meat on spits. Howice helped the *T'An* Roehmonde down onto his couch, and we all took couches round him. I noticed a prevalence of brown robes, both Earthspeaker and Wellkeepers. Maric came over with wine for Ruric and I.

'Verek Sethin Talkul,' Howice introduced the group. Sethin was a thin woman, neither young nor old. 'My sister. Sethin Falkyr, her son. The Earthspeaker Theluk. The Wellkeeper Arad.'

Falkyr was a neat cold man in his twenties, Theluk a darkmaned woman somewhat older; and Arad a contemporary of Howice, lean where the other man was stout.

'Theluk?' Ruric said as the *l'ri-an* were bringing round platters. 'I used to know a Theluk n'ri n'suth Edris up at Path-of-Skulls, a few years back.'

'I was your Second one winter, commander—*T'An*, I mean.' The woman shifted, embarrassed for a moment. 'The year the Simmerath nomads attacked.'

'I remember. Eight, no, nine winters back. Yes. And you're Earth-speaker now, and not Edris *telestre?*'

'Since six years ago. I was called. I mostly work down the east coast, but I've come upriver for the winter.'

'For the winter, was it?' the Wellkeeper Arad remarked, and the woman veiled her eyes. The food came round, and I heard Ruric quietly asking Theluk about conditions in east Roehmonde, but didn't hear the reply.

The *l'ri-an* served great steaks of *wirazu* and *zilmei*, with root vege-tables and black bread, and later fish from the coast, and *hura* clams from the river. I ate lightly and drank hardly at all, wanting a clear head. There's no Orthean tabu against talking business over a meal, indeed I sometimes think it's the only reason they eat together.

Iron stands held candles by the score, black iron wrought into eye-bending loops and curves. Candlelight glinted on rings and arm-brace-lets, on *harur* blades and buckles, and on crystal beads braided into Orthean manes. The stone floor was inset with patterns. It was warm where we were, by the firepit, but people had pulled their couches away from the chill at the doors.

'You had a long journey, envoy,' Howice said, as the second wine came round. 'How long does it take, travelling between the worlds?'

'Ninety days from my world to yours. Our days are shorter than yours, though.' He seemed satisfied. I wasn't going into details of FTL ships—the FTL drive is instantaneous in any case, it's getting far enough out of a star's gravity well to use it that takes the time.

'And to send word to your home?'

'The same.' There's no altering that, until we get a transmitter that works through trans-light space.

'A long exile.' He shook his head, sympathetic.

'I'm glad to be here.'

'And your *telestre?*' Sethin asked.

Orthean questions fall into a pattern after a while—what kind of *telestre* do we live in, why do we live apart from our families, what land do we hold (the term 'owner' passed out of my vocabulary), what weap-ons do we carry; how many *ashiren* do I have, who is my *arykei*, who is my *s'an telestre*, what is the custom of 'marriage', what is the Earth court like? I talked to Sethin without more than my average number of mistakes in Roehmonder terms and inflection.

There was an odd tinge to her skin, and sepia shadows under her clouded eyes. A little later she excused herself and left, and I saw Howice's eyes follow her anxiously. The old man, Koltyn, appeared not to notice; he was conversing with Ruric. I realized Sethin was a sick woman.

'No doubt we seem primitive to you.' There was an edge to Howice's voice. 'You and your kin who travel off the world doubtless have easier methods of doing things. Mining, for example. There are many forest *telestres* who'd like to hear of your methods of mining metal and quarrying stone.'

'I'm not an expert on that science, I'm afraid,' I said, taking closer notice of the man. 'One of my kin—my colleagues—in Tathcaer would be better qualified to tell you that.'

'Would they come here?' he asked.

'It's possible.' Ruric interrupted her conversation with the *T'An*. 'Once Suthafiori's had Christie's report. I don't agree with it myself, but—'

'You don't agree?'

Howice's pounce was indecently quick, I thought. His layer of charm was convincing, but very thin.

'Don't get me wrong. I approve of Christie.' Ruric grinned broadly at me. 'I even like some of her kin in Tathcaer. But letting her people—who we don't know at all—loose on the Southland, that I'm not so sure about.'

I hadn't been able to change her opinion. I wasn't sure that I wanted to. Orthe was a definite case for making haste slowly, and my reports were being coloured by that fact.

'We've much to gain by meeting Christie's people, I'm sure.' Howice was urbane. 'Though we're poor in Roehmonde, and have besides the Wall to guard, and tribes who envy us and would take what little we do have.'

'There again we come to methods,' the young man, Falkyr, said sardonically. 'Your people have weapons, I would suppose, that put our *harur* blades and winch-bows to shame?'

Howice gave him an angry glare. He was lean and crop-maned, Sethin's son, with something of a detached manner.

'None that we'd bring here,' I answered him, watching the quickly hidden greed on Howice's face. 'It's our strictest law.'

'So you carry no swords between worlds,' Arad's deep voice said, 'and yet you carry news of people who do not live by the Goddess's ways, and that may be fully as dangerous.'

I said, 'I can only tell you the truth.'

'Who said the truth wasn't dangerous?' Falkyr demanded, and laughed.

'Lies, also,' Theluk said softly, looking at Arad, 'and mostly they are dangerous to the liar.'

There was a circuit of hostility between them, Howice and Arad, Falkyr and Theluk; something they were aware of that we didn't know. I caught Ruric's eye. She gave a meaningful glance at Koltyn.

The *T'An* Roehmonde was propped up semi-reclining on cushions, staring abstractedly at the firepit. I put it down to old man's vagueness. Then I saw the thin thread of saliva leaking from the corner of his mouth. The membranes covered his eyes completely.

'The *T'An* sleeps,' Howice said, calling a *l'ri-an* who half-carried Koltyn from the hall. 'You'll excuse him tonight, I know, he is an old man and weary. I'll return in a moment.'

There was a brief hush in the hall as they left, and then the flutes picked up again, and there was singing over on the other side of the firepit, where the *ashiren* sat. Under cover of pulling the benches closer together, Ruric leaned over and spoke.

'Sleeps? That old man's senile! I couldn't put my finger on it till a while back, but when we were talking he thought it was nine years back, and I was commanding the Skulls garrison. Goddess!'

Her expression was pity mixed with disgust.

'He can't know it, can't realize it himself, or he'd renounce being *T'An* Roehmonde. But what's Talkul *telestre* thinking of? They must know he's in no condition—'

She broke off as Howice rejoined the group.

Theluk and Falkyr had been arguing heatedly for some minutes, and it was in the silence accompanying Howice's return that the argument broke surface.

'—nature of the Goddess—' Theluk stopped abruptly, with a glance at Arad.

'The Goddess being incarnate, then, on earth,' Falkyr pursued, as sceptical as I'd ever heard a Southlander be. 'In every generation?'

'Alive, and human,' Theluk said eagerly. 'Sometimes knowing Herself for what she is, and sometimes not aware but living as we live. And as liable to be a Roehmonder as an Ymirian, a woman of Kasabaarde as a man of the Rainbow Cities.'

I was all for staying out of religious arguments, but just then Falkyr gave me a superior smile.

'I suppose, then, that when She's here,' he said, 'She might very well come as an Otherworlder?'

There was an intake of breath from Arad. I swore mentally, cursing Falkyr. It was his way of annoying the Wellkeeper, but I didn't want it rebounding on my head. This was something to stop before it started.

'It's very unlikely, surely?' I said.

'But possible,' he needled Theluk. 'You said She is not always aware.'

'It's a question for the church,' Arad said harshly, 'and I agree with the envoy. In any case, the question is only ever settled with hindsight, after several generations.'

'You can answer me a question without waiting generations.' Ruric, distracting attention, stirring up trouble. 'The slums between the two rivers—eight years ago they weren't there, just a few landless men and women living round the barge-docks. Now there are shacks from the Berufal to the Beruth! What's happening?'

Theluk stared challengingly at Arad and I saw Falkyr watching with hooded eyes. Howice was apparently unaware of the whole discussion.

'The same problem, *T'An* Commander. The landless.' Arad was equally as hostile as Ruric. 'All the rogues and ruffians turned off their *telestres* come down to Corbek, and some ship out to the coast, and some stay and rot. What would you have me do, *T'An,* drive them out with swords?'

'If the *telestres* can't care for their own, they need looking to. In any case, the church has a duty—'

'And has performed it,' the Wellkeeper snapped.

'Are they *all* landless?' she asked, with that particular inflection that means Goddess as well as land. She was thinking of the *ashiren,* I knew.

'If a man or woman leaves their *telestre,* there must be a reason,' Arad persisted with the vehemence of an orator. 'We do not pick out of the dung-heap those who are too evil for even their own households.'

He glared round. People avoided his eye. Theluk looked as though she would have spoken, but then lowered her head.

'People must stay on their *telestres.*' Arad's gaze went past me to where Maric was pouring wine. 'When I was young, the *ashiren* didn't expect to be fostered hundreds of *seri* from home. We weren't made to become *l'ri-an* in other households. We stayed on the land where we belonged, forging the link with the Goddess. Now these rootless wanderers come to Corbek and expect us to take them in. No! Let them rot where they have chosen to be.'

Ruric turned on Howice. 'Does Koltyn agree with this?'

Faultlessly polite, Howice said, 'I'm afraid I can't discuss the *T'An's* policies in his absence.'

Not long after that, the hall began to clear. Maric whispered that he was staying to help with the cleaning, and I agreed that he should. Ruric went off in Theluk's company, and Howice—I wasn't surprised to see—spent his time soothing the Wellkeeper's temper.

'Sanctimonious landless *amari!*' Falkyr said under his breath. Then he saw I'd overheard and shuttered his eyes. Abruptly he said 'Ride out with me tomorrow. I know the city. And you might as well answer my questions as theirs.'

'I might as well,' I agreed, cheerfully.

'I thought you'd gone,' I said. 'The troop has.'

'I'll catch them up on the road. I've sent Ho-Telerit south,' Ruric added, 'but there's something needs doing before I leave Corbek.'

'Maric brought me your message.' I looked behind. The *ashiren* was holding the reins of Gher and Oru, and Falkyr was just dismounting.

'Don't worry about Sethin Falkyr, he'll do as a witness.' She turned, walking up the muddy lane. She wore a blue *becamil* cloak thrown back from her left shoulder, letting the drape of the cloth conceal the pinned sleeve and stump of her right arm. You wouldn't automatically have recognized the *T'An* Commander.

'Did you talk to *kir?*'

'About the *l'ri-an?* Yes.' Maric had come home late the previous night, very puzzled. 'He says they're afraid, but doesn't know of what.'

'Being *l'ri-an* has a bad name in Corbek—and *I* don't know why.'

Ruric stopped where a blank wall was broken by an ornamental gate, waiting for the young man to catch us up.

'*T'An* Commander.' Falkyr was cool, unhurried.

The iron gate swung open, and I saw Theluk in the shadow of the archway. She squinted up at the starbright autumn sky, eyes half-hooded.

'It's nearly time.'

'We're ready.' Ruric caught the challenging stare of Falkyr, and bowed, and ushered us both through the archway ahead of her. We crossed the tiny courtyard, and Theluk pulled open a heavy wooden door.

'Small, for a Wellhouse,' Falkyr commented, 'but a better-known one would not have suited you so well, perhaps?'

'Wellkeeper Uruth, here, is my friend,' Theluk said.

'And so lets you have the use of his house. What it is to have friends,' he said ironically, watching Ruric.

The room was small, domed, the stone walls lime-washed. A slot in the dome let in late morning light. The circle of the well mouth was black. We stood in a luminous twilight, except for one patch of white sunlight that showed dust on the floor, and flakes of lime.

'Who comes before the Goddess?' Theluk spoke formally.

'Lynne de Lisle Christie,' Ruric said.

'Who stands as her second?'

'*T'An* Commander *amari* Ruric Orhlandis.'

'Who stands as witness?'

Ruric glanced at him. 'The son of Sethin sees this.'

'I witness it,' Falkyr said grudgingly. 'If you bring me here to see your fool trick, I suppose I can't deny I've seen it.'

'I'm not sure what you're doing,' I said, 'but are you sure it applies to an offworlder?'

'If it applies to those outside the Southland, it can apply to anyone. And there may come a time when you need to answer yes, if they ask you if you've been recognized by the Goddess.'

I couldn't back out. Ruric had that look of abstract determination that meant she was plotting in advance of events.

'It's time,' Theluk said, approaching the well. The black water's surface was motionless.

There was a soundless explosion of light. I flung up one arm against the glare, and when I lowered it the room was pearl-bright with rainbow coruscations. Bells chimed across the city. The noon sun struck down through the slot in the dome, hit the surface of the well water, and dazzled us with luminosity.

'Here is Your daughter from a far—' Theluk hesitated '—a far world. Receive her name.'

Ruric's hand in the flat of my back pushed me forward. Theluk bent and dipped her hand in the well, lifted it dripping clear fire. She touched her wet fingers to my forehead, and both eyes. Momentarily I felt her heartbeat through her fingertips, the difference of her hands.

'The Goddess knows you,' she said, 'Lynne de Lisle Christie.'

'Witnessed,' Ruric said.

'Witnessed,' Falkyr echoed reluctantly.

Outside in the courtyard, I was still breathless and dazzled.

'If you need me, *t'an*, the Wellkeeper here will know where I am,' Theluk said awkwardly to me. She gripped Ruric's hand, and then made haste to swing the iron gates shut behind us.

'You think that will have any practical value?' Falkyr challenged Ruric.

'The point is, it's done, and I'm grateful.' I wasn't entirely sure for what, but her intentions were obvious.

She smiled, yellow eyes hooded. 'Torvern Forthweek,' she said. 'But you can always send a message up to the garrison. Though, knowing you, you won't need to.'

We walked down to where Maric held the *marhaz*.

Gher splashed mud as we cantered up beside the Berufal river. One of the rare autumn rainstorms had swept down the river valley and this was the first time in four days that we'd ridden outside the city.

The road was a morass. Shacks crowded close to it, sprawling wooden structures with board-tiled roofs. Some were old and disintegrating. In other places new, round, box-like rooms had been tacked on, two and three storeys high; staircases wound between them. Clothes hung on ropes strung between buildings. Steam went up into the rainwashed sunlight. The pig-like red guardbeasts, *kuru*, rooted in the dirt. Drab-clad *ashiren* played in the mud, or sat on steps blankly watching us ride by.

'You'd think they'd go,' I said. None of the structures were temporary. 'Why don't they leave?'

Falkyr shrugged.

'This doesn't happen in Tathcaer.' It was my only other point of reference.

'They don't belong.' Falkyr delicately edged his *marhaz* closer.

'To a *telestre?*'

'To anything or anybody.'

I'd been in the Southland just long enough to appreciate how atypical that was.

'Can't they go back to their *telestres?*'

For the first time in the several days I'd known him, Falkyr had no mordantly witty or sarcastic answer.

'There are certain new laws from the church. You heard Arad. We are not to leave our *telestres* without very good reason.' He didn't look at me. 'Having left for no better reason than that living there was impossible for them—they can't go back. And no one follows old custom and takes them in *n'ri n'suth*, or *l'ri-an*.'

'Because they're afraid?' I guessed.

'If it were Arad alone—or even the *T'An* alone—' His head came up and he straightened. 'I'll give my uncle his due: more people are prosperous because of it, because of keeping to their *telestres* and working; it's better for Roehmonde.'

'But some people pay a price.'

His eyes hooded. He smiled. 'There's always a price, *t'an*. Even your world's marvels come with a price on them, I'd say.'

He was formal again, irreverent and laughing; but I'd had a glimpse of an unhappy man. He'd said: leaving for no better reason than that living there was impossible. . . .

Was it impossible living with Howice, with Sethin, with the sick old man? I didn't ask. Loyalty is to the *telestre*. He wouldn't answer.

It was Torvern Firstweek Sixday, the day I returned to the *T'An* Roehmonde's household to find another guest. A gaunt whitemaned woman, whom I regarded for several minutes before I recognized her from our one previous encounter: Sulis n'ri n'suth SuBannasen, *T'An* Melkathi.

10

Arykei

SuBannasen was seated in a high-backed chair, her silver-headed cane resting against its arm. Facing her across a small table was Sethin, and a young woman sat in the window seat breast-feeding a baby.

'Excuse me,' I said, 'I was looking for *t'an* Falkyr. Sorry.'

'No, don't go, come in.' Sulis n'ri n'suth SuBannasen beckoned.

'I was just leaving,' Sethin remarked. Her face paled as she stood up. 'You'll excuse me if I don't finish our game, Sulis.'

'Yes, of course.' The old woman sounded concerned.

'It's time for the *ashiren* to sleep, anyway. Jacan,' Sethin called the young woman.

The window of this tower room looked north across the amphitheatre at the foot of the cliff, high enough to see across the city to where flat plains descended into cold haze. It was unusual in the Southland to have that exterior view. Thick, leaded glass kept out the chill.

SuBannasen watched Sethin and the woman leave. She frowned, shaking her head.

'It's a great pity,' she said, almost to herself, 'and she's a good woman. Will you be seated, *t'an* Christie? Do you play?'

A hexagonal *ochmir* board was set out on the table. It is the perennial game of the Southland, played on two hundred and sixteen triangular divisions of the board with an equal number of double-sided counters.

Unlike our games it is not based on territory but on manipulation. The counters are double-sided (traditionally blue-on-white and white-on-blue) and are of three kinds: the *ferrorn,* the *thurin,* and the *leremoc.* They are drawn sight-unseen from a bag in the course of the game. The object—which can take a remarkably long time to achieve—is to have all the pieces showing one's chosen colour.

To turn a piece, it is necessary to place a majority of one's own colour into the minor hexagons formed by any six of the board's triangular divisions. The minority pieces are then reversed to show the opposing colour. Now add to this that *ferrorn* may be placed and not thereafter moved, that *thurin* may be placed and afterwards move in a limited fashion, and that the rare *leremoc* can be moved as desired.

Add also that, as thought will show, the pattern of minor hexagons within the board is shifting, overlapping one. And that what is on the obverse of a *ferrorn* may not be another *ferrorn*, but *thurin* perhaps, or even *leremoc*. . . .

And you begin to see that *ochmir* is a game of labyrinthine and almost limitless complexity. Mobility, not rank; manipulation and not territory: the themes of interdependance and control are central to the Southland mind.

I knew just enough about it to see that Sulis had been winning.

'Thanks, no,' I refused her offer, 'I'm not very proficient at the game yet.'

'I sometimes think it can take a lifetime to master all the intricacies.' She smiled as I sat down opposite her. 'I'd heard you were here, and hoped we'd meet before I left.'

'You've come up from—' I remembered the name of her Melkathi city '—Ales-Kadareth?'

'I had a ship due to sail up the east coast, and then came upriver by barge. I'm a little old for rough travelling on Roehmonde roads—and land travelling is uncertain, they tell me. Besides, the sea is quicker.' There was amusement in her hooded eyes.

'The *marhaz* riding is tiring, yes.' I should have come on a ship, I thought, and then I wouldn't be in danger of becoming permanently bowlegged.

'But I wanted to see you,' she repeated. Her chicken-claw hands closed over the knob of her cane. She leaned forward. 'The last time we met, I was—a little formal, perhaps. Not because of yourself, envoy; but I dislike the company of grubby intelligencers.'

She was genuinely apologetic. There's no proof it was her behind the attacks, I thought. But no proof it wasn't. In this half-civilized land there's no lack of candidates. And yet if it wasn't SuBannasen, who was it?

'I don't know if you have plans,' she went on, 'but after you've finished here, perhaps you'd like to come south with me to Melkathi. I'm here because of my daughter's child Beris—*ke's* old enough to foster in the Roehmonde court—but I shall be going back towards the end of Torvern Thirdweek.'

'Fostering seems to be out of fashion here, lately.'

'This was a previous arrangement of long standing. Howice . . .' her brows quirked up. 'I have no mind to let Howice Talkul spoil my arrangements. And Koltyn was my friend.'

Despite myself, I was liking the old woman. But I wasn't anywhere near ready to trust her.

'It's a kind offer, *T'An* Sulis. Perhaps we could talk it over again when you're ready to leave, and then I'll have a better idea of what I'm going to do.'

'Certainly. I hope it's possible,' she said. 'My old bones won't put up with Roehmonder winters. They're bad for the health—so cold. But winters in Melkathi are mild. You'd find it much more comfortable there.'

I wanted to ask: is that an offer or a threat?

She reached out and fingered one of the *leremoc* counters. 'I might even have the time to teach you how to play *ochmir.*'

I came back one noon from riding with Falkyr to find Maric in a state of excitement.

'You've got a visitor, *t'an.*' He was grinning.

I pulled the embroidered hangings back and went into my rooms.

'Hello, Christie.'

'Haltern!' He gripped my arms. I must have knocked the breath out of him, thumping him on the back. 'Hal, I'm really glad to see you. When did you get here? What are you doing here?'

He laughed. His boots were muddy, his *becamil* cloak threadbare; I guessed he'd not long arrived in Corbek. There was some truth to Su-lis's jibe about grubby intelligencers.

'You can't have met Ruric's messenger,' I calculated. Ho-Telerit had only been gone fourteen days.

'I met no messengers.' He took a bowl of herb-tea as Maric came back with them. We sat on the couch beside the brazier. 'Suthafiori sent me—the Goddess only knows why it was me, I loathe the provinces—after she'd had a report from an Earthspeaker.'

'That wouldn't be Theluk, would it?'

'Some such name.'

Suthafiori would send Haltern because she trusted him and I knew him. And because, although Theluk had been opposing Arad before I ever arrived, I couldn't pretend my presence wasn't disruptive.

'I'm just going to nose around quietly,' Haltern said. 'But what about you, did you have a good journey up here?'

'Oh lord, you don't know about that, either! We've got a lot to catch up on. And you must tell me how Tathcaer is.'

'Better than the bug-ridden north,' he grumbled.

Maric scavenged round the kitchen and brought up food, and we were still talking when the midnight bell sounded, and the boy was curled up asleep on the pelts in front of the brazier.

'Unarmed,' Haltern said as I finished my story. 'Unarmed and against a hired sword!'

Displaying the pink healing scar on my palm, I said, 'I did that too, if you remember.'

'There you are. Normally it takes years of training to be able to cut yourself like that.'

I laughed so hard I woke Maric up.

'I've talked enough, I'm going to bed.' Haltern stood. 'For an envoy, you make a good intelligencer; you notice a lot of what's going on.'

Some of my guesses, then, must correspond with Theluk's report. I said, 'There's one other thing. Sulis n'ri n'suth SuBannasen is here.'

'Is she, now? That's interesting. Yes.'

I reminded myself, there are private feuds going on here that you know nothing about, envoy, and they might have nothing to do with you. You might be justified in trusting the *T'An* Melkathi.

'It's possible I'll go to Ales-Kadareth,' I added.

His eyes opaqued. After a moment, he said, 'Have you made a decision yet?'

'I'm still considering it.'

'You know your own job best. But I should think about it carefully,' he advised. 'Yes. Very carefully. Goodnight, Christie.'

There was the usual round of meetings and dinners in Corbek, meeting the *s'ans* from the Roehmonde *telestres.* Often as not, Howice or Arad were there, and there was always a large number of brown-robed priests. I found the Roehmonders asked far less about trade than the Ymirians, and far more about technology. I visited some of the mining *telestres* to the east with Sethin Falkyr. Falkyr seemed to have appointed himself the envoy's companion, but his contribution was mostly sarcasm. When I went looking for Haltern, Maric told me he was staying anonymously in the city. No doubt keeping his mouth shut and his ears open, I thought.

The weather turned cold, with heavy frosts, and the first snow fell in the dry air, powdering the domes. I found nowhere warm in all of Corbek and went round bundled up in one of the long *zilmei* pelts. Falkyr laughed at me for a southerner.

'You and your world of marvels,' he said ironically, one afternoon. We were in his high tower room. He was dividing his attention between teaching me *ochmir* and trying to understand Earth, and as a result doing neither particularly well. 'With engines to take you through the sky, and do your work, and keep you warm—and no doubt bury you when you're dead. What do you find to do with yourselves?'

'Much the same as anybody else.' I moved a *thurin* into a minor hexagon, giving me a 4–2 majority. His two pieces, reversed now and so mine, proved to be *thurin* and *ferrorn* respectively. 'Your move. And when we've got bored with our machines, we come and see how you live —and remember how lucky we are.'

'Are you sure you haven't played this before?' He regarded the board suspiciously.

'I'm sure.'

He got up and crossed the mosaic floor, bringing a wine jar back to the table with him. I refilled my bowl. He came round behind my chair, studying the pieces from my point of view.

'But you are different,' he said, as if completing a train of thought. It was unexpected, then: one hand that lifted the weight of my hair, one hand that stroked the bare nape of my neck. Smooth, instead of the Orthean mane. There was the shock of desire: flesh calling to different flesh. Some of my feelings over the past days were abruptly clear to me.

I looked up and saw his face human, not cold, not sarcastic; only asking—as we all ask—not to be hurt.

I saw him as human: it's the penalty of being an empath—and the reason why, although we're extremely useful to the ET department, they don't altogether trust us. Inside your head you are not man or woman, young or old, Western or Third World. So now I couldn't see the two of us as human and alien, but only as Lynne de Lisle Christie and Sethin Falkyr Talkul.

Falkyr with that brilliant, bitter mind; who moved with all the dangerous Orthean grace, who was born an outsider in his own land; it was inevitable.

'Christie,' he said, 'are we to be *arykei*?'

'That *ashiren* took long enough finding you,' Haltern grumbled. I was surprised to see him there in the main hall. The evening meal was just finishing.

'Don't blame Maric. He had to come over to Falkyr's rooms.'

'Sethin Falkyr? Yes, I've met him.' Haltern's expression underwent a sudden and total change. Then he grinned.

'Is it that obvious?' It seemed that it was. I was cheerful. 'Don't worry, Hal, it's all being done according to the *arykei* custom.'

'Congratulations.' He, like Maric, appeared to regard it as cause for public celebration. Being no Southlander, I wanted it kept quiet.

'What did you want to see me for, anyway?'

'What? Oh—yes.' He became serious. 'There's been a message received from the Skulls garrison. Ruric won't be leaving for a while. She's ill.'

'How bad is it? Serious?'

'Just a fever, from what I've heard, but they won't move her. The *t'an* Howice intends one of his physicians to ride up there and make sure it's nothing bad.'

I was quiet, taking it in; almost guilty to be happy while the Orthean woman was sick.

'Should we ride up there?'

'It's a week's ride . . . if the next *rashaku*-carrier brings no better news, I'll go,' Haltern said.

'I'll come with you.'

But the messages over the next week were good, and Howice's physician arrived at the garrison and pronounced it only a fever brought on by the north's unaccustomed cold after Tathcaer. Haltern grumbled something to the effect that anyone connected with Howice Talkul couldn't doctor a sick *marhaz*, but seemed content to remain in the city.

The first rush of duties being over, I was free to spend time with Falkyr. I avoided Sulis n'ri n'suth SuBannasen on the pretext that I was busy. Sometime soon I'd have to make a decision, but not yet. Not until I was sure Ruric was well.

Not until I understood what was happening between Falkyr and myself.

Any difficulties we had were habit and not physiology; Adair had been right about that. For the rest, it was the time you spend totally wrapped up in each other's attention, the best time, before doubts and practicality creep in.

And, as it turned out, it was only a very little time.

'Have I leave to go to the city, *t'an?*' Maric asked.

'What? Sure, I shan't need you this afternoon.' I pulled the fur robe tightly round me while I hunted for riding britches. Falkyr and I intended riding out to Delu *telestre* where they bred hunting *kazza*, trackers and killers. 'Have you seen my shirt?'

'It came back from the washroom, I hung it in the closet.'

If I'd had any sense, I'd have found my clothes before I undressed to change. Corbek wasn't getting any warmer.

'You remember the Wellhouse the *T'An* Ruric took me to, before she left?'

He nodded.

'Could you find it again?'

'Yes, *t'an.*'

'Well, if you happen to go that way this afternoon, call in on the Wellkeeper. Ask him if he knows where Theluk is. Haltern wants to know.'

He hadn't been able to find the woman priest for several days.

'I might happen to go that way.' Maric grinned.

'Well, go on, get lost before I think of something else that wants doing.'

He went. I sat down on the bed and began to unlace my boots. A few minutes later I heard footsteps. The curtain was pulled back without any preliminary call. Howice Talkul came into the room.

'Lynne de Lisle Christie, alleged Otherworld envoy—'

I stood up, barefoot on the cold stone, tugging the long *zilmei* pelt round me.

Alleged envoy. Trouble, I thought. And it's big.

There were half a dozen men and women behind him, with drawn *harur* blades. I recognized two of Falkyr's brothers. All had the Talkul face, younger sons and daughters of the *telestre.*

'—in view of the doubt cast upon the status of the alleged envoy, and certain allegations concerning the said Lynne de Lisle Christie and that most abhorred race, the Golden Witchbreed—'

Howice read stolidly from a paper. There was no trace of the polite and friendly man who'd been helpful to the Earth envoy.

'—my pleasure that she shall be conveyed to a place of safety, and there held until a trial may be convened on the matter. Given on Torvern Thirdweek Eightday, under my hand in Corbek: Telvelis Koltyn Talkul, *T'An* Roehmonde.'

Howice let the paper snap back into a roll, and tapped it primly against his hand.

I stood staring at him like an idiot.

'Are you saying you're arresting me?'

11

The Justice of the Wellhouse

The cells were cold.

Condensation ran down the rock wall. Dim light filtered down through roof-slots, and I saw bars and shadows.

A wooden bench hung on chains from the rock wall. I sat, feet tucked up under my robe, hugging the pelt round me. Bars divided the chamber into several cells, each with their bench and bucket. I couldn't see if there were other occupants, but no sound broke the silence.

Cold struck up from the rough floor, and seeped down through the air slots.

I lost track of time.

Noise shattered the quiet. I jumped up. It was the heavy outer door being opened. I limped over to the bars, legs numb from lack of circulation; and was dazzled by torches. The light was all but gone; it must be evening outside.

One guard unlocked the cell next to mine, ignoring me, and two or three more came in with a man struggling between them. They threw him roughly into the cell, and left. The oily black smoke of torches drifted in the air. My eyes readjusted to the twilight.

'Haltern?'

He got up. We touched fingers through the bars. Good Roehmonder ironwork. He looked unharmed, only a little more disreputable than usual.

'You all right?'

'Yes. I was planning on leaving Corbek, but I didn't go in time.'

'They're not serious, are they?' It was a rhetorical question. Some of my stupefaction wore off. 'How long are we going to be here? Can we get a message out?'

'Perhaps. Christie, it's not good. The nearest help is at the garrison.'

'And Ruric's ill.'

'Or else south, in Tathcaer.'

'Too far. Too long a time to be any use.'

He nodded. 'You have no . . . weapons? Nothing that would free us?'

'Nothing. All my gear is in my rooms.' A thought struck me. 'Maric?'

'I didn't see *kir* when they brought me in.'

'What are we going to do?'

'Wait,' he said.

The cell was small, three paces one way and four paces the other. The bench was barely large enough to stretch out on. We talked for a while, each on our separate benches, and the last of the light failed.

'Don't depend on him.' Haltern's voice came out of the darkness. 'First loyalty is to the *telestre.*'

'He'll find some way to get us out.'

I lay awake, waiting for Falkyr to come.

Pale sunlight streamed down the air slots. I chafed my arms and feet, half-paralysed by cold. It must be early, I thought. I'd slept in snatches, despite the hard bench, but it had been impossible to get warm and my feet had got cold enough to be painful.

Haltern was still curled in a foetal position, asleep. It gave me a chance to use the bucket in relative privacy; I still wasn't used to the casual Orthean attitude.

Then there was nothing to do but wait.

The light moved down the wall and reached the floor of the opposite cell. It lit up dust and dirty straw. Now I was certain one of the other cells was occupied, there had been sounds during the night. When the sun fell directly on the straw the heap shuddered and opened, and a woman stood up.

She took hold of the bars of the cage door, shaking them until the iron rattled and echoed.

Old white scars were visible on her dark skin. Her hands were thin even for an Orthean, all twelve claw-nails bitten back to the quick; and her feet had wide-spreading toes as gnarled as roots. She was naked. As she swung round, pacing in that confined space, I saw her bramble-thicket mane that was rooted down to the small of her back.

Her face was scratched, her mouth crusted with old blood, and her eyes were as expressionless as black glass.

'Goddess!' An amazed whisper. Haltern was awake.

At the voice, she froze. Watching us.

I said, 'Who are you?'

No answer. She backed out of the direct sunlight, back against the wall of the cell, fading into the dimness.

'That's no use,' Haltern said, 'she's a barbarian. From over the Wall. They must have sent her down from the garrison.'

We ceased talking as the main door opened. A tall and very thin woman came in, carrying her *harur-nazari* unsheathed. She unlocked the door of my cell. Others followed her, carrying blankets, furs, food and wine and, finally and most welcome, a brazier and a stock of coal.

'You have friends in the *telestre*,' the thin woman said. I recognized her, not from her face but from her expression, she was another of Sethin's children. 'Do not speak of this, if you are asked.'

'Is there a message?'

She shook her head quickly, re-locking the cell.

'Can you take word? Say that—'

The main door banged shut, and I heard the bars being slotted into their sockets on the outside.

I was able to pull the brazier close to the bars, where Haltern could feel the heat, and pass him some of the blankets. It was still cold, but I no longer felt that bone-penetrating chill.

'Your *arykei* is to be commended.' Haltern up-ended the wine flask and drank deeply. 'It's a risk I wouldn't take.'

I managed to toss a haunch of roast *wirazu* into the opposite cell. The barbarian woman squatted down, ripping it apart with her teeth. No one had fed her, or us, and the hard pain of hunger made it difficult to think.

'I should never have left Tathcaer,' Haltern said grimly. 'Cities are my business. Not grubbing in Roehmonde dirt. Have you got any money?'

'No, not one copper bit.'

'I've some silver. Next time I'll try and bribe them to take a message out.'

The barbarian woman said something, a short phrase. Haltern stopped, mouth open, and stared at her.

'Who are you?' I went to the bars. 'How did you get here?'

There was still no animation in her face, but there was a question in her tone.

'Ymirian?' I was incredulous.

'An archaic form, perhaps,' Haltern said, 'you're right.'

The woman pointed. 'Who?'

'Christie,' I said, and repeated it when she said it back to me. She came forward, wrapping her bony hands round the bars. Her voice was harsh.

'Who is thy friend?' she asked.

'Haltern.' I added, 'he's from the south.'

There was no telling how much she understood. Haltern came up beside me and asked questions, but she didn't reply. Before long she went back to the rear of her cell, ignoring us.

'How long has she been here, I wonder?'

'I don't know. Did I ever,' he went on in a plain attempt at distraction, 'tell you about my *telestre,* Beth'ru-elen?'

I settled back on the bench with three blankets and a *zilmei* pelt round me. 'No, you never did. Come on. Let's hear it.'

I ducked my head, flinching from the white light. There was a hand on my arm, halting me. Automatically I reached out to steady myself, and the metal cuffs cut into my wrists. The guard's hand caught me, and I was able to stand. Two feet of chain hobbled my ankles.

'Be silent in the presence! Be silent in the house!'

The hum and chatter died away.

A great dome towered above my head, the noon sun falling through the roof slot, blinding me. I squinted. Tall pillars edged the domed chamber. Beyond them were smaller domes, and in those alcoves a crowd of people.

I stood between two guards.

Noon bells cut across the silence; brief chimes echoing in the dome.

The guard pushed me forward. I stepped up onto a raised block. In front of me was an iron grating, circular, some sixteen feet across. I looked down. For a few yards the sun lit the rock sides of the great well shaft. Then there was darkness.

On the other side of the well stood Arad. There was another raised block, this one empty. He stood by a table on which were piled scrolls and documents, conferring with a young Earthspeaker.

Apart from us, I saw no one on the vast, tessellated floor of the dome. My eyes becoming used to the light, I made out how the natural rock amphitheatre was carved in rising tiers of seats, and how smaller domes clung to the sides of the main one. Between pillars I saw a multitude of Orthean faces, surrounding me on all sides.

'I have called you to the Wellhouse to consider a most serious matter.' Without being raised, Arad's voice penetrated clearly through the dome. 'The *T'An* Roehmonde has decreed that this is a matter for the Wellhouse and not the court. I call you all here to judge and witness.'

There were Earthspeakers in that assembly, and other Wellkeepers that I recognized from social functions, and *s'an* of the nearby *telestres*. I stood pinned under the spotlight of the noon glare. Peering past Arad I made out members of the Talkul *telestre,* and then all at once saw Howice, and Sethin, and Koltyn himself. The old man nodded at Arad, staring at me with no recognition.

'We witness,' Howice said, and other voices echoed him. Searching along the line I saw Sulis n'ri n'suth SuBannasen, her face impassive.

'The woman you see—' Arad's hand flicked in my direction '—has claimed to come from another world. There are certain things which would seem to support this. In Tathcaer, they believed it. But there are other explanations. There is evidence that she is the product, if not in fact the child, of that most ancient, bloody, cruel, and proud race, the Golden Witchbreed.'

This was what I'd expected, and now it came I was relieved. I said to the nearest guard, 'When may I speak?'

'You?' he stared at me. 'You're not here to speak.'

'What?'

'Keep your mouth shut.'

'But if I'm not allowed a defence—'

The hilt of a *harur* blade caught me high up under the ribs. I shut up. Arad was still talking. We were ignored.

'—having heard her freely confess to such machines and engines as are used on her world,' Arad said. 'Which indeed you have all heard, when she visited your *telestres,* making no secret of it. And these are familiar matters to us, who know how Witchbreed travelled between their many lands riding the air, we who know what weapons devastated the Barrens, we who know the legacy of desolation left to us. We, whose kin swore after that Empire fell, never again to permit such ruin of the earth.'

He was so reasonable, I found I was afraid of him. This was no savage, and this was no audience for my carefully-thought-out pleas for the benefits of science. And if I couldn't get a hearing. . . .

'There's no dispute about the existence of other worlds, I suppose.' Arad seated himself casually on the edge of the table. 'The stars being the Mother's Daughters, it were no great wonder if they also had children such as ourselves. Philosophers have often speculated that it may be so, and so it may; but I ask you, which is the more likely? That such people would find out a way to cross vast gulfs, and send this woman here—or that she comes from some untenanted part of our own world; perhaps even a known part, perhaps even Kel Harantish?'

I was surprised by the sophistication of the argument, even while my spirits were sinking lower. The quiet in the assembly chilled me. I thought, if it comes to it, can I prove I'm from Earth?

'You have the Crown's seal on my documents!' I sensed movement from the guards, but Arad signalled them to stand back. I didn't raise my voice. The acoustics were such that I was being heard throughout the dome. 'I'm an accredited envoy of my world.'

'Not all tales out of Tathcaer are true,' he said, 'and even the *T'An Suthai-Telestre* may be taken in by a liar. Be silent. The evidence will be heard.'

At his signal the young Earthspeaker picked up a document from the table, and stepped on to the raised block.

'The evidence of Kethan n'ri n'suth Renu, physician,' he read. ' "On being summoned to tend the *T'An* Commander Ruric Orhlandis, I found her to be suffering from a fever unknown to me. She presently lies ill here in the Skulls garrison. It is my opinion that the illness was deliberately caused, though I cannot say by whom, or why." '

As he stepped down, Arad said, 'The *T'An* Commander of the Southland's army lies sick, and this after—and only after—travelling to Roehmonde in the company of the alleged envoy.'

I missed the evidence of the next two or three, mainly *s'an* of mining *telestres* describing what I'd told them of Earth technology. Ruric? I thought. They suspect me of—that's crazy!

Kethan n'ri n'suth Renu, I remembered, is Howice's physician.

Questions were asked, some by *s'an*, some just from the assembly; and that quiet rational voice went on piling up circumstantial evidence against me. I shifted, easing my back, wishing I could sit down. When word of this got back to Tathcaer, and to the xeno-team—

If word got back. And suppose it does, I thought suddenly, supposing even a garbled version of the truth gets out, what could they do? What could they do in time to help me? Even if it ended in an execution, ultimately there was little that could be done; and I wasn't interested in posthumous justice.

'Evidence of conjecture, perhaps,' Arad said. 'However, I have a last witness, an eye-witness, a man who has seen this envoy—this alleged envoy—use forbidden Witchbreed science. Your name, *t'an.*'

'Aluys Blaize n'ri n'suth Meduenin, of the Mercenaries' Guild in

Rimon,' the man said, mounting the witness block; and the light fell on him, and I saw the ruined half of his face and recognized him. The face that had stayed with me from Terison, the hired sword, the nameless killer.

'I see you know him,' Arad remarked in my direction. It was too late to deny that.

'He made an attempt on my life. I'm not liable to forget him.'

'Nor I to forget you,' the man said. I realized I'd never heard him speak. It was a deep voice, speaking Roehmonder with a thick Rimon accent. 'I bear your mark still, Witchbreed.'

He held up his wrist, strapped and bound. I saw the *harur-nilgiri* slung for left-hand use.

'I was travelling east. Our paths crossed at a Wellhouse.' He stared round the assembly, his head up defiantly. Roehmonders have no love for mercenaries. 'We became friends, then *arykei.*'

Blood thundered in my ears. The faceless crowd narrowed down to one focus: Howice Talkul's smile. Plain as words it said: deny that's possible. Just try.

'She has an object about so big—' Blaise held his hands a little way apart '—the shape of a *hura* shell, grey and hard. When I saw it, I asked what it was; she told me it was a weapon. Weapons are my business,' he appealed to the assembly, 'I was eager to study it, she not at all eager for me to lay hands on it. We fought. She carries no sword, nor ever did while I knew her. Her sole weapon was that object. She used it against me—pointed it from a distance—called down forked lightning out of the air. My swordhand was useless: I fled for my life. When I knew where she had gone, it became my duty to warn you.'

As he stepped down, Arad picked up an object from the table. 'This is that weapon?'

'Yes.'

'You have leave to go.' Arad waited, then faced me again. 'You do not deny this is yours?'

'I deny that it does what he says, or that what he says happened took place.'

They'd searched my baggage. What else would they have found? The reports—no, they couldn't play them back, and it wouldn't make much difference if they did. The medic kit. That would puzzle them. And I didn't want to lose it.

Arad displayed it round the assembly as evidence against me.

'I demand the right to speak!' I controlled frustration. Talking was all I could do, and now I was denied even that. 'Have I ever said that

Earth is not a technological world? Have I ever denied we use our own science? Tell me how that makes me part of a race that's extinct on this planet! Can't you see I'm different from you? Use your eyes!'

'You're different,' Arad said, 'but such changes were always within the power of the Witchbreed, it proves nothing either way.'

'I'm under the protection of Crown law. This isn't justice.'

'But you are in Roehmonde,' Arad said over a growl of approval from the Roehmonders, 'and this is a Wellhouse, and you are under the justice of the Goddess.'

The guards took me out of the Wellhouse, and we waited in an outer chamber for the larger part of the afternoon. My protests were ignored. I was beginning to accept that.

When I was brought back in the torches were lit and the last afternoon light fell on the black well shaft. I stood at the edge of that dizzying pit.

'You have witnessed,' Arad said to the assembly, 'now judge.'

Eventually a woman came forward onto the floor, glancing back at the *s'ans* and priests.

'It's taken us a long time to confer,' she said hesitantly, 'and we feel the case isn't proved against her, but we're not convinced she's innocent. She may be Witchbreed, and she may not—we can't be sure.'

There was a murmur of approval. I sought out Howice's face. He wasn't happy about it.

Arad, after conferring with some of the Earthspeakers, said, 'This is my word, then. Let her be taken back and confined in the cells. We will search for new evidence. We will hear this again. Is this acceptable?'

I hardly heard their agreement. It was no more than time I'd gained, but it was better than what I'd feared.

I saw the scarred man across the hall. He never saw the sonic stunner, I thought, and certainly he never saw me use it. Someone rehearsed him very carefully with his evidence. Someone who'd previously hired him, and knew to bring him here. . . .

Old suspicions flared up, but I couldn't see Sulis now. Going down to the cells again, my mind made and discarded plans. If I could get a message out. If Ruric recovered soon, and returned. If Falkyr—

I didn't see Falkyr there, I realized.

'It's time,' I said, when I'd told Haltern about it. 'Surely we can do something?'

'We can be careful.' He was grim. 'They've given the envoy a hearing, and by the law of the Wellhouse they can keep you in the cells until they decide to give you another one. And wouldn't it be convenient if you sickened and died of the damp-lung sickness, or bad food—or the assassin's sword?'

I woke from a dream of warmth, of fingers knotting in the roots of a short-cropped mane.

The barbarian woman shook the bars, the sound echoing. Her face was turned up to the air slots.

'What?'

She said a word several times, but it was not until I looked up that I understood her. Morning: pale snowlight. She gave the bars a last kick and went back to her heap of straw. She had a tremendous capacity for conserving her energy in sleep.

Our talk never got much beyond the 'who are you?' stage. Neither mine or Haltern's versions of Ymirian and Roehmonder were comprehensible to her.

'What day is it?'

'Forthweek Fourday, I think.' I was pretty sure the hearing had been on Twoday. 'You all right?'

'We're almost out of fuel.' He ignored the question. I'd heard him coughing during the night.

'I can't believe this.' There was no way to work off my anger. 'I can't believe there's no way to protest. And I don't believe that travesty was due process of law!'

'It was informal, and it was Wellhouse custom.' Haltern pulled the blanket shawl-like round his shoulders. 'If it had been Crown law, you'd have been allowed to speak, and call your own evidence. Which, I suspect, is why the *T'An* Roehmonde turned it over to Arad.'

I refuelled the brazier, shaking the ash onto the floor.

'Howice. Not Koltyn.'

He nodded. 'Forthweek Fourday . . . if the *T'An* Ruric is well enough to return—'

'If.' The thought disturbed me. I knew Haltern was wrong, Howice wouldn't order me killed yet. Not yet: he would still be coming to terms with what he'd done—arrested an envoy accredited by the Crown. But if he was able to deceive Ruric about where I was, and if she went on south, *then* he'd think again. He might not be so chary of disposing of the envoy.

It was not being able to do anything that hurt.

Dampness hung in the air. Thin streams of water mizzled down from the air slots, pooling on the stone floor. The brazier held nothing but warm ashes.

The barbarian woman gripped the bars of her cage door, shaking it on its hinges. Monotonous, hopeless: her face with no more expression than it ever had.

'Stop that Goddess-forsaken noise!' Haltern added a curse in Peir-Dadeni. His hands were shaking. He threw the empty wine flask at her, and it struck the bars and skittered into the rain pool.

'Don't shout at her, it's not her fault we're in here.'

'It's not *mine*,' he said acidly.

'Bloody half-civilized savages,' I said. 'All of you.'

The rain eased. Moisture pearled the sleeping-furs. The cold of the iron bars bit into my hands.

'Haltern? I'm sorry.'

We touched hands through the bars.

'So am I. Sorry. These Roehmonders—' he shrugged. 'I thought I was too clever to get picked up like that, at my age.'

'It's not as if you are half-civilized.' I was pursuing my own train of thought. 'The Witchbreed are more than legends. And I'm not trained for post-holocaust societies.'

'Christie,' the barbarian woman called. She was backing away from the bars, watching the main door.

'What—?'

The door swung open. I expected either more of the food and wine that was anonymously supplied to us, or else the *T'An* Roehmonde's guards. Instead, a woman entered and swung the door closed behind her.

'Verek Sethin.' Haltern went to the bars.

'I've little time.' She unlocked the door to his cell, and then mine.

I said, 'Where's Falkyr?'

'With my brother Howice. There is a hunt, this being the Fiveday holiday.'

'He isn't here?'

She looked at me uncomprehendingly. I stepped outside the cell. I didn't want to ask the next question.

'Does he know about this?'

Sethin shook her head. 'My son is loyal to the *telestre*. *T'an*, you must come with me quickly.'

Haltern was rolling up the less bulky blankets. I watched him. Part of me had stopped thinking.

'She's got to come too,' I said, as Sethin passed the barbarian woman's cell.

Haltern nodded. 'You're right. They'll get out of her what she's seen if she stays here.'

His pragmatism shocked me.

The barbarian woman shied back, then stood still while I knotted one blanket round her under the arms and pulled another one over her head as hood and shawl. She might pass as a Roehmonder. I hoped.

She strode after Sethin and Haltern, blankets tangling her legs. I followed. Sethin had two of my packs waiting in the empty guardroom. We went through long stone passages and up seemingly endless flights of stairs.

'Sethin.' I elbowed past Haltern to speak to her. 'If he didn't . . . who was it saw to it that we were comfortable, down there?'

'That was Falkyr's wish.' She didn't slow her pace. 'He would do all he could for an *arykei*. Indeed, he did much. It was he who spoke to Howice of your recognition by the Goddess—'

'Hell!' How could I have forgotten? I thought. But I had, it had gone out of my mind completely. I suppose I'd regarded it as partly a charming native ceremony, and partly as one of Ruric's good intentions; but it had never crossed my mind, not even in the Wellhouse.

'It would have done you no good to mention it,' Sethin added, 'Howice knew, and Arad knew, and how would it have sounded to say that you were recognized by the Goddess, and that your second presently lies struck down with sickness?'

'But Falkyr—'

'He did what he could, within the law of the *telestre*.'

'And you?' What I wanted to ask was, why are you here instead of him?

'I do what I can,' she said, 'and I don't have strength or time enough to put it to the *telestre*, so I act now, for myself.'

The bluff hung above us. The damp air struck me as warm, coming up from underground. The sun was past noon, daystars were white over the towers of Corbek. We stood in the rutted lane, blinking at the light, breathing the wind, silent for long minutes.

Less than a week. Eight days. And yet it had changed. The trees in the gardens were changing colour: yellow to grey. The air smelled sharply of autumn.

'I'll do no more, and know no more,' Sethin said. 'Go. Leave Corbek.'

She stood in the doorway, the light cruel on the sharp planes of her face. Her eyes were dull, brown-shadowed, and the same colour crept round her pinched lips. Her clothes hung loose from her angular shoulders.

She had that cold and stubborn expression I had often seen on her son's face.

Falkyr. Who was Roehmonder, who was Talkul *telestre* above all else. Much as I'd disliked the thought of my freedom resting in someone else's hands, I'd still relied on him, imagining him working for my release. Now I was betrayed. Not by him. By me: expecting us to think and feel the same way. Thinking I understood the *telestre*.

'Thank you.' I took Sethin's cold hands. 'I won't speak of this, whatever happens.'

'In a while, it won't matter to me.' She smiled wryly. 'Have you any word for my son, Christie?'

Under the rationality, bitterness welled up. I shook my head. I couldn't trust myself.

'We're grateful, *t'an,*' Haltern said, 'and the Crown shall hear of this, privately if you wish. And if you'd send word to the *T'An* Ruric?'

'Not outside Corbek. If she comes here, yes.' Sethin regarded me. 'Don't think too badly of us. Arad is honest in what he does, he believes you are Witchbreed and a danger. Even Howice does what he does for us. He loves control, I grant you, and all that goes with it, but in all honesty he believes there are things he can do for the *telestre* that no other can.'

'Then let him wait,' Haltern said. 'When the old man dies, they may name Howice as *T'An* Roehmonde.'

'But then, you see, they may not. And he has waited so long.' Her face closed up and she was cold again. 'Now, go.'

The door shut behind her. I took the barbarian woman's arm, and followed Haltern down into the city.

12

Flight to the South

'Where are you going? We've got to get out of here!'

'Be reasonable,' Haltern said. 'The alarm will go out when Howice returns—say, sunset, or dawn tomorrow at the latest. He'll send fast riders out to warn the *telestres*. If you can think of a way to get out of the Roehmonde *telestres* by dawn—'

'All right. All right, but what do we do? We can't stay here.'

'That's just what we can do.' He was flushed, alert; freedom filled him with a sudden energy. 'For a time.'

The blank walls of the city *telestre*-houses shut us out. It was slippery walking, the mud was ankle-deep and the ruts filled with rainwater. I kept hold of the barbarian woman's wrist, not trusting her to stay with us otherwise. I carried the packs over my shoulder; they were light, and I was doubtful about how much of my property remained in them.

'Theluk,' I said.

'Go to a Wellhouse?' Haltern said doubtfully.

'She said that Wellkeeper could be trusted, and she's no friend of Arad.'

'If she's still in Corbek. . . .' He hesitated as we came to an intersection. 'Yes, but not to stay, that's too much of a risk.'

'You think this isn't risky? Let's get off the streets.'

I might pass for Roehmonder if lucky, keeping my eyes lowered and my hands out of sight. The barbarian woman, swathed in blankets, was already attracting stares. Now we were coming down into the Fiveday holiday crowds. And Haltern laughed. It was ludicrous: but I had to laugh with him, I was out of that filthy place, and that was all that mattered.

The Wellhouse was shut up, but Haltern rattled the iron gates until an inner door was opened, and then Theluk herself came running out.

'Inside. Quick! How did you—never mind, get out of sight.'

In the courtyard she stopped and stared at us, and used one or two expressions I'd heard from Ruric's troopers. She opened the door to one of the rooms beside the Wellhouse dome, then: 'What's *that?*'

The barbarian woman shied back from the door. I could understand her not wanting to go under a roof again.

'Thee will stay?' I indicated the courtyard, and she nodded. Theluk had locked the outer gates.

'Thou and thy friend . . . leave this—?' She used an expression I didn't know, but the comprehensive gesture of her gnarled hand took in all of Corbek.

'Soon, yes.'

I left her sitting cross-legged on the flagstones, blanket put back from her head, face turned to the sky.

Inside the ill-lit room, an *ashiren* rose from setting a fire in the hearth. *'T'an!'*

Maric gripped my hands. I was embarrassed: there was no reason he should be so glad to see me. He fetched food while Haltern sketched out events for Theluk, and I sorted through the packs.

The medic kit was there, half emptied; and some spare clothes and a handful of silver bits. No sign of the micro-recorder. But, at the bottom of one pack, wrapped in a *chirith-goyen* shirt, I found the sonic stunner.

I wish I'd thanked Sethin when I had the chance. There were no half measures for her when her conscience moved her. I hoped Howice wouldn't hurt her.

'There's no going by river,' Theluk said, 'I tried to get passage east on one of the barges, but they want travel permits signed by the *T'An* Roehmonde.'

'East would be best—take ship at the mouth of the Beruth for Tathcaer. Going south, too many *telestres* support Talkul.' Haltern scowled. 'Travel permits in the one province? I never heard of anything so against rule and custom!'

'That's Arad you have to thank.'

'Have we got enough money for *marhaz?*' I was counting my silver.

Theluk shook her head. 'You need also a permit to buy *marhaz* in Corbek.'

Haltern swore, outraged, then said, 'I wonder—a bribe?'

'I've tried. It was only luck I wasn't arrested.' Theluk turned to me.

'You can't stay here, *t'an*. I don't mean to be unfriendly, but Arad knows I oppose him, and they're searching all Wellhouses.'

Maric brought stone cups and a jug of gritty wine. Anxiously he said, 'What will we do, *t'an?*'

We're not so much better off, I thought, now that we're out of the cells . . . and that's ridiculous! There has to be a way.

'Can we do it on foot?' I was remembering the ride up to Roehmonde, with Ruric's troopers. 'East . . . or north, to the garrison. Or south, until we find someone who'll credit the *T'An Suthai-Telestre's* authority and not the *T'An* Roehmonde's. It's all that's left.'

'On foot through *this* country—?'

'It's not so mad an idea,' Theluk cut in. 'The weather should hold dry and cold now. We used to take out foot patrols from the garrison in Torvern, and we're a good few *seri* further south here. You're less likely to be seen, more able to hide.'

'If you think I'm walking to Tathcaer you *are* mad!'

The idea wasn't that crazy. I've done survival courses: I was fairly confident we could get out of Roehmonde, but it wouldn't be comfortable. And they would be looking for us. My mind flinched away from the thought. It wasn't until I was free that I knew: no one was going to lock me up again. Ever.

'They'll search the roads,' Haltern protested.

'Go west, where they won't expect to see you.' Theluk bent down and picked a charred stick from the fire, and scratched in the ashes. 'Here's Corbek, and the hills to the west, and the flat land to the north . . . the rivers and the forest to the south. If you were to go west, then southwest, you'd reach the Oranon river, and the *telestres* there are admitted Ymirian.'

'That's over a hundred *seri*,' Haltern said, aghast.

'Six days, maybe seven, given good weather; any trooper can do that.'

She was optimistic, I thought. But she knew the country, she'd been a soldier, she might be right.

I said, 'Maybe you should leave Corbek too.'

'Yes.' She put the stick down, the six-fingered hands linking before her. 'I've had to keep out of Arad's sight. He won't listen to reason, and he's heard much from me lately; I'd be safer out of Roehmonde.'

'You're both mad,' Haltern said testily.

'It'll do until we have a better idea. But if we can't stay here . . .'

'You can't,' Theluk confirmed. 'You'll have to come with me. Out of sight of the Talkul *t'ans*. I know where.'

Waking, I felt excited, anticipatory without knowing the reason. Then it came back: I wasn't in the cells. Apprehension returned. Leaving the city . . . could we do it?

A greenish light hung in the room. It was round-walled, all wood, even the low conical roof; rough stones were mortared together to make a chimney.

Still as a rock, the barbarian woman stood holding the leather curtain away from the doorway. Her head was up, her hands knotted into fists. The light shone on her unhuman body: the scarred ribs, small paired breasts and lower nipples, the unbroken sweep of smooth skin down to the hairless groin.

'Christie.' Her quiet tone woke nobody.

I got up, pulling the blanket round me, and went to stand beside her. Outside, the first twilight was giving way to sunrise. Ground mist rose over the shacks, hid the river.

'You'll have to come with us,' I said.

'What is thy road?'

'That way.' I pointed west, and her eyes were suddenly opaque.

'I will come,' she said, and turned away.

Breakfast was cold meat and herb-tea, most of our funds having been spent on gear for the journey. I let Maric work out loads and weights; he was more expert.

'There's Gher and Oru still up there,' I said, rolling blankets.

'Go and ask Howice for them,' was Haltern's acid advice.

Or Falkyr, I thought, and was still for a moment. It had a way of going right out of my mind, and then coming over me suddenly. I'd cried, and sworn at his memory, and it still came back.

'Are we ready?' Theluk wore *harur-nilgiri* and *harur-nazari* now, as Haltern did. Maric had a belt-knife. It was habit with me now to wear a short knife, but I carried the stunner holstered under a Roehmonder coat. Spare clothes were worn rather than add weight to the packs.

There's no reason for anyone to stop us, I thought. If they don't look too closely.

The morning air was chill. I climbed stiffly down the outside steps to the ground, adjusting the pack's straps. My boots sank into mud. Haltern and Theluk joined me, and then the barbarian woman—in a Roehmonder coat that did nothing to disguise her angular height, her wildness—and Maric. A hard knot of tension settled under my ribs, eating acidly at my stomach.

We set off on the river road. Narrow passages led between stacked rooms and rickety staircases, where stone chimneys breathed black smoke. *Kuru* rooted in the mud. There was an unidentifiable sour smell. We left the rooming-house—it would be charity to call it a companion-house—behind in the river mist.

This shack town was the first place that reminded me of Earth. It was a transient's town. No one had asked our names. More important, no one had asked about our *telestres*. My purse had been weighty enough to hire rooms. The people here had a restless look, they were drifters and strays; and being Orthean, they took it worse than I did.

Maric's shoulder brushed my arm. 'What do we do if they stop us?'

'They won't. If they do, run and hide. Wait for the *T'An* Commander to get here.' And just how sick is she?

The sun grew brighter. We followed the Berufal upstream, where water mills thundered and rumbled and speech was impossible. Turning north and west took us past the old city walls and out to where the northern roads begin. Walls went past, and lanes and passages; and people walking, and riding *marhaz,* and some with the Talkul insignia. I met no one's eyes. Tension silenced us.

Then we were past the *telestre*-houses, on cinder-track roads. I looked back and saw Corbek's terraces rising behind me, steps and stairs and towers; and crowning the bluff, pale in the morning light, the dome of the Wellhouse.

Haltern let out a long breath, scratched through his thinning mane and grinned. Theluk laughed. It was the first time I'd seen her anything but serious, it made her look as much an *ashiren* as Maric. Maric himself peered round the barbarian woman—we'd flanked her through the city—and gave me a hard look. There was something very determined about the boy: he didn't intend going back to Corbek any more than I did.

'That's the worst over,' Haltern said.

'Don't be too sure.' Serious again, Theluk stopped and rested her foot on a markstone, retying a sandal-thong. 'They've sent out the alarm, you can be certain.'

'We can avoid them in the forests.'

'So let's move.' I eased the pack again, tucking my thumbs under the strap.

And step by step, Corbek receded behind us.

The land was flat, with forested hills to the south of us, a pale mass broken by the blue and scarlet changing leaves of *lapuur* and *ziku*. The air was sharp. It was empty country. A few carts passed us, and one or two *marhaz* riders.

Is it that easy? I thought, as noon came and we turned to roads that went south and west. And tried to ignore the weight of the miles that lay between us and Ymir.

'There's a companion-house on the edge of these hills,' Theluk persisted, 'just a bit further on.'

'You've been saying that since noon,' Haltern grumbled.

It was the fourth day since leaving the city. The second day had been the worst, working off stiffness, but after that we made better time. To my surprise I was enjoying it. The walking was tiring, but not unduly so; the packs weren't over-heavy; and we fell into a routine. Mornings, the ground rang iron-hard with frost, and rime stiffened the waterproof *becamil* tent. The days were clear, skies that pale blue of an Orthean autumn, and the noon sun still had heat. We talked, walking through pale gold light in the hazy short afternoons; and sometimes Theluk scouted the hills to hunt, and sometimes Maric. Cleaning game was messy. The barbarian woman trailed us, staying off the roads. We didn't hurry. It snowed powdery dust on the third morning (and I discovered that *becamil*, as well as keeping out rain, keeps in heat); the wine was doled out more heavily that day, and we went on in breathy white clouds of cheer. That was the day we saw no one at all on the hill tracks, and—searching for water—disturbed a *zilmei* that reared up a good twelve feet, beating the air with wide claws, and was gone in a ripple of grey-white pelt and a hooting, mournful cry. We were more sober, after that. And today, for the first time, turned due south.

'We're still within fifty *seri* of Corbek,' Haltern guessed, 'but we need supplies, we need news—need to know where the search is.'

'You're coming to the end of the land I know,' Theluk said, 'but— ah, there, I was right!'

A low, flat-roofed building sprawled below us on the southern spur of the hill. Thin smoke went up from the chimney. I could just make out *marhaz* in the yard.

'I'll go down,' Theluk offered, 'all Earthspeakers are wanderers, no one will think it strange if I ask questions. Are you coming, *ashiren-te?*'

Maric trotted off down the rough track after her. We went back off the skyline, resting in a dip where the blue thousand-flower grew. The barbarian woman coalesced out of the wood's shadows. She was sucking her fingers. They were slimed with blood. She did her own hunting.

'We can't take her there,' Haltern said.

Attempting her archaic inflections, I said 'Will thee stay?'

'Not within walls.'

'You can't trust her. You don't know what these people are like.'

'Hal, what were you planning to do about her anyway? Not take her to Tathcaer with us?'

'There are questions she could answer.'

'Willingly?'

He shrugged. 'We should know what they're planning. A few quiet seasons . . . they may be massing for an attack. It's happened before. I wish I knew where Howice got her.'

'This direction, I think. I've had the feeling as we travelled that she recognizes it.'

'Don't be ridiculous, we're hundreds of *seri* south of the Skulls pass—'

There was crashing in the underbrush. We sprang up, Haltern with *harur* blades unsheathed. Maric tumbled into sight.

'We can go down! Theluk sent me back. She's hired rooms.'

'The search hasn't come this way?'

'Yes, been and passed a day back.'

Haltern sheathed the paired blades. He looked at the barbarian woman.

Tranquilly she said 'I will await thee, and the morning.'

And was gone.

The companion-house, kept by the two *telestres* Ereval and Irys, was not as small as it appeared. It was built into the south face of the spur, with six floors leading down to another set of stables on the main route from Corbek to Mirane. It was not crowded—most of the harvest markets were over by now.

'Shall you risk going south now?' Theluk asked as we ate, and then frowned. 'What in the Goddess's name do they put in this stew?'

'Customers who don't pay their bills, I should think.' Being under a roof restored Haltern's spirits.

'You're a Crown Messenger,' I said, 'send a message. Surely we're far enough away now.'

'Give it another day or two. There are no lines of communication to Tathcaer until we reach the Oranon river, anyway.'

'They're still expecting you to have gone east,' Theluk guessed, 'but give them time, they'll work it out.'

Our rooms were over the stables and grain-loft. The musky smell of *marhaz* got into my head, and I dreamed in the night of riding to the edge of the world. I woke once, and lay awake—paradoxically, now I was comfortable I had time to think, and couldn't sleep.

After a while I realized Haltern was awake too. He watched me. The starlight shone in his eyes, membrane retracted, pupils become velvet holes. He sees me better than I see him, I thought.

Softly he said, 'Did you ever ask him to become *n'ri n'suth* to your *telestre?*'

There was no question of who was meant by *he.*

'No, how could I?'

'Did he ever ask you to become *n'ri n'suth* Talkul?'

'No.' I hadn't known he was meant to.

'Then you were *arykei*, well and good, and it ended perhaps before you were ready; but for the Goddess's sake, Christie—when something's dead, leave it alone!'

Under the hectoring tone there was something very like concern. It kept me from telling him to go to hell.

'It's different customs, isn't it? And misunderstandings.' I was very tired. 'It's all right, Hal. I don't want to discuss it. But thanks for saying.'

'We need you here,' he said, 'and not with your spirit still in Corbek.'

The night was full of noises: *marhaz*, people in the companion-house, and one hunting night-*rashaku* with a call like rusty metal being torn apart. I smelled the chill of frost, and thought with a sudden longing of Tathcaer, and the sun, and how glad—how very glad—I would be when we got to the south.

I came back across the yard from the outhouse, lacing up my coat and shivering. The frost had gone, the morning was damp. From the top of the spur you could see for miles, the southern hills rolling down into haze. I traced the road. It was achingly slow travelling. Would they be willing to sell *marhaz* here, I wondered, or was it too risky to ask?

As I turned I caught sight of movement on the road. Riders. Light flashed from ornamented *marhaz* harness. Too far to make out insignia, or even the number of riders. My spine prickled. All the tension flooded back.

The first rain fell as I hurried back inside.

'Motherless, landless turds,' Theluk said under her breath. 'There they go. That's blocked the south road. Offspring of Witchbreed!'

'Do you think they know we were there?' Maric had a strained look about him.

'The keeper was bound to tell them. Hei, why did they have to come back this way!' She kept her temper on a tight rein. We wriggled down the slope to where Haltern stood guard over the packs. The rain was fine but persistent.

'The main force has gone south, they've sent out scouts.'

'They've guessed what we're doing. We'll have to go back into the hills, and west again.'

There'd been no opportunity to steal *marhaz.* We'd crept out as fast as possible, and as a consequence were underprovisioned.

'Check the path,' Theluk told Maric, and when he'd gone added 'One word: these are north Roehmonders hunting us, I have known them to use *kazza* to track down fugitives. We may be grateful yet for this bad weather.'

I'd not seen the hunting *kazza.* We never made that ride out to the northern *telestre:* I was arrested. But Falkyr's voice came back to me. Difficult as *rashaku* to train, he'd said, and difficult as fate to avoid.

'There's your barbarian friend,' Haltern said to me, 'if they take her —and Goddess knows where she is now!—they'll be certain it's us. Then we're finished.'

'*If* they catch her.'

Before midmorning, the rain turned to sleet.

'Christ!' I yelled ahead to Theluk, 'we can't carry on in this!'

I stopped, waiting for Haltern to catch up. I had my arm round Maric; he was huddled into my side, head down.

'Nobody's moving in this,' Haltern panted, 'them or us. Tell that woman we don't all have Earthspeaker's stamina—we've got to get under shelter.'

It was impossible to face into the wind. Frozen rain sliced out of the south. Mud clogged on boots, weighing them down. I felt water seep through layers of coat and tunics, cold against fever-hot skin. Uncontrollable shivers centred in my chest and stomach. Even through mittens my hands were numb; there was no feeling in my face.

'Get under the trees,' Theluk said when she was close enough to be heard.

The *tukinna* blocked some of the wind. I pushed on up the slope after the Orthean woman. The blue mossgrass broke away underfoot, leaving long skids of mud, and I had to let go of the *ashiren* and use both hands to climb. The pack overbalanced me. *Tukinna* bark peeled away wet and black when I gripped the tree boles.

'Come on.' I reached back and hauled Maric up beside me.

Haltern was fifty yards down the slope, labouring. Theluk skidded past me, crabwise down between the twisted trees, and got one of his arms over her broad shoulders. She was less protected than any of us: only a Roehmonder coat over her priest's skirt, and sandals, and yet she kept going. As if the cold didn't touch her.

'Further up,' she called, 'in the rocks.'

Water fell in streams from the trees. We were suddenly out of the wind. I scrambled up over ridges of earth, one of Maric's slender-fingered hands gripped in mine. The dim light outlined rocks. Rivulets drained between them, soaking knees and elbows. Twilight became shadow. I stood up. High outcroppings of rock hugged the ridge, split and fissured into blocks.

There were no caves. There were splits that went back into the main mass of rock. We tumbled into one that was wide at ground-level, narrowing as it went up. Damp mud, damp rock, but no wind or sleet.

Maric was shaking as hard as I was. Haltern, let out of the Earthspeaker's grip, pitched forward onto his knees. Theluk leaned against the entrance of the cleft. Her eyes opaqued, then shut.

It was cold. It was frighteningly cold. It hurt. People have died from exposure, I thought, and pneumonia.

It was a long time before any of us moved.

'Fire,' Theluk said.

'Give away our position.' Haltern's eyes opened. 'What would burn? Too wet.'

'Mossgrass. In the clefts.' She looked at me, and I slipped the pack off and stood up.

'I'll look.'

My feet slipped, struck rock; sometimes I fell. I was numb. I pulled mittens off with my teeth, so that I could strip mossgrass out of sheltered cracks. Some brushwood wasn't soaking wet, only damp; I took that too. Above my head the clustered leaves rattled to another onslaught of rain.

When I came back Theluk was using her *harur-nazari* to hack off bird's-wing bushes and pile them against the entrance to the cleft. I dumped what fuel I'd collected inside. Under a makeshift *becamil* shelter Haltern was chafing the *ashiren's* hands and feet. A wine flask lay open and empty.

'He all right?'

Haltern nodded without looking up. I forced myself to go back outside. Theluk had scaled the rockface and was putting brushwood over top of the cleft. Grey veils of sleet fell from the *tukinna* trees. The cold was so intense that it burned. And it was, despite the overcast, bright—the fierce Orthean sun blazed behind the storm clouds.

Theluk dropped down beside me, sure-footed on the mud.

'Shouldn't do this,' she said. 'End of Torvern, beginning of Riardh; it should be dry.'

'It—' I bit down on my temper '—it isn't, though, is it?'

She took hold of my hands. Her bare fingers were warm. Hot, against my numb skin. I stared at her. It was difficult for me to understand the Goddess's priesthood: they were not celibate, they carried weapons, there seemed nothing to distinguish them from other Ortheans. Except that Theluk was tired, not exhausted; cold, but not frozen. And serenely unafraid of this killing weather.

She managed to light the mossgrass with her tinder-box, and build a small fire. We gathered brushwood to dry. Then, in the firelit dimness, we clustered over the tiny flames.

The last wine flask was passed round and emptied.

(What would I take with me? I thought, half-tranced. If I had to do this again. Matches. Compass. Waterproof boots. A good pair of binoculars. Protein tablets. A brain that would keep me from getting into these situations in the first place.)

There were dried strips of meat to chew, and handfuls of the bird's-wing bush's berries. It was not satisfying.

'The rain's got into everything,' I said. 'Clothes, blankets, the lot.'

'Use them anyway,' Theluk fed twigs to the fire. Damp smoke coiled up, sifting out through the makeshift roof. My eyes stung.

'It's near second twilight.' Haltern's instinct for time was not dependent on the visual. 'What do you say, Earthspeaker, will the night be colder?'

Her nostrils flared slightly. The plump face was serious, concentrating.

'The wind to ease . . . the still air to be warmer, but cold towards sunrise. Tomorrow . . . no, I do not know.'

'Is she accurate?' I was too tired to be sceptical. Or polite.

'Most times,' Theluk herself answered.

'If not this time, you'll kill us all. Be sure,' Haltern urged.

'And if I am not sure, what will you do? Go out into the dark and seek Howice's riders?'

'It's the *ashiren*,' I said.

Maric opened dark eyes and said, 'You can't give in, *t'an*, I won't be the excuse for that.'

'When I give in, I won't need an excuse.'

He grinned weakly at me.

'I'll take first watch,' Theluk said.

At first light, there were five of us. Theluk pulled the brushwood away from the entrance and found the barbarian woman sitting cross-legged in the shadow of the rock. She was still wearing the torn Roehmonder cloth, blackened and flecked with *tukinna* bark. I understood none of her brief remarks.

The fire was ashes. We ate the last of the dried meat, and repacked the blankets. The packs were light.

'Weather?' Haltern asked. His thin fingers dug into his neck, trying to shift a cramp.

'I don't know. We're a long way out of the land I know . . .' Theluk peered up at the pale clouds visible through the *tukinna*. 'I think it will be dry.'

'I hope you're right.' Sleeping in damp warm blankets had given me stiffness in both legs, and a crick in my neck that meant I couldn't move my head.

'They'll be out looking,' Haltern said. 'We must stay off the roads, try and work south west.'

Maric fixed his sling-stones to his belt. 'We might be able to kill something for supper.'

It was slippery walking under the trees. The day advanced, and we travelled over sharp ridges. Weak sun broke through the clouds towards noon. We saw no one. No *rashaku* called. Twice I took the stunner and scouted round with Maric, hoping for game, but we saw nothing. Tracks were days old. We filled the water flasks after midday, leaving the rivers and coming into shallower hills.

Theluk cocked her head. 'Listen!'

We were in open woodland, bird's-wing growing sparsely under the *tukinna*. Haltern stopped, drawing the *harur* blades.

'What is it?'

A high-pitched whining came from all directions. Maric drew his belt-knife.

The first one left the trees as I groped for the stunner. I saw nothing but the movement. The boy screamed. The barbarian woman caught something in mid-leap and went over backwards. A snarl split the whining. Haltern yelled. Theluk's *harur-nilgiri* came free as she slipped her pack from her shoulders.

In that second I thumbed the stunner onto full strength and wide beam.

'Out of the way—*now!*'

Maric hurled himself behind me. I held the stunner two-handed and fired. Awls drilled into my ears. I heard Theluk scream, distantly. On widebeam, there's leakage.

I didn't miss.

I was suddenly aware that there was no sound except my harsh breathing. The whining had stopped. The stunner was quiet. It had been as natural as target-shooting on the practice ranges. Except that it was quite different, and nothing was moving now.

Haltern bent double, convulsed by racking coughs, leaning on the blade that held a corpse to the ground. Theluk sheathed first the *harur-nilgiri*, then the short *harur-nazari*. She turned one of the bodies over with her foot.

Deep red feather-pelt, black markings, no bigger than a dog. Large cup-like ears. A long weasel-body, short legs. A sharp-toothed bone jaw, lips drawn back from a swollen split tongue. The tail was short and not covered by the pelt. Black slit eyes were already dulling over.

Maric bent down, and Theluk swatted his hand away. 'Hei, what—?'

'Don't touch it. That's killpack fever.'

Soundlessly, the barbarian woman was with us. Sorting out memories, I realized that first hand-flick of hers had broken the spine of the beast that attacked her.

The bodies lay in a fan-spread between the *tukinna,* some forty in number.

'Vermin,' Haltern said.

'Let's go. They're sleeping, not dead.' I holstered the stunner.

'At least we know why game's scarce,' Theluk commented as we went on through the watery sunlight.

'They know where we are,' I said, 'and they know what we're trying to do.'

'We've *got* to go south. I don't know exactly where we are, but if we're caught between them and the Fens—' Haltern broke off, shaken by deep coughs.

'Between hammer and anvil,' Theluk agreed.

'I won't go back to Corbek.' My determination frightened me. It was fear: I wasn't going back in those cells.

'We'll fight them!' Maric insisted. 'That weapon you used on the killpack!'

'No. They're riding in companies, we'd never do it.'

The soft rain fell. We'd had three dry days, three days of looping south and barely avoiding the Talkul riders. Now, going north over bare hills, we trudged through mud. Perhaps they couldn't use *kazza*, I thought. Perhaps they'd lost us. We'd seen no one since the day before.

'Markstone!' Maric shouted. The first in days.

'Oeth,' Theluk read. 'No, I don't know it.'

The barbarian woman was missing again. I scanned the line of hills. The rain was easing. There was no sign of her. I wondered if this time she'd gone for good.

'*Marhaz.* Steal or buy, it doesn't matter which,' Haltern wheezed. 'Then make for Mirane as fast as possible, and hope we don't meet more riders than we can deal with.'

'We're not left with many choices, are we?' Theluk was gentle.

'I agree. Let's go.' I moved up beside her and when I had the chance asked 'What's he got?'

'Damp-lung. He needs to rest up a week or two.'

Oeth lay below us when we reached the top of the hill. A large *telestre* surrounded by outbuildings and beast-pens, almost a town. The pale sun picked out activity: carts, *marhaz*, people.

Beyond Oeth, stretching west to the horizon, lay the Fens.

PART
FOUR

13

The Lesser Fens

The lush mossgrass went down to clumps of weed, and then to vast beds of double-bladed reeds. Towards the horizon were stretches of standing water. Other species of mossgrass and fungi covered the acres of mudflats: black and purple, blue and green, iridescent as peacock's feathers. As we watched, a patch of sunlight swept across the desolate, flat marshland. Lurid colours flared. Water channels became silver threads, netting the sun: rivulets, ditches, pools, a web of outspreading waterways.

'The Lesser Fens,' Haltern breathed. 'Oh, that finishes it, we must go south now. *Now.*'

To the north and to the south, the hills came down like a coastline to that sea of quicksand.

Maric moved closer to us. 'Is it true—things live there that aren't human?'

Haltern looked at Theluk, who shook her head. 'We keep the edict that was made in Galen Honeymouth's time,' she said. 'We to our borders, and the fenborn to their own. No, I do not know if they are more than legend.'

'It's no concern of ours. We need *marhaz.*' Haltern stumped off down the track towards Oeth.

The main courtyard was a hundred yards across, *telestre* house on one side, stock-pens on the other three. The pens were full, an incredible hissing and bawling and stinking surrounding us; men and women shouting their bids for *kuru* and *skurrai* and *marhaz,* and for sacks of grain. Besides the fruit and bread-fungus stalls there were tables laid out with embroidered *chirith-goyen* shirts and *zilmei* coats; tunics, boots, and belt-buckles and jewellery; and the short curved *harur* blades of western Roehmonde.

'Don't stray too far,' Haltern warned, turning over in his palm what we'd been able to contribute: a few bronze bits, a silver cloakclasp, and Theluk's sea-ivory knife. 'I'll search out someone less fond of Arad's laws, honest enough to sell for an honest price.'

'Or dishonest enough,' I said.

We walked round the square while he was gone, looking at the stalls where Ortheans wove hurdles from the thin *tukinna* saplings, and watching the professional acrobats and jugglers. Once round then back to wait, trying to look like just another group of visitors to the market. Haltern was gone a long time. Theluk settled down beside a wine stall out of the press of the crowd and Maric and I sat beside her. There was a story-teller behind me, speaking to a gaggle of *ashiren:*

'—said to the Emperor Sandor, "Golden you may be, my lord, and Golden your empire; but because of what I have done, it will not outlast the reaping of this year's golden corn—" '

A man walked past, his hand twisted in the collar of a hunting *kazza.* He did not wear the Talkul insignia. The beast stood hip-high, heavily muscled, the short white pelt marked with blue dapples. The feathery tail lashed nervously. A leather hood covered the square-jawed head, with only slits for the eyes.

Maric yanked at my sleeve, pointing.

Haltern came running through the crowd, pushed past one man, knocked a woman aside, ignoring her curses, and came up to us out of breath and sweating.

'They're here,' he said curtly. 'I saw Howice. And that hired sword, from Rimon. They must have worked out we were being driven here.'

'Marhaz?'

'No one will sell—' he glanced over his shoulder. 'We've got to get out of here!'

As we left the courtyard a yell went up from the far side. I heard a strong voice bellow, 'Witchbreed!' Suddenly I saw Talkul's insignia, and ran. Maric darted off towards outbuildings. We pounded through narrow mud-tracks. Haltern was wheezing, Theluk had him by the arm.

Maric shrieked something lost in the din. Then I was clear of the outbuildings, running through thick blue-grey mossgrass that dragged wetly at my boots. Panting, sweating. I slowed to wait for the others. Between the wooden buildings, I saw a man bend down and unlace the muzzle of a *kazza.*

Marhaz dotted the hills round Oeth.

'They put a cordon round the *telestre.*' It was so simple. I should have known.

Haltern, speaking between gasps, said 'Too much. One day. Saw us. Yesterday.'

Maric drew his knife. *'T'an?'*

'Run!'

The ground was soft. We out-distanced them, but it wouldn't be for long. As I saw past the southern edge of the *telestre* I stopped, breath heaving, chest burning. There were riders to the south, too.

'Right.' Fear hid under determination. 'Let's go out towards the Fens, see if we can work round, hide.'

The yowling whine of a *kazza* rose over the shouting.

The ground turned to mud and the mossgrass to double-headed reeds, and we halted on the very edge of the marsh. Haltern clung to Theluk's shoulder. Maric went a few steps into the mud, lurched as he sank ankle-deep, and dragged himself back. The mud sucked hungrily at his boots. We stood close together.

'That's it.' Haltern sounded relieved. 'We can't go any further.'

I put my hand under my coat, feeling the hard shape of the stunner. On a tight focus . . . perhaps.

I dropped the *kazza* thirty feet from us. The closest men and women hesitated, the impetus of the mob was lost. I glimpsed riders forcing their way through. Even a powerpack wasn't inexhaustible: I couldn't take them all.

Theluk touched my arm and pointed. There was a speck, coming down from the north over the grassland. A human speck moving with such speed that it was deceptive: she seemed to float.

The barbarian woman. And *marhaz* riders behind her. So they had put a wide cordon round Oeth: I was sorry they were taking her in it.

Now I could see her clearly, running with her head high and her elbows tucked into her sides, never putting a foot wrong. Parallel to the reed beds. A last spurt of effort—wasted, there was nowhere for her to go.

She wheeled and ran into the marsh.

She's killing herself! I thought. She dodged and turned like a dancer, not sinking, not drowning. Following a route visible only to her animal senses, picking her way out across the marsh—

'Come on!'

'You're mad,' Haltern yelled.

'Maric, stay close behind me. Tread where I do.'

The mud was black: Stepped on, it sank. A wash of evil-smelling water submerged my feet. I splashed knee-deep in mud, tore myself out, and was suddenly on firm ground.

The barbarian woman was waiting a hundred yards on. I hoped she was waiting, and not stuck. I picked my way towards her with paralysing slowness.

Water plopped. I looked round. Something splashed into the mud beside me. Theluk wasn't far behind us.

'*T'an*, please. Hurry.' Maric's agonized whisper started me moving again.

'What is it?'

'Winch-bow bolts.'

My back crawled. It was nightmarish: I couldn't move faster than a slow walk. Theluk closed the gap, catching us up. *Marhaz* riders clustered on the edge of firm ground. *Kazza* whined. I couldn't see Haltern, there were reed beds between us. Now I recognized two riders. One was Howice. The other—utterly familiar, forking the saddle as if he were part of the beast—was Falkyr.

The barbarian woman moved again, picking a slow way between water channels. Searching out the spurs of solid ground that must underlie the marsh.

Now the winch-bow bolts fell short.

Step and look, step and test. Reed-mats sagged. Mud stank, gasses bubbling up. Iridescent blue weed masked treacherous ground. The last sunlight was swallowed up in cloud. Grey haze began to creep up from the water.

'Christie.'

I waited until Theluk caught up. Like Maric and myself, she was coated in black mud to the waist. Running had made me hot: now I felt the chill of the Fens.

'Where's Hal?'

She shook her head. 'We can't wait. I don't know what happened.'

'We can't leave him!'

'If they see us, they'll follow—edict or no edict.'

The barbarian woman wasn't waiting this time. It was follow her or be stranded. I didn't hesitate. We picked our slow way across the Fens, she and I and Maric and Theluk. Great flocks of long-legged *rashaku-nai* whirred up round us, until the sky was black with them.

'He's not following.' Theluk had ceased looking behind for Haltern. 'They must have taken him.'

'There's a simpler explanation.'

'You think he's dead?'

I didn't want to believe it, but these Fens were deadly. 'It's possible.'

I realized we were on relatively firm ground. Maric ran ahead to where the barbarian woman had stopped and squatted down. This was almost an island in the fenland, a few yards high, perhaps a quarter-mile long. Thick-boled scrub grew tightly on it, nowhere more than waist-high. The metallic green leaves shone in the evening light.

I saw her digging bare-handed, then the barbarian woman unearthed several large packages. They were bound tightly in something that looked waterproof—greased hide, I guessed. She unrolled one. It was a bundle of fist-sized lumps of paste, unappetizing and greasy. Already stuffing it in handfuls into her mouth, she pushed the other pack at us.

'Goddess!' Maric said a few minutes later, pausing in gobbling the fatty mess. 'This tastes foul. How can you eat it, *t'an?*'

'Cast-iron stomach. First necessity for a diplomat. You want to see some of the things they shoved at us on Beruine.' This was meat-based, I thought, and welcome; but water was going to be a problem. We couldn't drink fen water.

'How did you know?' I asked the barbarian woman.

'When—' her arm described an arc from the north-west back towards the hills '—then were many. Now—' her arm swept back, her fist closed and touched her chest.

'You left these? Caches of food?' Getting no response, I pointed north. 'There were many?'

'Dead,' she said simply.

Plain enough, if I was guessing right: a group of her people come to Roehmonde, all but her killed, and now she was returning the same way. Where, I wondered. Over the Wall, Haltern had said, Haltern who wouldn't see if his guess was right or not.

Surprisingly, the scrub burned well. Sap spat and hissed, the heat was intense. Maric joined me in pulling up bushes and dragging them into a shelter and firewood pile.

'Grief of the Goddess!' Theluk's face was stained red by the leaping flames. 'Damp it down, they'll see that twenty *seri* off!'

'Who'll see?' I watched the wood catch. It was more a bonfire than a camp fire. Standing as close as I could get to the flames, I was warm for the first time in ten days. The *ashiren* squatted down beside me. Even the barbarian woman edged closer. 'If they were going to follow, they would have by now.'

'There may be wild beasts.' Theluk was quiet. When I looked at her, I knew why. She was afraid. 'And . . . the fenborn may not be legends. Galen took it seriously enough when he was *T'An Suthai-Telestre*. In four generations no one's broken the boundary.'

Maric looked up dreamily and said, 'The High Hall of the fenborn in Tethi Starsmere is floored with skin, human and Golden. I heard that in a story somewhere.'

'That *is* legend.' As the fire died down, she kicked the outer fragments into the centre. We erected the little tent, damp-smelling, but better than sleeping in the open.

Night came, and the thick stars of the Orthean winter sky shone through the clear air. It was chillingly cold facing away from the fire. A while after dark, the tail of a nebula rose above the horizon. Filmy red and blue, it covered half the southern sky. It took me some time to think, *I've travelled past that. Out along the spiral arm, to Earth.*

The hills near Oeth still looked close, despite the *seri* we'd come. In the clear morning air I could make out each dip and hollow, white in the early sun, grey in shadow. Coils of mist hugged the fen water. Ice spangled the scrub.

Maric was coughing. Theluk took his head in her hand, peered in his eyes and nose, and down his throat. She patted his arm dismissively. 'You'll be all right.'

He began rolling the tent up. She crossed to me and said, 'Damplung. It's not surprising. Why you brought *kir* into this wet country amazes me.'

'I was supposed to leave him for Howice's people?'

'They'd have cared for *kir.*' Watching me, her expression changed. 'Who'd harm an *ashiren?* Who'd dare?'

'Anyway, *will* he be all right?'

'Not unless *ke* gets somewhere warm and dry.'

The night chorus of whoops and cries had stopped at dawn. It was quiet now, a white silence. In the faded blue sky the daystars were pinpoints of light. The Fens stretched out south and west and north, flat to the wide horizon.

Only, in the north there was a line of darker blue about ten degrees up the sky. I couldn't decide if it were low cloud or extremely high hills. As the dawn warmth drew the mist up, I lost sight of it altogether.

'I will not wait for thee,' the barbarian woman said.

'Oh—sure. We go that way.' I pointed south. We could parallel the Roehmonde hills most of the day, I thought, and hope Talkul's riders had lost us when we emerged.

'No.' She indicated north-west. 'That is my way.'

'Damn it, we don't want to go further into this!'

'That is my road,' she said, with the nearest to temper I'd ever heard from her. 'If it is not thy road, go thy way.'

'Theluk!'

But Theluk couldn't argue her out of it either. The barbarian woman was going home—wherever that was—and nowhere else.

'The other side of Lesser Fens, the Great Fens begin, and the other side of the Great Fens is Peir-Dadeni—and that is six hundred *seri*, skirting the marshes, and do you think we can walk six hundred *seri* through this? Can you?'

Eventually she gave up. 'Can we go south alone?'

'Can you find a path?' When that sunk in, I said 'If we lose her, we're stuck, it's that simple.'

'You may have killed us all, coming here.'

'So I may—but that doesn't mean I'll stop trying to get out.'

She turned her back on me. 'Load your pack light, *ashiren-te*, I'll take more in mine.'

My head was hot and heavy and thick. I couldn't stop my nose running, and I shivered continuously. Throat and lungs were raw from coughing. I chewed another of the bitter painkillers from the medic kit. It didn't lessen the pain, but it detached me from it.

Maric, when he coughed, spat pink phlegm. Even Theluk had the wheezing that marks the beginning of damp-lung.

The barbarian woman pushed on as fast as was possible. With all her circling and back-tracking, she was keeping us headed north of west on a direct course. It may have been fever, or empathy, but I was beginning to see the Fens as she must: islands of safe ground, of greater and lesser size, separated by rivers and seas of insect-ridden water.

Two days, or was it three? This was the first night we hadn't been able to light a fire. Fog drifted past us. At the arch of the sky it was silver. Moisture clung to the twisted branches of low trees. We sat among roots, on the highest spot of land in a flooded basin, wrapped in *becamil* blankets, boots almost in the water.

Luminous *siriye* darted past, multifaceted eyes glowing. Odd cries came from the reed beds. Maric leaned against me, sleeping with his mouth open, breathing harshly.

Darkness hit me. It wasn't sleep. There was no knowledge of being unconscious: it was as if time pleated itself. I woke with a headache that threatened to split bone.

An unhuman face stared into mine.

Time slipped again: totally disorientated. When I sat up, I held my head and whimpered. Phlegm loosened, I coughed and spat. Each spasm rocked my head. The pain almost blinded me.

At last I could sit quiet. The relief was incredible. I opened watery eyes. The light was green. Reaching up, my fingers met a yielding surface. Very slowly it dawned on me that I was under cover. The surface was leather. Pegged over—branches? And laying on more of the same: me, and others with me. The face I'd seen—or was that fever-dream?— that cat-eyed and prick-eared face stayed with me, with visionary intensity.

Theluk. Maric. The *ashiren* lay sprawled on one side, looking very young and vulnerable. Theluk's face was the colour of uncooked meal. Both were asleep or unconscious. The barbarian woman was missing. But on the other side of Theluk, a broad-shouldered man lay with his back to me. For a second I thought, *Haltern!* But as I knelt upright, I saw who it was.

Scarred face, the puddingy red and white skin masking half the forehead, cheek, and chin. That's a burn, I thought detachedly. Fair silver-streaked mane. The faint dapple of marshflower on his broad hands.

I saw the hired sword out of Rimon, Haltern said. In Oeth.

Did they all follow? Is he the only one? Why; who?

It was like coming out of anaesthetic, I didn't believe in the reality of the world. I'd had dreams in the dark that were coming back to me now. This might be another. There were long gaps in my memory. That last camp site was more than a day away, I thought.

I slept again.

Light flickered. I rubbed my gummy eyes open. There was a dim impression in my mind of being fed something liquid, and—perhaps of being carried, I wasn't sure.

Light was red, yellow, was firelight, and shadows moved on the sides of a tent. A much larger tent. There was a gap at its apex, and a glimpse of daystarred sky.

The barbarian woman sat cross-legged beside a firepit, feeding chunks of peat and wood to the flames. I moved, sat up, coughed. Physical misery rushed back. It was at the same time stuffy and cold in the tent, and difficult to breathe. I edged over on all fours to the fire.

'Thou?' She touched her throat, and then mine.

My head ached, my throat was sore, but my lungs had cleared.

Dopily I thought, I must congratulate Adair. The shots work. No pneumonia, no pleurisy. Christ. Lucky!

I said, 'Where are we?'

Her answer was unintelligible. I knelt over the fire for a while, and then stood up. My legs were weak. The tent stank of excrement and illness. I made my way over to the flap, gripping the struts for support, and picked at the lacings.

There was no warmth from the sun hanging low in the south. The pale sky dazzled me. I blinked. Outside, the chill struck into me. This was high land, a good yard above the water table level: an island larger than most. Scrub and twisted trees covered it. I went a little way from the tent to shit.

The Roehmonde hills were no longer visible. There was nothing, in all the vast circle of the horizon, except the Fens. Across a water channel were more of the dull green tents, blending into the background, and a few figures—I couldn't tell what they were at that distance. Quarantine, I thought. And giggled weakly. Whoever had us didn't want us.

Back in the tent I found Maric awake and huddled over the fire. Theluk was trying to question the barbarian woman. The man—Blaize n'ri n'suth Meduenin, it came back bell-clear from the trial—was muttering in his sleep, and twitching.

'They're fenborn!' the boy said excitedly. 'I was awake, I saw them.'

'Where are we?' Theluk asked.

'As near the middle of nowhere as makes no difference.' I had to sit down before I fell down, I had no resources of strength left. I wondered just how ill I had been.

'What's he doing here?' Maric jerked his head at the man. 'They've taken our packs, *t'an*, and the *harur* swords.'

The stunner was missing too, I realized.

Theluk bent over the fairmaned Orthean, rolling up his eyelids with her thumb. She frowned. Examining him, she sniffed his breath and peered down his throat. The puzzled look vanished.

'He's not sick,' she said, 'maybe a touch of damp-lung, that's all.'

'What's wrong with him?'

'He's *ataile* addicted. For some time, I'd guess. He won't find any in the Fens. Well, if he lives through this, he'll be free of it.'

'If he lives?'

'We ought to kill him,' Maric said. 'While we can. He's followed you to kill you, *t'an* Christie.'

And got picked up the same time we did? I thought. He must have been behind us from Oeth. What drove him to that?

'*Ke's* right,' Theluk agreed, 'we've little enough chance of getting out of here as it is.'

'No, we can't do that.' I had a sneaking regret they hadn't done it while I was unconscious. You can't argue with a fact. And I didn't need active malice on top of everything else.

There was a call from outside. The barbarian woman rose fluidly to her feet and left the tent. I followed her, Theluk holding onto the struts of the doorway behind me.

Fenborn.

He was not human, not even by Orthean standards, which were what I applied. The barbarian woman talked to him, standing on the edge of the waterway.

He was younger than she, slender, with stick-thin limbs, and not much taller than Maric. Pale, dusty-olive skin had, in the wintry sunlight, a bloom of gold on it. Green and gold, changing hue with every movement, as in the weave of a cloth. He was hairless except for a fine black down on his skull, a ridge from forehead to mid-spine. Obviously male. There was something wrong or odd about the jointing of his limbs.

Seeing us, he left the conversation with the barbarian woman and walked over to the tent. His eyes were black, slit-pupilled, half-veiled. As he breathed, I saw light and shadow chase each other over his skin.

He touched my hand (rough snakeskin feel) and snatched his fingers away. There were webs between them, pale dapples down his seamed belly. I wanted to laugh: hysteria. His fingers were ice-cold. He said something I didn't understand, repeated it, and turned away.

The barbarian woman was not having much better luck in making herself understood, I saw.

In one movement the fenborn slid under the surface of the channel, out of sight until the dark-ridged head appeared thirty feet away, at the far bank. With obvious distaste, the barbarian woman waded through the mud and swam after him.

She hadn't returned by nightfall.

We rested four days in that temporary camp. I often saw the barbarian woman among the other tents with the fenborn, though she mostly returned to us at nightfall. She answered no questions.

I wasn't sure at the end of that time if the fenborn were intelligent, or only animals. Their speech had nothing in common with any of the Southland languages, being only grunts. They pegged hides over branches as tents, and gutted the *rashaku-nai* and marsh beasts with stone knives . . . and yet beavers make dams and fieldmice weave nests. The fenborn were equally at home in water or on the low land, or —judging by the pack of young ones—in the twisted branches of the trees.

None of them entered our tent. One came as far as the entrance and had a chittering and growling argument with the barbarian—she was not much better understood in their camp than she was in ours—which ended in a scuffle. It was not until I studied the fenborn that I realized they had no use of fire. And the barbarian woman had Theluk's tinderbox, and a firm determination to keep the firepit going.

'We can't stay here,' Theluk said towards afternoon on the fourth day. 'They can't keep us.'

Westering light was lilac over the water, and the low trees stood black against the horizon. Wide-winged lizardbirds circled overhead.

'It isn't them—it's that.'

The Fens lay chill under the darkening sky. The days were noticeably shorter now.

'How's the kid?' She'd been caring for him; Earthspeaker duties included medical training.

'*Ke's* well enough, likely to recover if *ke's* kept warm. There's nothing else I can do.'

'The other one?'

'What's he got to do with me?' She was uncharacteristically savage. 'Hunts us half-way across Roehmonde, drives us into this Goddessforsaken place, and expects nursing? No, not from me. If it's his time, She'll take him; and if not, he'll live.'

Walking the perimeter of our island, we came back to the tent. It was no great distance. The woman stretched, linking her bony fingers; and then dug them into the roots of her mane, kneading the muscles at the back of her neck. She was tense all the time now.

'I don't feel for this land,' she said, 'it's too far from home. Perhaps Arad was right. Too much strangeness—there are some parts of Her that I'll never understand.'

She ducked under the open flap into the tent. I watched the fading light. A cluster of dark blobs in the water resolved themselves into fenborn young. They chittered, darted back to the opposite bank as swift as fish, and became a shrieking, tumbling mob.

'Tastes like *rashaku* droppings.'

'Eat it or starve.'

I woke to hear Maric quarrelling with the scarred man. We had no hot food or drink, only raw meat that could be scorched in the firepit, and a choice between fen water and leather containers of some milky liquid. Meduenin was right: it was foul.

Theluk rolled over, ignoring everyone. I saw the barbarian woman was missing again. On top of the cold, I was developing some kind of allergic reaction, my eyes and nose streaming, and a skin rash.

'You're dead,' the man said, 'all of you. You may be too stupid to realize it, but you are.'

The jeering note got to me. I sat up. He was propped against the tent strut, hands flat on the ground beside him. Sunlight from the open flap lit his dusty mane, and the red ruin of his half-face.

'You want this?' Maric passed over the leather bag. I sucked the milk, ignoring the taste.

'You were paid to kill.' My voice was rusty. 'Pity you got caught with us. Not too clever, was it?'

He looked pared down to the bone. All through the withdrawal fever from the *ataile* addiction, it had been impossible to make him eat. At one point Theluk had knotted a blanket round him, while he thrashed in delirium. Now he stared, cocky because he was alive. And wondering why none of us had knifed him, I thought.

'I'm going to see you dead,' he told me in a conversational tone.

'What good will it do you? Will it help that if you kill me?'

His left hand was rubbing his right wrist: he snatched them apart as if they burned him. The broken wrist had mended, though not set (Theluk said) as well as it could have been. He had the use of it.

'You won't find them,' Maric put in, seeing him looking round for his packs. 'The fenborn have everything.'

'Fenborn—' he glanced outside obviously remembering something of what had gone on round him. Seen in profile, he was young. Younger than Theluk: late twenties, perhaps, or early thirties. 'Well now: fenborn.'

'My government—'

'Is a long way from here, if I understand right.'

He was not impressed by Earth, by envoys. Obviously not, or he wouldn't have been hired as killer and witness against me.

'Leave it.' I stood up, rubbing my itching eyes, and hunched over the fire. The whole conversation was beginning to seem unreal. Events were hallucinatory. I thought, *how fit am I?* 'Just—leave it. We'll settle it later on. Not here. Not now.'

'Why not now?' he challenged.

There were four of us in the tent, and no one of us fit, but it was still three to one. I admired his nerve, if nothing else.

'Because I don't propose to do the fenborn's work for them. Because if they kill us, they won't leave you out. It's nothing personal—different customs, you might say. Let's call a truce.'

'Is it true you're Witchbreed?'

I shook my head. He sounded as though he hoped I was.

'Law doesn't apply here,' he said.

I was still trying to work out exactly what he meant, when the fenborn came for us.

14

Speaker-for-the-People

Orthe's pale sky gleamed like water, freckled at the horizon with needlepoint daystars. Pith-reeds spiked up out of frozen mud, brittle white spears. The ground creaked underfoot. Webs of ice edged the open water. The flat marsh went out to an infinite haze.

A fenborn gestured with her spear, and we huddled aside while the tent was ripped down. The firepit was given a wide berth. Two or three of them bent to paw and sniff the leather and struts. Eventually it was discarded, left in the mud. I felt homeless. Sweat, the lingering taint of sickness: it had enclosed a warm and somehow comforting smell of humanity, but the chill air dispersed it.

'What are they going to do?' It was the first time Maric had questioned or complained, though he'd been crying when he thought himself unobserved.

'I don't know. It's all right.' I put my arm round his shoulders, taking him under my blanket. I needed to hold on to somebody. We had the clothes we stood up in, and covers rescued from the tent; that was all. Theluk was barefoot, her sandals lost somewhere. We looked like refugees.

They carried spears and double-tined forks with stone blades and long shafts, and stone axes. Some flint-tipped spears lowered in our direction. I tensed. The barbarian woman appeared out of the mob, gestured towards the water, and a gap appeared in the crowd. I moved hesitantly in that direction. Theluk closed up the distance behind me, her eyes scanning rapidly. Herded, we reached the water.

There was a scuffle behind. I paid no attention. Blaise n'ri n'suth Meduenin cursed, and then was with us again, wiping a bloody mouth.

Flat-bottomed boats were piled with rolled-up tents and fish-spears. We sat among damp leather and gutted marsh beasts. A woman heaved us free of the mud, and we were poled across the deep water to the other side of the channel. Tall reed beds rattled in the wind.

A group of fenborn stepped lightly aboard. I could see six other boats from where I sat, all low in the water. Hides stretched over a wooden framework: I could feel the pulse of the water under me. Theluk sat bolt upright, gripping the sides.

'Can you swim?' Blaize said sardonically. 'It might be easier in the end.'

'They'd kill us.' Maric's eyes fixed on the fenborn, adult and young, who followed the boats, threading paths over the treacherous mud, or swimming and diving in the open channel.

'Quick, at least. There are harder ways of dying.'

'Be quiet,' I snapped. He shrugged.

We passed through deeper channels between towering banks of reeds, yellow-green and still with the husks of red bloom on them. Two of the fenborn stood at the rear of the leaf-shaped boat, digging long poles into the mud. A third sat in the centre, breast-feeding an infant. She had dugs like an old sow. Two others, nearer me in the boat, were trying to keep four or five young fenborn quiet.

One of the litter, about three seasons old, crawled over the tents to stare at us. The dark eyes watched us, nictitating membrane blurring the slit pupils. Broad forehead, pointed chin, and flat ears that came to a small point. The impression was half-human, half-batrachian, but not ugly. A changeling child.

The younger male swept it up and dumped it unceremoniously back in the stern, with the immemorial gesture of adults. Male? I thought. And stared. The belly bulged. Undeniably male, but to all appearances pregnant.

Settled back down again, the younger male and the female had their heads together. I saw him, slender webbed hands at his stomach; and then he was holding an oblate spheroid, and then another. The female took and examined them. They were greenish-white, fist sized, and with a tough flexible covering.

Terison, it came back to me; Terison, and the birth, and the babies born in a flexible membrane. The membrane that must be the last evolutionary remnant of this process.

The younger male was replacing the eggs in his pouch, and the other female giving suck to the child—or was it a different child? I couldn't tell. Ortheans don't pair, they group. This group, I thought, must be one unit; I wonder if it applies to the other boats . . .

'Are you all right?'

I hugged Maric closer, and managed to stop giggling. 'It's just funny, the things I still notice. When there's no need.'

Theluk's knuckles were white with the strain of gripping the boat. She didn't talk, only shaking her head in response to questions. Blaize n'ri n'suth Meduenin had a curious abstracted expression, almost a lost look, and his hands went to his belt-pouch as if he expected to find *ataile* leaves. It was not an addict's search. If he lives, Theluk had said, he'll lose the desire. I thought, he's trying to understand why he doesn't want it any more.

Towards noon I saw the shadow-line on the northern horizon again. It was too hazy for hills, unless extremely distant, but too solid for cloud. I lost sight of it after that, as we came among wider channels and higher islands covered with interlinking trees. Roots hung black into the water, contrasting with the chrome-yellow, plate-like leaves. The water was the colour of jade. *Kekri* flies hung in clouds in the midday warmth, glittering metallic blue and green. Other fenborn came to take over poling the boat. They swam in the stagnant water, catching their food live, and sometimes throwing mudcrawlers or amphibians into the bottom of the boat. No one fed us. I was too tensed up to notice.

I thought, if this is how they took us when we were first captured and drugged, we could be a hundred *seri* from Roehmonde. And if so, and if we do get free—where are we going to go?

Channels and mudflats: the monotony of the flat land bore down on us. The afternoon passed in a daze. The sun stood over my left shoulder. The boats crept on northwards, and a dark smudge grew infinitesimally until I could make out more scrub-covered islands. I began to see more fenborn, some in camps, some standing and watching as we passed. There were no hails. We drifted in a silence that lulled us into apathy, hid fear under temporary boredom.

Trees met overhead, enclosing us in a yellow twilight. Through thin gaps the afternoon sun dappled white on black water. I shook Maric awake.

'What?' He threshed upright. 'Where?'

'I think we're stopping.'

The trees extended roots into the water, black scaly bark covered with scarlet and blue mosses. Fenborn children crouched on the roots watching us, sometimes slipping under the surface and coming up beside the boat. They chattered, and gave high-pitched squeals. The adults grunted and swatted them away. The boat was poled into an apparent dead end, where other boats were moored. The charnel, spicy odour of the disturbed water was overpowering.

Fenborn slid lithely ashore, pulling and jamming the boat between roots. There was no earth visible. The roots and fibres formed a semi-solid mat. Maric looked questioningly at me. I tried to focus, to concentrate; I wished I could see the barbarian woman. One fenborn grunted, jabbing a spear in my direction. I reached out and hauled myself up into the roots, clambering, clutching at branches, and holding out a hand to Maric. Underfoot, the matted roots gave and swayed. Blaize followed, then Theluk. The fenborn chittered.

Theluk shoved me aside, breaking free. Scrambling over roots, clutching branches, hurling herself along the edge of the island—away from the fenborn. Maric called out. The nearest fenborn threw a stone axe with perfect accuracy, catching the Earthspeaker at the base of the skull.

She went forward as if her legs had been cut out from under her, hit the roots, spun sideways, then jack-knifed in a fold that slid her under the black water.

The ripples died.

I stared stupidly at the spot where Theluk vanished.

Two fenborn dived under the water, and reappeared moments later. As they climbed out, a swirl of water showed the soaked cloth of Theluk's coat. It sank again. The fenborn chattered at each other. The spears jerked with an unmistakable command: move.

'She—I—she wouldn't have felt—' I was blank. 'It can't have happened. It—must have killed her, she—'

Maric cried noisily and wiped his face, leaving smears of black mud.

'Do you want to end up with her?' Blaize shoved the *ashiren* forward. The fenborn's incomprehensible order came again. Spears raised.

Theluk. It was impossible to walk over the mass of roots without concentrating on not slipping. I thought of Theluk, and if branches were too weak to bear my weight, and of Theluk: never really known, only as the friend of a friend. Bemused, moving in a dream, under snaking branches and green and yellow leaves; and Theluk, competent, and a private person: *why* did she run, what panicked her?

Now we were surrounded by fenborn, male and female, old and young; with a pack of children underfoot. Barefoot, sharp-eyed, frighteningly silent.

Those seconds: so quick, so casual, if I'd had my head turned the other way I'd never have seen it. Theluk. The slung axe, the folding body. Barely a disturbance. And now wide-eyed and mud-throated down in the tangled roots.

'Christie.' Maric took my hand, and we walked onto firmer ground.

Shafts of autumn sun speared down into the gloom. The tangle of branches lifted, forming a high roof and the tightly woven roots were carpeted with skins. Fenborn sat and stood round the edge of this natural hall. The skins, two and three deep, made for firmer footing. They had a curious dusty gold sparkle to them. In the centre space, on a massive block of blue-grey stone, sat an ancient fenborn. Beside her was the barbarian woman.

I went up to her, pointing at the old fenborn. 'Has she thy tongue?'

'Yes. Little.'

'Then tell her—tell her there's been a murder.'

The silence was broken, the barbarian woman and the fenborn with us all screeching at the old fenborn woman. The assembly jabbered. A child's thin wail rose above the noise. The old woman raised her arms. The noise quieted.

'She is Speaker-for-the-People,' the barbarian woman said. 'Thy friend is dead?'

'They killed her!' Maric, shrill.

The fenborn woman grunted. I stepped forward. She looked down at me. She was dirty, faded, eyes filmed over with whitening membrane. A frown tugged at her forehead. She gestured.

'Show thy hands,' the barbarian woman said.

I put my hands flat on the shoulder-high stone. The fenborn woman put her hand beside them, prodding, counting over the fingers. Her hand was icy. She reached down, touching me on the cheek, staring into my eyes. I held still. There was nothing to do. It wouldn't bring Theluk back if I got myself killed.

A flare of empathy came through the old woman's touch. I knew beyond doubt that she would not order me murdered. It was so certain that I was not surprised when the barbarian woman said, 'Thou and thy possessions are free of here: she says, *Go.*'

'What's she going to do about Theluk?'

There was speech too swift for me to follow, part in the fenborn grunts and squeals, part in the barbarian woman's archaic conglomerate of several Southland tongues. Behind me, Blaize n'ri n'suth Meduenin swore.

'Never mind the dead,' he said, 'what about the living?'

The barbarian woman argued in the sun-striped twilight. Yells came from the crowd. The blue-grey stone, lit by the white sun, showed intricate carvings on its side. Too intricate for fenborn. Hunger buzzed in my head and settled in a knot of pain in my chest.

'She says, *Go*,' the barbarian woman repeated. Some of the other fenborn dragged packs out onto the floor. They'd been opened and picked through, some seams ripped, some clothes torn, and a lot of stuff missing. The medic kit was there, but empty. Surprised, I saw the *harur* blades had been left untouched.

I hesitated. It was failing Theluk not to push it further. But what good would it do?

I scooped up half the stuff and Maric grabbed the rest. As we turned away, spears lowered.

'You said we could go!' I called.

'Thou,' the barbarian woman said, 'and I, but not these others.'

Maric gaped. Then Blaize spoke.

'Possessions too,' he emphasized, 'and *ke* is her *l'ri-an*, and I am her hired sword; you must send us with her.'

The barbarian woman translated it. I saw Blaize keen and tense, half his attention on them and half on the discarded *harur* blades. He'll fight, I thought, if this doesn't work.

At last the barbarian woman touched her hands to the fenborn's, and walked swiftly towards us. She gestured us to follow, and this time they let all of us pass.

'Watch your back,' Blaize murmured, 'they've already killed once.'

'I don't need reminding!'

'Pity you didn't remind them.'

I nearly stopped to argue it out there, but we had to keep moving. The fenborn clustered round us. They were overhead in the branches, sure footed; close by, not quite touching.

'I should have talked to her,' Maric said. 'She looked after me. If I'd seen she was scared, if I'd listened, she might not have run like that. Do you think she would have run like that?'

'She misjudged, that's all.' Blaize was less sharp. 'There's no second chances.'

Out from under the trees, to a low muddy shore. The whole western sky was silver and indigo, reflected in water channels, gleaming on mud flats. The rushes rattled. The barbarian woman caught the prow of one of the shallow boats. I dumped the armful of stuff in the bottom of the boat, and Maric copied me.

Why they took us, why they didn't kill us, why they let all of us go —I can speculate, but I don't know. The barbarian woman and I still had a very imperfect understanding of each other. It was possible they thought the Fens would kill us. Or other fenborn. Or the barbarian woman herself. Or was it some blood-price for Theluk?

'Move,' I said, trying to keep balanced, and the barbarian woman and I clumsily poled the boat out into the middle of the channel. The fenborn watched us in silence. Blaize sat, sorting through the baggage for his own gear. Maric held the edge of the boat, staring back over the stern.

'I suppose it's different for an Earthspeaker,' he said, 'but everyone should go back to their own *telestre* when they die. For the fire. The Goddess is always the Goddess, but—I don't want to rot in these marshes.'

'Nor do I.' It was difficult to keep the boat from grounding. 'We'll stop when we're out of sight. See if you can't get *rashaku-nai* with that sling of yours. We've got to eat.'

The boy was expert with slingstones, and the barbarian woman had a remarkable ability to catch mudcrawlers. Blaize took a turn poling the boat. And I watched for the fenborn. I couldn't believe they'd leave us alone.

Second twilight showed, on the distant northern horizon, the faint shadow of hills.

PART
FIVE

15

Over the Wall of the World

'Can you use these?' I offered Maric Theluk's *harur-nilgiri* and *harur-nazari.*

He said hesitantly, 'I'm still *ashiren.'*

'And I don't know one end of them from the other—you do.'

He buckled the belt round his waist, drew the blades—that simultaneous flourish—and replaced them to make readjustments. I thought how he'd changed. He was skinny, a little taller, and the once cropped mane hung round his face in rat's-tails. But he was not a child. *Ashiren* or not, if he were human I'd have taken him for a young man.

'The packs are light,' he observed.

'Thieving savages.' I knew the fenborn had followed us, watching, to the edge of the Fens. Their light-fingered way with property didn't bother the Southlanders—who weren't particular that way themselves —but it annoyed me. All I'd got left was the stunner, and that only because it had no recognizable use. It was pure chance no one had tossed it in a ditch.

'Christie.' The barbarian woman came over with her arms full of the waxed food-skins. I used my knife to rip one open, and Maric and I ate handfuls of the cold greasy meat. It had been lean going the past five days. Most fen beasts and predators were hibernating.

'Which is thy way now?' I asked her, and the barbarian woman pointed at the Wall.

The five days in the boat had been mild for autumn, hazy skies and mist over the Fens, so it was not until today that we had gained a clear sight of the hills. I was curious: they were surely too low to have shown up so far across the marshes. Then, looking idly up beyond them into the hazed sky, I saw first blue shadow, then what I took for solid cloud, and at last glittering rocks and snow peaks. Breaking from the haze and showing itself clear across the northern horizon was the Wall of the World.

We camped on a low heath just out of the marshes, using the framework of the boat to fuel a fire. Low hills rolled up to the north, covered with a browngold mossgrass and outfalls of rock. About six *seri* away the foothills humped up, covered with dark trees; and the base of the Wall fanned up from them.

'You want us to *climb*—'

'There is a path.' Her hands moved narrowly apart. She must have come down that way, I realized. So there must be a pass.

North-east and south-west, the line of the Wall continued. There were peaks, headlands, crevasses striking back into the northern land. But in most places it was sheer rock face, heaved up like a snow-crested wave about to smash down on the Fens. Some gigantic slip-fault. We faced rock cliffs easily seven thousand feet high, and those further off— I squinted in the clear light—maybe twenty or thirty thousand.

'If you're going to have an unknown pass down from the Barrens, this is the place to have it.' Blaize n'ri n'suth Meduenin bent down to fasten his pack. He nodded at the Fens. 'Any barbarian army that can get through that and still manage to invade us deserves to win.'

Maric pointedly ignored him. 'Need we go, Christie? Maybe we could follow these foothills back to Roehmonde.'

'If it doesn't mean crossing fens again. If it isn't a great distance, which I suspect it is. If Roehmonde was any less dangerous than being here.'

He had to crane his neck to see the top of the peaks. 'Is that any better?'

'To be practical—while we follow her, we know there are caches of food along the route. We'll eat. As for getting back to Roehmonde,' I admitted, 'I'm lost.'

'What about him?' He indicated Blaize, who'd moved out of earshot, staring up at the Wall.

'Keep it as we've been doing it. Sleep alternate watches, and don't take your eyes off him.'

We paralleled the Wall all of that day, walking in a mild sun and a south wind from the Fens. Towards second twilight the barbarian woman turned from west to north, rounding a headland that flamed saffron in the sunset. Twenty *seri* away across low hills, the Wall stood black against the west. The crevasse ran up towards the north, so that we were walking with peaks on either side, and the ground was almost imperceptibly rising. We made camp in a shallow dip, burning strips of the brown mossgrass and eating cold rations.

I took first watch. The sun set abruptly behind an outflung spur of the Wall; second twilight was short. Silver light flooded the ground, inking in shadows, leaching the colours from the heath. The others huddled asleep in the dip, out of the night wind. I was alone.

The stars were so close and so numerous that they ran together in blazes of light, webs of blue-white spangled with darkness. The Fens lay hidden under pale fog. This barren land that went up between rock faces was rough-coated, a shaggy sleeping animal. And the Wall itself, the Wall of the World, blocked out the stars like a tide of night.

I came back towards the camp, lacing myself up. It was chill, the mossgrass was crunchy with frost, and the sun put long shadows into the west. The peaks and cliffs of the Wall stood out in minute detail. I paused, looking south over the Fens. Somewhere past them, past Roehmonde and Ymir, hundreds of *seri* from here, the same sun was gilding the ship's masts at harbour in Tathcaer, and now the dawn bells were ringing out over the island.

Light flickered in the corner of my eye. Reflex taking over, I ducked and fell and rolled away. Coming upright I thought, overreacting, you're getting nervous, Christie. And then I saw the knife at the base of the rock outcrop, and the white scar on the stone. Blaize n'ri n'suth Meduenin came lightly down the slope, *harur-nilgiri* carried in his left hand and *harur-nazari* in his right. The scar made something impossible of his expression.

Can I take him? I thought, and he circled round, and the morning sun was in my eyes. I dropped again, anticipating, and heard the spang of metal on rock: the *harur-nazari* thrown and lost. I backed into rockshadow. The steel glittered wickedly.

He closed in, and I rehearsed in my mind the methods for disarming attackers, feeling stiff and awkward in the cold air. And he came closer and I shot him.

The whine of high-pitched sound cracked the morning open. I heard Maric shout and then he came tumbling over the slope, drawing Theluk's *harur* blades, and stopped dead. The barbarian woman watched impassively from the top of the dip. I took my thumb off the stud, and the silence was frightening. The stunner was warm, comfortable in my palm.

'Is he dead?' Maric asked.

'I don't think so.' I knelt down and rolled the man onto his back. He was heavy. His arms flopped. I'd never used the stunner on an Orthean. If they were more sensitive . . .

A little blood ran from his ears and nose. But the heartbeat was strong under my hand.

'What am I going to do with you?' I was talking to myself. I left him, melted frost soaking into the back of his tunic, and went to pick up the knives. The blade a few feet from his outstretched hand was a slender Rimon *harur-nilgiri.* Maric eyed the man warily and came to sit on one of the rocks. I had to sit down. I sat rubbing the heels of my hands into my eye-sockets, trying to relieve tension. It was quiet. We were that way for some time; the shadows shortened as the sun rose up the sky, and the *rashaku-nai* hooted mournfully down in the Fens.

'What are you going to do?' Maric asked flatly. 'You—we—have to kill him. Before he kills us.'

It was logic, but I couldn't face it.

'Or we could leave him here. Just—go. Let the land kill him for us.'

'No, we can't do that. I know he's a good tracker. I can't be forever watching my back,' I protested.

'Spoken like a true Southlander.' Blaize's voice was a croak. He hitched himself up on his elbows, watching us.

'What the hell do you think you're playing at?'

'I was hired for a certain purpose,' he said.

'In the Fens you claimed to be my hired sword.'

'In Corbek I claimed you were my *arykei,* does that make it true?'

It made me furious. He grinned, sitting up and shaking his head to clear it. He rubbed his ears. Part deaf, I guessed.

'Of all the stupid . . . and we're miles from Melkathi.'

'Did I mention SuBannasen?' His head was cocked sideways and he was frowning. And watching lips, I realized, and deliberately turned my head when I spoke to Maric.

'Get the stuff packed. I think there's a limit to how long she'll wait for us.'

'Right. What about him?'

'Leave it to me.' I balanced the *harur* blades. I'd keep the throwing knife, I decided.

'You don't have to mention SuBannasen,' I told Blaize, 'I can add up facts as well as anyone. But what difference does it make, here?'

I had to repeat the question. He said, 'I'm a sell-sword. I make my living because I keep my word. Unreliable mercenaries don't get paid.'

'Is that what brought you into the Fens—money?'

He got to his feet slowly. I pushed the *harur* blades over to him. There was no point one of us being unarmed in this wild country.

'You're careless,' he accused.

'No, I'll defend myself when I'm attacked.'

'Oh, that I don't doubt.' A touch of the old acid.

'Shall I tell you one more thing? The damage isn't permanent, I shouldn't think. You'll hear clear by the end of the day.' It was impossible to miss the fear and relief in his eyes. 'But that's once—I can't answer for what might happen a second or third time; you seem to be more sensitive to high-frequency sound than we are. If it happens again, the damage might be permanent.'

He sheathed the blades and then looked at me, weighing up what I'd said. Maric appeared with the barbarian woman, and called to me. She was already turning away towards the Wall.

'You think you can cross *that?*'

'She did.'

'Ah, I see. Sooner than return south, you prefer a quiet death on the rock face. Understandable.'

'Well, never mind mercenary ethics. Am I going to have to watch my back all the time from now on?'

'That's rough travelling.' His gaze still took in the Wall. 'And as I thought before—laws don't apply out here.'

I didn't trust him. But we went on up the narrowing valley, between peaks spidered with snow against a glaring sky.

Walking was hell. The brown mossgrass here grew tough and springy and knee-high. Impossible to push through, it was necessary with each step to tread it down. And it hid potholes, ankle-wrenching rifts in the ground. The first half hour had me running with sweat despite the icy wind. Old dry shoots broke off as we walked and crept into everything; hair, eyes, shirt, and boots.

By unspoken consent we broke to rest every few miles. I sprawled belly-down and breathless, and thought that if the barbarian woman couldn't wait for us she could go to—but she sensed our temper, I think, and slowed her pace.

At second twilight I raised my head, having been walking all day, watching where I was putting my feet. It amazed me how close the mountains had come. No, not close, I thought. We're already in them.

Miles distant on either side, the great peaks rose up. This rough unforested land they held between them was an ancient geological split

—and must be the barbarian woman's pass. We were way above fen-level, and the land was still rising.

Mist gathered over a cold stream bed. The barbarian woman uncovered food and skin tents in a cleft slope that wasn't worth the name of cave. We cleared a space to burn mossgrass, and huddled out of the wind. Sleep didn't come easy. By now we were wearing all the spare gear we had, and it was still bone-chillingly cold. I woke several times to chafe circulation into hands and feet.

If the weather doesn't break, I thought, maybe we stand a chance. If the wind rises . . . if the chill-factor increases . . . if it rains . . .

If we don't get across this pass and down into the country beyond inside a day—tomorrow—then the chances are we won't make it.

I fell asleep without ever wondering what lay the other side of the mountains.

Dawn showed pale rock against a star-dusted sky, all milky shades of blue and pastel grey—soft, it looked; and yet as I saw it I could sense the knife-sharp rock, the razor-edged wind. Here the cold presence of the rock was closely felt: dark, wet, massive and solid. But ahead and all around, scarp-faces reared up into the northern sky. Ten, fifteen, twenty thousand feet in one sheer span. And the blue distance softened them to grey and white.

Dawn, and a long day coming.

The mossgrass grew sparsely as we climbed higher—it was a blessing to walk easy for once—and great broken boulders littered the steep slope. The chill of the rock struck through *becamil* coats; breath was white on the air.

Towards midday the first tendrils of mist crept down off the peaks.

Old brown snow, still frozen from last winter, clung to the northern shelter of the boulders. Sounds echoed. Somewhere I heard water falling.

A hot ache settled itself under my ribs. The air parched in my throat and lungs. Cold and the physical effort shut me off: we climbed each in our own world. The barbarian woman was always ahead, vanishing into the thickening mist and reappearing like a vision.

Putting one foot in front of the other took all my concentration. Mist pearled on my hair, soaking it; my lips froze with every breath. Twice when I sat down to rest I fell instantly asleep, but the cold woke me. Each time it was harder to get up again.

It frightened me that I was so exhausted, so soon. And there was a new sensation I felt but couldn't identify—more a vacancy than an exhaustion—that would have frightened me all the more had I been capable of worrying about it.

The mist boiled and shifted, soaking like a soft rain, and it was a long while before it mattered to me that the slope was now a downward one. I saw a thread of chill water flowing downhill past me, the mist thinned as we came out from under its ceiling, and all of us stopped to look in the long afternoon. The cold eased as the wind dropped. There was no joy in knowing we had crossed the pass, nor any point in looking back: now we could only go on.

'We're lucky,' Blaize said grudgingly as we rested, 'any later in the year and this would be blocked by snow. It must be Riardh Secondweek or Thirdweek now.'

Movement alerted me. The barbarian woman was on her feet again, and picking her way down the long slope. The rock went down into many gullies and long transverse hills. Clear light covered the tundra, pale gold. Even I could see that we couldn't survive here in bad weather, and not very long in good weather either. Nothing grew, and the hunting would be sparse. Here were the exposed ribs of the land, the bones of Orthe. An uncompromising country, we'd have to come to it on its own terms or it would kill us.

The barbarian went ahead, our only guide.

There was a food cache in the valley coming down from the Wall, but half of it was spoiled. Faint white plumes on the peaks became streams in the valleys, noisy and rushing, cold enough to freeze hands. We stayed there, in that air that seemed mild after the pass, for all the next day. We had come down no more than three or four thousand feet—the whole tableland was higher than the fen country.

'Where are you going?' I asked the barbarian woman in as many ways as I could frame the question.

'We are Kirriach people,' she said, and her brown arm swept out towards the north west. That was all.

We're coming to the end of it, I thought. One way or another. There's a limit to how long we can live rough. There's a limit to how long we can go on with never enough sleep—Christ, but I'd like one unbroken night! A limit to how long we can live half-starved. And sooner or later there's bad weather coming. She can survive. She's tough even for an Orthean. But we can't.

I spent most of the day sleeping. Every time I stirred, I saw Maric and Blaize dozing by the embers of the fire. Suddenly there was no question of watching each other. The barbarian woman was sometimes there and sometimes not, seeming unwearied.

Someone shook me, and I opened my eyes to twilight. The sun had set behind the peaks already, flushing the snow pink and saffron. Maric was leaning over me.

'I think she wants us to move. What shall we do, Christie?'

It was a minute before I collected my wits. I blew on my hands to warm them, and looked round for the pack.

'Could make sense—keep walking at night, sleep in the day when it's warmer. Better than freezing to death. Yes.'

' "Make sense"?' Blaize was incredulous. I ignored him.

We went on by starlight, bright enough for us to pick a path. The barbarian woman increased the pace, waiting impatiently until we caught up. A sense of urgency infected us. I didn't know what there was in this land that we should fear. As the night wore on, we tired. The long cold hours after midnight sap the strength. I trudged on beside Maric. We were leaving hill country, coming into flat land. If I'd thought, I might have wondered at the smoothness of the route.

Something angular blocked the starlight. Then the barbarian went in through an arch. A doorway. I touched a wall, wonderingly. Stone. Dressed stone, here in the Barrens.

Yellow light flickered, destroying night vision. A deadwood fire showed the limits of the broken-roofed stone room, and the barbarian woman, crouched down with Theluk's tinderbox. The fire was catching now. Blaize shouldered past me, dropping his pack on the flagstones, and hunched down, cupping his hands for warmth.

Water-skins. Fat meat sealed in waxed leather. I saw Maric slit the stitching with his knife, and was released to join in. We ate like animals, not sparing breath to talk, and soaked dry tongues in water. The wood crackled noisily. The barbarian woman laid strips of mossgrass on it, and it burned low and intense.

I saw her face by firelight, teeth gleaming. She leaned back against the wall, watching the smoke spiral up to the sky showing through the gaps in the roof. I'd thought her expressionless before. Now I could see that the strain had gone out of her face; she was relaxing.

I fell asleep as false dawn outlined the archway.

Something hard was jammed into my cheek. Warm and half-sleeping, I was reluctant to move. The discomfort roused me. I opened my eyes. It was a bootheel, belonging to the Rimon mercenary. When I moved, I banged my head against Maric's leg. Neither of them moved.

The fire was dead. The barbarian woman wasn't present. By the light through the arch, the sun had been up a good long time.

I picked my way across the floor—over blankets, foodbags, and firewood—and out of the arched doorway. Sunlight dazzled me. The stone was blue-grey, almost translucent in the light. I went outside to relieve myself. Then I took a bleary look round and realized what I was seeing. This was no isolated hut. There were dozens of buildings in my immediate view, and the wind blew dead leaves down paved streets.

It was a ruined city.

Ruined and deserted, that much was obvious at a glance. The buildings were all of the same stone and all of a pattern. They gave the impression of being curiously incomplete, mere shells. Reaching a crossroads, I saw one way led back towards the snowpeaks—that must have been the road we came in on. But in all other directions, the city stretched away as far as I could see.

I followed paths. Mostly there were triple junctions, and after I'd passed a few it became apparent that the prevalent shape of building was hexagonal. And the buildings lacked that central courtyard that I'd come to take for granted in Southland architecture.

'Christie!' The boy came scrambling after me. 'Goddess! It goes on for ever.'

Knife-edged shadows lay across our path, the straight-edged shadows that only occur in cities. The sun was low in the south behind us. Ahead, there was barely anything left standing. Walls jutted up from moss-covered hummocks. Pale-leafed scrub forced its way between the paving stones. The weather had rounded the edges of the slabs, worn them smooth. The walls might have been carved, once. Further on, open to the sky, there were only lines on the barren earth to show where walls had stood. A great flight of steps went down a slope, beginning nowhere and ending nowhere, grown over with a feathery silver-green weed. We stood on the steps. They were as rounded as if the sea had worked on them.

'It's old,' I said. 'Lord, it's old!'

'It's big.' Maric stared round. The ruins went on north as far as the eye could see. A few miles off were taller structures. I caught myself wondering if it would be possible to explore them.

'I don't like it,' he said quietly, trying not to disturb the silence. 'It's —this is what they warn us about. No wonder the tribes are barbarians. Living with this.'

'We don't know that they do.'

The circle of the horizon, with only a southern snowpeak boundary, cupped the ruined city in worn fingers. A wind blew across the desolate land and whined between the jutting walls.

'Let's go back,' Maric said. I agreed.

The barbarian woman was there, and Blaize was arguing with her. She watched him in total incomprehension. When she saw me, she pointed to the north.

'Our road.'

'We can't travel far.'

Her hands moved close together. 'Not far.'

'Days?' I indicated the sun.

A headshake. That was all I could understand. She waited impatiently while we packed all the spare food and water with our blankets. Blaize had the set look of a man dragged into something against his will.

He and Maric were alike in one thing, I thought, as the barbarian woman led us on northwards. Being in a city this size—even one that had been dead several thousand years—bothered them. The parts of the Southland that I'd seen had nothing as big as this.

Before mid-afternoon, we stopped. The barbarian woman led us past shallow dips in the earth that I realized were collapsed underground chambers, and into thick scrub. There she halted, casting about, and hauled a stone slab to one side. Worn steps went down into the dimness.

Inside was cool and dry. Light seeped in from gaps in the ceiling, a ceiling that must have been the floor of a great building but was now masked with the brown-leaved scrub. My eyes adjusted to the twilight. It was a huge hall-like space, stone-floored and with pillared walls. Stacked along the far wall were water skins, leather foodbags, blankets and pelts.

'In every stone place.' The barbarian's voice echoed softly. 'Enough for twelve—' she counted on her bony fingers so that I'd understand her '—twelve of us, for twelve sunsets. We must pass these lands.'

'You?'

'All Kirriach people.'

Maric was walking past the shadowy stacks. He came back with strips of mossturf in his hands and put them in one corner. The floor was blackened from previous fires. The barbarian woman crouched down with the tinderbox, striking flints over dry slivers of wood.

We ate. The short afternoon drew down to evening outside. At last the barbarian woman stood. She went to the steps. There was a cold wind blowing.

'Christie.'

I went over, waiting for her to speak.

'Thee must wait.'

'How long?'

She counted twelves on her fingers two or three times and shrugged. 'I will speak with Kirriach people. Thee must stay.'

'May I not come and speak with them myself?'

'They would kill thee. There is food. Wait. I will come to thee.'

I followed her up the steps. She pointed towards the less destroyed part of the city.

'There is well-water.' She put both hands on my shoulders. 'Stay here.'

'I'll wait,' I said. There was nowhere to go.

She dropped her hands from my shoulders, turned, and loped off into the second twilight. I stood in the cold until I lost sight of her, and then went below.

Both pairs of eyes fixed on me. The man and the boy, both with the same distrustful expression. I squatted down beside the fire.

'We wait till she comes back, I guess.'

'She's going to her people?' Maric asked.

'Let's hope she doesn't bring them back with her.' Blaize was as self-contained and sharp as ever. 'I'd sooner keep my head where it is, and not on a barbarian's lance. But then, considering she's gone south with a band of her own people, and come back alone with two Southlanders and you—'

'She'll have some explaining to do.' I regretted he'd heard Maric and I speculating about her origins.

We waited.

16

Kirriach People

'*How* long?' Blaize persisted.

'You can count, can't you?' Maric added the eighth notch to his tally stick. He'd tried scratching the wall, but the blue stone was diamond-hard.

'How long will you carry on this stupidity? The longer we stay here, the less we'll have to keep us on the journey. It's a long walk back to the Southland.'

'Any time you want to try it, don't bother to wait for us.' Maric went back to stirring broth in the small can hung over the fire on a stick wedged across the hearth-corner. It was the only utensil we'd saved.

Blaize lounged with his back up against the pile of scrub-wood, one booted foot almost in the ashes of the fire. His pale mane was dark with dirt. He was cleaning under his claw-nails with the tip of his knife.

'The first thing we'll run out of,' he went on, 'is firewood. There isn't that much growing hereabouts. Not water, I admit; there's the well. But food, now, and time—'

'If you think we're short on wood, why don't you go out and collect some more?' I couched it as a suggestion. To my surprise he grunted, got up, and went up the cellar steps.

'We—ah—we could pack what food we could carry.' There was a query in Maric's tone. 'We could walk. I don't know where. That garrison the *T'An* Ruric went to—it must be on the Wall somewhere.'

'East of here. But north-east of Corbek, if I remember the map. It's probably a good three hundred *seri.*'

His face tightened. 'We could try.'

'Look—' On the verge of hysteria, I said 'I don't know how to put this. I don't want to start walking again. I don't think I can. All right?'

'I don't want to either. But if we don't, what happens to us?'

'I suppose . . . we might have to stay with these tribes for a while.'

'You mean as prisoners?'

'There's worse things than that.' At the back of my mind was the thought that, the barbarian woman having gone down to the Southland with her own people and returned with three strangers, it might be much easier for her (and who wouldn't take the easy way out) if she just forgot we were here.

I heard footsteps, and Blaize reappeared with an armful of branches. I hauled myself upright and grabbed the wooden bucket.

'Going to the well.'

Outside there were coin-sized spatters of dampness on the grey stone. Flakes glittered in the air, not rain, not quite snow. The peaks of the Wall were hidden. Massive grey-white clouds hugged the horizon, looking as though their undersides had been soaked in ink.

I levered the slab off the top of the well, and lay flat to dip the bucket in icy water. The wind thrummed on the ruined walls. I sat on the stone slab for a few minutes. Sometimes the cellar walls closed in. I was irritable, partly because I was always hungry, and trapped in a circle of digestive upsets. But partly because I was here, miles from any kind of civilization, in a ruined city of the Golden Witchbreed. And I knew why.

I don't think I was less efficient in Corbek than I was in Tathcaer. But things were different in Corbek. If I hadn't been careless I would have realized what was going on; all the clues were there in Arad and Howice's behaviour. If I'd had more than half my mind on my job. Lover, *arykei,* under whatever misapprehension . . . when it's dead, Haltern said (Hal, I need you here), when it's dead, leave it.

Failure has its own heady excitement. Tried by church court, hunted across half a province—I fucked it up, I thought, but I'm still here, I've survived so far.

That wouldn't last, I knew; as I'd get used to it, it would start gnawing at me.

Falkyr, Falkyr at Oeth with the hunters. And Haltern—if he was dead, I'd make somebody pay. If I ever get out of here, I thought, I'll take it to Ruric, to the Crown . . . Ruric: I don't know if she's alive, any more than I do Haltern. And Theluk—

I can face her death now, I thought. I might die that way myself, sudden, unprotected. I don't want to, I'll fight to prevent it, but—it's possible. And if I can accept it for myself, how can I not accept it for her?

A dusting of snow fell the next day. Maric called me outside.

'Look at that.' He pointed.

Tracks feathered the snow: delicate claw and wing marks, heavier paws, sinuous trails. The sharp edges of the ruined city were masked.

'I thought there was no game here.'

'Oh, it's here.' Maric was frustrated. 'But I can't get close to it. Everything here is used to being hunted.'

'The tribes, I suppose.' I thought of the barbarian woman, and changed the subject quickly. 'I'll get the water. Can you check the fire isn't going out? It looked low.'

'Right.' He clattered back down the steps.

There was a thin film of ice over the water. I shattered it, kneeling, and then paused. Reflected in the black water: a face. I almost didn't recognize it. It wasn't just that I was filthy, my matted hair cropped back with a knife. I'd lost weight, had hollows under the cheekbones, my temples were sunk in. There was no mask left: I looked afraid.

I dipped my hands in the icy water, shuddering. It was too cold to wash. My old Roehmonder clothes had lost their original colouring, become a uniform mud-brown. Dirt flaked yellow on my skin. Lice-bites made red irritations. I'd torn my last and least filthy shirt up to bandage my feet; chilblains had burst and were running sore.

For pre-tech worlds, you don't have to be too fussy. Nobody likes dirt and discomfort, but put up with it. So he said: my uncle, John de Lisle, minister for the department. That was when I applied for off-Earth postings. I'd always sworn never to use family influence—certainly not the de Lisle family. That noble resolution lasted until I realized how badly I wanted in to the ET department. It wasn't fair; he was the only de Lisle who felt guilty about his family's treatment of mine. When I came asking—and I was qualified—he had to give.

Would I be here? I thought, shivering, still kneeling beside the well. Would I be off Earth without that influence? Yes. Would it have happened this soon? Ah, now, that's another question.

Hearing footsteps, I hastily scooped up a double handful of freezing water and rinsed my face. I choked and shuddered, wiping my eyes on my sleeve.

'Problems?' Blaize said.

'Nothing you haven't got as well.' I pulled the bucket up by its rope handle and started walking back towards the cellar. He fell in step beside me.

'Which one is it?'

'What?' I saw him point, indicating the few daystars still visible in the west. 'Oh. You can't see Earth's sun from here.'

The stone paving was treacherous under a slick coating of snow. I kept my balance with difficulty. The man made no move to help.

'What's it like out there?'

When I looked at him, I saw he was serious. Whether it was that— that he credited my alien origins—or the isolation, or simply that his attacks on me seemed to have been made a long time ago in a different world, for some reason I felt I should be civil to him.

'It's surprisingly similar. Given this kind of star—sun, I mean—and a world at a certain distance from it, all plants and animals and people are variations on a theme.'

The real aliens are the life forms of gas giants, and roving interstellar worlds and close-orbit planets; those we may never understand.

'Like that?' He stretched out his hand: thumb and five fingers.

'That's a minor variation.'

'And you live in high towers, and fly through the sky, and travel in carriages drawn by no animal.' His tone was mocking. 'You begin to make me think they're right, you are Witchbreed.'

'Who are "they"?' He didn't answer. My guess was SuBannasen. We came in sight of the cellar. A thin column of heated air rose from the concealed hearth.

'Why did you come? And what follows you—more 'Breed trickery?' He turned the scarred profile away from me. 'We have our life. It's the one we've chosen. Will knowing your Otherworld make our life better?'

For some mad reason—and this was the man who had twice tried to kill me—I thought I owed him honesty.

'My government talks about mutual enrichment of culture by contact between Dominion worlds. Which is true enough. Not to say that they won't enrich themselves, if a world has anything worth trading or buying. And if they can sell you anything, they'll do that too. There's also medical aid, improved agricultural methods, things like that— which you'll need.'

'We have all we need.' He was stubborn, and as certain as if he could say 'we' and speak for every *telestre* in the Southland.

'How can you say that?'

'We've seen the other. Your way. And it doesn't work.'

He was angry, and less protective of his pride than I'd ever seen him. Shabby, walking with his hands tucked inside his worn coat, ears and nose red from the cold, the mottling of his scar turned blue and purple.

'Because you've had one technological society on this planet that failed, it doesn't mean another will. And it's too long ago—'

His head came up, and all the old acid was back in his tone. 'I assure you, the 'Breed are as dead as their city—but not forgotten.'

He strode ahead. I shifted the bucket to my other hand, blowing on cold fingers, and followed him down into the cellar.

'Here.' Maric took the bucket, and handed me the small can. It was uncomfortably hot, full of the preserved meat boiled down into a broth. 'When you've eaten, I'll do his.'

'You've had yours?'

'While you were outside. What's it like?'

'Cold.'

'There's snow coming,' Blaize said contemptuously.

I settled down beside the makeshift hearth, picking meat lumps out of the can and sipping hot broth. Maric sat beside me.

'I wish I was back on my *telestre,*' he said. 'It was cold by the Oranon sometimes, but not as cold as this.'

'Maybe we should found our own *telestre*. Though this isn't exactly the best place.' It was weak humour.

The membrane slid back; his eyes were bright with astonishment. 'It took the Crown and church four generations to decide the Peir-Dadeni *telestres* were legal, *t'an.* You might have to wait a while.'

Something Haltern said came back to me: no *telestre* has changed its boundaries since it was founded, there have been no land transactions in the Southland since *amari* Andrethe founded Peir-Dadeni.

'But you must be able to . . . where do people live?'

'Three choices,' Blaize said, across the fire. 'Their own *telestre.* Or *n'ri n'suth* to another. Or landless.'

Maric snapped 'She is not landless!'

'She has no *telestre.*'

'But it's different for them—'

It was at that point that empathy, the xeno-team reports, and gossip came together in my head to give me an image of Orthe. Solid, unchanging, a totally static society. It appalled me, because it was by choice. They'd had the technological knowledge of the Golden Empire and they refused to use it. As I'd realized in Corbek: not a pre-technological society, but a post-technological society.

That put me in a bad position. I was trained for primitive worlds. The department's rule of thumb there was that a nonspacegoing race wouldn't prove a threat to the Dominion, and that one member of the Dominion can't cause major damage to a world. Inaccurate, yes, but good enough for troubled times. On Earth they called it the Dispersal, this headlong rush to explore space by the FTL drive, and their main problem was holding their own authority together.

But Carrick V wasn't pre-tech, not a world to scan and classify, and perhaps keep satellite surveillance over. Carrick V had had a civilization that could leave ruins like this city.

We've misunderstood them badly, I thought. What kind of a mentality leads a world (or is it only the Southland?) to prefer living in danger, squalor, and disease? That makes Wellhouses and *T'An Suthai-Telestres* suppress all of the knowledge that could improve conditions . . .

I looked across at Blaize. I'd had hinted to me often enough in Corbek that Wellkeepers and Earthspeakers hoarded all kinds of knowledge, including medical—the Witchbreed had been as advanced as the Dominion in that respect. There was no technology now to back up the knowledge, but it could be created. I could live with disfigurement if I knew there was no way to cure it, but if I knew there was a way, and it had been decided to forbid it . . .

On Earth such a society wouldn't hold stable for two generations, never mind two thousand years. It argued a more alien quality of thought than I'd anticipated, seeing humanoids in some respects so similar to ourselves.

'You finished with the can?'

I gave it back, empty. Maric was sulking. Obviously they'd been quarreling while I was lost in speculation. Given the circumstances, one was as sensible as the other.

Blaize was sitting with a wooden case on his knees. I'd seen it before in his pack and assumed from the way he guarded it, it was money or other valuables. It wasn't. He opened it out: a travelling *ochmir* set. It gave a board the size of a large plate. The pieces (in two bags, one for the version of the game with three players) were enamelled with the various script characters for *ferrorn, thurin,* or *leremoc.*

It took me back so hard I caught my breath. *Ochmir* games in Corbek's cold towers, that so often were left half-finished while Falkyr and I pursued more important matters.

Blaize gave me a hard look. He said, 'I don't suppose you do anything as civilized as play *ochmir?*'

It would take my mind off the waiting. And any break in the boredom was welcome. Even with Blaize n'ri n'suth Meduenin.

'Yes,' I said, 'I do.'

The snow came, and lay for a morning before melting. After that it was clear and cold. We left the underground chamber as seldom as possible. But it was necessary to go further for firewood.

Carrick's Star was an ice-eye low to the south. Clouds massed on a north wind. It was glittering, restless weather. Wet stone, far off, shone like silver. I used the excuse of firewood to explore, for as long as I could stand the cold. Seemingly endless, the city offered nothing but ruins. There were obvious subsidences where underground buildings had collapsed, but nothing left of the Witchbreed city except stone. And the three of us camped there, building fires on their tessellated floors, with no protection against cold or darkness—the barbarians were in the city and no mistake, I thought.

A call attracted my attention. The bundle of scrub-wood was difficult to manage. I climbed a flight of shallow steps to higher ground. It was Maric. He brandished the *harur* blades. But it wasn't a warning yell. Something was on the ground beside him.

When I got close I saw it was some species of lizardbird, the jaw long and toothed, the body scaled rather than feathered. Maric's stroke had severed one grey-webbed wing almost completely.

I put the bundle of wood down and took one wing-tip, while he took the other and stretched it out. The full wingspan was almost ten feet. Hand-sized talons bore vicious claws.

'It attacked me.' He grappled with the body, dragging it towards the cellar steps. 'Over where all the potholes are. I didn't see it. It nearly took my head off!'

Blaize never stirred from beside the fire. He eyed the corpse, and Maric. *'Kur-rashaku.* That was lucky.'

'It wasn't luck! I waited until the last moment, then I—' he let go of the lizardbird, illustrating a complex double flourish of blades. His hands were black with blood.

'Lucky for us, I mean. A change of diet.'

For the first time I saw a grave humour in the Rimon man's eyes, but he kept a straight face. To my surprise, he helped skin and cut up the body. Mercenaries' skills, I thought. They were beyond me. I trekked out to the well again.

After the meal we stretched out round the fire. Maric was attempting to clean the blood off Theluk's blades—or his, I suppose they were now—with a rag. Blaize watched with mounting impatience. He muttered something obscure, rummaged in his pack, and threw the boy some of the strips of oiled cloth he used on his own blades.

'Thanks.' Maric was wary.

'Mmmph.' Blaize leaned back into the shadows. When the metal was clean, he said, 'You favour the *nilgiri* too much.'

'Maybe,' Maric admitted.

Like most Ortheans, he was ambidextrous. The shield is unknown in the Southland, and *harur* blades in combination are lethal. And, like Blaize, most can switch the use of the *nilgiri* and *nazari* to either hand.

'You ought to practise.' He intercepted a hard stare from me. 'Don't you worry, *T'An* Outworlder. I'm not about to butcher your *l'ri-an.*'

'I never imagined you were.' Which wasn't entirely true.

'Need exercise, cooped up here.' He took Maric's blades, testing the weight. 'I was arms-tutor to a Morvren *telestre* for a year, once, before I went down to Saberon. Look, try this.'

He set the boy to doing some obscure exercise with the two blades, and then sat down beside me to watch him.

'You want to train?' A half-malicious offer.

'I know where my talents lie, and that isn't one of them.' I didn't plan on being careless enough to be on the wrong end of a Meduenin blade again. 'I'll stay with the less energetic sports. One of these days I'm going to beat you at *ochmir.*'

'Ah, you're thinking we'll be here all winter?'

As he went to retrieve the board and counters, I put more wood on the fire. He could no more help being sarcastic than he could help breathing, it came to me. But for all his bitching, he was pulling his weight. I wasn't sure precisely why.

We drew for the first move, decided by who gains the more mobile piece, and the game opened slowly. It was quiet in the underground room, the noise of the wind didn't penetrate down. Maric ended his blade practice and returned to the fire. It was our central reference-point.

Blaize put down one of the static *ferrorn* to open another area of conflict on the board. I studied the pattern, and moved a *thurin.*

'You can't do that,' Blaize contradicted. 'Only across a line, not across an angle—unless the piece is a *leremoc.*'

'You did,' I protested.

' "All *ochmir* players cheat," that's a proverb. Also . . .' he bent down, scrutinizing the board, and the firelight made an impossible mask of his scarred face. 'Also, "good *ochmir* players cheat only when necessary." '

'This, then.' I forced a reversal on one of his blue *thurin,* which proved to be a white *leremoc* on the obverse: a considerable advantage for me.

He drew another handful of counters from the bag, weighing them thoughtfully in his palm. His eyes were dark and clear in the dim light. 'I was in Kasabaarde once. In the trade city. That's where I got these.'

'That's not in the Southland?'

'No, over the Inner Sea, down past Bridge Alley and the archipelago. There was some fighting down the Desert Coast. About six years back. Quarth and Kel Harantish, I think it was.'

'You were fighting?'

A shrug. 'I was hired.'

'Is that the way you look at it?'

'It's a convenient way.' He put a piece down. I wasn't sure if it was a legal move, I'd been distracted. By now I was more interested in the conversation. And treading lightly.

'You came home after that?'

'Back to the Southland. As for home—it's a good *telestre*, but I was right at fourteen when I left it. I keep *telezu*, mind.' He referred to the custom of spending one season in the year at the *telestre*. 'When I can. No, that time I was in the Medued city Watch for a couple of years.'

'You sound like me. I move around. But that's less common here, isn't it?' I put down another *ferrorn*.

He moved for a majority in a minor hexagon, which shifted the balance in several of the overlapping hexagon-frames. By the time the implications had worked out to the edge of the board, I'd lost a score of pieces.

'Yes, it's uncommon. I went down the coast to Morvren again, after that. That's where I got this.' His hand strayed up to the burn.

'In a war?'

He laughed. It was loud, natural. Maric opened his eyes, then went back to dozing.

'In a companion-house in Morvren Freeport,' he said gravely, 'in a fight over nothing at all. Ten years overseas, then that. Some *amari* threw an oil-lamp.'

He lifted his arm, demonstrating how he shielded his eyes. The sleeve pulled back and I saw scar tissue from wrist to elbow.

'She won't do that trick again,' he added, touching the hilt of the *harur* blade. 'But I'm getting too old for this game.'

We carried on in silence, playing a game which was not the one he meant.

There were twelve notches on the tally stick.

The fifteenth day was bitter cold. Yellow snow clouds massed from the east, but no snow fell.

'It won't be long before it's winter.'

Maric nodded agreement. He hacked another root free with his knife and handed it to me. 'The passes are closed in winter, I've heard.'

'I expect you're right. Let's get back, that's enough wood. It's vicious cold out here.' I realized we'd come a long way from the cellar. The ruins were similar to the eye. I searched for landmarks.

'This way!' Maric called.

'Are you sure?' It wasn't the way we'd come. I followed him. The going was easy, he was keeping to the paved ways. We came up on the hidden entrance from a different angle, so that I didn't recognize it until we were on top of it.

'You're quick,' I said as we hurried down the steps and made for the fire. 'I was lost there, for a minute.'

He threw the wood on the stockpile. 'I'm not clever, it's just that I lived here before.'

My hands tingled with returning circulation. It was a minute before I heard what he said.

'You *what?*'

'Lived in this city. Under the 'Breed, of course.'

'Of course,' I said automatically, and met Blaize's eyes. I couldn't cope with delusions now.

'What's wrong with that? It's a coincidence, I admit, but—'

'You as well?' I suspected them of some elaborate charade.

'No. My memories show me no mountains, when I was in a 'Breed city.'

I rounded on Maric. 'You never mentioned this before!'

'I didn't realize, *t'an.*' He spoke with self-possession, as if it were a thing everyone would know. 'Since we came here, my memory-dreams have been stronger, and matching up with what I've seen. Only I think it must have been a long time ago. The city's larger than I remember.'

I appealed to Blaize. 'Look, I know we're all under a considerable strain—'

'You don't have them, do you?' There was no mockery at all.

'No past-memories?' Maric, frightened, looked at Blaize. That alerted me. This was no joke. We'd been close. Something that would make him turn from me to a hired sword, already proved untrustworthy . . . but a man of his own race.

'He's afraid,' Blaize said, 'because the Witchbreed, also, had no memories of their previous lives. And perhaps no lives to remember. Are you like the Witchbreed in that, you Otherworlders?'

'I can't answer that question before I understand it. Sit down a minute, I want to talk. Maric, for God's sake, I'm not going to hurt you!'

Shamefaced, he sat beside me. 'I know. I know you, *t'an*. But I thought you were—like us.'

'Tell me about it.' I faced both of them. There was that glance of complicity between them, that I had thought meant they were in league. It was for reassurance. This had hit them both hard.

'We live,' Blaize said simply, 'and return, under Her sky. That's all.'

'That's not all—it can't be—how can you be so sure? Oh,' I stopped Maric interrupting, 'I don't doubt you believe what you say. There are people on Earth who believe the same thing, equally honestly. But there's no proof!'

'We remember,' Maric said. 'We can't all be wrong, or else we wouldn't remember the same things, would we? We know about the Witchbreed because we remember being there, being their slaves. Christie, we know.'

'The church. . . .' It made an odd kind of sense. Why they weren't given to extravagant funeral celebrations. And Theluk had shocked me, once, when she seemed to approve of suicide. And Maric, who had hated this city when he entered it, was comfortable in it now.

'So you know what a technological civilization is like.' They were both watching me. I had to frame careful questions. If there was one thing the Ortheans were reticent over, it was this heart of their belief. Without the situation we were in, lost in desolate country, I could never have had the discussion at all.

'We know. I told you,' Blaize said, 'we've seen it and we don't want it.'

'But the Witchbreed, are none of them—reincarnated?'

'Yes!' Maric said. 'What about Kel Harantish?'

'No, they're human like the rest of us.' Blaize was sober. 'I've seen them. The 'Breed were exterminated, so it's said.'

'Said? I thought you knew.'

'There are those who claim to have been born after the Fall of the Golden Empire, but I don't believe them. It's too soon.'

I found I was walking up and down the floor. I came back into the circle of firelight. It was feasible. It would work as a superstition, or as a reality—and they were convinced it was reality. It was bedrock to them, I could see that.

Suddenly depressed, I squatted down close to the heat.

'If you know you'll be reborn, why put up with *this?*'

There was silence for a time. Blaize leaned forward, his silver-streaked mane falling over his eyes.

'When it comes to it—I won't stay longer than I have to.'

'But to leave everyone,' Maric whispered. 'It means losing all of them, all the *telestres,* everybody. And what kind of a world will it be to come back to? I know the Earthspeakers say it'll be the same, but it's so long . . . and I won't be Maric Salathiel then, I'll be another person, with some of my memories, born into a different world.'

'None of us wants to die.' Blaize was abrupt. Then he lifted his head and looked me in the face. 'Dying with no hope of return? You're a strange people, Christie.'

Bedrock, yes. It was too fundamental a difference to grasp completely. To have that certainty. . . . And because of the form it took, for it not to play a vocal part in everyday living, though it shaped the society in which that living takes place. No wonder the Witchbreed were a living threat, even though they were two thousand years dead. Or that the memory of the power of technology hadn't faded, nor the determination never to use it again.

'Perhaps it is the same for you,' the boy said hopefully, 'and you just don't know.'

'I *don't* know. As I'm beginning to find out.' And the more I did find out about Orthe, the more I was depressed by my total ignorance.

Blaize said nothing, staring past the child at me. He was shaken, because he could imagine what it would be like to die without knowing what follows—as much as any Orthean can imagine that. Maric, like the young of every race, didn't quite believe in death yet.

The crackling of burning wood sounded loud in the cellar. The walls gleamed in the red light. I came back down from the opening hurriedly. It was still snowing outside, and snowing hard.

The *ashiren* stirred, mumbled something, and rolled closer to the fire without waking up. I stepped over him and sat down by the wood-pile, feeding fragments onto the fire. It was not far off dawn, I thought. Not that it was possible to see any change outside, but it felt close to first light.

I thought, there's no point keeping a watch. Nothing's going to find its way down here and attack us. Nobody's here.

Realization crystallized. We had been abandoned. This was where we'd stay, if we didn't do anything for ourselves. What could be done?

Pack and start walking? Not back to the Fens. Look for a pass across the Wall? How far away is that, I wondered, and how far can we expect to travel now, in winter, without supplies? There's no reserves of strength left. It was all used up coming from Corbek to here.

Blaize grunted, and half-started up, one arm protectively over his head. He stared round with no recognition, and sank back. Head resting on his arms, asleep. I knew he had nightmares. Sometimes his mouth moved soundlessly as though he were shouting, and when he woke he didn't hear what was said to him.

The boy dreamed memory-dreams, becoming more remote from us as time went on. He looked at the city and saw more than I ever could, sometimes smiling and listening to the wind's voices.

Sixteen days. Part of it was hunger: the food was rationed now. And lack of various things in the diet, and boredom, and the thought that we had left it too late now to begin walking anywhere.

Stone walls merged with city streets, ruins became megalopoli. At the same time that I knew I was dreaming, I knew that this was not a Witchbreed city I dreamed of. It had aspects of Earth: London, maybe, or Peking, or Bombay. People lived there who weren't hungry, who weren't cold, who travelled without walking, and talked in a language that was bitterly familiar. And I was another person, one who had never left the safe earth. Dry sobs of self-pity woke me; I can never cry in dreams.

'Christie!' Blaize whispered urgently.

I sat up, confused. Maric lifted his head, frowning, listening.

'Can you hear that?'

'Blaize, I—' The stunner slid into my hand. 'What is it? I don't hear anything.'

My feet were frozen and sore, it took me a minute to stumble up the steps after him. Maric drew his *harur* blades. White light blinded me. I leaned on the ruined stone, rubbing water out of my streaming eyes. Blaize was black against the snowlight, the Rimon blades catching the sun.

'Cover,' he said to me sharply, pushing Maric towards the scrub that concealed the entrance.

'Wait a minute. Wait!' I shielded my eyes. Carrick's Star at dawn, on the new snow, was unbearable. 'What do you think you're going to do? I don't care who it is, it's a better option than starvation!'

He lowered the blades and nodded. Maric hesitantly came back to join us.

I said, 'I still don't hear anything.'

'Over that way.' Blaize pointed. Stark walls were plastered with snow, blocking the view. I strained, and heard something that I couldn't name.

'Let's go and meet them.'

The hired sword looked at me as if I were crazy; and he was nearly right, I'd stopped worrying about danger. He shrugged, accepting it. The boy walked between us, still carrying the naked blades. The stone was glassy underfoot, snow clogged my boots. Soon we were holding on to each other just to keep upright.

I hoped it was the barbarian woman come back, but I didn't care. Not then.

We rounded the highest wall, looking down over a stretch of old road, and came to a dead halt.

17

The Woman Who Walks Far

A dark-skinned man was riding over the virgin snow, following the unnaturally flat expanses that marked the old roads. Others rode behind him. The sky at their back was eggshell blue flowered with stars. The air was clear to the horizon, each snow-covered wall and hillock of the city distinct and indigo-shadowed.

As the riders approached, I saw they wore tunics and thick pelts. The high saddles were cushioned with furs, hung with glinting and flashing ornaments. The riderbeasts were nothing I recognized, certainly not *marhaz* or *skurrai*.

'Goddess . . .' Maric's breath smoked white on the air. He was open-mouthed. Blaize had his hand on his sword-hilt. His nictitating membrane protected his eyes against snow-glare. Our shadows lay black towards the west, towards the riders.

The size of the grey riderbeasts became apparent: six feet or more at the shoulders, and their slender tapering necks added at least another three feet. Reins looped down, knotted loosely on saddles, jingling with metal decorations.

'Look, I—' Blaize fell silent, staring west.

Behind the outriders, travelling slowly on the old road, was what I at first took for a sledge. Eight beasts were yoked in pairs in front of it, shaggy white-pelted animals, bulky, with short pairs of horns projecting from their broad foreheads. The vehicle travelled on what were obviously makeshift runners. It was bright against the snow, as bright as blood, crimson as a severed artery. There were people in it. It was bigger than any vehicle I'd seen on Orthe so far, and the shape was odd and familiar: a flattened ovoid, open at the top.

'Don't frighten them,' I said foolishly. 'Don't make them think we're dangerous.'

The first riders reached us, keeping a distance and circling so that we were surrounded. The grey-skinned beasts left delicate tracks in the snow. It didn't seem possible that such spindly legs could bear the body and long neck. The riders looked down at us, silent, dark-eyed. They carried short curved swords, I saw, and metal-tipped lances. Men and women both, as far as I could tell with Orthean faces.

The sledge approached, steam going up from the white beasts' nostrils, runners crunching through the snow. I caught sight of another, smaller, vehicle behind the first, pulled by a team of four beasts, skins strapped down over whatever it was carrying.

Maric said 'There are *ashiren* in that thing, look!'

The team-driver sat on a high perch over the shafts, reins in her hands. Behind her in the body of the ovoid vehicle, fur-clad children crowded at the rim, scrambling up on the high tailfins for a better look at us.

Blaize and Maric exchanged glances.

'Yes,' the hired sword said, 'but it shouldn't travel on the ground, should it?'

'They rode the air, when this was a city.' The boy's eyes were bright.

After he'd said that, it was obvious. It was aerodynamic, a shape I should have recognized myself; but my mind couldn't accept its existence. Not here. Not now.

The shaggy beasts stopped, snorting white jets into the frosty air. The high sides of the vehicle towered over us. Morning sun turned it crimson and gold. A rope-ladder unrolled over the side, and a scramble of *ashiren* and adults came down it, one woman elbowing her way to the front.

Her mane was glossy and her skin oiled. A great white pelt was belted over a supple leather skirt and a curved knife stuck under the jewelled belt. But she was barefoot, and white scars seamed her ribs, licking down between breast and second nipple, familiar on the dark skin.

'Peace!' the barbarian woman shouted. The *ashiren* were silent. She smiled broadly, reaching out to grip my hands. I stared, numb. 'Ah, thy choice was good; I feared thee would not wait. I was sick, and could not come to thee. But now I am here!'

'Thank god for that,' I said; and then we were in the middle of a crowd of *ashiren,* pushing close to touch us, and the riders dismounted

and crowded round, gabbling in their archaic tongue. I was dazed and
dazzled: after the long silence, it was too much.

'Peace,' Blaize was laughing, 'we could have guessed; not even the
tribes bring *ashiren* to a battle, Christie.'

I put my hand on Maric's shoulder for support. He couldn't stop
grinning. It was confusion for a while, it seemed everyone had to touch
us, finger clothing and flesh, before they believed we existed.

'My brothers.' The barbarian woman pulled forward two young
men, who veiled their eyes, embarrassed, and then jabbered at me faster
than I could comprehend. 'And this, my sister's *ashiren;* and mine.'

I couldn't pick them out from the other children. Manes were dark,
smooth skins black or brick-red except in a few cases—I saw one milk-
skinned child with silver mane. They were curious, forward, self-reliant
as all Orthean children are.

'What—I mean, where—?' It was overwhelming.

'Come,' the barbarian woman said, 'and thy friends, also; thou must
ride with me.'

It was not until then that I realized she was no plain tribeswoman,
but a leader, or chief, or both. She'd never said more than was absolutely necessary; that kind of reticence is easily mistaken for stupidity.

'We have to trust them, don't we?' Maric said.

'Yes. Run and fetch anything you want to bring with you. Quick.'

I touched the side of the ovoid vehicle. It was neither wood nor
metal, having a texture that reminded me of plastic. And light, judging
by how far it pushed down the snow. The colour was integral. Up close,
I could see that it was pitted and worn. How long could something like
this exist? On Earth, glass is still found from Phoenician times, plastics
from the early twentieth century. But to survive from the Golden Empire—two thousand or more Orthean years, perhaps two and half thousand Earth-standard—that was incredible. Yet it looked to be moulded
in one piece, it was conceivable such a framework could last. . . .

'Christie.' The barbarian woman held out the rope-ladder.

The team strained, the team-leader whooped, and the vehicle crunched
free of the thin film of ice and began to glide. I settled back on the pelt-
strewn wooded bench. The barbarian woman sat next to me, one of the
many *ashiren* in her lap. Maric sat on the bench below, next to Blaize,
his back against my knees. The cold wind took my breath. We pulled
the feather-pelts round us. Oblivious to cold, the older *ashiren*
screeched and hung over the side of the vehicle.

An old man, who the barbarian woman called from his grey beast to ride with us, spoke a passable Roehmonde. With his interpretations and her accented, antique tongue, we understood each other as far as was possible.

'Thee and I must talk,' she said. 'Thee and Kirriach people.'

At the name, Maric looked up. He said 'The city Kirriach, which was called aKirrik.'

'That is so, aKirrik was the name of this place.' She glanced at the old man.

'He remembers being here,' I said carefully, and their faces cleared.

'Does thy memory tell thee what else was here?' she asked.

He twisted, pointing back eastwards. 'There was another city, S'Imrath.'

She nodded, pleased. 'Simrathan people. That way we do not go, we are enemies. And this way?'

The boy frowned. 'A . . . a river. I don't know how far.'

She looked at the old man, who translated, and she nodded again.

The vehicle bucked slightly on its runners, and we followed the long curve of the road north-west. The snow had been heavier here. Sunlight glittered on icicles hanging from broken walls.

'Thee must talk,' she repeated, intense. Her expression was never easy to read. She spoke slowly, darting looks at the old man to supply her with words. 'I have spoken of—of thy Otherworld. Thy people. Of thy journey here, to the Mother—to the world. Thy speech has been to lowlanders. Now it must be to us.'

I was staggered by how much I'd underestimated her. And yet we'd talked in front of her, Haltern and I, as if she was an animal. The Southland term was always 'barbarian.' For the first time it dawned on me that they might be wrong. And it brought me back to what I'd forgotten, being solely concerned with survival: I was still envoy.

'I'll talk to anyone who'll hear me,' I promised.

'Thee must go soon,' the barbarian woman said. 'Winter is soon this year. The passes will close. Thy friends also must go.'

Rain lashed the terrace. The snow was gone. Grey clouds veiled Kirriach, hiding the river and the distant plains. I squinted out at the slanting water. My eyes were puffy and swollen. Something in the barbarian's diet was causing a histamine reaction, but it was mild. The choice between starvation and allergy was an easy one.

'I've only been here a few days. It isn't long enough to explain—'

In one of her rare interruptions, she said, 'Go, or spend winter here.

And then thou must be fought over, Simrathan and Yrythemne and Giryse-Acha will hear of thee, and raid us.'

'Could I not speak to them, as I've spoken to your people?'

'There is no debt between thee and those others. They would kill thee. Or else take thee for Goldens, returned, as stories say they will.'

Wind gusted rain across the terrace, and the barbarian woman reached out to pull the wooden shutters closed and bar them. The stockade walls and beastpens were hidden from sight.

I went with her down the stairs to the main hall. It was similar to the other halls of the Kirriach people: the shell of a Witchbreed building, in which were wooden platforms and partitions and cubicles, and a generation's worth of murals fading on the walls. They had painted in and outlined the worn carvings of the original stonework: symbols and hieroglyphs that, while incomprehensible, teased the mind with the strange geometric relationship between them.

I never saw all the Kirriach tribe in one place to estimate their size, there were always hunting and raiding parties absent. This hall held some fifty people, and I'd talked in at least six other halls.

Maric came up. 'What's happening?'

'I think we're leaving when the rain eases.' I saw Blaize solemnly playing a kind of *ochmir* solitaire by the hearth. 'Tell him, will you?'

The barbarian woman was smiling. Reflectively she said, 'There were those who bade me kill thee anyway, Christie.'

I didn't doubt that. She was not the tribe's leader—I don't think they had a leader as such, all had an equal voice in the argument. But as there was a broad-built man with a bushy mane who was acknowledged expert on the hunt, and another man expert in the preparation of grain and dried meat stores, and a woman in the managing of raiding parties, so the barbarian woman was acknowledged expert on anything that came from 'the lowland' beyond Kirriach.

'But you didn't kill me.'

'If thee was dead, who would carry word of us to thy people?' A lithe shrug. 'And in the lowlands, thee and I . . . but there must be messengers sent to us from thy Otherworld; do not forget, but do it.'

'It may take time.'

'We are Kirriach people. In winter we are here. In summer—' her hand flicked out northwards, towards the great plains, as if she could see beyond the grey stone walls. They spent the fine season in crop growing and hunting in the north, returning to the city in the harsh winter, treading a fine line between poverty and starvation. 'Thy people will find us.'

'We'll try.'

'And perhaps thee will trade with us? Perhaps,' she said, 'we will trade for such weapons as I have seen thee use?'

A silence spread out from where we stood, as the tribe broke off from eating and talking to listen. Maric and Blaize came over the dirty moss-strewn floor, looking round with concealed anxiety.

Many of the tribe's weapons had a Southland look to them; I didn't need to be told they raided to get them. I rubbed my eyes, cursing the irritation. These were not people to quote Dominion law at, especially the laws about importing high-tech weaponry.

'No,' I said, 'and I'll tell you why. You've seen me use this?'

I held out the stunner. The barbarian woman nodded.

'Show,' she demanded.

Some *kur-rashaku* nested in the high roof of the hall. I raised the stunner and sighted on one. The narrow focus of sound produced a high whine. The lizardbird thudded down on the stone floor. As I thumbed it off people drew away, expressions of pain fading, talking and shouting. The barbarian woman's yell produced silence.

'We would trade for those,' she said, 'many of those, and then let Simrathan raid us!'

'Take it.' She hesitated, then did. I held her hand over the stud. 'You saw what I did. Point it, then press down.'

The interpreter was called over and the idea translated. The barbarian woman gripped the stunner two-handed, held it at arm's length, and fired at another of the lizardbirds. Not having my bio-patterns, she got no response. Before she could do more than spit and swear, I took the stunner back and threw it to Blaize.

'Look!' I got her attention. 'It's the same for South—for the lowlanders. Go ahead,' I invited him, 'try it on me.'

The eyes veiled, lines tightened round his mouth. It might have been amusement or irony. I didn't underestimate Blaize n'ri n'suth Meduenin, he was capable of that.

He aimed as carefully as if he thought it would work, and thumbed the stud down twice. Nothing happened. The stunner was passed round from hand to hand while all the tribe confirmed its lack of function.

'Our weapons don't work for you.' I hoped it sounded convincing.

'Thy people are cunning,' the barbarian woman said quietly. 'I knew it would not live in my hand, I took it from thee in the wetlands, when thee slept. But it is dead to all: *that* is cunning.'

She might have killed me in the Fens if it had worked, I thought; no matter what debt there was between us over Corbek. (I assumed it was over Corbek, she never made it clear.)

'The rain will end by morning,' she said. 'I will gift thee food and *lahamu* for the road south.'

'We'll go no further,' the old man said in his accented Roehmonde.

'The lowlanders are near. That is thy road to them.' The barbarian woman indicated the ancient stone, all but covered under mossgrass and rockfalls.

The riders of the grey *lahamu* beasts gathered round the vehicle as we dismounted. This was another relic of the Witchbreed, an ovoid whose use I never discovered, fitted with a wooden axle-frame and wheels, and drawn by the shaggy *muroc*. It had been better for sleeping than the cold ground, but rough travelling over the old highways.

Kirriach lay five days to the north. Its blue-grey stone walls, with their curiously fused appearance, were left behind; remote as Earth's pyramids. We followed the thread of a road south until the peaks of the Wall crept up over the horizon, and the air became colder the further south we went. It was rising ground all the way with the mountains ahead of us, until this last day when I realized that we were travelling up between spurs of the Wall itself to a pass.

'Follow the road,' the barbarian woman said, 'and when there is a place where *lahamu* may not easily go, turn them loose. They will return to us.'

I took the reins of the grey beast. It had a musky scent, and a cold reptilian hide. Blaize and Maric could mount theirs without help; the *ashiren* aided me. Even though the saddle was built up at the back, I still had the feeling of slipping; the *lahamu* barrel-body slopes towards the hindquarters.

The riderbeast skittered sideways and I stayed on with some difficulty.

'Christie,' the woman said. She stood up in the vehicle, on a level with me. 'I have thy name.'

'Yes.' None of the Kirriach people gave names outside the tribe.

'I am Gur'an, the fighter; I am Alahamu-te, racer-of-*lahamu*.' She leaned forward, six-fingered hands gripping the rim of the vehicle. 'I am O'he-Oramu-te, the woman who walks far. There is no debt between thy people and Kirriach!'

The *muroc* team wheeled, the vehicle turned on the long road that led away from the mountains; and as they cantered off, the *lahamu* lifted up their long-muzzled heads and belled like hounds.

Mist hung over the damp rocks, glittering where the sun found rifts in the clouds. The air was chill. Dark mossgrass and lichen grew over the old road. Its shape was clear, winding upwards. Scree slopes went up into the cloud. Boulders the size of houses dotted the slopes. Somewhere there was the sound of running water.

'Nearly noon,' Maric said, without sky or sun to guide him. 'We can't spend the night in a place like this, Christie.'

'We could go back to the plains, try the crossing tomorrow,' Blaize suggested.

'Keep going a while yet.' I concentrated on keeping the *lahamu* under control. 'There's time.'

Snow spotted the mossgrass, clinging in crevices of rock. It was a fresh fall. Have we left it too late? I wondered. I dreaded the pass being blocked, or us being lost; I was determined to get where I could see.

If I have to go back . . . I don't know if I can do this all over again. We're running out of strength, of time, of everything.

The cloud came down. I pulled the *muroc* pelt round me and tugged the hood up. We rode on, searching out the thin outlines of the ancient road, up among naked glistening rock. Damp cold slicked the feather-fur. The high altitude was winter-cold. The track was steeper now, and the *lahamu* picked their way delicately over lumps of frozen snow.

Pale light made the mist luminous. It was white, pearl, then pale blue; and the sky opened out over us, and I looked back on the mist that lay like the surface of a lake behind me. All the Barrens were left behind under that mist.

Framed in a double horn of snowpeaks, we sat looking south over the edge of the Wall.

'Jesus! You can see half the world!'

Even Blaize was silent. Maric edged his *lahamu* closer to mine.

The vast distance of empty air turned my stomach. Such space, such emptiness. The eye focused gratefully on the land below.

From this height it looked flat, brown and beige and white rectangles fitting into each other in an interlocking quilt pattern. Fuzzy whiteness bothered me until I saw it moving, and its shadow moving over the tiny fields below, and I realized I was looking down on cloud. Dots like clustered poppy-seeds were copses of trees, their infinitesimally small black shadows pooled on the earth. I followed the sweep of the land out to where a lake, long and narrow and impossibly blue, lay in its cup of white sand.

Details became clearer the longer I looked. Not flat land, it swelled here and there into hills, and in some places the exposed biscuit-coloured face of rock cliffs. Thread-thin divisions between the rectangles were paths, roads, tracks. And tiny clustered squares, flat roofs white in sunlight and sides black in shadows, must be a *telestre* . . . so far down.

Distant, panoramic: beyond the lake, hills and more water fading into the blue haze. And beyond that—the pass opens to the southwest—the Wall of the World went down into mountains, white like crumpled bedsheets: the Northern Wilderness and the Kyre. I turned, taking in that vast panoramic landscape, seeing the mountains fade down until the southern horizon shaded off into level distance. I was half-deafened by the drumming wind.

A haze of cloud surfaced the sky, and down over the mountains flat-bottomed cumulus clouds piled up in white masses, and cast blue shadows on the land.

'The Southland,' Maric said. 'Christie, look. We're home.'

'Not yet.' Blaize reined his *lahamu* in close and slid down from the saddle, throwing the reins to Maric. He strode to the highest point of the Witchbreed road, where it made a sharp turn and vanished over the edge.

I dismounted more cautiously. I'd already fallen off the beast twice, knocking the wind out of myself. Like all the *lahamu,* mine had the habit of bending round and nipping your leg or unseating you.

Snow dazzled against the blueness, thin threads of spray blown off the high peaks. Indigo shadows haunted the rockface. The air was thin and cold, and there was a wind here that scraped the lungs. I went over to where Blaize was standing.

Relief surged through me: it was a pass. Far higher than the rift leading up from the Fens, the Wall here dropped a sheer ten thousand feet.

'It has to be the Southland, doesn't it?'

Blaize nodded reflectively. 'There's only one pass so far to the west. This must be Broken Stair.'

A memory of Theluk came back to me. The other side of the Great Fens, she'd said. Peir-Dadeni. One of the Southland provinces. It's true, I thought, it's true, we're safe, we're home.

'There's the road,' he pointed.

It angled sharply right from where I stood, sloping down the face of the Wall, and then doubled back on itself, zig-zagging down in quarter-mile lengths, down to a thread's thickness, ten thousand feet below. It was cut into the rock; in some places the blue-grey stone paving was still intact. Further down I saw where rockslides had flaked away, taking the roadway with it. Passable? Yes, on foot.

'This is where we leave the *lahamu.*' The beasts were mouthing the rock with their long pointed upper lips, searching for edible lichen. Maric clucked softly, affectionately, and they lay down to have their saddle-packs removed. His ability with riderbeasts always amazed me.

'What shall I leave?'

'Take as much as we can comfortably carry.' It was easier to think ahead now. 'We don't have much daylight left, there might be another night in the open before we get to inhabited country.'

He rubbed the *lahamu's* muzzle. 'Will they be all right, do you think?'

'They'll find their way back.'

Blaize was still staring south, booted feet apart, head thrown back. I wondered if the height bothered him. Height and cold air and silence, and the soaring rock cliffs that went up to either side of us. It was harsh country. He spat carelessly over the broken edge of the road, and came to get his pack.

Chill wind dried the sweat on me. My stomach churned. Sun reflected off the fractured rock. My fingers were stiff and numb with cold.

'Go left. . . .' I coughed, throat dry, and reached out a hand to Maric. 'There's a ledge under your foot, there . . . That's it.'

Our hands met, and I pulled him across the gap. Behind him, Blaize spidered across the rock. I kept my eyes on him, ignoring the vast empty spaces of air. Fragments shaled out from under his boots. Spots of brown, half-melted snow clung to the rock, moisture dripping in the shadows. I reached out again and he heaved himself up onto the ruined road, holding my arm.

'Is that the worst of it?' He looked down over the edge; more than I could do. 'Well, maybe. It's a shame your barbarian friends never gave us any rope.'

'I'll try and remember that, next time.'

One of his sharp looks was followed by a reluctant smile.

After that, there were fewer gaps in the road; in places we could almost have walked abreast. The sun was going down behind mountains that lay west and south, still the Wall of the World. The air had been thin on the pass. Coming down, it was like descending into a sea of oxygen. And warm, after the rock's chill. We made our descent at that time when it is winter on the Barrens, but still autumn below in the Southland.

The checkerboard fields vanished from sight as we climbed down. The last remnants of the road disappeared in the foothills that washed up against the skirts of the mountain. Rocky slopes gave way to moss-grass and streams, and brown bushes that had edible blue berries. Maric coaxed a fire out of the tinderbox, and the last of the barbarians' rations were eaten.

Tomorrow is soon enough to cast about for another path, I thought; there's bound to be a *telestre* in walking distance.

'I'll take first watch,' I said. 'Then you, Maric?'

'Yes.' His eyes were shutting despite his efforts to stay awake.

I banked the fire. The others rolled themselves in their blankets. We were out of the wind in a dip between the hills, out of the bitter cold. It was barely sunset. I walked around for a time to keep awake, watching the last light golden on the snowpeaks, and the plumes of falling water.

'Christie!'

I sat up in a panic, shaken out of sleep. Bright cloudy light dazzled me. I couldn't focus.

'What? *What?*'

'He's gone,' the boy shouted, 'he was here for last watch, and now he isn't, he's gone—'

I knelt upright and wiped dew-wet hands over my face, bringing me coldly awake. A headache throbbed behind my eyes. When I'd got rid of the night's stiffness, I staggered upright. The fire was ashes. The packs were open, empty, strewn on the mossgrass. Except one. That was gone.

'He took everything he could carry.' I wanted to kill Blaize n'ri n'suth Meduenin. We had the clothes we wore, the blankets we slept in; that was all. No—he'd left the *harur* blades, the sonic stunner. But only because we slept with them on us, I thought.

'He took the tinderbox.' Maric was crying openly, but it wasn't for that.

I said 'So much for a mercenary's price. He's gone looking for the quickest way back to SuBannasen.'

PART
SIX

18

Shiriya-Shenin

Streams fell in spate from the peaks, so cold their water burned the mouth; water that whitened the skin and was fire on open cold sores. But there was nothing to eat. The foothills of the Wall are barren. Bogs and ponds made the valleys impassable. Sparse brown mossgrass grew between outcroppings of rock on the hills. Maric and I went hand in hand, supporting each other. At the crest of a ridge, we stopped. The boy knelt, leaning against a grey boulder.

I squinted upwards. The cloudy dawn cleared to a blue and silver day, stars freckling the west. Mountains hung gold and white in the sky to either side, the foothills lost in haze. High overhead, *kur-rashaku* circled. Shrill cries drifted down. I had no idea of direction, except to keep the dip of the pass behind us.

Bone-weary, hands and feet swollen, I felt afraid. Hunger made a hard pain under my ribs. How much permanent damage have I done? I thought. And the *ashiren* . . . but Ortheans are tough, aren't they?

The earth, damp under my numb hands, became alien soil. The cold air sang. The wrinkled hills might rise up, I thought, vaguely aware that I had fallen; the hills might shake us off their hide, and we'd be lost forever.

'Riders!' Maric said, head cocked to one side, listening. His voice sounded thin. 'Coming this way!'

We both stood and walked a few yards down the far side of the ridge. An old track ran south. Now even I heard it.

Marhaz scattered mud: horns burnished, pelts shining. The riders wore horn-mail over dun uniforms, slit to mid-spine, braided manes flying. The high-backed saddles' leather gleamed. Bright spears glittered. The first rider reined in so sharply that her *marhaz* reared in a

tight circle. She shouted an unintelligible demand. Maric and I uncon-
sciously drew closer together.

The second rider dismounted, unsheathing a curved blade. He was
jet-skinned, a sleek copper mane pulled up and braided into a horsetail
on the crown of his head. He was afraid. I saw the membrane of his eyes
retract so far that the whites were visible. He glared, repeating words I
almost understood.

It shattered the quiet: the shouting, the hoofbeats, the smell of *marhaz.* The Barrens and the Fens left a silence in me. Now I felt the world
break and come together, changed.

'I'm Lynne de Lisle Christie, Dominion envoy.' I repeated it in
Roehmonder, and a spattering of Melkathan and Rimon, and then
again in Ymirian. They stared at me uncomprehendingly. The man
peered at us, and abruptly backed off.

The woman spoke sharply and he remounted, clapped heels to the
marhaz flanks, and scuffed up divots of mud along the track towards
the Broken Stair pass.

'Maric?'

'I'm a southerner.' He shook his head wearily. 'But I think she
wants us to go with her.'

The spear came down, bright point lowering towards me. We began
to walk ahead of the rider.

Walk long enough to get weary, and keep walking after that, and
you fall into a curious frame of mind. Movement becomes involuntary.
It's a trance state: the earth is very distinct, all physical sensations are
exaggerated, the senses reach out to the world. So, following the track
with the rider and *marhaz* behind us, I was remembering going to
Kirriach—the sheer distance of the flat horizon. The depth of the pale
sky. The cold wind and glittering daystars. The moss and rock of the
Barrens were part of my mental landscape now. Tired muscles, light-
headed with hunger, feet rubbed raw by stiffened leather boots, one
undershirt sleeve ripped loose and tied over nose and mouth against the
freezing wind—it merges, becomes part of the sunlight and the silence.

The hills gave way to open land. Rutted earth tracks ran ruler-
straight between drystone walls, and the chessboard pattern seen from
the pass resolved itself into thin pasture and the stubble of harvested
ground. Flat land and straight track: it seemed we walked and walked
and never gained an inch.

The plain was deceptive. I came out of a daze to see that we approached rising ground; crowning it was a winding brick-built wall with
flat-roofed brick buildings beyond it. Sunlight glanced off lichened walls

and iron gates. Traders booths were being dismantled by the gate, and merchants and *ashiren* turned to stare at us. My face felt bare, as if anyone could read my thoughts for the looking. Even Maric was alien.

The place wasn't as large as it first seemed to me, fresh come down from the Barrens. A fortress, not a *telestre*. Colours were faded. Only the steel of sword and axe were bright.

'They'll have someone to interpret,' I said optimistically. Maric gave a subdued nod.

The rider dismounted, speaking at length to a woman with troopmaster's belt-badges. Now, to me, none of the troopers looked clean, and they oiled their braided manes with a pungent oil. When Maric attempted to interrupt, the gate-guards moved forward drawing curved *harur* blades.

I didn't blame them, considering how we must look. A skinny *ashiren* in filthy clothes, mane in rat's-tails, brown skin caked with dirt; and an equally dirty woman, hair hacked short with a knife, boots splitting at the seams. Out of place: this land—ochre and umber, high and infertile—had a feeling of cleanness about it. Or perhaps it was only sterility.

Other Ortheans drifted through the gates for a closer look. Beyond them, inside the walls, I saw a courtyard surrounded by armoury and stores and kitchen. Familiar. The few practice bouts were breaking up, now they had another source of interest. The troopers linked spears horizontally, blocking the crowd from us. Merchants, soldiers, insular hill men, all in brilliant clothes. Slit-backed *becamil* robes, *chirith-goyen* sashes, loose britches and short boots, and slender curved blades. Most had manes braided down the spine but pulled up into a cascading horsetail on the crown of the head. Quartz beads and bracelets gleamed. I watched their bright alien eyes; surprise and distaste shadowing them as clouds shadow the sun.

The crowd began to scatter as an Orthean male came through, giving sharp orders. He was tan-skinned, stout, in his forties. Rank-badges made him a commander. Of this garrison? I wondered. With him was a younger man in the brown robes of an Earthspeaker.

'Well, now.' The commander's accent when he spoke Ymirian was new, but intelligible. 'Who are you, and where do you come from?'

'Achil Maric Salathiel, of Rimon,' the boy said quickly. *'T'an,* where is this?'

'Ai Garrison. North Peir-Dadeni,' he elaborated. 'How is it you don't know, *ashiren?* And does your companion speak?'

'We've come from Roehmonde. I'm Christie, the envoy from—you call us Outworlders.'

'Huroth said she found you up near Broken Stair.'

I was too tired to lie, or to make it sound less incredible. 'We came down the pass yesterday. We came from Roehmonde across the Barrens.'

The whites of his eyes showed momentarily. He gestured the Earthspeaker forward. The young male, not coming close, sniffed the air. Then he went to Maric, looking into his face, thumbing back his eyelids and looking into his mouth and nostrils. I kept still for a similar examination. The Earthspeaker said something and the nearest troopers relaxed, laughing and commenting.

'They are neither of them fit, but the *ashiren* carries no disease. As for the other, *t'an* Shaid, I can't say. I'm not certain the woman is human.'

I saw them note eyes, hands, differences. 'I'm the Dominion envoy. From Earth.'

'If she were diseased,' the *t'an* Shaid said, 'the *ashiren* would be ill.'

'Yes, that is likely.'

'So, not dangerous that way. But in what other ways?'

'She is—' here the Earthspeaker used an unfamiliar term '—with the earth.'

'We're not dangerous,' I said. 'Tired, yes; dangerous, no. All I want, *t'an,* is to get to the Crown at Tathcaer.'

Some kind of recognition seemed to occur to him. 'So you expect to be fed and kept while messages are sent halfway across the Southland, do you?'

The urbane sarcasm riled me. 'I'm the envoy. Haven't you got eyes?'

'I've seen freaks before. If you were that clever, you'd know that this envoy—whatever it was, and I had my doubts—died of the snow-fever in Roehmonde last Torvern. Ah, that's stopped you. We're forewarned: a messenger changed mounts here this morning, and gave warning of suspicious travellers coming down the Kyre. Broken Stair, my sire and dam!'

I didn't have to ask. A 'messenger' with a scarred face, lying to get a riderbeast to take him south.

'He didn't have to do that,' Maric whispered. 'He could have left, he . . . not to us, he shouldn't have.'

'I'd keep you in the cells,' the commander said, 'but that's a waste of supplies. You have a choice: the road to the Kyre or the road to Shiriya-Shenin. I suggest you take one and start walking.'

I realized he was serious. He didn't believe me. He intended to throw us out, back on the road, where footsteps ate up the miles in infinitesimal fractions.

'You listen to me, *t'an.*' My voice sounded disused, hollow. The wind swept dust against the garrison walls. Now there were only half a dozen troopers round us, but I was aware of eyes watching from the walls. Temper made me breathless, dizzy. 'I'm Christie, envoy of the Dominion, which Suthafiori will confirm. This is my *l'ri-an,* Achil Maric Salathiel. Your informant was a hired sword in the pay of the Crown's enemies. I've been hunted out of Roehmonde, I've crossed the Fens, I've crossed the Barrens and come down Broken Stair—and believe me I don't intend walking one *seri* more! Now either you keep me here until Suthafiori is informed, or you provide me with transport and an escort to go south. One or the other!'

The commander shook his head, more in frustration than anything else, watching me with a clear topaz gaze. The Earthspeaker said something in the Peir-Dadeni language.

'Yes. Of course,' the commander said, keeping eye-contact with me. 'It's Riardh Sixthweek. The *T'An Suthai-Telestre* will have moved to winter court in Shiriya-Shenin by now. Two days downriver, Outlander. What do you say, shall I send you there?'

Later, I realized that was the point he expected me to crack. It's easy enough for an imposter to ask to be taken to the Crown when the court is half a continent away.

'Only—two days?' The flare of energy died. I nodded weakly. 'Yes. Both of us. The *ashiren* stays with me.'

He was puzzled, he still didn't believe me. But he wasn't going to risk being wrong.

'You,' he said to the woman who had brought us in, 'take an escort, go down to Shiriya-Shenin on the water-caravan. As for these two, feed them, but nothing else. Let them go to the *T'An Suthai-Telestre* as beggars, if they're so certain of belief. And keep close watch—see they get to Shiriya-Shenin, and nowhere else.'

Because of the plain it was impossible to see the river until we were on its banks. It was wide, even here, and sluggish; a loop meandered up close to the Ai garrison and then drifted away southwest. Broad flat-bottomed boats were drawn up to wooden jetties. Brown water swirled round the piles.

I was tired of being filthy, resenting the commander's spite—it would have cost him nothing to let us wash, at least. Back of that was an irrational hurt. Despite my better judgement, I'd trusted Blaize n'ri n'suth Meduenin.

'I thought we'd done with trouble when we left the Barrens,' Maric said quietly, 'but it isn't over yet, Christie, is it?'

'Nearly,' I said, and he smiled ruefully.

A damp cold hazed the flat horizon. Traders were loading the boats, lashing crates to the rails. Bundles bound in waxed cloth filled the holds past deck-level. Six or seven boats were moored together, painted in rainbow colours, beaked rudders jutting from the river. Ortheans shouted in the Peir-Dadeni tongue.

We were pushed aboard the last boat, then ignored while the troop-master had a long, incomprehensible argument with the crew. I sat down under the deck awning, leaning back against the bales in the hold. Maric, sighing, eased himself down beside me.

I must see if I can make that woman understand me, I thought. What did the commander call her—Huroth? Meanwhile I can at least unlace these damn boots.

And in that moment between sitting down and bending forward, I fell asleep.

A sour taste furred my mouth. Cramp caught me as I moved, grunting, and opened my eyes. I lay skewed against the cargo bales. Water hissed against the hull, inches from my head. Someone had thrown a blanket over me and—I raised my head, wincing—over Maric too.

The garrison escort squatted on the other side of the deck, playing *ochmir;* and the traders sat on cushions under the steersman's awning.

Midday sunlight reflected brilliantly from the smooth water. When I sat up I saw we had come out of the plains. There were low hills to either side—brown, sparsely vegetated, dotted here and there with *marhaz* and *skurrai* herds and sprawling *telestre* buildings. Some of the slopes were terraced. Perhaps it was only that this was the time after harvest, well into the dead time of winter, but it looked a harsh land to me.

'Christie?' Maric sat up, blinking; then relaxed and scratched his matted mane. 'I thought . . . I've still got the flask here, do you want a drink?'

It was unwatered wine. I coughed. The sun, I realized, was in the wrong position. 'Have I slept the day round?'

'Not all of it. Remember last night?' Seeing my blank look, he added 'The *telestre* we stopped at, where the herds of wild *skurrai* were. You woke long enough to eat.'

It was true, the ravenous hurt was eased. 'I guess I wasn't as awake as I looked.'

A shadow fell across us. Maric looked up. *'T'an* Huroth.'

'Troopmaster,' she corrected, squatting down by him. She avoided looking at me.

'Salathiel *telestre?*' she said at last, in accented Rimon.

'Tathcaer westbank. We run the ferry.'

'Yes. I thought I knew the Salathiel face. I've a sister who's *n'ri n'suth* Lyadine now, I used to visit them there.'

'You'd have passed us on your way up the Oranon, then.'

She grunted. When she did meet my eyes, it was with her own veiled.

'You have your *ashiren* well versed in *kir* story.'

I said, 'You don't believe he's lying.'

'Ah. Well.' She stood. 'You're going where you wish. Isn't that enough?'

The boats kept to the eastern side of the wide expanse of water, passing terraced hills. Every scrap of earth was hoarded. I watched the narrow ochre strips pass, seeing the pale stone walls retreat back up from the river's edge in steps. Noon shadows pooled black under the occasional isolated *tukinna* tree. *Telestre* buildings were stone-walled, stone-roofed. It was land worn down to the bone, a land that had been scoured clean.

Ribbons of sunlight stretched like tapes from the broken cloud cover, sinking into the silty river. The sun never got as low in the sky as I was used to in the British Isles, but nevertheless the pale star was hanging close to the southern horizon. Southward the river valley wound between shallow hills, diminishing into golden haze.

Huroth talked a little and some of the traders spoke Ymirian, so I got some idea of where the water-caravan was heading. Shortly after noon on that second day the river curved westward. We passed a burning-ground, flat cremation stones set in a valley close to the water, and I guessed we must be close. Then the river turned south again into higher, hillier land, and I saw the city.

The river is narrow here, between hills that rise up steep to either side; mossgrass turning from summer browns and blues to winter's ochre and umber. I saw *tukinna* trees in clefts so deep their crooked branches hardly reached up to the open air. And then, ahead, was Shiriya-Shenin. Ridged hills went up from the eastern bank. For a moment I thought—map changed to territory—that every hill had contour lines on it. Then that they were stepped, like pyramids. And then I saw that these cone-like hills were terraced, the low walls following every fold and dip and ridge. In all that massive natural amphitheatre that holds an eastern meander of the Ai river, there is not one yard of uncultivated soil.

Shiriya-Shenin sprawled on the plateau a little above the river, brown as the hills surrounding it, long and low and cornered with ziggurat towers. As we came further round the bend in the river, I saw how far it stretched: a city larger than Corbek, larger even than Tathcaer.

Numerous docks and jetties were crowded with the last of the season's riverboats. We came under the city wall, glowing honey-coloured in the winter sunlight, loaf-shaped bricks gleaming with thick glaze. Squat towers spaced along the walls opened slit windows on the riverside.

The crew of the water-caravan steered the boats in, taking ropes thrown from the dock, and each vessel was moored. Huroth curtly directed her troopers to guard us, and went ashore.

Finally we were herded off the boat. The wooden dock was hard underfoot. I found it difficult just to walk. Maric groaned, held my arm, and cursed under his breath. Huroth beckoned us forward.

Between two ziggurat towers, great painted wooden gates stood open. Stone plinths on either side supported statues of *zilmei*, painted very lifelike: one on all fours, ears flat against the wedge-shaped skull, showing tusks in a snarl, the other rearing up and clawing the air, head back as if to give out its whooping cry. So it was that the *ashiren* and I came into Shiriya-Shenin by the great Fifthwall *Zilmei* Gate.

Muddy streets were flanked by boardwalks at the rivergate. It was an effort to walk. The troopers jostled close, afraid of our vanishing into the crowd.

Don't you worry, I thought as we stepped on to brick-paved ways further in. We're not going to escape, no indeed.

I plodded on behind Huroth. Even Maric, Orthean and *ashiren*, was at the limit of his endurance. Damp wind chilled between blank-walled *telestre* houses, whipping down narrow streets—and they really are streets, I thought. The same secretive houses faced inward to courtyards with pools and cisterns, but they were set out on a grid system. *Kurrashaku* wheeled and perched on flat roofs, their harsh cries sounding over the crowded passages.

It was not only that these people spoke a different language—they seemed alien even to Corbek and Tathcaer. The *ashiren* ran barefoot, ceramic beads woven into braided manes. Adults sported uncut six-clawed hands. There was not a street in which you could not hear singing. There were no bells. Cages hung by the gates, and squat-bodied lizardbeasts gripped the bars with spatulate fingers and sang shrill warnings.

At each wall—the city has outgrown its boundaries four times— Huroth showed authorization at the gateways, and wrangled interminably with the city Watch. From Fifthwall to Firstwall took most of the afternoon.

At the L'ku Gate, guards clustered round a brazier, stamping their feet against the cold. Beyond them lay a warren of single-storey buildings, yards, raised walks and hexagon-shaped halls: the old Firstwall city founded by *amari* Andrethe. Huroth argued with what I gathered were aides and ministers of the *tha'adur,* the Peir-Dadeni court. Eventually, half asleep on my feet, I interrupted in Ymirian. Someone must understand.

'You,' I said, picking out a pale goldmaned Orthean at random, 'tell the *T'An Suthai-Telestre* that the Dominion envoy is here.'

He gave the slight inclination that passes for a bow in Peir-Dadeni. He was not young, a tall Orthean in scarlet slit-robe with sash and rank-badges and curved Dadeni blades. The diamond-scale pattern of his skin was more pronounced, changing with the winter. One six-fingered hand rested on a *harur* blade. Gold flashed. Like many Ortheans he had the atrophied remnant of webbing between his fingers, and the thin sections of skin were pierced with gold and quartz studs. Orthe's streak of the barbaric.

'Cethelen Khassiye Reihalyn,' he introduced himself measuredly, speaking Ymirian with a south Dadeni accent. 'You understand, these things take time.'

'I understand that Suthafiori will lose little time in making her displeasure known, if this is kept from her.'

'That is easy to say.'

'Then say it to her!' I snapped. 'I haven't come halfway across the Southland to stand waiting at the gates of Shiriya-Shenin.'

'It's true, *t'an,'* Maric said to him. 'We have come across the Barrens from Corbek. The Otherworld envoy *lives;* it is for the *T'An Suthai-Telestre* to know this as soon as possible.'

'Keep guard on them. Wait here.' Khassiye's gaze flicked over us before he went back through the Firstwall gate, and I saw subliminal recoil. Well, we're not pretty, I thought, but we're alive, that's something.

City sounds quieted. Smoke went up grey into the second twilight.

The Nineday fast would be broken now, I could smell evening meals cooking. My gut contracted: I was hungrier than I knew. The streets were emptying, and oil-lanterns were lit and hung over *telestre* archways.

'I've had enough of this,' I said.

'They might kill us if we scare them,' the *ashiren* said thoughtfully, 'considering where we've come from. I never heard any good of these northern lands. Best to keep quiet and wait, *S'ar-anth.*'

'We'll go in under guard,' I said to Huroth, 'but I'm going in to find someone who knows me, or we'll be here all night.'

She was no keener on being kept waiting than I was, and the troopers wanted to spend what time they could in Shiriya-Shenin before they returned to garrison duty. She endured the remarks of the city Watch only under protest.

'Yes,' she said, 'it was commanded we take you to the *T'An Suthai-Telestre,* not stand outside the L'Ku Gate. You there, stand aside! Goddess! they're under guard, aren't they? Stand out of the way.'

There was no troopmaster present, so she outranked them. I'd counted on it.

The garishly-painted gates had lost their colour in the twilight. The city smells dispersed on a cold wind. A light rain began to fall. Windows shone yellow in the low mass of brickwork that was the Firstwall city. The gateway was a tunnel: footsteps echoed as we went through.

One gnarled *tukinna* grew in the centre of a hexagonal courtyard where shallow steps went down to a covered well. Lanterns hung at intervals shed yellow light on the brown flagstones. I saw the same expression on Maric's face that I must have had on mine—intimidated, overpowered by the age and arrogance of the secretive walls. Diamond-slit windows lined the low flat-roofed buildings.

Huroth strode past tree and well, her back stiff with tension. As I caught up, intending to speak to her, a woman in a green *becamil* cloak came out of the far building. Silhouetted against the open doorway, then resolving into recognition. The cloak's hood was thrown back, disclosing cropped black mane, gaunt dark face. She moved abstractedly, head down, left hand tucked under her belt. The cloak hung flat from her right shoulder. I almost didn't know her: she must have been desperately ill, I thought.

'Ruric!'

Her head came up and her face went blank. The yellow eyes veiled, then became clear. Am I that different? I wondered, seeing how very slowly the recognition came. But it came.

'Christie? Grief of the Goddess, *Christie!*'

Then we were embracing, swaying in the rain and twilight; and she was laughing and pounding me on the back in her single-armed embrace. She put me back to arm's length, and we grinned foolishly at each other. Her gaze took in Maric, the Ai garrison troopers.

'Wha'?' She shook her head ruefully, and wrinkled her nose. 'Goddess, Christie, but you stink!'

'I have an excuse for that. A number of excuses. The Fens, the Barrens . . . this is my escort from Broken Stair, by the way.'

She shook her head again, still grinning. 'I have to hear this. And so does Suthafiori . . . You—troopmaster—I want your report. Christie; dear Goddess, what a story!'

I rescued my knife and the sonic stunner, but the rest of my clothes and gear had to be burned. Their state was unbelievable, even to me. I peeled off wrappings from sore hands, and when I finally did remove my boots and the makeshift bandages, two or three nails came away with them. Open coldsores smarted in the hot bath water. I spent a mindless, comfortable time in near-scalding water, ridding myself of scurf and dirt and lice; it took four baths to go from black-brown to scrubbed pink. *L'ri-an* took me to a set of rooms in the quarantine hall and a woman came to clip my hopelessly matted hair. It was cropped shorter than an Ymirian's. I sat in front of the hearth, wrapped in a soft robe, listening to the rain beat at the narrow windows.

'Christie?' Maric came in, belting a *chirith-goyen* robe round him. His skin was pale tan again, the winter scale pattern quite distinct. 'It's quieter in here. All these people . . .'

'Hard to take, yes. We'll get used to it, I suppose.'

He shuttered the diamond-shaped windows. The small room was warm, lamps and firelight bright on the tapestried walls. It would have been easy to sleep. Maric sat by the fire, cradling a wine jug. Clean clothes were laid out on the bed, and I limped across to dress.

Maric leaned forward, running fingers through his mane in the fire's heat. 'Will you braid it when it's dry, *S'aranth?*'

'Sure, in a minute.' No Orthean can reach properly to braid its own mane, and his had grown long enough out of the cropped style to go in Dadeni braids. The implications of that came home to me: in these close-knit communities an Orthean is never without brother or sister, parent or offspring, to perform that simple task.

I'd put my shirt on and was lacing up my britches, when I heard the door open.

'Now it starts, I suppose. Questions. I—'

A middle-aged Orthean came in, fair mane wet, rain darkening on his shoulders. Coldness hit me. For a second I was deaf and blind with a surge of adrenalin, back in the marshes, back in Oeth.

'I came as soon as I heard.' The grip of his six-fingered hands was dry, firm. 'You're not hurt?'

'No, I . . .' Easy tears blinded me. I blinked clear of them, grasping his hands to keep back hysteria. 'No, we're all right. Hal, it's good to see you.'

There was no need to say more. We had entered in to our old friendship as soon as he walked into the room. I remembered Ruric saying, He's a good man, don't trust him. I didn't know about good—he had all the Orthean addiction to intrigue and untruth—but I could trust him.

'Now,' he said as we sat by the hearth, 'now let Howice and SuBannasen lie to the Crown: we've got them!'

'They're here?'

'The *T'Ans* travel with the court. But Howice is here for the Crown's inquiry into Corbek. *T'An* Ruric and I,' he said, 'she got down to Corbek about the time they dragged me back there, we've been stirring scandal ever since. But I never thought we'd have a witness back from the dead.'

I laughed with him. Then, 'Does that mean I've been reported dead, to Earth?'

'Your people were notified, yes.'

'That's going to cause some bureaucratic confusion.' It was a difficult concept to translate. Then, making the connection, I said, 'If Howice is here, does that mean Falkyr is?'

He nodded, eyeing me warily. 'Somewhere, yes.' A pause. 'Sethin's dead, and the old man Koltyn; which makes it difficult for us.'

Relief, sorrow: I didn't know what I was feeling, or for whom.

'What happened to that barbarian woman?' he said avidly. 'And— where's Theluk?'

Now I knew I was back in the world again, and I took the weight of it. Maric was looking for me to answer.

'The fenborn killed her,' I said. 'Theluk's dead.'

19

Echoes of Corbek

Towards the end of that week I attended the inquiries (having spent most of the intervening days asleep). There were two, called quickly because of the speed with which the scandal spread through the city: an inquiry into the report of my 'death' in Corbek, and into the hiring of a mercenary assassin by person or persons unknown but widely supposed to be SuBannasen *telestre*. I had hopes of uncovering a multitude of injustices.

Both courts being there—the Dadeni *tha'adur* and the Ymirian *tak-shiriye*—the inquiries were presided over by the *T'An Suthai-Telestre* and the Andrethe, and given in both languages. The Andrethe's investigator turned out to be Cethelen Khassiye Reihalyn (who made no mention of our meeting at the L'Ku Gate); and for the Crown, the First Minister of Ymir. Despite lines of age, his face was familiar. I was not surprised to find he was Hanathra *telestre*, Hellel by name.

'How much do I have to say?' I asked Haltern as we filed into the low-roofed hall on the second day.

'Very little. You'll be called on to affirm the statements you've made.'

Haltern was working with a knife-faced man I recognized. He'd been at the disastrous dinner at Hill-Damarie: Brodin n'ri n'suth Charain. I eased back on the carved wooden seat—it was near one of the hall's ornamental iron braziers—and rested my feet on a cushion. There was still no way I could get boots on my swollen feet, they looked and felt like slabs of raw meat. So I had them bandaged and swathed in several pairs of stockings.

'For *telestre* Talkul: Verek Howice!'

The Orthean stood, was acknowledged, and came forward. He wore

Roehmonder dress, dull against the bright Dadeni robes, and he was just as I remembered him.

The light through the lozenge-shaped windows dazzled me where it fell on the mosaic floor. The Wellhouse, the cells: it came back with a bitter taste. Clear-eyed and guileless he looked across the hall at me. The shock of hatred was like cold water. I loathed him. No, that was unprofessional. Nonetheless. . . .

He said, 'Can I be blamed for the actions of an old man and a mad Keeper?'

They couldn't shift him from that defence.

'Koltyn was an old man,' he said, soft voice clearly audible through the Hexagram Hall. 'Now it seems he was a senile old man. I could deny that I realized it, but it wouldn't be true. We all knew. He was an old man, but he had been a good *s'an* to us, and it would have broken him to know that he was no longer capable. We—let me be honest, we imagined he would soon die. We didn't know he could do so much harm before he did. We kept him as *s'an,* we obeyed him as *s'an*—both wrong, perhaps, but wrong for the right reason.'

It went down well with the Ortheans.

'Lying little shit!' I said under my breath. In English.

'Yes,' Haltern whispered back, recognizing the tone, if nothing else. 'But how are we going to prove it? Koltyn's dead, and Sethin.'

And Theluk, I thought. It doesn't leave much credible evidence.

'Arad,' Khassiye Reihelyn queried. His six-fingered hands flashed gold as he gestured. 'What of him?'

Howice shrugged. 'The church in Corbek is asking that very question, and I can't anticipate their answer. All I can say is that I think he was misguided, but he believed in what he did.'

At that point I realized that this inquiry was anything but a foregone conclusion. Here was I, worn raw from Howice hunting me across Roehmonde, but pinning him down . . . it was going to be harder than walking across the Barrens.

It broke up inconclusively again, and I sat there while the hall emptied. Eventually I limped across to the ornamented fireplace to be introduced to the Andrethe, who sat there talking with Ruric and the Crown.

'Envoy, be welcome.' Suthafiori studied me as if there was some change apparent. I sat down. I'd seen her the day I arrived, but didn't remember making too much sense at the time. 'For a dead woman, you look well.'

'Andrethe,' Ruric used the formal inflection, 'this is Christie S'aranth of the British Isles.'

Kanta Andrethe was mountainous, her coffee-coloured flesh enclosed in a blue and gold robe belted with a wide *chirith-goyen* sash; the robe split down the spine to show her brown mane in elaborate braids. Her arms were hams, her legs tree-trunks. But her face—unveiled raisin-eyes in wrinkled flesh—showed an odd mixture of maternalism and shrewdness.

'Outworlders, is it? I'm not convinced. Some adventurer out of Saberon or Kel Harantish.' She gave me a very direct look. 'My dear, I don't apologize, I like your style.'

'I also make no apologies, excellence, that I come from a greater distance than Kel Harantish or Saberon. May I present the greetings of the governments of the Dominion to the Andrethe of Peir-Dadeni.'

She hesitated, then gave a snorting chuckle. 'My sire and dam! Yes, you may.'

A *l'ri-an* came in to rake the fire into life, and serve bowls of hot herb-tea.

'The SuBannasen awaits your inquiry, *T'An,*' Haltern said to Suthafiori, 'but there again we are robbed of witnesses.'

'The Meduenin hired sword,' Kanta Andrethe's black eyes veiled 'He is here. With Sulis, Brodin tells me.'

'So arrest him,' I said, rather too bluntly. Meduenin in the city—no, I didn't want to think about the past.

'Ah, he will have closed the contract by now if he is wise, and then there is no questioning him.' The Andrethe glanced at Brodin, who nodded. 'But still, we do know what Sulis n'ri n'suth SuBannasen did in Corbek.'

'Yes, bribery; and how?' Suthafiori's head lowered as she stared at her linked hands. 'Melkathi is poor, and she has spent gold on this. Where did that come from?'

'Who knows? But it went to Howice,' Ruric observed, 'he could tell much, if he would.'

'If! Mother, yes, *if* he would.' Kanta's heavy head swayed from side to side. 'And if Corbek is questioning that Wellkeeper Arad . . . we will see.'

At her gesture the *l'ri-an* brought forward a table. A map of the Southland *telestres* was inlaid in enamel on its surface. (The sheer permanence of political divisions impressed me—coming from a world where atlases are liable to be out of date almost as soon as they're printed). Haltern and Brodin conferred. The women studied the map, slender fingers pointing. The Andrethe wore gold studs between her plump fingers. Brown, massive, a woman ruling a province the size of Ymir, Melkathi, and Roehmonde put together. Beside her, silvergilt and slender, the Crown seemed almost childlike.

'Melkathi, Roehmonde . . .' Suthafiori touched Ymir, that lies between them. 'There are quarrels between *telestres* of Ymir and Rimon that might be revived. And you say the SuBannasen fosters *ashiren* at Corbek, envoy? Yes . . . but Morvren Freeport will not fight the Crown, nor you, Andrethe, nor the Kyre.' She was grim. 'On your Otherworld, envoy, what would this mean?'

'I'm not sure. War, perhaps.' There was no literal translation. 'If they attacked. . . .'

'Raiding, you mean?' Ruric sipped from her tea-bowl. 'Then they'd have the whole Hundred Thousand in arms. No, SuBannasen's not stupid, nor is Howice.'

The Southland's standing army puzzled me at first, being no more than the few thousand necessary to man the garrisons at Ai and Tathcaer and Path-of-Skulls. Then I realized that Southlanders are trained fighters from *ashiren* onwards: a force which is, by nature, defensive.

'I'll tell you, Dalzielle.' The Andrethe rolled back in her chair, fixing her gaze on Suthafiori. 'Next year, yes, comes Midsummer-Tenyear? Well, then. When it comes to naming the Crown again, how many *T'Ans* will you have that favour you?'

The small woman nodded. 'If the *s'an telestres* should name the SuBannasen again for Melkathi, and Howice for Roehmonde; and if those two gained the support of Rimon, say, or Morvren. . . .'

'Then you have lost the Crown, and must go back to being Dalzielle *telestre* Kerys-Andrethe. Last Tenyear you were lucky, that was the year you beat the barbarians at Skulls. This Tenyear—this is the year you brought Golden Witchbreed back to the Southland!'

'Your pardon, *T'An*,' I said, 'we're not Witchbreed.'

'It's what they think you are that matters.'

Ruric widened yellow eyes. 'Oh I agree, Andrethe.'

The woman snorted. 'So, all that's gold may not be Witchbreed, I'll grant you that.'

'Should there be a different Crown, that will cause problems for you and your people, envoy.' Suthafiori paused. 'But I think you need not be concerned. I am Crown, and mean to be so after Midsummer-Tenyear.'

It was after the midday gongs sounded across the city that I left the Hexagram Hall.

It can drag on all through winter, I thought. Howice is as slippery as a fish. And will it be any better with SuBannasen?

I walked through the passages to the Hall of Mosaics, meaning to go and check on the progress of the Crown's inquiry. A group of Ortheans were talking, brightly illuminated by the hall's coloured glass windows. I avoided them. One drew his sword to demonstrate a stroke and parry. A Roehmonder *harur-nilgiri*, I noted; the group were mostly in Roehmonde jackets and loose trousers. Cropped manes had rock-crystal beads knotted down to mid-spine. Then the sword-wielder's head went back as he laughed, and a familiar voice made some barbed comment. He sheathed the blade, turned, and saw me.

'Christie,' he said soberly. 'I heard you were here. I'm glad you're well.'

Sethin Falkyr, Falkyr of Corbek.

Was that only last autumn? I thought. It seems years ago. Was that woman really Lynne Christie?

'I heard about Sethin,' I said. 'I'm sorry.'

'When the sickness was advanced, she came to me,' Falkyr said, 'and asked what a mother may demand of her sons. So I made it painless. Death was easy for her. May we meet again.'

It was the traditional acknowledgement of death. It wouldn't have surprised me to hear that Sethin had taken her own life, but it shocked me that she had asked Falkyr, and he had done it, and seemed to regard it as a mark of favour. How close were we? I wondered. How far did we ever understand each other?

'Koltyn should have done the same,' he added, 'but She took him at the beginning of Riardh Secondweek.'

An awkward silence fell. There was nothing in his expression to say that we had ever been *arykei.*

'And you, you're well?' I asked.

'Yes. I travel with *t'an* Howice now. Who knows, I may become one of the *tha'adur.*' Something of the old sarcasm sounded in his voice, but his eyes were veiled.

When it's dead, someone said to me, then leave it. We'd been joined in nothing but flesh. Looking back, I couldn't recognize us in the two people standing here.

'You're thin,' he said, 'you should rest. They tell me you crossed the Barrens, that's hard country. When you're well, perhaps we'll ride out round Shiriya-Shenin.'

'Perhaps, *t'an* Falkyr, but I am kept fairly busy here.'

We parted bewildered on both sides.

It drew on towards Orventa, the winter season. I took rooms in Firstwall, not far from Ruric. There wasn't a two-storey building in Shiriya-Shenin, with the exception of the ziggurat watchtowers; seen from the nearby high ground it resembled its own terraced hillsides, each long low line of *telestre* buildings forming a step up from the river. I could have done with less walking in the interminable maze of passages. Not until the late season storms struck did I appreciate the advantage of being under cover, as a wind came upriver that would have stripped any tower off the hillside.

Rain lashed the lozenge windows, the last snarl of a storm, and Haltern walked into my rooms. I was attempting, again, to write out a report in longhand.

'Where are we today, then?' I asked cheerfully. It wouldn't surprise me to hear they'd moved the inquiry yet again.

'Nowhere.' He crossed to the window and looked out at the falling rain. 'They've closed the Corbek inquiry.'

'They've done *what?*'

'Closed it. It's finished.'

I heard shouts in the courtyard outside. *Ashiren* beginning the celebrations for the end of Riardh, and for winter festival.

'So what happens to Howice?'

'Nothing. He's left, gone downriver; plans to get back to Roehmonde before winter makes travelling impossible. Most of his *t'ans* have gone with him.'

'Shit!' And a few other English expressions.

Haltern shrugged. 'Arad must explain Corbek's poverty, and that is church business. All Howice did he claims his *s'an telestre* ordered him to do. No, by spring Howice may be *T'An* Roehmonde himself.'

I remembered Sethin. 'And then again—he may not.'

There was a pause.

'I see you're busy with the *t'ans* here,' Haltern added, 'but spare us a little more time, Christie. I need to call you for the inquiry on Sulis n'ri n'suth SuBannasen.'

20

The Answer of SuBannasen

'We won't get many more boats downriver before the freeze.' Ruric hitched her cloak one-handed round her shoulders. A keen, damp wind blew off the river, and the sky was heavy with unshed snow.

'I want to get a message to Tathcaer—get them to pass word on to the Earth ship that I'm not dead.'

It is a curious fact that it is quicker to travel the nine hundred *seri* down the Ai and the eight hundred *seri* up the Rimon coast by ship than it is travelling the mere five hundred odd *seri* across Dadeni Heath and north Rimon on land. Especially the way Southland roads are in winter.

The river dock was half deserted, the warehouses shut up, the shipping *telestres* closing down for the day. Maric was with me. Neither he nor I wanted to walk far.

A raw cold came up off the grey water.

'How about it?' I asked Maric. 'You want to send a message to your *telestre*, let them know you're all right?'

'Yes, I do.'

'Or do you want to take the message in person?'

His head came up, his eyes were bright; there was no need to ask if that was what he wanted.

'I'm still your *l'ri-an.*'

'Of course. I'll send my message to Tathcaer by you, then you winter over at Salathiel. I'll be downriver again in the spring.'

'It's good of you. But I'll stay here if you want me, Christie.'

'This is most convenient for both of us, I think. Though I suspect I won't find out how much you do until I have to do it myself—and I don't know one end of a *marhaz* from the other. Speaking of which, do they take riderbeasts on the riverships?'

'They do,' Ruric put in, 'and I have your two in my stable still, Christie, I brought them back with me from Corbek. There was no one else . . .'

'No, of course not. Can't have you walking, though,' I said to Maric, 'so you'd better keep Oru, and take one of the *skurrai* for baggage.'

He thanked me, grinning.

We turned to walk back along the dock to Fifthwall's Silver Gate. When the boy was a way ahead, Ruric said, 'You should call in on Salathiel in the spring—explain to the *s'an telestre* why an *ashiren* comes home with *harur* blades and a *marhaz*.'

'Did I do wrong?'

'No.' She laughed. As we came to the Silver Gate she looked at me seriously. 'You're still going to need a *l'ri-an* this winter. Will you do me a favour?'

'Sure, what?'

'My *ashiren,* Rodion. Will you let *ke* do it?'

Even Ruric isn't above using her *telestre* to keep an eye on the envoy, I thought, but at least it's a friendly eye.

'Yes, of course.'

'It might not be easy,' the Orthean woman warned, 'but you do need a *l'ri-an,* and Rodion needs something—I'm not sure what.'

The SuBannasen trial—because that was what it was turning into— continued into Orventa at the usual slow Orthean pace. I attended, fitting appointments with *s'an* and *t'an* of the court into my spare time, and studying to become reasonably fluent in Peir-Dadeni. The envoy was becoming known in Shiriya-Shenin.

'Rodion?' It was towards the end of a cold morning. 'How long ago did this message come?'

Eventually the *ashiren* slouched out of the back rooms, eyed me up and down, and said, 'Not long.'

'Well, couldn't you have given it to me? Now I find out they want me at the inquiry again!'

Ke shrugged. Gawky, long-legged, this one was all adolescent, and well past the age for an *ashiren* to become adult.

'I didn't ask to be your *l'ri-an, S'aranth.'* The use-name had all its old insolence.

There was some expression in *kir* face that reminded me of Ruric, but that was all the resemblance. Pale mane braided to midspine, slick diamond-patterned skin with a flush of gold to it, and tawny-gold whiteless eyes . . . *ke* was very much as the Witchbreed are always described. The other *ashiren* called *kir* Rodion Halfgold: an intimation that somewhere in *kir* ancestry was Witchbreed blood (but I was also told that interbreeding between Ortheans and that extinct race was never possible). Whatever the truth, it didn't make *kir* life easy.

'Find Haltern, tell him I'm on my way.'

'Yes, *S'aranth.*'

As Rodion left, I realized something. I'd always seen *ashiren* as either male or female. Even Maric, who a year from now might be man or woman, I saw as a boy. (Once I came on them together, bent over an *ochmir* board, and—before I recognized him—saw Maric as a lean dark-maned girl.) But Rodion was neither, not in appearance or behaviour. In Dadeni robes, *ke* might be female, in Ymirian dress, male; and since those were purely Earth preconceptions I had to disregard them. I was forced into use of the neutral pronoun, and it was becoming natural to see all *ashiren* that way. I found it unsettling and a little frightening.

Ruric met me in the entrance to the Hexagram Hall.

'Inquiries!' she swore. 'If it was up to me I wouldn't inquire, I'd slit SuBannasen's throat. I hear they want our evidence again?'

'For all the good it'll do, yes.' The old woman's defence so far consisted of a flat denial, and an invitation that anyone prove any of their accusations. Which was proving remarkably hard to do.

I saw Rodion out in the courtyard; *ke* ducked *kir* head and scuttled off.

'Is it any easier?' Ruric asked.

'Not so's you'd notice.' I was truthful. 'That child thinks it's got a grudge against everyone.'

'That's my fault,' the Orthean woman said, yellow eyes half veiled. 'My Desert Coast mother must have come from Kel Harantish, I think, and the Witchbreed blood's strong there.'

'*Ke* must be—what, nearly fifteen?'

'Yes, and still *ashiren*. That doesn't help. When I was fifteen . . .' She shrugged as we entered the main body of the hall, taking seats by the *T'an Suthai-Telestre's* table. 'That was the year I came to Tathcaer, worked in a companion-house to save money to join the army. Straike was in the same house. Oh, he was proud, you'd think he was the first boy to father an *ashiren*. And the first year in the Guard is theory and study, I was able to keep Rodion with me.'

'He had that colouring?'

'Straike? No. Redhead, and pale as I am dark; I'd hoped Rodion would take after him. I got him to join the Guard. Bullied him, really. He was my Second all through the Quarth raids.' She paused. 'When he died in Melkathi, I had Rodion fostered up here. It isn't easy for a Halfgold anywhere.'

I saw Khassiye Reihalyn and Hellel Hanathra in one of the Hexagram Hall's many alcoves, and then Brodin passed me; and Sulis n'ri n'suth SuBannasen. The hall was crowded. I was aware that Haltern and Brodin had their own systems of intelligence; many of the seemingly unimportant members of the *tha'adur* and *takshiriye* brought information from other parts of the Southland. Of necessity, I would be ignorant of much that went on.

One face briefly glimpsed in the crowd was familiar. Fair streaked mane lit by sunlight falling through lozenge-windows . . . Blaize n'ri n'suth Meduenin.

'Ah, you're here.' Haltern, emerging from another of the alcoves, interrupted my thoughts.

'Is there new evidence against SuBannasen?'

He smiled, as noncommittal as an Orthean can be, and exchanged polite formalities with Ruric.

The air in the Hexagram Hall was chill, despite the fires of slow-burning mossturf. Shiriya-Shenin's river mist combined with the smoke to make a dense fog and the thin winter sunlight vanished. *L'ri-an* lit oil lamps. The yellow glow added to the claustrophobic atmosphere. All but the centre tables were now occupied.

Aliens, I thought again. It was more noticeable in Shiriya-Shenin: their slit robes, curved pairs of blades and manes braided with ceramic beads, their habit of going barefoot on tessellated stone floors.

'I hear the Andrethe is tired of the delay,' Ruric said, 'and so's Dalzielle. I—yes, Oreyn, I saw you: hello.'

The man nodded acknowledgement and passed on. He was old, thin and white-skinned. The Orthean mane receded from his forehead and back from his ears, leaving a cropped crest. Narrow forehead and bright eyes gave his face a singularly insect-like appearance. With his slender six-fingered hands linked before his chest, he resembled nothing so much as a praying mantis.

'Your *telestre?*'

'Hana Oreyn Orhlandis,' she said quietly. 'The last of Hana's birth now alive. He was brother to my father. And now his place is as SuBannasen's first minister.'

'But you said—the uprising—'

'Orhlandis and Ales-Kadareth have always had strong links,' she said wryly, and laughed. 'They won't change that for one member of the *telestre*, even if she is *T'An* Commander.'

Suthafiori and the Andrethe entered the hall, talking, neither taking their places at the central table. I despaired of the Orthean sense of time. A buzz of talk rose. Ruric leaned over and questioned Haltern in a fierce undertone.

'Envoy.'

An old woman's voice. I stood, looking round, and saw that it was SuBannasen herself. She was in the nearest alcove. Oreyn Orhlandis left her side as I went over.

'*T'An* Sulis.' I found it hard to be impolite to the old woman.

She was seated on a window bench, by a glazed ceramic wall that showed a pattern of stars. Her hands shook faintly as she poured wine from a flask into glass goblets.

'Drink with me,' she said, friendly, peremptory, as I sat down beside her. 'It's a shame you never came to Melkathi, *t'an* Christie.'

Her pale eyes, hooded and alert, gazed past me into the body of the hall. Oreyn was in conversation with another Melkathi man—Santhil, was it?

'I wish that I could have visited you, *T'An.*' For a moment, seeing the humour and sadness in her face, it was the truth. 'But I think, perhaps, not now.'

'No. They'll find some excuse,' Sulis said. 'Some excuse to take Ales-Kadareth from me. Ten years ago I would have fought . . . but I'm tired. Perhaps I shall go home to SuBannasen. Come, Christie, drink to the *telestres* we've left.'

It was the honey-thick wine of south Dadeni. A familiar scent rose from it—much clearer to a human, I think, than to an Orthean. I knew it now. Certainly there was less of it in the wine than there had been at Hill-Damarie, but it was unmistakable: *saryl-kabriz.*

The old Orthean woman smiled.

'Thank you, *T'An* Sulis.' I put the glass down untasted. 'Forgive me, I must go back to my place now.'

She picked it up, swirling the contents thoughtfully. It was impossible to resent her, though I had every right.

'I will play you at *ochmir* if you ever do come to Melkathi,' she promised. Then—the inquiry being opened by Suthafiori—she made her way to her seat in the hall.

And there was no shifting her from her defence. No proof of bribery in Corbek: Howice had his own reasons for being absent. No proof of hired assassins—even Haltern couldn't break the Mercenary Guild-house's code.

She'll do it yet, I thought. Goddammit, she will, she'll do it like Howice!

I realized that I was far from safe in Shiriya-Shenin, for the winter, with SuBannasen.

On my way back across the courtyard I saw Blaize n'ri n'suth Meduenin again. He nodded civilly. *'T'an* Christie.'

The sky was yellowing. A cold wind scoured the yard, swirling the fog, and I was instantly back in the ruined city of Kirriach, smelling bad weather coming.

'You've got a brass nerve,' I said.

'T'an?' He appeared puzzled.

He must know I still carried the stunner. But he knows I'm envoy, I thought; and self-defence—he's not going to give me an excuse.

'You got here quicker than I thought.' He grinned, showing teeth stained with *ataile* juice. His eye membranes were retracted, the pupils enlarged. 'You must have been in Shiriya-Shenin before I closed contract.'

'With SuBannasen.'

Another toothy smile. 'I'm not obliged to say.'

An Orthean proverb says of someone that their word is as good as a sell-swords', and it's a compliment. And also, I suppose, a necessity.

'If I were you,' I said, 'I'd get out of Shiriya-Shenin.'

'That's wise advice, but I won't take it.'

'If I were Orthean, or prepared to use Orthean methods—'

'Why?' Genuine surprise showed on his scarred face. 'In the Barrens there's no law, but in the Southland I had a contract to keep. I'm a hired soldier.'

'Hired for assassination?'

'Kill one, kill many—it's the same job.'

There was no answering that. I said, 'You could have killed me easily at Broken Stair.'

'I could have done it, but not easily. You recall I've had experience of your Outworld weapons. I preferred not to take the risk, and that cost me fee-money; but it would be strange if I couldn't find another employer in Shiriya-Shenin.'

If I was angry, it was more at myself than at him. He was acting morally, according to Southland custom.

'You might need a hired sword yourself,' he said blandly. 'Not all your enemies are as cautious as my previous employer. I'm open to contract, *t'an* Christie.'

'Go to hell!' There was no translation for that, but he understood the tone. Seeing him walk away I thought, no, it's culture shock, I should be used to this by now.

'You wait,' I said, and he turned and faced me. 'Suppose I say, you stay in Firstwall and keep your ears open, tell me anything I should know about, and I'll pay you a retaining fee?'

I half expected him to be insulted. Instead he looked at me as if I'd finally done something sensible.

'Better hire me for more than that, or they'll know I'm your intelligencer. Call me your weapons tutor, *t'an,* I've done that before.'

'No other contracts while I employ you.'

He inclined his head. 'The price increases for that. Yes.'

I wanted to laugh. It had just occurred to me to wonder how I'd justify this to the ET department's financial section. It was hardly textbook envoy's behaviour. Doubtless any department psychiatrist would tell me I was heading for paranoia. I don't know any psychiatrists who've been hunted the length of the Southland.

'All right,' I said. 'All right. Where are you staying?'

'Down in Fifthwall, the Mercenaries' Guildhouse.'

'I'll find you space in my rooms here,' I decided. 'Maybe weapons training is no bad idea. Who knows, I may need it.'

The SuBannasen trial was abruptly reconvened a little after winter festival. I arrived at the Mosaic Hall with Ruric and Haltern just as the Crown was taking her place at the centre table.

'Well,' Suthafiori said, 'what now?'

Khassiye Reihalyn approached her table and bowed. 'There is new evidence to be heard.'

'On this matter of assassination?'

'On a different matter,' he said; and the hall, which had been resigned to the tedium of more endless wrangling, was loud with chatter and then quieted.

'I thought it better you hear this.' Kanta Andrethe for the first time used the formal inflection to the *T'An Suthai-Telestre*. A milky membrane slid over her eyes as she watched SuBannasen.

Suthafiori nodded and gestured to Khassiye to continue. He called forward another of the Melkathi men.

'What is your *telestre?*'

'Rimnith,' the man said calmly. He was in his middle fifties. 'I am Nelum Santhil, Portmaster of the city of Ales-Kadareth.'

'Santhil Portmaster, do you recognize these papers?'

He took them from Khassiye Reihalyn, scanned them briefly, and then raised his head. 'I do. They are lists of cargo for ships entering the port of Ales-Kadareth over the past three years.'

Unlike the previous days with their long-winded formality, this session was short and to the point. Ortheans favour group discussions and argument carried to great lengths. This degree of straightforward questioning argued a crisis.

'And these, also, do you recognize?'

He took time before answering. 'Yes. These are the true cargo lists for those same vessels, signed by the *T'an* Melkathi.'

I could see SuBannasen where she sat on one of the front benches. She made no movement, but she seemed to lose colour.

'You are aware that there are discrepancies between the two?'

'I am,' Santhil said, 'that is why I made them known to you.'

Khassiye signalled, and the man returned to his seat. Both sets of documents were passed to the Crown. She went from one to the other, the Andrethe sometimes pointing items out; and all that time there was no sound in the hall.

'They have in common, these ships, that all came from or called at the port of Kel Harantish.' Suthafiori's voice was quiet. 'It seems to me, Sulis, that you were less than wise in taking—gifts—from the Emperor-in-Exile.'

'Does that say I did?' She fussed with her cloak, then settled with her bony hands clasped on her stick. A gold-rimmed goblet stood on the bench beside her. I thought, gold is the heart of it. And remembered them asking where she had got gold for her bribery.

'This is your seal,' Suthafiori said, 'and this is your name put to it, and this your *telestre's* marksign.'

'Let me see.' The old woman peered at the papers when Khassiye gave them to her. I saw her expression fade, seeming to lose direction.

'That is your authority,' Suthafiori repeated.

SuBannasen folded the papers, handed them to Oreyn Orhlandis, and sat back silently. But she's old, I thought suddenly, and she might —she just might—have authorized things without checking them. And if that's true, she has too much pride ever to admit it.

'Do not be so swift to call me traitor,' she said at last. 'If I took gold from Kel Harantish why would I keep such evidence to betray me?'

'Perhaps to make that very excuse,' the Andrethe put in.

'Do you deny it?' Suthafiori asked.

The hesitation stretched into silence. The old woman cleared her throat, sipped from the goblet, and said, 'It may well be true, and if it is not—it will serve.'

The small, gilt-maned woman leaned back, her unblinking gaze fixed on Sulis. 'I must house you in the Kuath-Re,' Suthafiori said, naming the Secondwall prison.

'Wherever the *T'An Suthai-Telestre* pleases.' The old woman's expression was serene. She lifted the goblet again, and drank wine.

Our eyes met. I knew then, remembering the drink that she had offered me, that I was not mistaken. Her gaze was amused, half regretful, and totally without fear. The impulse to stop her faded. It's her right, I thought. She put the goblet down empty, reached for her stick, and walked slowly out of the hall between the guards.

'I don't trust that woman,' Ruric grumbled under her breath. 'Vermin don't lose their poison when they grow old, and she—'

A stir outside in the lobby: I heard the confusion of voices that I'd been waiting for. Ruric sprang to her feet. Through the doorway, a press of people blocked my vision. I saw the silver-topped cane laying on the tiles, trodden underfoot. *Saryl-kabriz* has that virtue, that it acts instantly.

21

Winter in Beth'ru-elen

Messages continued to arrive, though the last ship had gone south and the river was frozen. The Dadeni Wellhouses train a species of *rashaku* as carriers, and the bird-relay serves the length of the Ai river. Duplicate authorization papers came from Tathcaer, with a promise of medical supplies as soon as spring thaw came, and with the news that a message contradicting my demise had been sent off on a ship to the Eastern Isles. I used bank-drafts to replenish my finances and, set up with *marhaz* and wardrobe and offices, began meeting Ortheans again as the Dominion's representative. In short, I was much as I had been in Tathcaer.

Except that, even to myself, I wasn't recognizable as the same woman who'd come to Orthe the previous summer. It wasn't just physical appearance, being worn bone-thin. The ground under my feet was shifting.

'Won't thaw before mid-Orventa,' Ruric observed, looking out of the glazed lozenges at the falling snow. She put a *ferrorn* down on the *ochmir* board to open up another area of conflict. From where I sat by the fire, sorting through the bundle of messages, it looked likely to be a long game—it had lasted five days, on and off, already.

'*Leremoc.*' Haltern reversed her piece, having gained a majority. 'Did your kinsmen leave before the freeze, *T'An* Ruric?'

'Oreyn's on his way to Ales-Kadareth to tell the *s'ans* they've to name a new *T'an* Melkathi.' She leaned back in the low chair, hand rubbing the stump of her arm.

'Who'll be named?' I asked. Most of the other communications were from downriver *telestres,* inviting my presence in the spring. 'Do you know?'

'It's sudden, *takshiriye* and *tha'adur* are both here, not there; we've left the game a little late for the playing. Still,' Haltern observed, 'I shall be interested to see the outcome.'

'Not that Rimnith man, Santhil,' Ruric studied the board. 'If he'd betray one *T'An*, he'd betray another. It wouldn't surprise me if it were an Orhlandis . . . yes, Hal, I know what you think about Oreyn, and I agree with you, but he is popular in Melkathi.'

Haltern's pale eyes veiled. 'Is that necessarily a recommendation?' Ruric chuckled.

It was pleasant to be there with them. Empathically, it felt right. And recognizing that, I saw the truth; and stared into the mossturf fire.

I thought, I'm afraid of Orthe.

Afraid of being taken over, irrevocably involved. And I don't know Orthe, only the Southland, and that's a dangerous bias . . . If it was up to me I'd terminate this mission now. Get another envoy to take over. He wouldn't have my contacts or experience. But then he wouldn't be so personally involved.

Even with Falkyr I never considered resigning as envoy and trying to make a life here on Orthe. But it's coming closer, that desire—and it's impossible. If only for the fact that I've spent my formative years half a galaxy away from Carrick's Star; there's no way I can be an Orthean.

'I'm in a bad position here.' Ruric's long clawed fingers hovered over the *ochmir* board. 'Christie, do you want to come and make it a three-handed game?'

'What? Yes, sure. Just let me finish opening these.' I picked the wax seal off the last paper and unfolded the outer wrapping. Not English, but the curling script of the Southland. I studied it, less happy with the written than with the spoken word.

' "Kasabaarde",' I deciphered.

'What?' Haltern sat up.

It was a city on the second continent, on the far shores of the Inner Sea: I couldn't trigger any more hypno-details.

I was in two minds about doing it but I needed the information, and so handed the parchment over to Haltern. 'What do you make of it?'

It was quite short. He read it aloud. And for once the mask slipped, and I saw the avid curiosity of a very clever man.

' "To Lynne de Lisle Christie, envoy in Tathcaer and now in Shiriya-Shenin: greetings.

' " When the time comes that you must take ship, let it be

to the Brown Tower in Kasabaarde, there to meet and speak
with—

—The Hexenmeister.' "

'Who or what is that?' I asked. 'And to know that I'm in Shiriya-
Shenin . . .'

'He has his methods,' Haltern said, 'and the time can't be until after
the thaw. It's uncommon . . . I know of no direct word out of
Kasabaarde for some years, but I think this is genuine.'

'So?'

'So,' he said, 'when the Brown Tower calls you, Christie, you can be
certain it's wise to go there.'

But there was other unfinished business, as I found out when I accepted
Haltern's invitation to guest at the Beth'ru-elen *telestre*.

The eastern slopes of the Shiriya-Shenin hills are grown over with
hanelys, the tanglebush: stems as hard and angular as wrought iron
grow up to nine feet high, and the twining branches form an impenetrable roof. A comfortable morning's ride through *hanelys* from the city
lies Dadeni Heath, and Beth'ru-elen *telestre* on the edge of it.

The *marhaz* stepped high over fallen barbs and thorns. Branches
shoot down roots at intervals, so that a whole hillside might be one
plant. Almost no snow had penetrated through. As the sun rose higher,
snow and ice began to melt a little, and I saw the sky through ice-glazed
gaps in the *hanelys*. The *marhaz* belled as drops spotted them. Rodion's
mount skittered down the hillside. *Ke* rode lightly robed, not bundled in
furs like me, and left *kir* white mane unbraided. Even Haltern tended to
avoid *kir*. White and gold: Witchbreed. Well, I had thought to do *kir* a
favour bringing *kir* out of Shiriya-Shenin and trouble with other
ashiren.

We came out from under *hanelys* cover on the next ridge and Haltern reined in, pointing. 'There—Beth'ru-elen.'

Where the plain sloped down, a vast tract of bog, heath and moorland stretched flat to the eastern horizon, rough contours hidden by the
dimpled snow. Thin plumes of smoke rose from a fold in the land,
where flat roofs were visible. We rode down, the *ashiren* far ahead of us.

'Beth'ru-elen,' Haltern said again, softly, and then smiled. 'The
church's *telestre*, they say.'

'Is it?'

'There's some truth in it. Beth'ru-elen *Ashirenin* founded it, and many Beth'ru-elen go into the church—my mother was Wellkeeper for Kyrenden.'

The *marhaz* negotiated a slope treacherous under snow, highstepping and tossing their horned heads.

'I've heard you called Priest,' I said. It was in much the same way as they called Ruric Yelloweyes or myself *S'aranth.*

'I did train for the church.' He was thoughtful. 'With my *arykei.* Hanat was born L'Ku *telestre.* He became *n'ri n'suth* Beth'ru-elen. That was a good time, we were young, I could see us Earthspeaker and Wellkeeper together . . . but he died, and I had no heart for the church after that. Perhaps I never did have.'

'I'm sorry.'

He unsnapped one of his belt-ornaments. The Dadeni robes and pelt changed him, he seemed more alien, less devious, than in Tathcaer. The worn pendant opened to show an etching of a young male Orthean's face. Careless, sardonic, an adventurer.

'Hanat,' he said. 'Twenty five years ago. We have each our griefs. But there is always the *telestre.'*

We came in sight of the *telestre*-house as he spoke. Beth'ru-elen has all the antiquity of Firstwall, but without that city's quality of intimidation. Multiple linked buildings, bronze and flame-coloured bricks bright in the morning light. Snow clung to the roofs. Following the track round we passed long low brick halls and barns, and beastpens. *Marhaz* bugled, and our borrowed mounts answered them. A warm beast-smell was on the wind. An *ashiren,* not more than four or five years old, picked up the hem of its robe and ran shrilly towards the main gate.

Rashaku wheeled overhead, fluttering in and out of the birdcotes, fluting their weird water-pipe songs. Somewhere a hammer clanged on an anvil; weaving shuttles hummed. *Kazza* prowled, white pelts invisible against the snow, blue summer markings fading. They were muzzled. Slit eyes watched us. I shivered, caught Haltern's glance, and knew we shared a memory.

Guardbeasts hung in cages by the gate, squat-bellied and chirruping loud warnings. Their azure eyes followed us as we rode in under the arch.

'Hal!' A young man hailed him. A crowd collected as solidly and imperceptibly as salt crystallizing: old men and women, young ones, *ashiren,* babies being carried. The babble of voices confused me totally. The Beth'ru-elen have accents varying from incomprehensible southern to impenetrable northern Peir-Dadeni.

I slid down from the *marhaz* and scratched the beast's cold hide between its horns. It nipped at my arms. A tiny *ashiren* pushed its head aside, grabbed the reins, and led it towards the stables. Snow was trodden into slush in the paved courtyard. Sparks from the smithy were orange, gold, sputtering on the stone. A spring-fed pool bubbled in the centre. I smelled cooking, heard voices; the organic machine that was the *telestre* ticking over.

'*S'an*, this is Christie.' Haltern's use of the respectful inflection was for once, I judged, genuine. 'Christie, Arak Haike, our *s'an telestre.*'

Haike was the young man who'd met us: surprisingly young, with the Beth'ru-elen fair colouring, tending to the obese. His arm was bandaged.

'Come inside,' he said, 'there's food. Christie, you are welcome.' He saw Haltern's questioning look, and rubbed his arm. 'This I got from walking too close to a colt *marhaz;* still, we've an Earthspeaker here to care for us—yes! I almost forgot. Christie, it was known you'd be coming, and this one said he would wait to see you. I believe you have business with the Corbek Wellhouse?'

Beth'ru-elen's Earthspeaker courteously offered me a medical examination, and I was curious enough about Southland healing techniques to accept.

'Change the dressings on your feet again tomorrow,' the old man said. 'The nails should grow back, and the skin become a normal colour —this I would say for one of my own people.'

I re-laced the leather slippers. Beth'ru-elen's tiled floors were hard. However accurate this old man might be—and I didn't doubt that he was, with his own species—I missed Adair's diagnostic machines, micro-recorders, and allergy shots.

'Thank you for doing this.'

'Shall we say professional curiosity—for us both, *t'an* Christie.' He seated himself on the window-couch. Thick glass behind him distorted the snowlight. 'You have done much, though, and should rest.'

'I'm not planning anything strenuous.' What I worried about were deficiency diseases, malnutrition, exhaustion; and for these I had only the traditional Orthean cure. Time.

He looked shrewdly at me. He was a neat man, age showing about his mouth and his crest-mane. '*T'an*, you're young, so far as I may judge you're healthy, but I must warn you that you're approaching your limit. You were nearly six weeks living rough, you tell me. You have to build up resources.'

From Corbek to Shiriya-Shenin it had been five weeks and seven days, Torvern Fifthweek Fiveday to Riardh Sixthweek Twoday. Seven or eight weeks Earth-standard: it felt longer. And I knew it was that season, dry and cold, that had let us live. Summer's fever, winter's storms; they would have finished us.

'I'll be careful,' I said. '*S'an* Haike said that you wanted to speak to me. What's it about?'

His face changed to an expression as clear as cold water. 'I have had messages from Corbek. We must have the death-words for Theluk, and the *ashiren* cannot give them, nor the hired sword. We must have that for the Edris *telestre*. They will have their grief.'

'And you won't?' It was an unfair comment, but he was stirring up something I didn't want to see.

'Nothing ends,' the Earthspeaker said, turning to look at the sun through the glass, open-eyed to that pale blaze. 'Some say we spend our other lives in fire, visible here only as the face of the Goddess. That other order of being has its echoes here, its links and connections. We are a small land in a sea of fire, shot through with that invisible flame. She'll come scoured free by that fire, come again; knowing, breathing, living. No, we do not grieve.'

Ortheans burn their dead and cast the ashes into rivers: fire and water mark their passing. None have more of a grave than Theluk has.

'Tell me how she died,' the old man said. 'We will pass the word to Edris, and they will remember. You cannot give her the passing of fire, but this you can do.'

But I never knew her . . . and then thinking back, I realized I knew more than I thought.

'She was a brave woman,' I said, 'though having been a soldier at the Skulls garrison, I suppose that was never in doubt. She opposed Arad, Wellkeeper in Corbek, though he had great influence there. She had sense and endurance, she travelled up from Roehmonde's east coast, and knew then that the only person who would heed her was the Crown. Many of us benefited from her messages to Tathcaer. And she was generous: I don't believe she was afraid to stay in Corbek and face Arad, I think she knew Haltern and Maric and I wouldn't get out of the province without her help. When she died, it was because she was faced with fears that were special to her—even legends of the fenborn offended her—and she preferred to risk her life on the chance of getting free. She was tough, but she had less feeling for the marshes than for any part of the earth. She had the right to take the chance that she did. And it was only chance that it failed.'

The old Earthspeaker was quiet for a time, then he nodded. 'I have

it. That was well done, for an Outlander. It is a good word to take to
Edris, and a true one.'

It was only after he'd gone that I began to appreciate the custom.
Much of the weight of Theluk's death has lifted from me.

The guesting custom at Beth'ru-elen was that visitors worked. Being
singularly untalented, I usually ended up gathering and chopping
hanelys wood, or washing dishes, or mucking out the *skurrai* and *marhaz* pens. There were always two or three Earthspeakers at the *telestre,*
and I often saw one in the main hall practising the common script;
those *ashiren* who felt an interest copied her. It was some time before I
realized this was as close to formal education as they got, and joined in.

It wasn't difficult to live at Beth'ru-elen, and ride back to Shiriya-
Shenin on business. Nor difficult to find an excuse for not riding back—
snow and hail and rainstorms were frequent. The *telezu* custom that
Haltern was following, spending this season on the *telestre,* was elastic
enough to include the envoy.

Orventa is the longest season, twelve weeks from winter to spring
festival. Towards the end of that time I had become fluent in two or
three of Peir-Dadeni's complex dialects, including the southern. Back at
Shiriya-Shenin's Firstwall library I studied books on Kasabaarde, mem-
orizing fragments of that language. I had no orders to make contacts
outside the Southland—but I'd been contacted myself, and it might pay
to follow that up at a later date.

And that Orventa, at Beth'ru-elen and in the city, I began to play
ochmir in earnest. It hurt. It reminded me of Falkyr, of the Barrens city,
of that dead woman Sulis n'ri n'suth SuBannasen; and of the malice
against the envoy that was, like the Southland in winter, only quiescent.
Maybe that's why I played it with such intense concentration. With
Ruric, with Haltern, with Rodion, Blaize Meduenin—anyone. It has a
resonance with the Southland: the *ferrorn* static like the *s'an telestre,* the
thurin mobile as the *t'ans* are, and the *leremoc* rare and powerful as the
T'An Suthai-Telestre. The areas of conflict shift, what is yours may at
any moment be reversed and prove to be playing against you.

I learned a little: how to think ahead, spot the patterns, remember
what hieroglyphs the reversed counters hid. Most of my games still
ended in an avalanche of reversals spreading out from some minor lost
hexagon, but a few were hard-fought. I was learning.

Orventa in closed Shiriya-Shenin is a time for indoor pursuits to flourish: plays are written and performed, *arykei* courted, weapons tourna-

ments are devised, and there are the inevitable marathon games of *ochmir* that last the nine-day-week from Feastday to Fastday. Gossip, satirical songs—and scientific experiments, under the close eye of the church.

After I'd seen steam and clockwork mechanisms, weaving machines, gun-powder and primitive electric motors, I decided that the Southland could have an industrial revolution any time it liked. And after I'd seen the devices dismantled and ignored by their inventors, I understood why they would not. The ghost of the Barrens hung over Shiriya-Shenin, and what I had learned of past-memories came sharply back to me.

In Orventa Eightweek came a slow thaw that isolated everything, and caught me at Beth'ru-elen. The rivers were in flood, the roads impassable. It was Orventa Tenweek before things dried out enough to make travelling possible.

I added more laboriously handwritten pages to the report I was compiling. It was difficult to pin the Ortheans down to an official view of the Dominion. Individual views, yes, from Ruric's acceptance of mutual kinship down to the anonymous stones shied at me in backstreets. But no one would commit themselves to a coherent policy I could pass back to Earth.

The winds turned southerly, the air warm. I rode back to Shiriya-Shenin through slopping mud, Rodion with me. *Hanelys*, black all winter, broke out in a fur of tiny scarlet flowers. The brown dead moss-grass, scuffed up, disclosed new grey-green spring growth. *Kekri* flies in hoards hummed on a pitch that would shatter glass. The terraced slopes round the city were thick with new shoots.

Expectancy was in the air.

'Duined wants an appointment.' Rodion sat down at my desk as *ke* sorted through the pile of messages. 'Downriver man, wants to talk about trade.'

'Much good it'll do him. Make it for Fiveday. What else?'

The tawny eyes flicked up. 'Berun n'ri n'suth Sarsyan again.'

'What does she want?'

'She wants to be your *arykei*, of course.' The *ashiren* grinned. 'You can't blame anyone for being curious, S'aranth.'

'Can't I, though?'

'Here's something.' *Ke* read briefly. 'A note from *t'an* Haltern, dated noon. A meeting in the Andrethe's Hall—they've had news through from Melkathi about the new *T'An*.'

The hall was large, built of yellow glazed bricks. A double row of forked pillars supported the low ceiling. The lozenge-shaped windows had hanging curtains of silver discs on cords, twisting and flashing in the spring sunlight. It was still wet outside. Muddy six-toed tracks crossed the geometrically patterned tiles. Silver bead curtains hung in the doorways, fastened back in the spaces between the pillars. A raised platform at one end held padded backless chairs. The wall behind me was patterned with the spiral symbols of the Goddess. The hall was filling with *tha'adur* and *takshiriye,* but at the moment the platform was empty.

Rodion was missing, as usual. I couldn't see Haltern or Ruric, so was pleased when I did find a face I knew.

'T'an Brodin.'

'Christie. You have heard the news, then?' He drew aside to let several *t'ans* pass.

'Melkathi have chosen their new *T'An,* yes. Do we know who?'

'No, this has been kept secret until the Crown should make the announcement.' He shrugged. 'Myself, I would say another of the SuBannasen *telestre.'*

That was news I didn't want to hear. 'Not Oreyn Orhlandis?'

'I doubt that—' he broke off. 'Here they are.'

My position close to the pillar commanded a good view of the now crowded platform. The Andrethe stood with Suthafiori and many of the *takshiriye.* One of the Crown Guard beat on a drumframe, and the talk died.

'Hear me!' Suthafiori's voice penetrated effortlessly to the back of the hall. 'I call you together, you of the Hundred Thousand: hear what I say and carry the news. The *T'An* Melkathi is named.'

The drum beat once and was silent.

'The symbol of Melkathi is returned from SuBannasen *telestre.'* Oreyn Orhlandis stepped forward with a plain silver circlet in his hands, and gave it to the Crown.

'Called for Melkathi, called by the *s'an telestres,'* Suthafiori said, 'is *amari* Ruric Orhlandis.'

'What?' Brodin said, his usual poise gone.

'Ruric?' I was astounded. 'Lord, I knew she said Orhlandis, but— good grief!'

The first buzz of surprise broke up into the scattered hissing and hand-beating that is their applause. I saw Ruric then, walking with her dark head up and her shoulders taut. A night-blue cloak draped her.

She wore a single silver *harur* blade. The *tha'adur* and *takshiriye* drew aside and she stood alone before Suthafiori.

'*Amari* Ruric Orhlandis,' Suthafiori said in the formal inflection, 'do you accept the office named?'

'I accept the office of *T'An* Melkathi, laying down all other offices I now hold.' There was no detectable nervousness in her voice.

'*Amari* Ruric Orhlandis, *T'An* Melkathi,' Suthafiori pronounced. 'By the power of the earth that we all return to, by power of fire and water through which we pass, I bid you take this outward symbol of the Melkathi *telestres* and bear it well. Their kin are your kin, their wishes your wishes, their welfare your own.'

'I receive this into my care,' Ruric answered, 'holding the land as the hand of the Goddess on earth. I will act to each *telestre* as if it were my own. This shall endure until the *s'an telestres* revoke it. Be it so, in Her name.'

'In Her name,' the Crown said, and placed the silver circlet on the dark woman's head. Against the black mane it caught the light and blazed like a star.

It was some time later, during the celebrations, that I finally got to speak to Ruric.

'*T'an* Melkathi.' I managed a respectable bow.

'What? Christie, you—' her dismay vanished. 'Sunmother's tits! I thought you meant it.'

'How about that?' I said after we embraced. 'Now I have to bow three times before speaking, and watch out for the assassin's blade.'

'Lackwit Outworlder,' she said goodnaturedly. Haltern was beside her, his pudgy features fixed in a smug grin. She gripped his shoulder hard.

'You and Oreyn, you've left me a job—Melkathi, grief of the Goddess! And I suppose I shall have to live in Ales-Kadareth, and let Asshe have the Guard.' She pointed Asshe out to me, a grim, grey-maned little man with a bantam-cock air. 'He's Skulls commander, I dare say he can handle it. Mother! I wish I thought I could handle Melkathi.'

Haltern, I thought, and Oreyn, and who else? Hal's a Crown Messenger, no need to ask if Suthafiori supports this.

'You'll manage,' I said.

'*S'aranth!*' Rodion yelled.

I came out of the *jayante* courts sweating and rubbing bruises. Blaize's efforts to teach me the use of Orthean weapons had largely been a failure, simply because Ortheans fight ambidextrously and I remained obstinately right-handed. The only weapon I showed any promise at was the *jayante,* a short, weighted quarterstaff, and I practised with all the more determination for knowing that the single remaining power pack for the stunner was half exhausted. Blaize's bruising enthusiasm I put down to revenge.

'Well?' I said.

'The Andrethe wants you,' *ke* said, 'in the Crystal Hall.'

'What does she want now?'

The *ashiren* shrugged. Kanta Andrethe monopolized the Dominion envoy in the same spirit that she studied new animals in her menagerie. I sighed and headed back to my rooms to change. Halls, corridors, courtyards: and never a place in all the Firstwall warren to be private.

'Where's my knife-belt?' I demanded, hurriedly lacing on a clean *chirith-goyen* shirt. 'Have you seen it?'

'I expect someone took it,' *ke* said, 'I'll try and get it back.'

Dadeni has no word for 'steal', only less welcome inflections of the word for 'take'. When it comes to property, all Ortheans have a very imperfect idea of mine and thine.

In Dadeni the coinage consists of metal discs or beads threaded on cords, traditionally worn round the neck or waist. I'd had to adopt that custom in lieu of a wallet, after mine went missing. As for my property —that refined itself down to personal documents, reports for the department, and the stunner, all of which I kept in a pack; and the only way I could keep Rodion's fingers out of it was to tell *kir* it was dangerous. True, in a way. If *ke* pilfered those from me, *ke'd* be in as great a danger as *ke* was ever likely to be.

I turned over a few pillows, books from the Firstwall library, but couldn't find the knife-belt. I gave up: I'd have to be informally dressed.

The door of the Crystal Hall was ajar when I arrived. I knocked— never having been able to break the habit—and went in. Spring twilight filled the chamber, the quartz windows gleaming. No lamps were alight. The braziers were red embers.

Did Rodion tell me the wrong place? I wondered. There was a sharp familiar scent in the air.

The Andrethe had her back to me, sitting in a chair facing one of the dying fires.

'Excuse me, excellence . . .'

She made no sign that she heard me. She was leaning back, one fat arm over the side of the chair. Asleep, I thought, now how do I do this tactfully? As I stepped round her, over the dappled furs, the spring light shone on her dark face and red-and-white robe. Her fingers held reflected red firelight, streaming on the furs and stone flags; and the smell came up in a wave.

Firstwall's kitchens and slaughterhouses.

Not a red robe. A white robe, sopping red from shoulder to lap to hem. Running like water, soaking into the furs. Grey cold air, and the stink of blood and faeces. Blood dripping from her curved fingers, covering the gold studs. Her open unveiled eyes stared at me—she must be alive, she moved! I thought. And then realized it was illusion. Not breathing, not blinking. Jammed under her chin amid rolls of flesh, a knife-handle kept her head back. There shouldn't be so much blood, blood shouldn't be so thin—

Jack-knifed forward, acrid liquid spilling from mouth and nostrils; I heard noises from the corridor. Then the room was full of people shouting.

22

Berani's Lament

Ruric's single hand shook me. I tried to tell her it was unnecessary. I knew what was happening.

'I found her,' I said.

'Found her? Killed her!' Brodin stood by the chair, hands red, tears streaking his face. Good-natured lampoons linked he and Kanta as *arykei*, I hadn't credited them until now.

'Is that your knife?' Khassiye Reihalyn demanded.

'I—yes, I had a knife taken: Rodion will tell you—'

'I expect *ke* will. Being Halfgold.'

Suthafiori was there, Hellel Hanathra was there; I didn't remember seeing them come in. I wanted to avoid looking at the dead woman.

'Listen,' Brodin faced Suthafiori angrily, 'this thing comes to you, it says: I'm from another world. And you sit there and you believe it! Even when you hear the truth you don't believe it. Witchbreed! Look at her *l'ri-an*, look at her companions—'

'I know your grief.' Ruric bent over the body, studying it with a clinical detachment. 'I'll say I didn't hear that.'

Someone's gone to a lot of trouble to make me look guilty, I thought. I felt dizzy. 'Why should I do this?'

Brodin ignored me, still speaking to the Crown. 'Leave Dadeni without the Andrethe, now, when she's most needed—she was your equal, now who is there to prevent you? They call you mad, believing in other worlds. You're not mad, no. And not above using Witchbreed to further your own purposes.'

'Mourn the dead later, and I will join you.' Suthafiori spoke mildly. 'If I have been mistaken in these people, it will be seen. Keep the envoy under guard.'

'Your pardon,' Khassiye interrupted, 'I've arrested her already under Dadeni custom.'

'And I under Crown law,' Suthafiori said. 'Ruric, take her. Khassiye, I give you acting authority for Shiriya-Shenin until this is over.'

It was quiet outside the Crystal Hall.

'Go back to your rooms and wait,' Ruric said. 'I'll find Asshe, get him to send a couple of guards along in a minute.'

'I didn't do it. You know that.'

Her yellow eyes glinted. 'I know. If it were you, she would have had a broken neck—S'aranth. As for being a true Outworlder . . . if you're a liar, you're an exceptional one, none of your stories contradict each other. No, the guards are for your protection, Christie. When this is known, there'll be many won't wait for the trial to decide on their verdict.'

Unconcerned faces passed me. How long would that last? Time's deceptive, it was only a few minutes later in that spring afternoon. Alone now in an alien land—news wouldn't take long to get out, would it?

Someone already knew. The killer.

Blaize n'ri n'suth Meduenin stood up as I entered my rooms. 'I've heard some disturbing rumours—'

'Too late, as usual. I don't know what I pay you for.' A kind of manic hilarity succeeded the numbness. I acted purely on instinct. Took the ET report from my pack, handed it to him. Unlooped a cord of silver coins from my neck. Gave them to him.

'Take Gher from the stables—don't let anyone see you—and go overland to Tathcaer. Give the report to the xeno-team. You're a Rimon man, you must know the country. Go.'

He didn't ask questions, just took the cord of money and slipped out. I picked up a hooded becamil cloak, the pack, and then the jayante in its backstrap. I might have been expecting this, I realized suddenly; this or something like it. All my personal belongings were in the pack. It was only necessary to pick it up and leave.

No one gave me a second look. I pulled the cloak on while I crossed the muddy courtyard. If I could beat the news to Fifthwall, leave the city—

'S'aranth,' Rodion called, 'where are you going?'

I touched the jayante. But fighting would attract attention, and I couldn't fight ashiren. The goldskinned face was bland. Ke hasn't heard yet, I thought.

'Come with me.'

Envoy and *l'ri-an*, that was a familiar enough sight in the streets of Shiriya-Shenin. Wind flayed my face as we came out from under the Firstwall L'ku Gate.

'Are there riverships leaving today?'

'It's Fiveday holiday . . . but yes, I think so. Why?'

'I'm leaving the city,' I said. A route sketched itself in my mind, familiar from maps. Down the Ai river to Morvren Freeport, then up the Rimon coast to Tathcaer. Safer to be on the Crown's island—if I could get that far. If nothing else, Tathcaer had ships for the Eastern Isles. For Earth.

'I'll come,' Rodion said.

'You don't know why I'm going. It's too dangerous to involve *ashiren.*' If I'd been thinking, I wouldn't have said that.

'Is it my fault I'm *ashiren?* I'm your *l'ri-an*, and I'm coming with you. If I stay, they'll make me tell where you went.' *Ke* eyed me. 'Why do you have to leave, *S'aranth?*'

Secondwall, Thirdwall, and still the Watch passed us through. And now we were lost in the Fiveday holiday crowds round the markets.

'Because I don't propose to be locked up again, certainly not for a murder I didn't commit.' And because it's too easy for one minor Dominion official to just vanish, I thought, and because the Southland has nothing resembling justice.

Kir eyes widened, clearing. 'Murder?'

I pulled the cloak's hood up, protecting against the wind and prying eyes. People jostled past.

'You come,' I said. 'When I get far enough downriver, I'll pay your passage back here. You'll bring messages from me to the authorities, saying what I'm doing and why. By that time it won't matter. You do what I say, Rodion.'

Ke looked as though it was difficult to take in the facts. Uncertain, now, whether *ke* wanted to accompany me.

'I'll do it,' Rodion said. *'S'aranth*, you have to keep me quiet one way or another. This is the best.'

Forthwall, Fifthwall, the ziggurat towers squat against the sky. The city opened out to grey gleaming river. Cold water lapped at the wooden piers. Now it was a matter of chance, finding out if there was a ship going downriver. Leaving immediately, I thought, looking back at the city, imagining the alarm going out even now.

The rivership's hull sliced through brown water. Twigs swirled in the wake. Brushwood clumbered the bank, left behind from the spring floods. I leaned against the rail, facing away from the people on board.

'The shipmaster wants half-fee now,' Rodion said. 'Where do we want to go to?'

'Where's a large river *telestre,* one that has many ships calling?'

'Kepulanan,' *ke* suggested. 'Hassichil. Pel'shennin.'

'Hassichil.' Unknotting a cord, I counted off silver coins. 'Tell the shipmaster that your *t'an* suffers pain from an old wound, and will likely stay in her cabin for most of the trip.'

'They'll wonder,' *ke* said, 'and when the word goes out, they'll remember us. *S'aranth,* what did you *do?*'

'Nothing. Do what I say.'

Twilight drifted blue over the terraced land, mist rising on the reed-choked banks of the river. I kept the cloak's hood up and avoided meeting anyone's eyes. Below, in the tiny cabin, I discarded the pack and *jayante* and lay back on the bench-bed.

'*S'aranth,*' Rodion said, 'are you sick?'

Ke thought *ke* was on a voyage with a madwoman. I closed my eyes, feeling Rodion's gaze burn into me. Not mad, I thought. Maybe a little unstable at the moment—but not mad, no indeed.

'Where is this?' It was nearly second twilight, a day downriver from Shiriya-Shenin.

Rodion peered at the markstone by the landing stage. 'Baharu-bazuriye.'

'Go down and get my pack. See you're not noticed.'

Beyond the landing stage, masked by giant reedbeds, rose the flat roofs of a large *telestre* house. Town-sized, with warehouses and companion-houses. Good. One of the trade *telestres*—pottery, glass, *becamil* and similar—who'd be used to travellers.

Rodion followed me off the rivership into the crowd at the landing stage. No one saw us go. There's a good chance they won't miss us here, I thought, then they won't know where we disembarked. They're expecting us to go to Hassichil. . . .

'Are we staying at a companion-house?' Rodion asked.

'And have them remember us?'

'Where, then?'

There were market stalls set out under *becamil* awnings round the *telestre* walls. I saw no uniforms of the Crown Guard or Andrethe city Watch, but that meant nothing. Will this count as Wellhouse business? I wondered. If it does, they'll send the news out on the *rashaku* relay. And there's no chance of outdistancing that.

'The market first. Blankets and provisions.' I thumbed the cord of coins. No, not poor yet.

The twilight faded quickly. I kept on the move, spine prickling with apprehension. The companion-houses were small, both were likely to note and remember us. I wanted somewhere crowded enough to be lost in. I retraced my steps, back down muddy tracks near the landing stage. There was an alternative. Long, low warehouses stood untenanted, some half-demolished by the winter storms. One door swung open when I pushed.

'It's going to be cold,' Rodion objected.

'The beginning of Hanys. It shouldn't freeze.' I laid out blankets under the soundest-looking area of roof. Rodion unrolled the spare cloak on the wooden floor. I was asleep before *ke* finished muttering complaints.

Wood scraped as the door opened.

Rodion was up and moving and the door was opening and someone came in and *ke* struck once, bare-handed, without even time to draw *kir* knife. Then someone grunted and fell heavily, Rodion was standing wringing *kir* hand, and I staggered up and pushed the door to.

I limped back. The cold had numbed my feet, woken me six or seven times. Now I felt disorientated.

The Orthean wore drab Dadeni work-robes, and he—no, she—lay on her back, a thick slug of blood creeping from her nose, in a vile parody of sleep.

I must have stood just looking at the woman for several minutes. Sleep froze my mind. That blur of movement—but violence is always quick, unexpected. I blotted out memories of Shiriya-Shenin.

She breathed shallowly, damply, on my palm. I wiped my hand, rolled her eyelid back with my thumb, the whiteless eye was opaqued by the nictitating membrane. Her skin was rough, winter-patterned. One outstretched hand twitched, claws scraped the hard wood.

What did you come here for? Tools, a place to be private, what? Was it just another misty chill morning, and did you step in here a moment out of the wind? And now all changed, in the fraction of a heartbeat, forever different.

'*S'aranth,* what are you doing?' Rodion was at the door, with the pack and cloaks.

'She might need medical attention—'

'She'll come to in a minute,' the *ashiren* said. *'S'aranth,* we can't stay here!'

It was true, there was no way out of it. Rodion looked at me anxiously and without a trace of regret.

The dark blood—darker than human—was stilled, drying. And I left her there, hurt; not without a second thought, it's true, but what use is thought without action? I never sent help, I never spoke of her. I still regret that.

Outside, river mist hid us from casual eyes. Carrick's Star was rising, saffron over the eastern plain. The tracks confused me in the half-light. After a few minutes—seeming like hours—I found the one that followed the river south-west.

'Do you know how far until we come to another *telestre?*'

Rodion shook *kir* head.

'Until the next landing stage?'

Another headshake.

'Then we'd better keep walking.'

Double-bladed reeds hid the river's edge. As the sun rose higher it shone on the desolate land a few *seri* to the west. Then, as light filled the vast dome of the empty sky, smoke trails went up from the opposite bank. Sails of early riverships showed white.

'I'm hungry,' Rodion said. 'We should have bought more food in the market.'

'The next place we see,' I promised. Thinking, how long since I ate? On the riverboat before Baharu-bazuriye . . . yes, once yesterday. Not today.

My mind closed down to narrow focus, only aware of the rough track. Winter had left it rutted, pocked with deep holes; obviously none of the *telestre* road-gangs had come this way yet. I felt dimly sorry that Rodion should be hungry and tired—*kir* eyes were showing their whites with sleeplessness—but I was riding some adrenalin-high, and feeling nothing at all.

That day was long, and I couldn't have foreseen its ending.

The morning sun was warm. A chill wind rattled the new growth on the reeds. No one passed me. I searched ahead, trying to pick out the hearth-smoke of a *telestre.*

'S'aranth. . . .'

'What?' I snapped irritably.

Without hysteria, but with complete determination, Rodion said, 'I have to sleep.'

'Now?'

'I shouldn't—' *ke* blinked, rubbed *kir* forehead, and without any warning pitched forward. I caught *kir* as *ke* slammed into the earth, the warm heavy body limp in my arms.

'Rodion?'

Dirt clung to grazes in *kir* golden skin. Hunger, was it, or fatigue? But the scale-pattern skin was rough, damp to the touch. When I thumbed *kir* eyelids back the membranes were retracted, the eyes rolled up to show half the whites.

The wind blew, and *rashaku* fluted, too high to be seen. Blood drummed in my ears. I slapped *kir* face lightly, holding back fury—I couldn't afford delay now! Had I asked to have an *ashiren* with me?

Ke didn't wake. I abandoned all but my pack, hoisted *kir* over my shoulder, staggering—*ke* was all but adult height and weight—and plodded on down the road. There had to be a *telestre* up ahead. There had to be.

A cluster of small buildings hugged a landing stage. Noon sun made me sweat. Rodion's body was a dead weight. Truly? I thought, close to panic, but then I felt *kir* ribs moving with shallow breaths. I might have come two *seri* or three, in fits and starts. I was ready to collapse myself.

A man left the yard, halted, and came running.

'Can you help—'

He helped me to lower *kir*. He was a dark Orthean, with broad shoulders under his work-robe. All his attention was on the *ashiren*.

'How long has *ke* been this way?'

'Up the road—a way back—' I couldn't get my breath. 'Is there a physician? An Earthspeaker?'

He nodded sharply, scooped Rodion up in his arms, and I followed him in through the door of the *telestre*-house. For a time I had no strength to do anything. One of the old women gave me a wine flask, while shouting to an *ashiren* to fetch the Earthspeaker. I found myself in a side room, while the man who carried Rodion was putting *kir* into a cot-bed by the hearth there.

Rodion's head rolled from side to side, making guttural noises in *kir* throat. Midday sun came through the narrow window and gleamed on gold skin and pale hair. I heard muttered comments. And kept my hood up, hoping that *kir* appearance as Halfgold would keep them from seeing I was Outworlder.

'Is *ke* late coming to this, *t'an?*'

An ebony-skinned male in Earthspeaker's robes examined Rodion, holding *kir* six-fingered hands in his.

'Late?'

His pale eyes unveiled, hearing my accent. Disguise doesn't depend on concealment but on attitude. Not to look him in the eyes, not to think differently from an Orthean.

'You're Outlander,' he said.

'Yes, from—' the lie came seamlessly '—the Desert Coast. But the *ashiren?*'

'*Ke* has come late to the change,' he said, turning and giving sharp orders for blankets. An old woman returned with them and a double handful of herbs. I sat in the shadow by Rodion while the Earthspeaker set them boiling in a pan over the hearth. The *ashiren* twitched, eyes half open, mumbling inaudibly.

If *ke* dies? I thought suddenly.

The Earthspeaker cleared the room of people and tied the curtain shut. He brought the steaming pan over to the bed, and while I held *kir* shoulders he bathed *kir* with the infusion.

'Now cover *kir,*' he said, and we wrapped *kir* in pelts. 'It's hard when it comes late, but over sooner. One way or the other.'

'Will *ke* be all right?'

He shrugged. Noting cloak, pack, and *jayante* he said, 'You must break your travels here until it is over.'

Noon declined towards evening. I heard others come in, voices beyond the curtained archway, but we were not disturbed. Sometimes Rodion thrashed in pain, so that it took the Earthspeaker and myself all our strength to hold *kir* down. At last *ke* appeared to sleep.

'Now we wait. Will you eat with us?' the Orthean asked. 'Or if your customs demand you eat alone, Outlander, I will have a meal sent to you.'

'Thank you, yes, if you will.' There were many Outlanders on the Ai, that river they call the highway of Peir-Dadeni. The Earthspeaker's tone had all the insular Southland dislike for the Desert Coast.

'Where are you from, *t'an?*'

'Kasabaarde.' It was the only Desert Coast city I knew the name of, besides Kel Harantish. And that, with Rodion Halfgold there, didn't rate a mention.

'You are not bound to wear your masks always, then?'

Masks? The lie came as easy as breathing. 'Not outside the city. You are a traveller also?'

'On the Ai. I'm Pel'kasir,' he said, 'from the Hassichil Wellhouse. You know Hassichil?'

I shook my head. Fencing with him, not easy. 'We may have seen it from the ship, coming upriver.'

'To Shiriya-Shenin?' he guessed.

'My companions go there. I had a fancy to follow on land and join them there. But now . . .'

'The change is under way,' Pel'kasir said. 'If *ke* passes midnight, it will be well.'

I dozed as the evening wore on. Rodion's cries woke me. Pel'kasir soothed *kir* again with the herb-solution. I tried to keep the pelts over *kir.* The silverwhite mane matted, coming loose from its braids. Tendrils clung to the rough skin surrounding the tawny eyes. *Ke* stared without seeing me.

Sometime in the late hours *ke* lapsed into a deep trance-like sleep.

'It's over,' Pel'kasir said with relief. He drew the pelts back, wiping the infusion over newly-smooth skin. 'There'll be internal changes for a while yet. Some days rest. Don't move . . . yes, *ashiren-te,* yes . . .'

There was not much to see. A swelling round the upper pair of nipples, the genital slit more pronounced. But it was an unmistakable change. Pel'kasir drew the furs up over the gold-skinned shoulders, and the tawny eyes opened and knew me.

'Ah, she will have *ashiren* of her own someday,' the Earthspeaker said, brushing the mane back off her forehead. The expression in his eyes might have been envy.

'*S'ar*—' a smile shone out, then her lids came down. She slept again.

'Now you may sleep,' Pel'kasir said. 'She is safe.'

'Thank you.' Exhausted, I had no words for gratitude.

'She should not be moved for several days.'

'No. No, we'll stay here.' I stood stiffly. 'Is it possible to borrow paper and a writing-stick? I must send word upriver so my companions don't worry about us.'

The Earthspeaker nodded. 'Many boats pass here; one will surely take your message in the morning.'

Morning came: I hadn't slept. The urgency of getting downriver was obvious, and I was acutely impatient.

'Where are you for?'

'Downstream.' The Orthean woman leaned over the docked ship's rail. 'Lei'eriel *telestre.*'

'How far is that?'

She stepped back to avoid two of the handlers stacking bales of *becamil*-wrapped pottery. 'Forty, maybe fifty *seri.* Well, Outlander, are you coming?'

'Yes. Wait.'

'Not long!' she called after me.

Rodion was sleeping when I left her. I took pack and *jayante*, pulling on the heavy cloak. Her face was untroubled. I knotted a cord of silver and copper coins round her wrist, and re-read the short message I was leaving her.

Rodion—

I intend going on as planned. When you are well, continue on to Shiriya-Shenin. You will have much to tell our companions there. But do not on any account go before you feel ready. I have left you enough money to pay for food for two weeks. Hoping to see you fully recovered when we meet again,

—C

Hanys Firstweek Sixday.

You'll take the hint, I thought, looking down at her. And by the time you get to Shiriya-Shenin I'll have taken ship from Morvren, and by then it won't matter. No one will blame you for anything.

I got aboard the rivership while they were loading water casks. No one saw me go. Mooring ropes were cast off, a distance of water opened between ship and landing stage.

Maric had taught me not to take *ashiren* where I went. Granted Rodion was adult now, but this might prove more dangerous than the journey across the Barrens. There, there was only the land to fight. Now I faced the Orthean game, directed against me alone. And I was no expert player.

With the landing at Lei'eriel, I began to come out of the trance of panic that had surrounded me since Shiriya-Shenin.

'Outlander?' a young woman said. 'You'll have come to see Berani's Watchtower, then. They all do.'

The gates of Lei'eriel *telestre* stood open. The woman was sitting in a low chair, robe unlaced, feeding a baby. Two others kicked on the *zilmei* pelt spread at her feet. They were bare to the afternoon sun. Thin down marked their spines. To me they looked tiny, lizard-like.

'You can just see it from here.' The woman pointed towards the western hills that were closer to the river here. I squinted, could just distinguish angular lines.

'Is that the actual tower?' It seemed a safe thing to say.

'Yes, the one in the "Lament".' One of the *ashiren* rolled over, its mouth squared and it began to howl. She scooped it up, putting the other one down on the feather-fur. 'Sssh . . . Terai, *ashiren-te.* . . . '

'If I go up there, will I be able to get a boat downriver this evening?'

She frowned, humming under her breath. The child squalled. She sang ' "Thousandflower, bird's-wing, and sweet mosseye; sweet wine and sour wine where tall ships go by. . . ." oh, you brat.'

It dribbled milk on her shoulder. She pulled up the hem of her robe to dab it dry. 'There're no downriver boats till morning,' she added, having thought. 'Most Outland folks stay over here.'

I took a room and—more to keep myself out of sight for the afternoon than anything else—walked the two *seri* up into the hills. They were desolate, stony, flecked here and there with brown mossgrass. A path had been hacked through stunted *hanelys.* It was dusty walking.

From the Watchtower knoll I saw the Ai valley laid out below me. Eastwards was fat land, pasture and newly-ploughed grain country, growing on the river's silt. Terraces had been replaced by irrigation channels. Downriver the view was blocked by a spur of these hills. Rounding the knoll, wind blew dust over cracked flagstones.

The remains of the brickwork ended abruptly on the scarp side. There had been rockfalls. A ring of the outer wall was standing. The steep western scarp fell two or three hundred feet to a plain, desolate as the hills, that stretched out to the horizon.

Berani's Watchtower . . . yes, one of the wailing atonal Dadeni songs mentioned it, I remembered at the court. I'd paid little attention.

The sun reflected off something in the western distance. At first I took it for water, but it didn't end as water does. Where it touched the brown heath—seven or eight *seri* out on the plain, I estimated—it ended it streaks. Sharp edges, like cat-ice on a puddle, like splinters. With the sheen of volcanic glass. Then the sun cleared the haze, and all that horizon blazed with unbearable light.

I walked round the ruined tower, blinking the spots out of my vision, and came to where a newer stone had been set up. Common script was cut into it:

'Here was Berani's Watchtower, where of old they kept lookout across the Glittering Plain towards the danger that lies in Eriel.'

Orthe defeated me. I admitted it then, confronted with my ignorance. I sat down on old steps. Nothing was left of the hall but a
depression in the ground. My back against sunwarmed brick, I looked
down at the Ai.

Berani's Lament. Bits of it returned to me. There was a flavour of
betrayal about it, though whether Berani had been betrayed or betrayer
I didn't know. A flavour of treachery. Very apt, I thought.

So I let my mind go back and touch what it had been avoiding for
days. Kanta Andrethe's butchered death. Somehow I needed to grieve.
I let the release come, weeping. For her. For Brodin, that bereaved man.
For myself. If there was self-pity, now was the time to get rid of it.

Self-pity. Haltern: why couldn't he have helped me? Ruric. What
did she mean: *if* you're a liar . . . and the arrogance, expecting me to
wait, unguarded, for Southland justice. The old childish complaint: why
didn't somebody *do* something?

Feeling faintly disgusted, I wiped my face and relaxed back in the
sun. Whatever: the events at the Andrethe court had occurred. Now it
was up to me to deal with it. Haltern and Ruric had been caught as flat-
footed as I had. No one's fault.

Yes. One. The killer. Could I speculate who it was? Another of the
SuBannasen? Howice? An enemy in Shiriya-Shenin? No, that was part
of the game of intrigue: it could be any one of a hundred people. . . .

What to do now, though? Tathcaer's still the safest place for an
Outworlder to be. Is Suthafiori still supporting the Dominion? I wondered. If not, ships to the Eastern Isles might be hard to come by.

Lord, Christie! I thought, laughing to myself. A few weeks ago you
were planning to stay on Orthe, and now look at the panic when you
think you might have to . . .

I woke when the sun had moved off the wall. A blue twilight hung
in the river valley, and lanterns glowed like *siriye*. The sky was clear,
purple in the west, star-speckled in the east. For a minute I was anxious
that I wouldn't be able to see my way back. Then I realized I only had
to wait out the second twilight, and Orthe's stars would be bright
enough to show me the path.

PART
SEVEN

23

Freeport

A watery haze hung over the river, softening the edges of riverboat sails and the last, dimly visible ridge of south-Dadeni's hills.

'I go no further south,' Dennet bawled. She was a leathery-skinned Orthean woman from south-Dadeni, running her tiny boat between there and the Morvren *telestres* with a crew of two *ashiren*.

'How far to the city?'

'About two *seri* down that way—you'll find a ferry to take you across.' She turned and spat *ataile* over the side, and yelled at the child on the tiller to bring the craft in to the landing stage.

Landing stops dotted this eastern bank of the Ai, mostly where tracks from distant *telestres* came down to the river. The far bank was invisible in the haze. Here the Ai runs out into estuaries and sand-bars and backwaters, the great river spidering out between flat slabs of low-land to the sea. I breathed deeply, catching the warm sparky tang of the ocean. It was subtly different from seas round the British Isles, less salty, less harsh. A warm wind blew off the land. *Rashaku-bazur* screeched. The water turned yellow and brown with the sand of Orthe's solar tides.

Southern latitudes. I thought us a good two hundred *seri* south of Tathcaer. I'd caught the spring weather, running downriver into it. Now it was Hanys Thirdweek, still liable to rainstorms, but hot.

The *ashiren* unloaded crates on to the jetty. *Marhaz* were visible on the upstream road and one of the riders waved a greeting. I paid the woman, mostly in coppers—it wasn't wise to appear too rich.

'There's unchancy folks in Freeport,' she said by way of farewell. 'Goddess give you a safe journey.'

'And to your mother's daughter, Dennet.'

I set off walking on the southward track, but stopped after a few minutes to take off the thick *becamil* cloak and strap it on top of my pack. The *jayante* settled awkwardly beside it.

Siir choked the riverbank. I walked between the thick, grey-silver stems. Like *hanelys*, it hugged the ground. Great trunks thick as a man's body grew up three feet or so and then looped over to lay along the earth, winding among other *siir* stems. Rosettes of chrome yellow leaves grew on the sunward-facing side of the stems. Bread-fungus hugged the ground under them, together with spring flowers, blue and purple and white. Down on the sandy earth of the river's edge were carpets of the black-centred flowers with ragged orange petals that Ortheans call City-in-Flames.

Close by a junction of tracks, a man was fishing.

'This the right way for Morvren Freeport?'

He looked me up and down, grunted, and waded back to his net. He muttered something about Outlanders that I didn't catch. Some Southlanders' tolerance stops dead at the *telestre* border.

Over the water, I began to see roofs shimmering in the haze, and the tall vanes of windpumps. There was no high land. If it had been clear, I could have seen for miles. I walked on. The pack-straps chafed my shoulders. Apart from sweating in the unaccustomed heat, I had an allergic rash from the river's eternal diet of *hura* stew and bread-fungus. It seemed to last forever, walking over that flat land.

Approaching the coast, I found myself in company with *skurrai* carts and *marhaz* riders, and men and women walking in towards the city. No one paid me any attention, except for the inevitable glances that labelled me as Outlander. Morvren Freeport was clearer now, visible across a stretch of water. It looked to be built across several of the flat islands out in the estuary. Low, biscuit-coloured buildings rose above jetties, where many small boats were sailing. All the traffic on this bank was heading down towards a cluster of wooden shacks.

Eighteen days from north Dadeni down to here. Going southwest all the time, between fat eastern lands and desolate western hills. Days and days of sailing past *ziku* and *lapuur* forests. Days and days of south Dadeni's wealthy river-meadows, thick with grazing *skurrai* and *marhaz*. It was too early to get a passenger ship clear down to Morvren, so I boat-hopped. Sometimes on cargo ships or slow barges, sometimes on tiny boats like Dennet's. Once or twice I saw Crown Messengers. More often I heard *rashaku* relay gossip about the Andrethe's death. But I was ahead of it, travelling incognito, the cords of money growing lighter round my neck, the stunner close at hand.

I thought, *what am I doing here?*

Travelling down the Ai had been good. Conversations with shipmasters, landholders, traders, in company with those who collected orders for glass, forgeware, grain, cloth . . . Dadeni waking from its winter stillness, re-forging the ancient linkage of trade and barter that connects all the river *telestres.* Unknown among them, travelling unrecognized on an alien world . . . that was adventure in the old sense! Even as I laughed at the thought, I enjoyed it.

Only now I was coming to a city again—and I was beginning to share the Orthean fascination with, and distrust of, cities. I had to enter the Freeport to get passage on a ship. To where, though? Tathcaer might be no safer than Shiriya-Shenin. The longer I was out of sight, the more chance they'd find the real killer . . . or would they? They were convinced it was me. And I couldn't function as envoy until the matter was settled.

I shouldered through the crowd, blinking in the heat. Sheds and stables edged the river, and a disreputable-looking companion-house. Carts queued on a slipway where a floating platform berthed. Smaller ferries were plying for hire. It didn't take long to find one willing to take me across the water.

Ship's fees and companion-houses eat away at cash. I might still have enough to book passage for the nine hundred *seri* up the coast to Tathcaer. Certainly I couldn't afford to stay long in the Freeport.

The boat rocked in the deep channel, the rower's stroke strengthened. Spray tasted metallic on my lips. We docked at the end of a long jetty. This was a walled city: sunbaked brick to a height of six feet, with one main gate choked by carts, and several smaller ones jammed with pedestrians. Men and women in sandy-coloured uniforms guarded all the gates.

They were checking papers. By the time I saw that, there was nothing to do but go forward.

'Permit,' a tall woman demanded, eyes veiled against the dust stirred up by the carts.

'My companions have them.' I made a vague gesture back at the river. My accent puzzled her, I saw. 'In two, three days, they come. I wait in the city.'

'Shadow take all Outlanders,' she said, barely under her breath; and then as if explaining to the slow-witted, 'No permit—no go into the Freeport. Go back. Wait. You understand me? Wait until your people come with permits. Then you come in. Understand? Sunmother's tits!'

I bowed, said something in English that didn't match the polite tone in which it was said, and backed off. She was watching me. I hung round a ferry queue until her attention was distracted, then slipped off to look at the smaller gates. They were guarded too.

The Crown's permits were useless. They'd remember Christie's name—they must be already on the look-out for it.

'You have trouble?' A pale-maned *ashiren* regarded me gravely. 'You want to enter Freeport, Outlander?'

'Go in the city? Yes.'

'I know a way,' the *ashiren* said. *Ke* wasn't more than five or six. 'A broken part of the wall. For a silver piece, I'll show you.'

Reluctantly I unknotted one and handed it over. The *ashiren* slid off *kir* seat on a mooring bollard and glanced round.

'I'll see if the way's clear. You wait here.' *Ke* vanished into the crowd. I waited. The pale sun blazed, unsoftened by the heat-mist. All but the brightest daystars were masked.

It took me longer than it should have to realize that the *ashiren* wasn't coming back.

I tried two or three more gates with no better result. Then—as I heard midday chimes from inside the walls, and began to smell cooking —I came to a shabby, land-side gate, deserted but for two troopers playing *ochmir*.

'I come in,' I said hopefully, with a worse accent than usual. The older of the two women slouched upright.

'Papers,' she said idly. I repeated my story. The younger woman also stood. Her face was masked with marshflower dapples, and raisin-dark eyes glowed.

'No papers? Maybe we can make an exception, Caveth.' She nudged the older woman with her foot. 'Of course, there's a fine you'll have to pay.'

'Fine?' With a show of reluctance I brought out a cord and began to count coins.

'And the tax,' she added, 'the—ah—tax on Outlanders entering the Freeport.'

'Steady, Zilthar. Even Outlanders aren't that stupid.' The older woman's south-Dadeni accent was thick. Southlanders, finding you can't speak their tongue, tend to assume you can't understand it either. 'Keep it low or she won't pay.'

'Some Seamarshal's guard we are.' Zilthar grinned briefly. 'That'll be five silver pieces, *T'An* Outlander.'

'Suppose they find out?' Caveth worried.

'Who'll tell? This one can't even talk properly. What—? Have I to count it out for you?' She bent over the handful of silver and copper I was offering her. 'Three . . . four . . . five; there.'

'Is that right?'

She looked at me, highly affronted. 'What do you think I am—a thief?'

As I went in under the brick and plaster arch I heard her add 'What does it matter, Caveth? When they throw her out under the nine days law she'll—'

The rumble of carts drowned her words. I went on into the Freeport. The *telestre* houses were low and sprawling, pale plaster reflecting back the glaring sun. Their walls had no windows except for slits on the first floors. Windpumps rose out of the dusty air like broad-petalled flowers. Creepers flowed down from rooftop tubs, crimson-leaved, bright with spring growth of blue and white blossoms. Through open archways I saw sunken pools, mosaic courtyards, Ortheans sleeping in the sun after the noon meal.

None of the streets were straight, so I was at the docks before I saw it. A brisk wind, still cold, blew whitecaps on a sea that stretched endlessly south. After all the long and land-locked winter—the sea.

Islands formed a sheltered harbour here. I saw how the Freeport hugged every scrap of land above water. Ships were moored along the quay, painted sails furled. *Fath* ships from Ymir and Rimon, some others from the Melkathi peninsula; some I didn't know. Ortheans pushed past me, Southlanders and others. Dialects and foreign tongues assailed my ears.

Back of the *chirith-goyen* cloth warehouses I found a companion-house willing to serve a late midday meal. *Skurrai* mare's milk and cheese, and the tough-fibred bread-mushroom. Tired, hot, I sat under the street-awning and drank cold herb-tea.

Ships for Tathcaer, that's next, I thought. Assuming the Portmaster isn't on the lookout for one Lynne de Lisle Christie. Assuming I can afford passage.

If Tathcaer's safe . . . at least I can talk to Eliot and Huxton, I reflected. Set diplomatic processes going. If the late Andrethe's *telestre* don't assassinate me, that is. Lord, how did I get into this mess! What I need now is someone who knows the country . . . I didn't realize how easy it was being made for me, travelling with Ortheans.

'Are there rooms here?' I asked the keeper of the companion-house.

'Maybe. Where's your permit?'

'My what?'

He looked suspiciously at me. 'Haven't you registered with the Well-house yet? You'd better, before one of the Seamarshal's guard stop you.'

'I don't understand. I've only just arrived.'

'You register. They give you a pass. It's good for nine days. Then you must go back to your *telestre* or Guild—but I forgot, you Outlanders don't have that.' He sniffed. 'You'll have to leave the city at the end of the week, then. But I can't take anyone without a permit. My *telestre* wouldn't allow it.'

'I'll register,' I promised, and received copious directions to the nearest Wellhouse. I paid and left, taking care to avoid that direction. The church would be looking for Christie.

Someone who knows the country, I thought as I stepped over the covered channel that served as the street's sewer. Someone to know custom, be an extra pair of eyes to warn against assassins; someone who —a sell-sword, yes! The only question is, can I afford to pay one? I began enquiring the way to the Mercenaries' Guildhouse.

'There is the list of the Guild members presently in the residence,' the Guildmaster said. 'Not all are available for contract, of course.'

She was a tan-skinned woman, strikingly beautiful despite her obvious age. A scar licked up from the corner of her mouth to her eye, giving her a sleepy, sardonic expression.

'You'll have the Seamarshal's permit,' she added casually, 'for an Outlander to hire a mercenary from the Hundred Thousand.'

'Mmm . . .' I studied the list of names on the parchment, mentally cursing Morvren's paranoid Seamarshal. A number of men and women passed through the low-ceilinged entrance hall. I couldn't guess, from looking, which were mercenaries and which were not.

'You're looking for a bodyguard?' The Guildmaster had the air of one trying to be helpful. 'Or one skilled in certain weapons—'

'This one.' I realized I'd interrupted her, but it couldn't be helped. I didn't believe what I was reading. She peered over my shoulder.

'That one's not presently available for contract.'

'I know. I'll wait.'

She shrugged. 'He's in the city, I believe. You may wait in the courtyard, *t'an*, if you wish, until he returns.'

Sand grated underfoot on the tiled floors. Windows laid narrow strips of white sunlight across the interior gloom. The courtyard was roofed with a cloth awning; benches stood by the walls, and desultory weapons practice was in progress in the centre square. I took a seat on one of the benches. The burst of enthusiasm sparked off by the entrance of a potential customer faded, as they saw I wasn't interested.

I didn't wait long.

He came into the courtyard with the familiar light tread, agile for his build. I saw him momentarily as a stranger would: a broad-shouldered Orthean male, not tall, in old mail and scuffed leather boots, worn _harur_ blades at his belt. Fair mane, silverlock, and the appalling mottled scar: Blaize n'ri n'suth Meduenin.

'I've been looking for you all day,' he said as he sat down beside me. 'Saw you at the gate, but then I lost you.'

'So much for disguise.'

'I'd know you anywhere,' he said simply.

Can you buy loyalty? I thought. Or am I being obtuse again? Ortheans!

'You couldn't have known I was here,' he added. 'What brings you to Duvalka's Guildhouse?'

'Planning to hire help to get me to Tathcaer. What interests me is what you're doing here, Meduenin.'

He nodded. There was dirt ingrained in his pale skin; he had the look of a man driven hard.

'I got as far as Afrual before the Crown's riders turned me back.' The pale eyes opaqued, cleared. 'Truth told, I think they thought I was you—riding your Gher, they knew the tracks. I went west to avoid them, couldn't break through. When I got as far as Charain I sold the beast to an Earthspeaker travelling north—I owe you that money—and came down on a rivership. Saw you as I came in this morning.'

'How close are they?'

'Close enough,' he admitted. 'They'll be hunting you all the way to Tathcaer, and further.'

'With nothing friendly in mind, I'd say.'

Scar tissue contorted. It was a moment before I recognized it as a smile. 'The consensus opinion is for slitting your throat without benefit of trial—which would suit a number of people very well.'

'You thinking of anyone in particular?'

'Whoever killed the Andrethe.' He sprawled back, tucking his hands under his belt. 'Someone _knows_ you're innocent, Christie. At the moment you've been convicted by popular opinion, but if it came to a trial it might not look so convincing. Safer if you were dead.'

'Do ships go from here to the Eastern Isles? No, forget I said that. Blaize, do you have any idea who's behind this?'

'Anyone of the _tha'adur,_ the _takshiriye,_ or the people in from the

Dadeni *telestres.'* He looked up. 'You think I should have warned you. It's what you hired me for. But there was no whisper of it until that last day, it must have been planned at a very high level.'

SuBannasen's dead, I thought, with the ambiguous pang that remembering her death always caused me. And Howice is in Roehmonde . . . but that doesn't rule him out. Who else?

'It's no excuse,' Blaize said. 'I did all I could. Don't you believe that?'

'What?' My train of thought vanished.

'After Broken Stair—but you never will credit a sell-sword's word, will you?' He grinned, the scar turning it into something merciless.

'Is it important that I believe you?'

He was silent a while. 'I take your gold, deliver what you require me to deliver to Tathcaer. No, what do I want with belief?'

This from a man who twice tried to kill me. So why was I feeling guilty?

'I don't doubt you,' I said slowly, trying to think it out. 'I wish I could be as certain of other people's honesty as I am of yours. You're honest where you're paid.'

He took it as a compliment, eyes veiled, embarrassed. After a pause he said, 'What will you do now?'

The *jayante* dug into my back. I eased the strap. 'I still want that report to get to Tathcaer. Is it safe to try and board a ship?'

'Safer for me, I'm an unknown in this. But I may have led them down on you here, they'll be watching.' He shrugged. 'You'd have a better chance if we were together.'

'And you'd have a worse one.'

'You hired me, didn't you?'

'That may be the most ungracious offer of help I ever had. Thanks.'

He laughed briefly. The courtyard was emptying, and the bells sounding for evening.

'Where are you staying?' he asked.

'At the moment, nowhere. Seems you need a signed permit to breathe in this city.'

'The problem of being a Freeport—if you let everyone in, you have to know who they are. You can stay here, Christie, I'll speak to the Guildmaster.' He stood up. 'You'll have to make a decision soon. There isn't much time.'

'There never is,' I said, 'and what there was has just about run out.'

'That's the Portmaster's office.' Blaize pointed down the quay towards a three-storey building. Despite the cold spring rain, the entrance hall was full and the crowd spilling out into the open. 'We should have come earlier.'

'You've been here before,' I remembered. His knowledge of the city was accurate, taking us from the Guildhouse across several ferry-channels to this outermost island.

'Best I go in,' he said. 'They might have your description.'

'If you can get in. Looks like a longish wait.'

One of the quayside awnings sheltered us. Rain pocked the sea. The pale plaster buildings across the water had a luminous sheen, and a distant spire was alternately veiled and revealed by low cloud.

Blaize touched my arm and indicated a ship. 'That's a Saberonisi vessel, look. From the Rainbow Cities.'

A party were going aboard, their faces caked with blue and scarlet paint, thread-thin chains girdling their dark robes. Saberon I dimly remembered from maps, several thousand miles south.

Despite the rain, there was no atmosphere of impatience in the crowd. A steady trickle of people came out of the building, and just as steadily we edged towards the door. The midmorning chimes sounded.

An eddy: people drawing back instinctively, others peering forward. I heard raised voices, a note of excitement. A group of people were leaving the Portmaster's office.

'Freeport, yes,' came a snatch of conversation behind me, 'but there are limits on who should be let in—'

Two, three, five of them: dark robes over bronze scaled tunics, high-arched feet bare, thin-hafted throwing spears strapped across their backs. The movement of the crowd left me close enough to touch them as they went past. The sea wind blew in their white unbound manes, where bronze and gold pins were tangled. Their skins glowed dusty gold. The brilliance was such that it was a minute before I realized they walked on the same dung-spattered paving as the rest of us, through the miasma from the dirty harbour. They were dirty, tunics foodstained; unintelligible voices harsh. Brown eyes flickered haughtily over Morvren's people. I had expected golden eyes. Some of the bleached manes had dark roots.

'Halfbreeds,' Blaize said in my ear. 'Kel Harantish. Wait here.'

He was gone inside the building, while the crowd's attention followed the Harantish people along the quay out of sight.

By the time he reappeared, I was edgy for no good reason. Perhaps a reaction to the Goldens. We retired to a dockside companion-house for an early dinner, discussing Blaize's news.

'There's two would take passengers,' he reported, 'and two that want deckhands. That we might try, if you've ever done any sailing. All those leave before the week's end.'

'I'm no sailor. What are the passenger fees?'

I listened to him recite figures. This division of the companion-house (a restaurant) was clean and well-lit compared to most of the Freeport. The rain had lessened, and intermittent watery sunlight shone through the stained glass windows.

A hand tapped my shoulder.

'What the—'

'No harm, *t'an;* I would speak with you.'

Alarm faded, replaced by a new disquiet. The man was dark-skinned, wearing sailor's britches. Off one of the docked ships, then. Yes, the accent was foreign. The sun laid white bars across his scarred ribs, nipples, corded throat. A soft leather mask covered his face from mouth to forehead. His dirty mane was roughly braided.

'What do you want?'

'Give me your hand.'

'I think not.'

The lips curved, smiling. Something darkly transparent blocked the mask's eyeholes. I couldn't see his eyes. But he saw mine.

He said 'I have a message from the Hexenmeister, to the woman not born of this world.'

Blaize had *harur-nazari* in his left hand, I hadn't seen or heard him draw it. I put my hands out of sight under the table, feeling the sonic stunner under my tunic.

'The Hexenmeister?' I recalled, then, an earlier message.

'It is this,' he said quietly. ' "Envoy, spring weather is uncertain travelling. If you take ship, be aware that you are welcome at the Brown Tower." That is all.'

'Wait,' I said as he turned to go. 'How . . . how did you find me?'

'All who left the city this season carried such a message.' Another eyeless smile. 'If you were here, you must come some time to the office of the Portmaster. From there I followed you.'

'Do you know who I am?'

'I know the signs to recognize you, and the words to compel your attention. The Tower told me. *T'an,* I have no other answers.'

He left, and I became aware that my hand was clenched on the stunner. It left a white impression when I released it. Blaize sheathed the *harur-nazari* and let out an explosive breath.

'Sunmother! Is the Hexenmeister interested in you now, Christie?' He sounded awed. 'Kasabaarde's an unchancy place, and not to be trusted. If I were you—'

'Yes?'

'I'd settle this mess before I got into another one.'

Being a companion-house, more or less anything was available. I requested parchment and a writing-stick, and they were brought to the table.

Twice this place called Kasabaarde had found me with a message. Even for curiosity's sake I wanted to know why. Besides that . . . I tried to get my thoughts into coherent form. It would be wise to leave the Southland for a time. Wise to diversify, the more contacts the Dominion had on this world, the better. Particularly as we weren't very welcome in the Hundred Thousand at the moment.

Or is that rationalizing cowardice? I thought. Am I just plain scared of going back to Tathcaer? Yes, true. Not that that makes my other reasons any less valid.

I scribbled furiously, folded the sheet of parchment, and sealed it with wax. When I looked up it was to see Blaize leaning back and scuffing his boot on the floor, seething with impatience.

'Are we going to Kasabaarde?' he demanded.

'I am. You're going to Tathcaer. You can take this letter with the report, it's an update to let them know what I'm doing. Naturally you won't deliver it to anyone except a member of the xeno-team. And should anyone ask, you don't know where I am.'

He grunted, then nodded. 'Now you're thinking like a Southlander.'

The spire became a pylon-shaped building jutting up out of the sea into a clear sky. As we came closer I tried to judge the height, revised my estimate upwards several times when I saw the buildings clustered round its base. Skyscraper height at the very least. No, larger. And— when the sun gleamed on it—it showed the blue-grey fused stone that meant Golden Witchbreed.

'Spire Gate,' Blaize said laconically, 'lots of island ships put in there.'

Coming closer now, and it was neck-stretchingly high. The ferry boat berthed in its shadow. Now I could see it was not simply a feature-less tower. A third of the way up, a thread-thin structure jutted out horizontally. It went south, straight as a die, over the ea; and every so often a support pillar soared up to seamlessly join it.

'Dear god,' I said, 'is that a *bridge?*'

The Meduenin man grinned. 'Rasrhe-y-Meluur,' he said. 'Otherwise known as Bridge Alley. I've been along it as far as Goldenarch and Stonefire. They say you can get clear to Kasabaarde.'

'Kasabaarde—' Which must be, if memory serves me, on the long side of two hundred *seri* distant.

'It's covered,' he said, rounding his hands to indicate a tubeshape, 'but not safe. Shall I ask round the ships?'

'What? Yes, do.'

Presumably it followed the chain of islands, the Kasabaarde Archipelago. To construct it argued an engineering skill not just staggering, but—for it to exist intact thousands of years—plain frightening.

Eventually I reached agreement with the master of an island ship, not much larger than a fishing smack, but willing to carry passengers down the Archipelago. Being in a hurry, I paid more than seemed strictly necessary. Freeporters, perhaps because of their contact outside the Hundred Thousand, have a clear idea of personal property. The ensuing casual dishonesty reminded me sharply of Earth.

'You could hire someone else to take that report to Tathcaer,' Blaize said. His eyes veiled in the bright sunlight. I had my pack, the *jayante;* there was nothing to do but go aboard.

'Who else can I trust?'

He reached out and gripped my hands, nodded once, and then strode off down the quay. And I went on board the *Mosshawk.*

Going south, spring comes all the faster. Each of the islands we put in at seemed to boast a greater amount of new-leafed *siir* and flowering *lapuur.* Hanys and the first weeks of Durestha often bring storms sweeping in from the Western Ocean, but the *Mosshawk* had a voyage of such balmy uneventfulness that we had nothing to do but watch the Archipelago glide past in daylight, and the starfire swirl in our wake during the cloudless nights.

The *Mosshawk* carried three passengers besides myself: a Desert Coast woman on her way to Quarth, and two men robed head to foot in scarlet who spoke no intelligible tongue. Being Orthean, they gambled. The cabins were cramped and dark and we spent our time on deck, well forward out of the crew's way, playing *ochmir.* After the first couple of days there was nothing new.

South, into warmer waters. Stopping over to pick up or deliver cargo, wine and pottery and seedling plants. It was shirt-sleeve weather when we made brief excursions onto the islands. And the sky grew paler, and the sun hotter, and all the time the pylons of the Rasrhe-y-Meluur cast their unbroken shadow on the ceaseless waves.

Slow travelling, the last few days of Hanys and well into Durestha Secondweek; but one morning I woke to white acid sunlight, and a dark line in the south.

'The coastline of Kasabaarde,' the Desert Coast woman said.

24

The Brown Tower

The sun flashed off a sea like broken glass. A grey-green fuzz covered the nearer coastline. Sepia mountains haunted the far south, desolate moonscapes and deserts that might have been anything up to fifty *seri* away. We sailed in towards a tall pylon marking the end of Bridge Alley, Rasrhe-y-Meluur.

Blobs of colour swam in my vision. I retreated below decks again, rubbing reddened, irritated eyes. My skin, already tanned, peeled. The hazy days had been bearable; with the protective haze gone, there was no avoiding the searing light of Carrick's Star.

If this is what it's like in Durestha, I thought, I don't want to be here in Merrum.

Wood creaked, waves hissed; gaps in the decks let through sunlight like molten metal. By the time I'd packed, the ship had docked and the other passengers were disembarking. I paid the shipmaster the remaining half of the fee and went ashore.

The land was utterly flat. Carts rolled down a wide quay that was inches deep in fine white dust. I tasted grit on my tongue, the metallic taste of Kasabaarde. The Desert woman and the two red-robed Ortheans were ahead of me at the pale mud-brick wall where several gates opened into the city.

'You wish to enter the trade city or the inner city?' the older of the Kasabaardeans asked the Desert Coast woman. They spoke the trade-tongue mentioned in the books I'd studied; I could just about make myself understood in it.

'The trade city,' the woman said.

'Pass, then.'

The books had been full of information on the trade city. Of the inner city they said nothing, except that the Brown Tower was there.

'You wish to enter the trade city?' The Kasabaardean studied me closely. 'Or the inner city?'

'The inner city.' The accent was manageable.

A young man barred my way with a staff. The group had the tan manes and bleached skins of the Desert Coast. They wore short, rope-belted tunics, and were barefoot.

'Touch the earth,' the Kasabaardean commanded. She had albino dapples down her bare arms, and on her hands the veins stood up with age. Like the others, she was masked.

As was the custom, I knelt to put both hands palm-flat on the dry ground, and then stood. Another woman offered me a bowl. Grey, ceramic, half full of water. They watched me expectantly. I took a small mouthful, hoping I'd avoid any infection. It had a flat taste.

'Have you edged weapons?' the woman continued the ritual.

'No—yes, a knife.'

'That shall be returned when you leave,' she said, taking it. The staff no longer barred my way. Under the mask's edge, her mouth smiled. 'The *jayante* you may keep with you. A welcome to you. I will take you to the inner city gate.'

'I'm looking for a companion-house,' I said as we walked beside the wall. The sun on the white dust and brickwork was painfully bright. 'Or somewhere I can stay.'

'You may stay among any of the Orders.'

'Somewhere cheap. I don't have much money.'

'You will not need money.' Her dry voice might have held amusement. It was difficult to tell, with her eyes hidden. 'In the inner city, all food is free, and all drink, and all clothing and shelter.'

Fitting my steps to her slow pace, we came to a squat gatehouse.

'For Kasabaardeans, you mean?'

'No, for all. For any who come here.'

'You mean anyone can just come here and ask, and get fed and housed?'

'Yes, certainly.'

That's impossible! I protested mentally. We entered the gatehouse. After the sun outside, I was blind. Vision clearing, I saw the Kasabaardean woman handing my knife over to another man. This was a weapons store. The man was jotting down an inventory of my possessions.

'What is yours, you may keep,' the Orthean woman said, pulling off her mask. So it was protection against the sun? I wondered. She had an angular face, and clear-water eyes. 'What is ours—you may leave with no more of that than you may carry on your back or in your stomach.'

I shook my head. Yes, she was amused. She must have had this reaction from strangers before.

'It's not—' I couldn't insult her, so began again. 'Don't you get people coming here and living off you, and not doing anything to earn it?'

'Is that so bad?' She bent over the list the man was making, and indicated I should open my pack. There was no option. She continued, 'All may live here, though none grow rich. That is for the Orders to do in the trade city. We will house you, feed you; if you wish to work in fields or city then you may. If not, then do not.'

'People can't just do nothing!'

Her veiled eyes watched me. Seeing me as an individual, I thought suddenly, not just another stranger.

'Why not?' she said softly. 'Perhaps if they do not toil, they learn some value from the Orders' teaching. Or find some clear vision of their own. Time is what we give, for self-searching or for idleness. And we give choices.'

'I still don't see how you can do it.' I was looking for the catch, as Southlanders and Outworlders do.

'The fields feed us, we have rivers; such wealth as the Orders have comes from trade and taxes. To stay here costs nothing. To pass through, much. And all that comes from the Rainbow Cities and Desert Coast must pass us to go north, and all the Southland must pass us on their voyaging, and there is the Rasrhe-y-Meluur besides.' Her thin lips moved, smiling, her eyes were bright. 'My Order is Su'niar, if you wish to go there. Tell them Orinc sent you. Or there are other Orders, Cir-nanth and Gethfirle, Thelmithar and Dureitch. But it would be a plea-sure for me to talk with you further.'

My pack was returned to me. The woman replaced her mask over her loosely braided mane.

'Yes,' I said. 'My name's Christie. Where is—Su'niar?'

'Along past Cir-nanth Way, anyone will tell you.' She pointed from the doorway. As I left she said, 'Christie, what's your business here?'

'The Brown Tower.'

I left her staring after me.

After the weeks on the ship, my legs weren't steady. I walked on into the inner city, adjusting to the solidity of the world. The white light leaked through my slitted eyelids. The heat sucked strength. Sweat dried immediately in the dryness. Ortheans jostled me, many in Kasabaardean robes, many from the other lands of this second conti-nent. I heard a babble of talk.

Low domes lined the curving streets, windows ebony in the expanses of white and sand-coloured plaster and bricks. Broad cartways gave way to narrow passages. Cloth awnings stretched across the alleys at roof-level. Bead-tapestries sheltered doorways.

Perhaps because it was impossible to see more than a few streets ahead at one time, the city seemed to go on forever. Occasionally I glimpsed the distant peaks of the desert land. Sometimes a road opened on to the brilliant sea. But the curved roads and passages had no discernible pattern. Between my version of the trade-tongue and people's attempts to give me directions, I was soon lost.

Vaned windpumps glittered as they turned. They jutted above the domes of this one-storey city, the only landmarks. Coming at last to a broad roadway, I stopped almost in the shadow of the vanes. The road surface sparked up light, dazzling noon fragments. Somewhere I heard water running. Then, as I walked out among the crowds on the scored, worn surface, I saw that the water was underfoot. A covered channel, roofed with semi-opaque blue-grey stone. . . .

The last pylon of the Rasrhe-y-Meluur towered in the north. Witchbreed again: another of Orthe's communities flourishing in the ruins of the Golden Empire. I thought of cold aKirrik in the Barrens, Kasabaarde on the searing equator. Not mere archeology, this, you couldn't separate Orthe from its past.

A number of Ortheans were sitting outside one building, their backs to the curving dome wall, in the shade of an awning.

'Where is this?' I asked carefully.

A few looked at me. Like all I'd seen, their eyes were permanently shielded by the nictitating membrane. One trickled dust from hand to hand. It was quiet.

'Thelmithar,' one said at last.

Inside was cool, dim, spacious. A man with blue threads woven into his rope-belt came over to me.

'The food is almost ready, do you wish to come down and wait?'

Hunger, thirst; they had been masked by the newness of Kasabaarde. I nodded. He led me down steps, into wide underground rooms where a few Ortheans already sat at tables. I smelled cooking. The light was diffuse, reflected down from the outside world by mirrors. One wall was blue-grey, half transparent, water moving there in the cool shadows.

Black hard bread, some unnamed fruits, and watered wine; and a stew that seemed to consist mainly of fungi. I ate slowly, watching the Ortheans that were there. Some were unmasked Kasabaardeans, some from other Desert cities, one looked as though she might have been a Southlander. As I was leaving, a fight broke out between two of the Desert men. No one attempted to interfere. Pausing on the steps, I watched while one beat the other unconscious. Then I went up into the searing light.

It wasn't possible just to walk out. Something in the back of my mind howled *thief!* While I hesitated, the same man returned from the street.

'Is there something else you desire?'

'No. Yes,' I contradicted myself. A certain freedom made itself felt. And a desire to test to the limit. 'A mask, one of those with the eye-shields. And can you tell me how to find Su'niar?'

'I'll take you there,' he said, returning from a storeroom with the mask in his hand. It felt suffocating at first, then ceased to be noticed. The dust-shields gave the world a sepia tint, but at least I could see comfortably.

The sun declined, a white-hot coin in a pale sky.

The face was thin. You could see the skull's shape under the tanned skin. And the eyes, half white, hard as marble; like nothing on Orthe. And laughing. I laced the mask on, turning away from the mirror.

Good grief, Christie! I thought. What did Blaize say? Finish this mess before you get into another. The department won't like this messing about with 'primitives' on the second continent, not while the Southland's like it is . . .

And anyone who stands there laughing at themselves in a mirror is in no position to question anybody else's sanity. Not even someone who calls themself Hexenmeister, and sends messages halfway across the world. Who's crazy—the one who calls, or the one who answers? What do I *say* to him, I wondered.

I went upstairs. Orinc was in the outer room, sweeping the tiled floor clear of the ever-present dust. Her movements were lethargic. It was that time when afternoon becomes evening.

'Why hurry?' she asked, seeing me masked for the streets. 'Stay here in Su'niar a while, child.'

'I'll be back,' I promised. 'Tell me how I find the Brown Tower.'

'Between Stone Gate and the gardens,' she said resignedly, and loosed the bead curtain behind me as I stepped out into the street.

Rounded shadows patched the streets, blue and soft. The furnace-sky cooled, minute by minute. Crowds dispersed, seeking food and shelter for the night in the houses of the different Orders. I went down by way of the seaward wall, walking until I came to a sandstone-block gate, and then turning back into the city towards the gardens. Scrub vegetation grew by the pools, ash-grey and milky blue leaves quivering in the light breeze. Creepers covered a wall on the western side of the gardens, and over it rose the broad square shape of the Tower. The arch in the wall had no gate. Beyond it I saw courtyards, fountains.

A man stepped out of the archway and spoke. When he saw I didn't understand, he repeated it in the trade-tongue.

'What do you want here?'

'Is this the Brown Tower?' Now it came to it, my guts were snake-knotting.

'Yes.'

'I've come to see the Hexenmeister.' Then it hit me where I'd seen that dark otter-sleekness before. Webs marked hands and feet, the skin was green-gold. In spite of the masked face, there was no mistaking it—this was one of the fenborn.

'The Hexenmeister?' he said, unconsciously arrogant. 'Why?'

'I don't know. You'd better ask him.'

He hesitated, staring at me. At last he said, 'What—who are you?'

'Christie.' At last the laces of the mask unknotted and I was free of it. 'Envoy from the Dominion.'

The evening's brilliance stung my eyes. He made some gesture I didn't recognize, ritualistic and formal.

'Outworlder,' he said, 'be welcome: you are expected.'

I left the sunlit courtyard, the flickering brightness of the fountains and the scent of grey-gold creepers, entering into the shadow of the Brown Tower.

Set into the soaring brown brick wall was a metal-studded door. The fenborn touched one of the studs and it glided open. We stepped through into a dim hallway. The door slid shut and a sourceless light sprang up, illuminating smooth walls and floor and ceiling. I touched the wall. The pale material had a slick feel, warmer than stone.

'Come,' the fenborn said.

Weights and pulleys? And the lighting, concealed mirrors again? As we passed through several doors and along corridors, I realized I was grasping for explanations. The place had the look of high technology about it. Another door slid open at our approach.

It was a library. Bookshelves from floor to ceiling; never since coming to Orthe had I seen so many books in one place. The dusty scent of old parchment filled the air. Evening light fell on woven mats, a blocky table and chairs. There weren't even bars on the windows.

'You're careless,' I said, still stunned by the contrast between city and Tower. 'Anyone could come here—'

'If you had not been desired to enter, you could not even have passed the gardens.' An old man came from behind one of the bookshelves, and placed the scroll he carried on the desk.

'Hexenmeister,' the fenborn said. 'Christie, the Outworlder.'

'Ah. Thank you, Tethmet. Leave us now.'

Like most Kasabaardeans he was a head smaller than me, and bent with age besides. His hands were bird-claws, his skin a diamond-pattern of wrinkles, and his mane gone except for a crest from forehead to spine. A brown sleeveless robe covered his tunic.

'You are the alien?'

'You want to count fingers? Yes, that's me.' I tucked the mask under my belt, and then had nothing to do with my hands. Nervous, fingers twisting together; I wanted to laugh. 'But anyone who can send me two messages across half a world, sight unseen, knows enough about me for my liking. Now I'm here, suppose you explain who you are, what you're doing, and what's so important I have to travel two hundred *seri* to get here?'

His puckered mouth wrinkled and a wheezing sound issued from his chest. I realized he was laughing. Using both hands to support himself, he lowered his body into a chair.

'What do you know of me? I don't wish to reiterate details you may already have.' He spoke fluent Ymirian, possibly choosing that because I still have that accent.

'Know? I don't *know* anything. The books say plenty about the trade part of the city, nothing about the Brown Tower. As for rumour —no one seems sure in their own mind if this is a good city to come to, or a bad one. And for yourself, Hexenmeister—'

'Yes?' he prompted, still short of breath from laughing.

'That you dream no past-dreams because you're immortal, that you see all that passes in the world, that the archives of the Brown Tower hold all knowledge.'

'Such superstition,' he said mildly. 'Well, you and I have much to speak of, envoy, and I will tell you why. I know much of what passes in the known lands, because most news comes either here to this city, or is heard by my people who travel. And it has been the custom—since before Tathcaer was a city—that they bring such news to me. The archives hold much knowledge, but not all. No, not all. And as for the other, that is answered more simply: yes, I am immortal.'

'I'm sorry, I don't believe that. I can't.' It hurt me to be rude to the old man. He had a kind of stillness about him, a solidity, that made it difficult to believe he was only a mad old man living in the ruins of Witchbreed technology.

'You *must* believe,' he said. 'Or else you'll believe nothing I tell you. And what I tell you may affect the relations between our two worlds. I know you've seen much of the Hundred Thousand, but do not suppose that they can speak for all Orthe.'

'And you can?' The sharpness was unintentional.

His white-filmed eyes met mine. 'You see, you have no proof that what I say is valid. So, though I don't normally deal in personalities, I think I must prove to you what I am.'

He eased forward in the chair, lifting himself with the weight on his wrists as the old do. I automatically moved to help him. His warm hand closed over mine, a many-fingered grip, and then he was standing upright.

'If you will lend me your arm . . . thank you. Lynne de Lisle Christie—and what is the correct usage: *t'an* or landholder, or something from your own world?'

We moved towards the door at his slow pace, and it opened to let us through.

'Christie will do,' I said. Wondering, is it beam-operated? Or—no, it can't be; not even Witchbreed technology lasts forever.

Along a diffusely-lit passage, passing more doors. Slow, at an old man's speed. His weight, leaning on my arm, was considerable.

Another door opened. We stepped into a small chamber, and the door slid shut. There was pressure underfoot, a sickness in the stomach; I realized we were descending. Then it stopped, the door opened, and we walked into another and slightly larger room. The light changed quality. The air felt dry, cool. Then a section of the opposite wall split and slid aside.

'That causes you no fear,' the old man said, 'you have seen such things before. Well, it is not to be wondered at, coming from the stars.'

An elevator. A sterile air-lock. Cool air hit me from the room beyond. Disbelief paralysed me. Kirriach was awesome enough. But Kirriach's safely dead, I thought, and this . . . he said: if you had not been desired to enter . . . Lord, what kind of defences does a place like this have?

'Christie?'

His warm grip on my arm was the only link with reality. Veiled eyes looked up. His skin was webbed with fine lines, the crestmane thin and wispy. Not a strong old man.

'Seems Witchbreed technology isn't as dead as it's thought to be.' My voice croaked, dry.

'The Brown Tower has stood for ten thousand years,' he said softly, impossibly. 'And hasn't been above borrowing Golden Empire technology when needed. Machines fail, you see. Even these. Though not for a time yet, I think.' He took a few unsupported steps into the room, resting his hands on the edge of metal casings. 'These are precious to me beyond all price, their like is not to be found in the world today.'

A long windowless room, underground. Banks of machinery—I presume it is, I thought—and screens, and cubicles like sarcophagi; and less recognizable objects. Quiet, chill, a subliminal hum.

And one object was familiar. I went forward, examining the table and the headrest—shaped for Ortheans—and attachments that might be electrodes; and connections to other banks of what might be computers. . . .

'That is known to you?'

I stood up, sighing. 'I don't know. Chance resemblance, I expect. Except that certain things are common to all worlds—including the laws of science. We have something very like this for teaching under hypnosis.'

We struggled with respective vocabularies, not sure if we were talking about the same thing. All the old man's words were unfamiliar. Kasabaarde, unlike the Hundred Thousand, has a technical terminology included in its language. Some things we certainly misinterpreted.

'You have heard,' he said at last, 'of those of us who possess a perfect memory?'

'Yes. Some humans have that.'

'These transcribe, store, and transfer such a person's memory intact to another person.'

That isn't possible, I thought. Even we can't do that. The hypnoteachers might pass as a prototype of that—a primitive prototype—but if it's true . . . what level of technology did the Witchbreed have?

'So you can record memory.'

'Record and transfer to another person. And that person, also, to another and another.' He smiled. 'With no loss of detail, down through the generations.'

'Someone said to me once—' it was the Desert Coast woman on the *Mosshawk*, I remembered '—"the Hexenmeister has a peculiar kind of serial immortality". No one in the Southland mentioned it.'

'Oh, I am not approved of in the Hundred Thousand.' He gave an old man's chuckle. 'If I hold a hundred generations of memory, then where are my own memories of past lives? No, I am not liked there, but then there are very few who know.'

'It's not immortality.'

'Not for me,' he touched his thin chest. '*I* am not immortal, but the Hexenmeister is. Look.'

He laid his palm flat on a cube-structure. As I watched, it cleared from the centre, as if viscous compartments became transparent. Evening light glimmered in what must be the outer courtyard. A girl was sitting on the fountain's rim, her arms cradling a child perhaps a year old. She was pale-skinned, tan mane braided with beads, wearing the brown robes and rope-belt of the Brown Tower. Just past *ashiren,* not more than sixteen. Her face was unsmiling, bent in concentration over the child that played with her six-fingered hand.

'There is one of this generation's,' the old man said. 'She has many of the memories stored in her mind. Another few years—when I die—and she will be the Hexenmeister. And she'll remember speaking with you, Christie, remember this moment as I do. Since there's no difference in my memory and hers, then she will be me—as I am all who went before me.'

The cube darkened, precipitating me back into the cool room. The evidence of alien technology surrounded me.

'Now do you see?' the Hexenmeister asked. 'Kasabaarde is the oldest city in this world, and I am the oldest person. I know this world. Perhaps I am the only person who does. So when Orthe comes to deal with other worlds—I am the only one qualified to speak for us.'

25

The Golden Empire

'That's all very well, but—' I realized I was pacing, and came to a halt in front of the old Orthean male. 'It's incredible! What real *proof* do you have?'

He spread his hands, indicating the Brown Tower in all its undeniable existence. 'If it were proved to your satisfaction that these machines act as I claim?'

'I don't have the technical training to prove or disprove it.' And where this was concerned, I thought, it might puzzle a few Dominion scientists to prove anything.

He sat down slowly on one of the metal fixtures, watching me. When his eyes unveiled they were black, bird-bright. Seeming to change tack, he said, 'The Southland is for the most part against contact with your world, I believe.'

'The majority? I don't know. And that may change.'

'They fear technology, the Witchbreed come again.' Slowly he shook his head. 'And all the danger that entails, though it's only a danger to them because they still desire it.'

'And Kasabaarde doesn't?'

'We are perhaps poor in material wealth, but there are other kinds of well-being. If I were to ask you your beliefs?'

'I . . .' It floored me. 'Beliefs?'

'Of the spiritual.'

'I don't know . . . agnostic, I suppose.' The department favours that, as being less likely to be offended by other worlds' religions.

'There are answers to be looked for,' he said, 'in the mind and soul; that is our choice in Kasabaarde. And you may believe what you will, or nothing at all. That is why these—' the protective hand on the machine '—don't touch us, as they would the Hundred Thousand, or Kel

Harantish. We have all made our choices. Now we face this new thing, your world. That brings other choices.'

'You,' I said, 'do you believe in a god? The Goddess?'

An expression crossed his face, it might have been surprise or satisfaction. 'You are god, Christie. I am god. So are we all.'

I was lost. Kasabaarde's orientation is radically different from the Southland's. An envoy would have a different job here.

'I—excuse me—I'm still not sure just why I'm here.'

'That, you may discover after you've spent time in the inner city. But as for why I requested you to visit me, that's simpler. The main business of the Brown Tower is knowledge. I want knowledge of your world, Christie. Of Earth and the Dominion.'

I shrugged. 'That's my job. I'll be glad to tell you all I can.'

'Language is inadequate,' the old man said. 'Perhaps we misunderstand each other more than we know.'

'Isn't that inevitable? At first, anyway.'

'Not necessarily.' He stood, his hand grasping my arm for support. 'It will be obvious to you, I suppose. I wish to record your own memories, Christie, so that I will know your world. And, as trade is the mark of Kasabaarde, I am prepared to offer you access to some of my own memories of Orthe.'

'Why do you doubt him?' the fenborn said as we went through the corridors.

'Do I?'

'Yes—or you would not speak the way you do. None of us would.' A note of outrage crept into his voice.

Stick-limbs, slit-eyes, the cool snake skin . . . it was incongruous here in the dusty, scorched south, to see a fenborn in the robes of the Brown Tower.

'Tethmet, how did you get here?'

He manipulated a fixture on the wall, and the outer doors slid open. The round roofs gleamed white beyond the gardens, white in the starlight; and the pungent smell of night-blossoming creepers drifted in.

He said, 'When I was young, men caught and caged me; took me down a great river to show for their sport. When I grew old enough I killed them, fled down the Rasrhe-y-Meluur—*he* found me.'

The sky was a silver blaze, bright stars merging. Without the mask, the city was as clear as daylight.

'You'll come back,' he said.

'I promised to give a decision. I will do, when I've thought it over.'

As I crossed the courtyard the fenborn stepped out of the Tower and called after me.

'Christie—he knows how it is to be a stranger, and an exile. You should believe that.'

Kasabaarde's streets are dangerous, even by clear starlight. Meditation, as Orinc says, turns some to wisdom, and some to idleness and violence; I had no desire for trouble. But in that rootless city there was no need to return to Su'niar. Other Orders were closer at hand.

Days passed, scoured by dust storms from the high lands, dry as a furnace. On the sixth day after my visit to the Tower, the wind swung round to the north. Bitter rainstorms whipped in off the Inner Sea, turned the dust in the streets to ankle-deep mud, and the Ortheans retreated to their dry underground dwellings. Vicious and short, the storms passed. Steam rose from the streets. And the sun blazed, and the grit drifted down from the High Desert . . .

I waited for the Hexenmeister's summons to the Tower to give him my answer. And tried desperately to think what answer I could give.

'Put that down,' Orinc said, exasperated.

Orinc's *ashiren* took the two covered buckets from me. It was a few hot yards' walk down to the street-pump and back. I sat down on the inner room bench beside the old woman.

'I like to be doing something.'

'Su'niar doesn't accept payment,' she said, and then chuckled and coughed, dust in her throat. 'You Outlanders can't do nothing, can you? You've to be fidgeting and working, and—ach! go out and sit under the awning. Do nothing. Then you'll see.'

'See what?'

Her mouth quirked under the edge of her mask. 'Can I tell you? No. If it could be told, it wouldn't be the true illumination. You must find out.'

Her insistence drove me out at last. I sat on the steps, masked against the acid sunlight, the awning's shade falling across me. Dust was warm under my bare palms. As always, a scatter of Ortheans were sitting with their backs to the dome-wall of the Order house. Some muttered, some sang, some stared; most were filthy, and all were incomprehensible. The trade-tongue was frowned on in the inner city.

Assuming it's true, I thought, and assuming Witchbreed technology can be adapted for human use as well as Orthean—how dangerous would it be? Physically, mentally, politically? The problem is simple, do I do it or don't I? I'd be a fool to do it. And a fool not to.

It's beyond my brief as an envoy. Have I the right to pass on information about Earth? But then, have I the right to refuse a chance to get information about Orthe? It's what I'm here for. And I don't know, in either case, quite what information will be gained, or what it will be used for . . . and there's no one I can ask.

Daystars were half-invisible points of light over the domed roofs, the glare of Carrick's Star drowned them. I moved as the shadow moved. Some tightness inside me I identified at last as terror.

I thought, if Kasabaarde is important, the department will condemn me for not getting all data when that's possible. If it isn't, I'll have been wasting time on trivialities—according to their way of thinking—and giving away facts about Earth's defences. So it's a no-win either way. That's assuming shock doesn't kill me—even with the hypno-teachers they have to be so damn careful . . .

Durestha's spring days lengthened, and I learned Orthean patience, waiting for the summons to the Brown Tower.

The young woman lay in the cubicle, head resting back on a mobius-strip tangle of machinery. I watched her face alter with emotions that were centuries dead. Tethmet held her baby, and it mouthed fruitlessly at the front of his tunic. The Hexenmeister sat upright on another cubicle's edge, bird-bright eyes watching.

When she was lifted free of the machine, she took the child and left. Old tears ran unchecked down her face.

'Well?' the old man asked.

'Yes,' I said. 'Now.'

The cubicle was slick under me, with a sensation unlike metal or any plastic. A hum that might have been sound or vibration surrounded me. I closed my eyes, sick. Panic told me this was a mistake, this trusting to an alien science. But it was too late.

There was a sensation that—if it had lasted any longer than a micro-second—would have been intolerable agony. There is no way to describe how that feels: as if the closed confines of the self had opened and become infinite, and the mind fragmented into pieces in an ever-expanding maze.

Total fear: I grasped in panic at some remembered snatch of conver-

sation, and what happened then happened with all the force of synaes-
thesia—

Pain.

—sitting opposite me in antique armour with a double-bladed axe at the
belt. He—or was it a young woman?—has the dark skin of a north-
erner; thin, ashbrown mane cropped short, long-fingered hands clasped
in her—or is it his?—lap.

'You will allow me to leave?' Direct eyes, unveiled. 'You'll understand I'm in something of a hurry, being what I am.'

Ashirenin, I realize, not recognizing it at first because of its rarity.
Ke is aged around twenty-seven or eight, by *kir* face. And still unchanged, unsexed, un-adult.

There are those who remain *ashiren* long past the time for change.
When the change to male or female comes, usually no later than the
mid-thirties, it invariably kills them.

'You are from the Freeport?' The word from the Order house where
ke stays is not detailed.

'From Morvren, yes. I've friends there, as well as enemies.' *Ke*
smiles. 'Good friends. Andrethe. Lori L'Ku. We may go upriver—they
say there's wild country there that could be tamed. If you let me leave
your city, master, that's what I'll do.'

'And you'll tell them what you've learned here?'

Kir eyes are bright with amusement. 'What have I learned, master?
Tell me.'

Sunlight filters through the window, patches the slick wall. It is
quiet enough to notice the subliminal hum that is the heartbeat of the
Brown Tower. This library room holds the smell of old books, of dust.
The *ashirenin* sits facing me, with a similar quiet serenity.

'You have been speaking in the Order house of Thelmithar.'

'Some have listened,' *ke* admits.

'Saying that the Southland's church is false, that the church of the
Goddess was set up only to prevent the rule of technology.'

'The second, yes, but not the first. Is it not true, master?'

'That Kerys Founder had such a purpose in mind? It may be so.'
And I would like to know where *ke* learned that, but truth has a habit
of coming to light in Kasabaarde. 'It is not my concern—'

'Then let me go.'

'—except so far as I have the friendship of the *T'An Suthai-Telestre.*'
I watch *kir* face. 'Will you return and tell the Hundred Thousand their
belief is a lie?'

'Most know what I know, master, or suspect it to be true. But no, that is not what I'd tell them.'

'What, then?'

Kir expression lightens, serious, but with an undercurrent of laughter. *Ke* leans forward intently. 'I'll tell them that Kerys, telling lies, came at last to tell the truth. The Goddess is, and we are the Goddess. The earth is. The stars are. Life is. What else should we require?'

Ke has found something in one of Kasabaarde's Orders, or in the inner city, or in the air itself: it's visible in *kir* face. I feel loss, because I'll never wholly understand it.

'I haven't long, master,' *ke* says. 'Not with the Hundred Thousand to preach to, and all the church for my enemy. Will you let me go?'

'I am not *T'An Suthai-Telestre,* to exile you from the Southland. You have your own destiny. Leave Kasabaarde. I confess I was curious, hearing from Thelmithar of this Beth'ru-elen. But I will not stop your leaving.'

'But is the Hexenmeister ever curious without reason?' *ke* asks wryly, in that archaic accent. Beth'ru-elen *Ashirenin* stands, with a last glance round at the imperishable walls of the Tower—

An instant's agony. The ancient sunlight fading now, and further falling into other reality:

speaking to a messenger. The man finishes talking, returns to squat by the fire, warming his broad hands over the flames.

'Gone into the High Desert.' He raises his head, fire-dazzled, looking to where the edge of the plateau rises against the stars. Around us, Kel Harantish burns. Wind brings ash, and skirls of dust. Men and women shout. The last fugitives are discovered, their screams hoarse.

'Not all, *s'an* Kerys. You have won a victory here.' Wondering, as I speak, how true that is.

'Have I, master? We have the city, but what use is that? I shall not keep it. We have a few of these half-breed Golden, but not the leaders.' He stands, walks a few paces into the star-lit, fire-lit darkness. Then, turning, 'Tell me, master of Kasabaarde. Tell me they won't build their cursed city up again, tell me there'll be no 'Breed science discovered again on the Desert Coast.'

'As to that . . .' Our eyes meet; his are humorous, thinking of 'Breed science in another city: Kasabaarde. 'I cannot promise, *s'an* Kerys. What is done in Tathcaer and the Hundred Thousand you may command. I have but a small city, and no warriors to crusade against Kel Harantish or Quarth or Psamnol if they rediscover 'Breed trickery.'

Some of his Seconds are here to consult him. I wait while they speak. They avoid looking at me. Kasabaarde's reputation is not entirely wholesome. Kerys returns, rubbing his hand across his eyes. Night darkens as the fires fail. He holds his cloak round himself. Desert nights are cold.

'It must go no further. This—' his arm sweeps out to include the ruins '—is the first step on the road, and the road ends where? At the Glittering Plain? In ruined Elansir? With the Hundred Thousand as dead as Eriel? No, master. We remember that destruction too well, and it must never come again. And—I do not believe we can choose, take what's good and leave the bad.'

'Another way, then?'

His face is shadowed, but the voice is clear. 'I can keep all 'Breed science out of my Hundred Thousand, make it forbidden by the church; I can begin to find that other way, yes. But what of the Desert Coast? If I forbid such weaponry, then we're defenceless. I'd let Kel Harantish do what it wishes in its own borders, why not? But would it end there; what would we do, finding them at the gates of Tathcaer? You cannot send swords against weapons that melt stone.'

'So you'd keep 'Breed weapons for their attack? And they, likewise, for yours?'

'And there is the road again, and destruction at the end of it!'

The stars are blotted out over the city by the pall of smoke. Flashes of blue light and sharp explosions mark the destruction of hoarded Golden technology. Kerys beckons. I rise and walk beside him, over pavements cracked by heat. The acrid smell comes on the wind, and the sound of flames. This garrison city: shattered with explosions, obscured by drifting smoke, and choking with the stink of burning—and worse.

'Easier to follow the Golden way and hope to avoid their end. Harder to make our own way. But still, master, we must try. And if we have not the weapons to defeat 'Breed technology, then we must do it by cunning and misdirection and stealth.' He smiles. The humour is genuine. 'Our ancestors deceived the Goldens themselves. Surely we can outwit this so-called Emperor-in-Exile.'

'It would be no advantage to Kasabaarde to see the Golden Empire come again.'

'Nor any advantage to Kasabaarde's Hexenmeister.'

'That too, s'an Kerys. I cannot control Kel Harantish, but I think it unlikely that any Desert Coast city would ally with them, no, and no Rainbow City either.'

'And this is done—how?'

'They must trade, *s'an,* and they must pass Kasabaarde. And we are always open—to those who abhor Witchbreed and all their works.'

Kasabaarde's power now is an accident of geography: to reach the Southland ports from the Desert Coast, ships must sail up the coast to Kasabaarde, re-provisioning, and then on up to the Archipelago. This is not to say that certain ships can't sail across the ocean to the Eastern Isles and thus directly to Ales-Kadareth—only that such ships must use all their hold-space for provisions, and thus cannot trade. Ships that go that way are passenger ships, or warships. Warships have no need to reprovision at Kasabaarde: another welcome accident.

Kerys stops, one hand on my shoulder. 'We too must trade. But we are a rich land. I think we could survive without Kasabaarde's blessing if we had to.'

Conscious of the pressure of his hand, of being alone and far from my people, I am careful in answering.

'Would you have to, *s'an* Kerys? There has always been friendship between the Brown Tower and the White City.'

'Kasabaarde and Tathcaer, yes. Yes.' His hand moves, links into his belt beside the *harur* blades. 'Sometimes, master, I wonder if we are wiser trusting you than we were trusting Kel Harantish.'

'Would you be here otherwise?'

'Perhaps, and perhaps not.'

He does not look much, this man, to have pulled order out of the long chaos after the Empire's fall. A tan skin, a brown braided mane, and whiteless sea-blue eyes; the diamond-patterns of care incised deeply on his skin. But to see him move, act . . .

And he will create the *telestres* out of chaos, the church out of necessity, and be remembered not for what he did, but—in the manner of legends when past-dreams have not yet made them clear—also for what he might have done. I alone will remember, and know.

'You may trust Kasabaarde,' I say, 'for as long as I am Hexenmeister of it.'

By his glance, I can tell that some rumours have come to his ears. And Kel Harantish burns—

The birth-pains of antiquity:

'—cheated me!' the voice echoes in the vast hexagonal rooms. 'And so I destroyed him.'

Turning from the shattered instruments of glass and copper, I watch Santhendor'lin-sandru. A few sphere-lights glow blue, bobbing in the still air, clustering to follow him as he paces. Others are only blackened sphere-shells, burnt out and clinging in the upper angles of the halls. Tenebrous darkness webs itself into those corners of translucent grey stone.

'Cheated you, Emperor?'

'I gave him everything!' Santhendor'lin-sandru faces me. Tall and slender, gold-skinned, his unbound mane like white fire. Yellow animal eyes in a face so beautiful that it is desecration for it to look angry, greedy, petulant—as it does now.

'How long did he work, and feed me promises? How long?' The cold-toned voice speaking the liquid, multisyllabic tongue of Archonis. 'And for nothing! So that it comes down to this, you cheat me no longer, Eyr'ra Thel Siawn. Never, no, never again.'

He steps through the vast span of the window-arch, seemingly into void; but a chill shimmer of air supports him, the bubble-field that keeps out the bone-cold northland wind. Archonis lies like a well of light, holding in its stone hand the Six Lakes and the river that flows through them to the inland sea.

'And did he fail, Emperor?' Which, I realize, is what I've come to discover; having spoken with Thel Siawn before that erratic genius's death. Was he allowed time to complete his work?

'He brought me nothing!' The beginning of that hysterical anger to which the Emperor is prone. His back to the sprawling city, he throws out an arm, animal-graceful, pointing into the blue glow of the wrecked chamber. Precise machines lay warped and shattered. 'All this I gave him! The first beastman to lay hands on the old science—irony, that!— so that what we created becomes itself a creator . . . and *nothing!* Am I to be put off, delayed, lied to?'

Behind him, Archonis's lights burn in the crepuscular northern night. Strings of sphere-lights; the hills above the lakes are speckled, freckled with blue, the sky beaded with towers of light that drown a skyful of stars. And for all that, the light is like a single sphere in a great dark hall: it serves barely to illuminate the edges and lower storeys of the city's cyclopean architecture.

Low towers border the nearer lake. Black beads line the rims, like shrivelled fruit. Severed heads. Closer, and you would see how many are wind-dried and dessicated, how many yet bleed.

I follow Santhendor'lin-sandru back into the chamber. The stone echoes as we walk: the brush of footsteps, the low hums and clicks of machinery, the roar of distant flyers in the night sky. There is a taste of dust in the air, despite all that the force-fields can do. A taste of chill, as if the lake-mist could creep inside.

'So Thel Siawn is dead.'

The angel calmness returns to his hawk-face. 'But I should never have trusted him. They are nothing more than animals, these beastmen, they never will be. Never let them into your bed.'

He watches me, and I am careful to give nothing away.

'*You* are some kind of friend to them, I've heard.'

'Friend? No.'

But I know now that Thel Siawn did succeed. Succeeded, and made use of Santhendor'lin-sandru's desires. Perhaps he was the genius I call him. Certainly he in his short life made more use of the old sciences of biology and gene-sculpting than we have since the Arrival.

'Cousin, you are quiet.'

It smells dry and arid here. Sphere-lights tingle on the skin, the links of metal-cloth slide as I walk. No scent-fountains play. And it is free now of that rank mustiness that no scent-fountain can ever disguise, that of our creations, the beastmen, the slaves.

'It occurs to me . . .'

'Well?'

'You allowed him experiments sculpting viruses, and it is true that many cures for beastmen's sicknesses have come from here. And yet—if that were not all? If there were diseases here to harm *us,* and they were let loose on the world?'

Which is an irony he might appreciate, if he ever knew, having bedded Thel Siawn and thus almost certainly begun the long spreading of a sculpted virus and a certain effect.

'I shall have these halls decontaminated, cousin; and—for your excellent advice—you may stay here and oversee the work.'

There are tendrils of darkness in the city, patches of shadow on the massive stone. Or do I dream, and is Archonis still as he sees it: the brilliant beating heart of the cities of the world, the fountainhead of the infinite sun of Golden rule?

Santhendor'lin-sandru will sire no more children, nor will any whom he beds, nor any whom they touch—spreading out from the middle lands to all the reaches of the Empire. They will turn on each other when they know, fight bloody wars; the Elansiir will be desert, this a barren wasteland of dead cities; the north will become the Twilight Shore, and Eriel pass to leave only a glittering plain. Sterile, this Empire, and terrible its passing.

'There is something else we might do, first.'

'Kyrianshur'na-rian, yes.'

There are places in the south, I've heard, where a Golden woman might find refuge, beyond the Rasrhe-y-Meluur. And we will need refuges when the last of us—long-lived as we are—fall into the hands of Thel Siawn's people.

His embrace is cruel, rapid, welcome. When I leave him I will bear a gift he knows nothing of. In the slick angles of the hall I see our merged reflection, Golden woman and Golden man, and Thel Siawn's ghost with us for ever.

Santhendor'lin-sandru, who in the beast-tongue is remembered as slavemaster and roadbuilder, and as Sandor, the Last Emperor.

Pain:

And I am not made up of these brief interruptions, these turning-points, however vital. I am the sum total of thousands of winter days walking the sleeping fields, of summers in the ships on the Inner Sea. Uncounted thousands of days: eating, sleeping, working, coupling; and coming at last to the Brown Tower. These unnoticed days touching the earth, under the changing sky; these made me.

And I am the constructed beastmen, offspring of Golden and fenborn; and all their long descendants in the south. And I am Witchbreed, in the infinite summer of the Empire; a golden richness that lay on the world uncounted thousand years.

In the cold reaches of my memory there is more:

—stars visible even at noon. Our shadows fall blackly to the pole of the world. The fierce sun that parents this world makes life impossible for us at the equator.

Wind rustles the vegetation. The others of the Set are down by the water, overseeing the servitors. I scuttle towards them, hesitate, then pass them and go on to the hilltop.

The pillars of the henge gleam in the sun, the capstones black and dead. I pick my way over the mossy ground to the centre of the circle and rear up into the rest-position. Empty archways surround me. Through them I see lowland, river, distant hills, and the few of us who remain alive.

I have seen these archways when they glowed, each one opening to a separate world, a jewel-box of landscapes, skies, stars and seas.

—It's useless, Keeper—

The Second has followed me, glitter-eyed as she has been since the catastrophe. I answer gently.

—There are too few of us, we cannot activate the Set. No one will pass through. The worlds are closed to us—

Claws strike chitin, she is grieving.

—Singer is dead—

—It is better, I think—

Emergencies happen, accidents happen. But to lose First, Third and Fourth in one contact; to have the Flyer and the Focus mindless, and the Nightsearcher and the Singer dead. . . .

—We'll never be a Set again, Keeper. We're on this world for good now, aren't we?—

—Yes—

—And our lives?—

There is no kindness in untruth.

—We're too far from the centre to reproduce. This is all there will ever be of us. But even this far from the centre, our lives will be long—

—Longer than we wish?—

—Perhaps so—

She shivers down her whole length, and turns to watch the few of us that are left: the Favoured, the Breathstealer, the Shadower. And, of course, the servitors.

—Will the servitors adapt to this world, Keeper? Will they breed?—

—I think so. In any case there is life closer to the equator, biped humanoid, very similar to the servitors. We can adapt them to our needs—

—That is good. I would not spend my last aeons alone—

The light, the cool wind, the scent of running water; all are strange to me. I wonder how long it will take for them to become over-familiar.

—We must leave the histories here—

She clicks scorn, her faceted eyes brilliant in the sun.

—Who will find them, Keeper? Who? We are the only travellers. The servitors have no mind-talent. They cannot contact, or connect. None will follow us. None will find us. The worlds are numerous as dust-specks in a sunbeam—

—Nevertheless, I am Keeper. The histories will be preserved—

A servitor comes stilt-legged up the hill, calling us to feed. Small, thick-limbed, wingless; its maned head on a level with mine. Will we change them to live on this world? I wonder; and will they, with their swift generations, outlive us at the last?

Having no power of contact, it bends its jointed stick-thin limbs to approximate the gesture of respect. It has jelly-eyes, with little intelligence in them, but evolution can play strange tricks and flukes. Strange if they were to survive, and raise up empires after we are gone. Eyes like beads, yellow as suns that—I am reminded—we will never see again. I drop out of rest-position to scuttle down the hill. . . .

Micro-pain: rejection: fear.

—slick walls, semi-metallic, and the carefully hoarded remnants of technology that remain in the Brown Tower. Moving stiffly, I sit up. The air is cool. There are levels under this, I know, down in the bedrock below the inner city. And above these protected walls the scorched dusty streets of Kasabaarde: I should like to walk in the open now, though I still hold the tactile memory of mossgrass. . . .

'Christie, hear me.'

When is this? I wonder. No time feels like the past when experienced. There is only ever Now.

'Are you well?'

A fenborn beside me, mask removed. Were the fenborn ever in Kasabaarde, or is this somewhere else? No, I know his name: Tethmet. The expression on his face is jealousy. And the old man—the Hexenmeister?

How can there be two of us?

He says again: 'Christie?'

'I think . . . I'm not sure. Is this another memory?' I rub my temples, trying to shift the pain. 'When am I going to wake up from this one?'

The fenborn hands me a bowl of liquid; hot, sweet, and stinging. It scours my throat. The physical sensation is an anchor to reality. The old man watches me anxiously.

'That is an effect I didn't anticipate, I am sorry. Believe me, you are out of the machine. This is your direct experience, not my memory.'

'Your memory? Not my memory?' My body aches: bones, joints, tendons, muscles. Looking down, I see unfamiliar hands clasped round the bowl. Stubby short-fingered hands, skin burned dark by Carrick's Star. 'How long . . . how long did it take?'

'It's noon,' the fenborn says, 'you began a little after sunrise.'

The old man reassures me. 'Not long, though it seems long to you.'

Details are coming back to me. My head clears. There was something else, wasn't there? Yes. 'You said you wanted to record my memories.' Aware of tension that is fear. 'We'd better get it over and done with.'

'Not necessary, Christie. It was done while you were here.'

'Already? I—'

'It's done,' the old man says. It takes the incomprehension on the fenborn's face to make me realize the words are English. And the old man is looking at me with an expression at once unfamiliar and known, that I have seen before.

In a mirror.

26

The Players of *Ochmir*

The sunlight outside the Tower's entrance dazzled me. I blinked water out of my eyes, blinked again—and realized I expected that to dim the brilliance, wanting human muscles to do what they couldn't: bring a third eyelid down. Hastily I put on my mask.

'I need you to come to the Tower again,' the Hexenmeister said. The shadow of the archway hid his face. But the voice, the phrasing, it was too familiar. 'What I know about your world, I find I need explained to me. Perhaps it's the same for you?'

'Yes, I—I'll come back, yes.' Tense, nervous, I waited for something —a needle of pain, maybe, that would wake me to a different reality?

'Be easy,' the old man said. 'It fades, after a time.'

I promised to return, and left him. Walking across the gardens, I was still conscious of unease. Peripheral memories haunted me. Pale-robed Ortheans passed me in the dusty streets, and I stared after them.

I know how it feels to be you, how you carry yourself, veil your eyes with darkness; how fear raises hackles down your spine, stiffens clawed hands. How you breathe and walk, I know.

The walk back to Su'niar was long. I felt uneasy in my own skin.

There were no writing-sticks or parchments available in the Order houses—they're not considered necessities of life—so I paid toll and entered the trade city. It was necessary to make some kind of a report before I lost all the details, I don't have the Hexenmeister's eidetic memory. Grasping remembered visions is clutching at sand.

Back in Su'niar, while they were strong, I wrote them down. The sexless, illuminated face of Beth'ru-elen, in the days before Peir-Dadeni was founded; Kerys and burning Kel Harantish, at the Southland's birth. And the Golden woman's stark insanity, uncounted ages past in the last days of the Empire. And the Keeper. Whatever it was. Spanning the ages—but that was rationalization: it felt like yesterday, like today.

Examined from a human point of view, they were often incomprehensible. Memories, like dreams, have their own internal logic.

Stone tubs stood on the flat roof of the tower. Ash-grey and violet-leafed shrubs grew in scarlet moss. Between them were benches, under awnings, and it was possible to sit and look out over the round domes of the inner city to the harbour. Haze hid the daystars.

A humming sound broke the silence. The Hexenmeister glanced at the small dome in the center of the roof-garden. It split open to disclose Tethmet on the lift-platform. The fenborn came towards us, with his usual stare of disapproval for me, and handed a message to the old man.

'This might interest you, Christie,' he said, reading slowly. 'The *T'An Suthai-Telestre* and the *takshiriye* have returned to Tathcaer . . . Durestha Firstweek, yes, three weeks back.' He smiled. 'News travels slowly. Sometimes.'

'Any news about the Andrethe's murder?' If they'd caught the killer . . . sudden excitement seized me.

'No, nothing of that. As to the rest of this,' he glanced up at the fenborn, 'say I shall come down to the meeting hall in a short time.'

The fenborn bowed and returned to the lift. I realized I was picking the scarlet moss off the tub beside me. Fragments littered the slick surface of the roof.

'Don't worry,' the old man said, 'they'll discover the killer. She was the Andrethe, she had her guard. She was in the Crystal Hall where she met with her intelligencers—the only time she would be unguarded. And it must have been someone she knew and trusted, else she'd have fought.'

'You're pretty sure I'm innocent.'

'You forget,' his hand tightened on my arm, 'I was there.'

There wasn't the same cross-identity that there had been directly after the transfer, but the closeness still shocked me. When his grip loosened, I stood and walked towards the edge of the roof. The atmosphere shimmered. Sweat dried immediately in the dry heat. I rubbed the back of my neck, where the sun beat down—cropped hair wasn't long enough to be a protection. Phantom sensations plagued me: I expected to scratch clawed fingers through the thickness of the spinal mane. Down in the inner city the streets were quiet, but I saw dust rising from the carts in the trade city.

The same scattered crowd sat under the street-awnings. The individ-

uals changed, but there were always people there. Why not, when the
Orders fed, housed, and clothed them? I pulled robe-sleeves down over
sun-blackened arms. It was an awkward feeling for me, being a head
taller than anyone else. It marked me out: that and my Outlander appearance, and visits to the Tower. And I no longer expected to be
different.

The city is a disconcerting place to live. I stood a while longer,
looking out over that city where all beliefs are possible: a place of
mysticism, idleness, violence, and vision.

'Come inside,' the Hexenmeister said. 'I have a meeting to attend
that will also interest you.'

He was painfully slow when he walked. At last we reached the lift-
dome, and the light of Carrick's Star gave way to the diffuse illumination of the Tower. I couldn't tell precisely where we stopped; my ac-
quired knowledge was sketchy.

Several of the brown-robes came up to give the Hexenmeister messages. He acknowledged them, continuing towards the meeting hall. It
was as bare and functional as all Tower rooms, apart from the old man's
quarters. Tethmet supervised the setting of chairs round an oval table,
and the provision of herb-tea.

'Let them enter,' the Hexenmeister said, taking the carved chair at
the head of the table.

A group of people came in. I recognized Ymirian dress—uncomfortably hot, I thought, and then realized: the Southland, here? Several
in Crown Guard uniforms ranged themselves either side of the square-
arched door. They were weaponless. The main party entered: a tall
woman with a curiously familiar face, some others I'd seen at court, all
attended by the Tower's brown-robes.

'Dalzielle Evalen Kerys-Andrethe,' Tethmet announced. *'T'an*
Evalen, you are in the presence of the Hexenmeister.'

'Goddess give you good day—' the well-known accents of Ymirian.
And the face of this young woman was Suthafiori's, thirty years ago.
She looked at me and stopped.

'You have met the Dominion envoy?' the old man inquired.

'I have with me some who have,' she said grimly. 'Haltern!'

He looks harassed as ever, was my first thought. And I'll take bets
that he hated every minute of the journey. And coped. And heard every
rumour between Tathcaer and Kasabaarde.

'Hal.'

He looked uncertainly at the woman, then at me; then stepped forward and gripped my hands. I thought, has my reputation sunk *that* low?

'I had no news of you after Morvren Freeport. To find you here—' he shook his head. '*T'an* Evalen, this is Lynne de Lisle Christie.'

It wasn't just the heat that was making the Southlanders uncomfortable. Evalen's narrow fingers linked in her belt by the empty scabbards, and she stared round at the bare brown walls of the Tower before she spoke. Bright clothes that suited Tathcaer were anachronistic here.

I missed Tathcaer's white stone walls, and the northern sea; missed them more than I would have thought possible. The Desert Coast's hot season grated on me.

'Master,' Evalen said, 'you'll understand my reluctance. I refuse to discuss the business of the Hundred Thousand in the presence of the Andrethe's murderer.'

He gave an old man's wheezing chuckle. 'I can answer for nothing else, *t'an,* but of the Andrethe's murder, at least, she is not guilty.'

The woman looked, looked again: a perfect double-take. Exclamations from the other Southlanders were quickly hushed. She said, 'You're telling me she didn't do it?'

'I know she did not.'

An incredulous grin spread over Haltern's face. He looked from the Hexenmeister to Evalen Kerys-Andrethe, and his hand came down on my shoulder in a congratulatory slap.

'Perfect,' he said under his breath, 'perfect!'

'If the envoy didn't do it, who did?' Evalen demanded.

'That I do not yet know, or I would have sent word to your mother.' Recalled to her duties, she executed a formal bow. 'The *T'An Suthai-Telestre* sends her regards and greetings to you, master.'

He acknowledged that, and gestured at the table. 'If you will be seated.'

She took the chair at the foot of the table. In the confusion as the Southlanders arranged themselves, she leaned across to me.

'I apologize, *t'an,* for what I said. News of this hasn't reached Tathcaer, and I still believed—'

'That's all right,' I said hastily. 'We'll discuss Tathcaer later, if that's possible.'

'Of course.'

When I could speak to Haltern without being noticed, I said 'Will they credit it in the Hundred Thousand, just on the Hexenmeister's word?'

'It carries weight with some. Though not in Peir-Dadeni, you'll find.' He pushed a six-fingered hand through his pale cropped mane, blinking worriedly at me. 'And they'd be better pleased knowing who is guilty, if the envoy isn't—but a clever move, nonetheless.'

I smiled.

He said 'You've changed.'

He didn't seem displeased. I wondered what he saw, shrewd as he was.

'Meduenin said he left you at the Freeport,' he added. 'I thought we might find you somewhere on the Desert Coast, though not here.'

'You've spoken to Blaize?'

'He's with the rest of *t'an* Evalen's company, back in the trade city. Your young *l'ri-an,* too.'

'Rodion's here?' I want to talk to them, I thought. 'Listen, Hal, what's all this about?'

He shrugged, amused. 'The Hexenmeister seems to require your presence in our discussions, and the Southland commonly humours his eccentricities. If you stay, Christie, you'll hear.'

Not like this I won't, I thought. Formalities between the Hundred Thousand and the Brown Tower are lengthy and formidable, and Evalen seemed determined to plough through all of them. The Hexenmeister's interviews were short—I tended to forget quite how old he was—and if they weren't finished soon, I could see nothing constructive being done before tomorrow.

'So what does Suthafiori want with the Brown Tower?'

Haltern's veiled eyes resolved into clarity. 'What anyone requires of the Hexenmeister—knowledge. Knowledge of Kel Harantish. It's apparent now that SuBannasen wasn't the only Southlander taking gold from the Emperor-in-Exile.'

The meeting reconvened after the noon meal (and after the old man had slept for a while, I think). This time it took place in the library, being less formal, and a lot of the Southlanders' tension vanished on finding they were not underground, and had windows open to the sunlight. It could have been any library in the Hundred Thousand, that room, and no one surrounded by books could fail to be reminded of the Tower's reputation for knowledge. The old man set his stage very carefully.

Afternoon sun illuminated the table, and the tea-bowls and fruit and sweetmeats. Tethmet stood behind the Hexenmeister's chair, watching us with the silent dislike for strangers that many of the Tower brown-robes had. His devotion to the old man was fanatical. Evalen bowed as she entered, and motioned the two Southlanders with her to sit at the table. Both took notes throughout. Haltern joined us, leaving the un-armed Crown Guard outside the chamber. The door slid shut behind him, and he flinched.

'Now,' the Hexenmeister said, 'what does Suthafiori say to me?'

'You'll have heard of unrest in the Hundred Thousand,' Evalen said, with complete confidence that he would know as much about the Southland as the child of the *T'An Suthai-Telestre.*

'Yes, and—if I may say this, Christie—much of it centred round this matter of other worlds.'

Evalen nodded. 'It's natural there should be those for and against the matter. But if it were only that, the *T'An* Suthafiori would not need to fear the loss of the Crown at Midsummer.'

'The loss—' I broke off at the Hexenmeister's gesture.

'It has always been the policy of your land not to obstruct the opinions of the Hundred Thousand. If they do not desire contact with the Dominion . . .'

'If that was all it was!' She glanced at me. 'And even so, if the Southland wants nothing to do with Earth, that's not to say Earth won't go to other lands on Orthe. Isn't that so, *t'an?*'

'That's so,' I agreed.

'Saberon, Kasabaarde, Kel Harantish even,' she elaborated, 'all will-ing, for their own reasons. And there's the Hundred Thousand left to come in rag, tag, and bobtail after the crowd, on Earth's conditions and not our own! Because it *will* come, we can't ignore it. All we can do is try and control the speed of it.' Her hands caught the sunlight, skin gleaming with a grainy quality. Faint marshflower-dapples were visible on her bony wrists. 'Whatever eventual relationship there is between our worlds, envoy, the changes should be introduced gradually. Perhaps over generations. That's always been the way with change in the Hun-dred Thousand.'

'I can't say yet what the Dominion's policy will be. It's part of my job to gain information to help them decide.' They'd pay lip service to sociology, I thought, but the truth of it was that Orthe was a backwater world, and liable to remain so. Or *was* that true, with the remnants of Golden technology left here? 'One thing occurs to me, *t'an* Evalen, and that's medical technology.'

The Hexenmeister said, 'There is much you have that we need des-perately. Most knowledge was lost when the Witchbreed fell. I grant there are physicians, the best of them in the Southland's church; but fevers and pestilence, wounds, sickness, childbirth . . .'

Steam coiled up from the bowls, and the scent of *arniac* herb-tea permeated the still air.

'If you have aids against such things on your world,' Evalen said, 'would they be acceptable to us here?'

'High level medicine demands high level technology to back it, *t'an,* and your church may object. Unless you'd keep it on a basis of trading for medical supplies . . . but that brings me back to my original point,' I said, 'which is that Orthe isn't a densely-populated world, and any Earth disease you have no immunity to could prove very serious.'

The old man nodded. 'Another year of the White Death could reduce us to Barrens savagery, and who's to say there aren't such plagues on your world.'

'Therefore you need restricted contact with the Dominion. Ideally Orthe should have some kind of quarantine.' That was a familiar concept to the Southland, at least, and I saw Evalen nod agreement.

'And for that you must have a Crown who supports Earth,' she said. 'Suthafiori bid me say it need not be her, but in truth I think there's only she that can do it.'

'It's not my business to fight Suthafiori's battles for her,' the Hexenmeister said testily. 'The Tower doesn't interfere outside Kasabaarde's walls. If she's to be named Crown again, then let the Southland name her.'

'If it was the Southland alone, I shouldn't be here,' Evalen persisted. 'Admitted, there is a strong faction who hold out for no contact with Earth at all—Howice *T'An* Roehmonde for one, and Thu'ell *T'An* Rimon, and perhaps the Seamarshal of Morvren Freeport.'

He chuckled. 'I know the Hundred Thousand too well to be concerned over a few of the *T'Ans*. The *telestres* are quite capable of going off and constituting themselves a new Crown and *takshiriye,* and leaving you and Howice and Suthafiori looking silly.'

'That is their ancient right,' she said stiffly, over the laughter that went round the room. Then, as she relaxed, genuine concern showed on her face. 'Yes, I think—I hope—most are opposed to Earth out of their own convictions. But some aren't, master. There's evidence that much of that party's support doesn't come from the Southland, but from Kel Harantish and the Emperor-in-Exile.'

It was quiet enough to hear boots grate on the smooth floor as one of the guards fidgeted. The Hexenmeister's eyes became bright. 'Now is that so?'

'Several minor affairs point to that city.' Evalen watched me, still speaking to him. 'It occurs to me, master, that if the envoy is guiltless of the Andrethe's death, that too might find a home in Kel Harantish.'

He lowered his hand as if to strike the table, touched it softly instead, and swore archaic oaths under his breath. His fingers moved blindly, following the grain of the wood. 'Now that's not proved.'

'Not proved, but likely?' she appealed.

'It must be looked into,' he said absently. 'Yes . . . Harantish behind a Southland conspiracy? You know your own people, *t'an* Evalen, is it likely?'

'I would have said nothing was less likely,' she admitted, 'nothing—unless it was visitors from the stars. So, one being possible, why not the other?'

'That's supposition, not fact.'

'I have details that my people will give you later. What Suthafiori asks is this, master: knowledge of Kel Harantish's affairs, and, I'm now forced to add, knowledge of Kanta Andrethe's murder. Will you help us?'

'I'll see what may be discovered.' He was sitting hunched up, mouth puckered with weariness. A tendril from his crest-mane strayed down towards the veiled eyes, deep in their nest of wrinkles. His hands shook. 'I'm not convinced of Kel Harantish's involvement; you must show me your evidence.'

I got bogged down in the talk of corruption and past scandal that followed. Names and places were familiar to me—but not from my own memories. I nibbled one of the edible fungi, with its pepper-and-spice flavour. It tasted subtly different. My standards of comparison were Orthean.

And I thought about Sulis n'ri n'suth SuBannasen, and treachery, and the game the Hundred Thousand play that isn't *ochmir.*

Evalen was stocky for an Orthean, broad across the shoulders. Her mane, growing out of a short crop, lay damply against her brown skin. Most of Suthafiori's gestures found a muffled echo in her—the way she sprawled back, fingers linked, slurring an Ymirian-accented version of the trade-tongue. But the blunt plodding manner she had was all her own, and concealed a surprising, if slow, intelligence.

'We'll continue later, master, if we may,' she said. 'I'm at your direction, of course, but I should see my company settled in their quarters. Tomorrow?'

He inclined his head. 'The Tower will investigate further, *t'an.* And the envoy, also, will stay in the city? There should be further discussions concerning Peir-Dadeni.'

'Of course,' I agreed. As things stood, Kasabaarde was still safer for me than Tathcaer.

I walked back with Haltern as far as the gate to the trade city.

'You'll stay with our company?' He squinted at me, in the glare of that long spring afternoon.

'No.' I saw an expression on his face that was half personal disappointment, and half professional curiosity. 'It's more practical at the moment, the way my finances are, if I stay in one of the Order houses.'

He laughed. 'You know we'll loan you whatever you need.'

'I know, but I'd as soon not be in debt. In any case . . .'

'Yes?' he prompted.

'Not being practical, there are still reasons why I'd like to stay in the inner city.' I couldn't frame them, somehow. But I found the words that made sense to Haltern: 'Your Beth'ru-elen stayed here, after all.'

27

News from Tathcaer

His fair-maned head towered over the crowds as he came up the covered street, obviously searching for something. He was barefoot, the white dust crusting on his skin. Empty scabbards hung at his belt, and his shirt was unlaced, I saw him pull it off and sling it across his shoulder. Paired nipples showed under the dust that grimed him. His mane straggled out of a crop-cut, rooted down his bony spine. Eyes alert, nictitating membrane closed against the bright evening light.

Even in that city of masks, he left his scarred face uncovered.

'Christie!' he called, coming over and dropping down on his haunches beside me on the Order-house steps. 'Sunmother! What are you doing in this madman's city?'

'Waiting,' I said. 'You took your time. Haltern tell you where I was?'

'If I depended on *him* to know what's happening—' he stopped. 'I forgot, he's a friend of yours.'

'Mmm. What do you reckon on him?'

'Haltern n'ri n'suth Beth'ru-elen?' He shrugged. 'If you played *ochmir* with him, you'd never be able to catch him cheating.'

It might or might not be a compliment. It was certainly true.

'So how's Tathcaer?' I asked.

'I saw your *t'an* Huxton, he took your package. And I think kept silent that he'd had news from you, it wasn't known in the city when I left.' Blaize sat on the steps, removing a leather pouch from his belt. 'He sends this to you. There's a letter in your own tongue, he'd not send a message by word of mouth.'

Huxton had obviously written at a near-hysterical pitch of anger. He wanted to know where I was, what the hell I was doing there, and in any case I should stop it and get back to Tathcaer at once, and for god's sake have a good explanation for what happened in Peir-Dadeni. I read it and chuckled. Whether the head of a xeno-team had technical superiority to an envoy or vice-versa was open to doubt, and I was going back to Tathcaer only when I considered it safe.

'I've another message,' he said.

'Who from?'

'The *T'An* Melkathi Ruric Orhlandis.' He rubbed the bridge of his nose with his fingers, eyes tightened with concentration. 'She says, The envoy's supposed murder of the Andrethe is a major scandal in Tathcaer now, and will be until after the naming of the new Crown. There have been attempts on the lives of some of Suthafiori's party. Advise you to stay overseas until the matter's settled, and the killer found.'

'Mmm . . .' Investigating the pouch further, I found cords of silver and bronze beads. That was one worry off my mind. 'Is she well?'

'She seems so, yes.' He gave a scarred lopsided smile. 'As to that about Suthafiori's party, that's true enough; there have been assassins sent against Orhlandis and Hanathra. All failed. And, being a known associate of yours, I found no employment myself until *T'An* Ruric hired me to travel with Rodion.'

If Tathcaer was that dangerous, I could see why Ruric would want Rodion as far away as possible. Although, being Orthean, she'd also use Rodion as her eyes and ears on the *t'an* Evalen's delegation.

The Meduenin looked tense. I said, 'What's the matter with you?'

'Me?' He seemed surprised. 'Nothing.'

'You think all of Evalen's party are trustworthy?'

'Yes, that's safe enough. As far as it's possible to tell.' One of the Su'niar Order brushed past him, going into the house. He moved aside quickly. The curved shutters were going up in the street as the evening shadows lengthened. Like most Orders, the Su'niar lived on the house's lower floors, but slept in the ground level domes. Blaize said, 'Why do you stay here, Christie?'

'That's the second time I've been asked that. I like it here.'

'It bothers me,' he said, and I remembered he'd been in Kasabaarde before. 'No decent food, no music, and crazy-headed lunatics for company. No, give me the trade city every time.'

'I admit I could stand a drink and a good game of *ochmir* from time to time.'

'No *ochmir,* not in the inner city. It's under ban. You'll have to come to us for that.'

'I will,' I said, affectionately. He was sitting with shoulders hunched, hands linked between his knees. 'Blaize, I'm glad you're here. I wish you'd tell me what's worrying you, though.'

He lifted his head. 'Christie, can I ask you something?'

'You can ask me anything.'

He still hesitated. Then at last said, 'Your *l'ri-an,* Rodion.'

'You've seen her more recently than I have.'

'I suppose I never took much notice of her at Shiriya-Shenin—her being *ashiren*—but now coming from Tathcaer, she's . . .' he moved his hand helplessly, searching for words. 'I didn't think I'd ever . . . but she's so young. And now I . . .'

I thought, she's still a child! But that was a human attitude, and my instincts now were for the Orthean.

'Are you *arykei?*'

He didn't answer directly. 'I can't take her back to Meduenin, even if it is my *telestre.* And how will it look if I come grubbing round Orhlandis to become *n'ri n'suth?*'

Looking at him, I was conscious of a regret that I'd sent him to Tathcaer. I felt as if I'd been shown a possibility and had it denied, all in the one moment. Rodion . . . ah well.

'How would it look?' I threw the question back at him.

'It'll look like some out-at-elbows mercenary come cap in hand to the *T'An* Melkathi's *telestre,* that's how.' One hand rubbed his scarred face. 'Christie, what do I do?'

'What does she say, herself?' Then, seeing his face, 'You've spoken to her, haven't you? Blaize, have you told her any of this?'

'I was waiting—I don't know what I was waiting for.' He sounded angry with himself. Then his eyes cleared. 'You're close to me as any kinsister. If you get the chance, will you talk to her? Don't say anything about . . . just see what kind of a woman you'd take her for.'

'Sure,' I said. 'You think I'm the one to judge?'

'You're the one I'm asking.'

'All right, all right. Shall I see you up at the Tower with Evalen and her people?'

'Not if I can help it.' He stood up to go. 'I wouldn't enter the Brown Tower for all the gold in a Mercenaries' Guildhouse. See you in the trade city, Christie.'

The discussions resumed on Sixday, again in the Tower's library. The *t'an* Evalen brought Haltern with her, as a scribe; and the Hexenmeister kept Tethmet-fenborn by him.

'Regarding Kel Harantish,' Evalen said when the formalities were over, 'and the matter of the Andrethe's death, it seems to me that the solving of the one would do much to counteract the influence of the

other. If the envoy were *proved* to be innocent—and the killer found—
that would remove much of the prejudice against Outworlders, and so
make it more probable that Kerys-Andrethe retains the Crown.'

'You'd be well-advised in any case to discover the real murderer,'
the old man said, and the sly humour in his voice went unnoticed.

'So,' Evalen went on doggedly, 'can you help us, master?'

'I know a little of the matter.' He proceeded to outline events as he
(or rather I) had seen them. It wasn't something I enjoyed recalling.

My seat was opposite the window. Chill air drifted in, with the scent
of *arniac* flower on it. The sun had barely risen. I couldn't see it, the
window faced west, but the light sent damp shadows across the city's
straight roads. Far in the distance, beyond the domes and the last pillar
of the Rasrhe-y-Meluur, the pylon tipped with gold, a blue haze hid the
High Desert. Soon the sun would burn all the coolness out of the air.

'I'll say this,' the old man observed, 'that if it were done by order of
the Emperor-in-Exile, then he could hardly have chosen a better victim
than Kanta Andrethe. She was loved beyond the Peir-Dadeni *telestres.*'

Haltern inclined his head respectfully to the old man, then to
Evalen. 'Your pardon, but it was not so in one case. SuBannasen *telestre*
have no cause to love her, and though Sulis is dead, there are still others
who bear the name. Remember, the Kel Harantish gold came by ship to
Ales-Kadareth; SuBannasen is close to the city.'

'They'd not risk it now, not with the Orhlandis named *T'An*
Melkathi,' Evalen objected. 'But . . . I wouldn't like to say that
Witchbreed gold isn't still finding its way to the Hundred Thousand.'

'Could a SuBannasen have murdered the Andrethe?' the Hexenmeister wondered aloud. 'As revenge for Sulis's death. And then seen
an opportunity, and put the blame on the envoy?'

Evalen frowned. 'You said the killer would be one she trusted. She'd
never trust any SuBannasen so close, then.'

Haltern said, 'She sometimes saw her intelligencers in the Crystal
Hall. That's why there were few guards, so they could come and go
secretly. That might have been known to someone, and so they could
come upon her when she was unprepared.'

'Now, was it planned or unplanned?' The Hexenmeister shifted in
his chair, and the fenborn bent over him and tucked the pelt close
round his knees. At a quiet word, he left the room. The old man continued, 'By that I mean, was it a chance killing, and the blame afterwards
put on the Dominion envoy because that was convenient? Or was it
deliberately planned to discredit Christie's people?'

There was some speculation, inconclusive on both sides. Tethmet returned with bowls of hot *arniac* tea. While we were drinking, I had to go over all the circumstances of my last day in Shiriya-Shenin.

'Someone knew your movements,' Haltern said. His hands cupped a blue glazed bowl, steam coiling over the surface of the crimson liquid. 'Someone knew you were at court, not at Beth'ru-elen, and that you were close at hand in Firstwall.'

'You saw the body?' the Hexenmeister said suddenly to Haltern.

'Yes. I was present when it was examined.'

'What were the precise nature of the wounds?'

Haltern's eyes clouded, cleared. 'The knife had been driven into the throat, severing the great vein—'

'Whose knife, is it known?'

'Mine,' I admitted, 'it went missing some time before.'

'Planned, then,' the Hexenmeister said over the talk, as they realized what he meant. 'Planned beforehand to discredit the envoy. What other injuries were there?'

Haltern gave him a curious look, as if he had not expected that question. 'The skull was bruised, there were scratches and contusions on the arms, and some claws broken on the hands. It was assumed she fell when she was struck with the knife, and then perhaps was dragged to the chair where she was found.'

I sipped from the tea-bowl, then put it down. Nausea made me dizzy.

The old man scratched absently at the thin crest of his mane. He seemed shrunken with age, especially in the company of tall Southlanders, but he dominated the room with his presence.

'Could it not also have been,' he suggested, 'that she was struck first on the head? And if so, and if that did not make her unconscious and she fought her attacker—there were other injuries, you say—perhaps she was only killed as a last resort. Perhaps,' he said into the quiet of that morning-chill room, 'she was only killed because she recognized the woman or man who struck her.'

After a moment Evalen said 'For what purpose?'

'I know Southlanders, and the Peir-Dadeni. I do not think anyone she trusted to come to the Crystal Hall would normally have killed her. After all,' he said, turning to me, 'if the envoy were found to have attacked the Andrethe, that would have been sufficient to turn many against the Dominion.'

'What reason could they possibly give?' I was bewildered. 'I've no more reason to attack her than I had to kill her.'

'They would have believed it,' Evalen stated. 'All Outworlders are

crazy—pardon, *t'an* Christie, but that's a popular view among the ignorant—and they would not have lacked people to credit the story.'

The Hexenmeister roused himself from his thoughts. 'So. We have a
murder possibly done on the spur of the moment, but since it's done, it
can still be blamed on the envoy. So they must have Christie there in
that room within a very few minutes. They call you to the Andrethe's
presence—'

'No one called me,' I said. 'Rodion told me I was wanted . . .
Rodion! But she couldn't commit murder!'

Haltern shook his head. 'She was *ashiren* then, and that was a blow
needing full strength.'

'Perhaps they planned to call you,' the Hexenmeister continued to
speculate. 'Then who comes? The Halfgold, the envoy's *l'ri-an,* who can
be trusted with a seemingly innocent message . . . yes, it could have
happened that way.'

'Meduenin said—'

'Yes!' Haltern set his bowl down with a clatter, turning to Evalen.
'T'an, there were assassins sent against Orhlandis *telestre,* as you know.
It was assumed they wanted the life of the *T'An* Ruric, but maybe that
was wrong. It could have been *t'an* Rodion.'

Her pale brows came together. 'Why has she never spoken?'

'She may not realize what she knows.'

'That's quickly answered, then.' Evalen called one of her guards.
'Find Ruric Rodion Orhlandis and bring her here. Now!'

One of the brown-robes accompanied the guard out.

It took time to find her. The fenborn brought fresh bowls of *arniac* tea,
while the company discussed those *telestres* that had had representatives at Shiriya-Shenin that winter.

Apprehension turned me cold. I don't believe it, I thought. I don't
believe I'm going to find out the answer. And if I do, will I like the
answer I get?

The sun dispersed the haze, and pale buildings reflected back fierce
light. I leaned against the edge of the window. We were high up. Among
the domes and alleys, the broad covered canals formed a grid, bright in
the morning sun. The air felt dry, motionless. I thought about Shiriya-
Shenin, about the Fifthwall docks where the north wind could snatch
the breath out of your mouth and leave you gasping. And here—still
Durestha Fourthweek, the beginning of spring—sweat collected in every crease of flesh, and the day's heat reflected back from brick walls to
glare in unprotected eyes.

I heard a stir outside, and made my way back to my seat. The doors slid open and the guard and brown-robes returned.

Blaize n'ri n'suth Meduenin followed them. Unarmed, light-footed, tense. I saw him glance once round the book-filled room, eyes wide enough that the whites were visible, and then he stood back against the wall by the door.

Of course, I thought. Hired to guard her, so he has to come.

Rodion halted in the doorway. The fenborn drew in breath, even the Hexenmeister stared. I hardly recognized her. Only six weeks, I thought, marvelling. The first time I'd seen the swift Orthean change from child to adult.

She had her mother's slender wiry frame and alert attitude, but the poise was all her own. The fine silver mane was cropped in Ymirian style, framing her high angular face, and her yellow eyes were wide. A sleeveless tunic laced over Ymirian britches, and empty *harur* scabbards hung at her belt. Taller than when I'd left her, sleeping out the fever of the change; narrow-hipped and high-breasted as Orthean women are, and with something entirely new in the way she carried herself.

The memory brought fear so strong I could taste it: Sandor's hawk-gold face. Evalen, Haltern, the Hexenmeister, did they also have that resurrection of ancient memories? Inhumanly beautiful, a Halfgold more than ever the image of the Witchbreed.

Then she looked round nervously, swallowed, and it became apparent that we had to do with a young Southland woman and nothing else.

'Rodion,' the Hexenmeister said gently, 'I have some questions about the Shiriya-Shenin court that you can perhaps answer.'

'Yes, master,' she said dutifully, curiosity and fear mingled in her voice; the effect of the Hexenmeister's reputation outside Kasabaarde.

I stared at the table while he asked her innocent questions. I didn't want to look at her, be accused of prompting her; I wanted to hear the truth. *T'an* Evalen waited quietly, betraying no impatience. Haltern sat with eyes hooded, studying her urbanely.

'—you told Christie that the Andrethe wanted her.' The Hexenmeister paused and, almost as an aside, said, 'Who gave you that message, by the way, do you remember?'

'Yes, I remember,' she said with the untempered honesty of the young. 'I met him outside the Crystal Hall. It was Brodin n'ri n'suth Charain.'

28

Havoth-jair

The air was still.

Ridge-backed lizards crawled on the stones at the edge of the road, basking in the heat. Their movements were abrupt, thin tails flicking like whips. Our footsteps grated on rock. As we approached, their ridged crests rose, opened, and became wings, and the whole flock skittered into the air. Wings hummed in the silence. Then there was nothing but the noise of footsteps and the rustle of cloth.

Blaize looked up at the hazy sky. 'There'll be no wind today.'

'Nor tomorrow, nor the next day, nor the next.' Rodion's voice gritted with irritation. 'How long are we meant to wait?'

'As long as it takes.'

'If there was a wind,' I said, 'you wouldn't be walking the country round Kasabaarde, you'd be on the *Child of Methemna* and halfway back to Tathcaer by now.'

'Ahh.' She made a disgusted sound, and shrugged. 'Conjure up one of your magic ships, *S'aranth,* fly us home.'

'I wish I could.'

The road led between irrigated fields, where pale green *del'ri* already had half its height. Dusty crimson *arniac* shrubs grew among the slender knobbed *del'ri* stems. The land was flat, and the road—the beginning of the great trade routes down the Desert Coast—was raised only a few inches above it. Across the miles of *del'ri* fields, the crags and dunes of the High Desert shimmered in the heat. Shining mirages of water patched the road ahead, only to vanish as we came closer. Kasabaarde glimmered, small in the distance.

'I'll check ahead,' Blaize said. The dust of a train of carts was visible, coming from the city. He increased his pace.

It was mid-afternoon. The days were lengthening now. I'd never had any problems coping with the extra hours of darkness—perhaps because I was so starved of sleep before I came to Shiriya-Shenin—but the extra daylight hours proved wearying. I usually slept an hour or two around noon to compensate. Besides, it was too hot to do anything else.

Rodion walked without speaking. Was she thinking of Brodin, I wondered, hawk-faced Brodin a murderer? One of the Andrethe's intelligencers, yes. But—he was Kanta's *arykei*. And his grief had been real.

The *jayante* strap tightened across my back; I eased it. Sweat ran under the mask, but the sun was too bright on the road without it. Rodion also went masked, and outside the city wore *harur-nilgiri* and *harur-nazari*.

'S'aranth . . .'

'Yes?'

'What did you feel like,' she said, 'the first time you killed someone?'

Blaize was a diminished figure on the road ahead, and the dust-cloud was drawing closer. It'd be safer to wait and let him check them out.

'Let's rest for a minute.' The rock was hot under me. Rodion hitched the *harur* blades back out of the way and sat beside me, still waiting for an answer. I said, 'Tell me how it happened.'

'In the street. Four of them.' She pulled the mask down and rubbed her face tiredly. When she looked at me, her eyes had the deep colour and clarity of a baby's. 'The guards killed one, and Meduenin—my sire and dam! he can fight—he killed one and disabled another; and I, I killed a man. It wasn't two streets away from Orhlandis *telestre* house up on the Hill. It was . . . crazy. Just like weapons practice. I kept expecting him to get up and say, No, you don't do it that way, your wrist should be higher. But he kept throwing up blood and then he died.'

The shock I felt was muffled. To an Orthean, it was not unusual for a child to kill. Yet it was Earth perception that saw her as a child; and cultural reactions against murder lie deep.

'How do you feel about it?'

'I didn't want to do it.' She shook her head. 'He was going to kill me. I was so afraid! I never gave him a chance, I was so scared. And that's wrong, he should have been questioned.'

'Everyone's afraid,' I said, and she nodded. She didn't ask the original question again; maybe she only needed to say how she felt.

'Where I come from,' I said, 'we don't teach children to fight.'

'Then how do they learn to defend themselves?'

'They don't. Well, they do. They don't need to!'

She laughed, throwing her head back, and slapped the rock with her open hand. *'S'aranth!'*

'I just wish you didn't make it sound so logical.'

She stretched lazily and stared down the road. Blaize was just visible, walking back in company with the traders. Their images wavered. I heard lizards chirruping in the distance. Heat struck up from the rocks.

'It's safe.' She pulled up the mask to shield her eyes again, and stood and brushed dust off herself. 'We'd better go.'

I'm getting suspicious as a Southlander, I thought. I'd been assuming, as they had, that there could be danger on any open road. In Tathcaer, maybe. But here? No, that was just Blaize n'ri n'suth Meduenin: a hired guard has to make the assumption of danger.

There was no shade, and my mouth was dry. It's time we got back to the city, I was thinking; and then Rodion spoke.

She nodded at Blaize, still a good way off, and said, 'What's he like —is he a good *arykei?'*

'What?' Startled, I said, 'How the hell should I know?'

'You're *arykei,* aren't you? At Morvren, everyone says.'

I managed not to smile. 'Everyone's got it wrong, then, for once. He's close as a brother, but he's not my *arykei.'*

'Ah.' She scuffed at the loose rocks as she walked, and then raised her face to the sun. Eventually she looked at me, a smile visible under the edge of her mask, and looked away again.

The carts rumbled past, drawn by the plodding sand-coloured beasts the Desert Coast call *brennior.* Their short flexible snouts quested blindly from side to side, the musty smell of them hanging in the still air. Blaize came out of the dust-cloud and offered a water flask to us.

'Traders aren't waiting for a wind,' he announced, 'they're risking the land route south. Might be some time before we get back to Tathcaer.'

Ships crowded the harbour. Frustration hung over the trade-city like a sandstorm, and tempers were short in the heat. We came in by the eastern gate, paying toll to enter as we'd paid toll to leave.

'Don't go back yet,' Rodion said. 'Evalen's quarters aren't far, *S'aranth,* come and visit.'

'Sure.' I'd as soon have been in the inner city's quiet. The trade city was crowded down here at the waterfront. Ramshackle, drystone barns hugged older, domed buildings. You could see that there had been Order houses here once, when the city was larger.

'I'll beat you at *ochmir,'* Blaize offered.

'I might surprise you there.' Now there were awning-covered streets again, narrow and winding, and we left most of the people behind. Entering the shade was for a minute like entering cold water, and then as hot as before. High curves of buildings shut out the sun, and any breath of air.

Blaize said something I didn't catch. When I turned, he wasn't there. Several streets converged here. I saw Rodion step back, both hands flashing in the cross-draw of *harur* blades. Then earth gritted under my hands and a wall slammed into my shoulder, and I got up on hands and knees without knowing I'd been knocked down. Someone grunted. Boots scraped on the hard earth. The *jayante* was in my hands, its hard weight comforting. I struck out. Something caught the side of my head, and I blinked water out of my eyes, and was blinded by sunlight: mask gone. The scuffling was punctuated by an abrupt cry. Something struck at me too fast for recognition, and the *jayante* caught the upper arm as I aimed, but I fumbled the blow that would paralyse the leg and he—she?—scuttled back into the shadow clutching one arm. A short curved blade lay on the earth, leather-wound grip dark with sweat.

Blaize stood up from bending over a sprawled body. Rodion shouted, high-pitched and harsh as a bird. Footsteps clattered past me. The stunner was in my hand and I sighted, fired—there's no charge left, I thought—but a brief sound split the air, and the running figure skidded forward onto knees, hands, face; and was still.

Rodion stood holding her arm. Dark blood welled and suddenly ran black between her fingers, dropping on the dusty street. Her indrawn breath was sharp.

'Christie—' Blaize glanced at me, sheathed *harur-nazari,* and went after the one I'd shot. He turned the body over, felt the throat, and smiled.

My hands were shaking and cold. I had to lean against the wall a minute before I could put the stunner away. The *jayante* lay a few feet away from the sprawled body.

There were more than two, I thought, searching the confused minutes for the memory of how many had run. It was only then, after it was over, that I began to know what had happened.

Blaize stood up, supporting the unconscious body of the attacker on his back. Rodion was panting hard, swearing and close to tears.

'Evalen's people—'

'No.' I cut Blaize off. 'I know where we are. Come with me.'

Rodion held onto my arm as we went. It was not far to the gate. As I'd hoped, it was Su'niar's Order on guard.

They let us through, dishevelled as we were, Rodion bleeding from a slash low on her side as well as from her arm, and Blaize with the unconscious assailant over his shoulders. A little way into the inner city I heard a scuffle behind me, and someone slammed between me and Rodion. She cried out with pain. Blaize ran past, vanishing in the narrow darkness of the alleys.

'Where—' Rodion's breathing came harshly.

'Come on.' I took her unwounded arm.

Blaize rejoined us, out of breath, scarred face unrecognizable with anger. He shook his head mutely. When he could speak he said, 'I didn't think he'd recover—not so soon—'

'It's lost power.'

'I should have made sure.' His tone was chilling. 'Christie, where are you taking us?'

'There,' I said as we came out into the gardens, and with my free hand pointed at the Brown Tower. Blaize grunted, but didn't object. Seeing Rodion's head hanging down, her feet stumble, I picked her up and carried her the few yards into the Tower. Blaize came behind, both *harur* blades drawn.

I am not naturally a brave woman. Having been attacked, my one idea was to get to the safety of what was undoubtedly the most impregnable structure on Orthe.

'You're all right?' Haltern asked again.

'Few bruises, that's all.' Experimentally I flexed one arm. Several muscles felt as though they'd been pulled in those hectic minutes. I saw Rodion, now with her wounds salved and bandaged, talking energetically to the *t'an* Evalen. Blaize stood with them.

I tried to reconstruct it in my mind, searching for details. They'd waited for us. Blaize had spotted them first, I think, and yelled for us to get back to back; and it might have been him or the first attacker who bowled me over. Were there three or four of them, and how had they been dressed?

'They were from the trade city,' I said. 'That won't be much help to you, Hal.'

'It won't be up to me.' His thin fingers picked at a worn place on his belt. 'They must be desperate, Christie. Try and kill you in the Hexenmeister's own city? They should know better than that.'

'They won't get another chance. We'll stay in the Tower until the *Child of Methemna* sails.'

'All of you?' His gesture included Blaize and Rodion. 'I don't like to say this, but I think you should be very careful, even when you get back to Tathcaer.'

I grinned. It was a light-headed reaction to the attack: I just felt good to be alive. 'Kasabaarde's full of people who don't feel safe in Tathcaer, isn't it?'

Tethmet-fenborn entered the library, stopped for a quiet word with Evalen, and then came across to me.

'The Hexenmeister requires your presence, envoy.'

'Yes, of course.' I stood up, still shaky. Evalen and I followed Tethmet to the meeting hall. Blaize supported Rodion, who was becoming drowsy from the herbs given to her.

The old man looked up. '*T'an* Evalen, good. Christie, I believe we have one of your attackers.'

So soon? The Hexenmeister's spy system was impressive, I thought.

Brown-robes brought in a struggling Orthean in torn shirt and britches.

'Is this one who attacked you?'

'I . . . can't say for certain. I'm sorry. It happened too fast.'

'Could be.' Blaize took another look. 'Can't say more than that.'

The abrupt tone wasn't meant for rudeness. This brown slick room was no comfort to a Southlander. Even in the days of the Golden Empire, it came to me, the Witchbreed kept much of their power secret from their slaves; Blaize would have no past-memories to soften the shock of the Tower.

'*T'an* Evalen?'

'I know her,' Evalen answered the old man. 'She's one of the *Child of Methemna's* crew. Are you telling me she—'

'*T'an*, why have they brought me here?' the woman interrupted. 'I've done nothing, tell them to let me go!'

Her accent was Desert Coast, clipped and slurred, all the emphasis different when she spoke Ymirian. She had the bleached skin of the Coast, and a rough dark mane coming down from complex braids; I suppose she was in her forties.

'My people found her running from the Landgate quarter where the attack took place. She has a mark on her that could be from a *jayante*.' The Hexenmeister nodded, and one of the brown-robes pulled up the woman's torn sleeve. A bruise was already yellowing, darkening.

'I fell earlier,' she said, '*t'an*, let me go back to the ship.'

'If you're innocent you have nothing to be afraid of,' Evalen said. 'No one will harm you if that's so, no, not the Hexenmeister himself.'

That dogged defiance in the heart of the Brown Tower touched me. Evalen was nervous as Blaize, nervous as any Southlander.

'But she *was* there,' Rodion said clearly. 'I saw her. She fought with *S'aranth* and then she ran away.'

'Are you certain of this?'

'Yes. Certain.'

The Desert woman said hastily, 'If you must hear it, *t'an* Evalen, it is this: I was in the Landgate quarter, yes, and I saw the attack happen. I said nothing because I—well, because I didn't go to help them. I don't know why. Afraid, maybe. There were many of them. And then I ran because I thought I should be blamed for that.'

Evalen frowned.

The Hexenmeister said, 'Will you let me question her?'

At that there was a silence, and the white membranes slid down over Evalen's bright eyes.

'I'm not wholly sure of her guilt.'

'Then be sure. I can uncover the truth.'

'I have heard,' she said with her still-veiled eyes on the Desert woman's face, 'that those whom you—question—are not unchanged by it. Some say it's possible to recognize them forever after, because of what they become.'

'*T'an,* you can hurt her greatly and she will perhaps tell you the truth, and perhaps a lie. I will hurt her not at all, and to me she will tell only the truth. But—'

'But?'

'But it is true she will be changed.'

The subliminal hum that underlies the Brown Tower intensified the silence. Cool air, with only the odours that the Southlanders brought in from outside—dust, spices, the sea. In artificial light, in that windowless room, the claustrophobia was almost tangible.

'Havoth-jair, I *must* know.' Evalen turned from the Desert woman to the old man. Her eyes cleared. 'You will question her, master, and I will witness it.'

'No,' the Hexenmeister said, 'you may not be there, *t'an.*'

'If I'm not, then you don't take her! How do we know what—' she broke off. 'Pardon me, master. There are those who will say she was forced into a lie, not the truth. I must be here and see it!'

About that time I realized that, whatever he might conceal from the

Southland, the Hexenmeister wouldn't hide this from me. Because I already knew.

'*T'an* Evalen, would it be satisfactory if I were to witness the interrogation on your behalf?'

She could hardly insult the newly-proved-innocent envoy; besides, her mother trusted me. And though I wasn't from the Southland's point of view the best possible witness, it was plain from the Hexenmeister's expression that I was the only witness they were liable to get.

Unexpectedly, Evalen smiled.

'Yes,' she said, 'we would agree to that.'

We went down into the maze of the Brown Tower among the masked brown-robes, the Desert woman pulled roughly along. I walked behind, the old man's hand on my arm. And we came to a familiar entrance, and a cool dry hall lit with faintly blue iridescence, and sarcophagus-machines.

I thought, I don't want to see this.

After sending the brown-robes away, the Hexenmeister turned his attention to the Desert woman. She stood with her arms across her body, hands clutching her upper arms.

'Havoth-jair,' he said, 'of what city?'

'Quarth.'

'That is a lie. I know when you lie. You know of me,' he said, and there was nothing frail or old about him. 'You know who makes the law in the city of the Brown Tower.'

'Don't try to frighten me,' she said harshly, in the Desert Coast tongue. Wrinkles showed round her eyes when she looked at him, membrane-covered as if she stared at a bright light. She was not young. It showed in the way she slumped.

He was mild. 'Tell me how you came to do this thing, Havoth-jair.'

Terror forced her words out, though you wouldn't have guessed it to look at her. But I'm practised at making the paralysis of fear look like the stillness of relaxation, and I know when someone else is doing it.

'I was bribed,' she said at last. 'Someone saw I was on the *Methemna* with the Halfgold, I suppose. They offered me money to kill the Orhlandis and the Outworld envoy. It was easy enough to find others to help me.'

He only watched her.

'Give me protection, master,' she said. 'There are names I might remember, but not under sentence of death. Keep me out of that and I'll tell you.'

She was aware, I think, that he could force any information out of her; but she had a streak of toughness that made her bargain even on the edge of desperation.

I wanted to say, can't we accept that? Can't you let her walk out of here unharmed?

And I couldn't say it, there were too many good reasons against her. Sometimes you play and you lose. The Desert Coast woman lost.

The Hexenmeister shook his head.

The brown-robes gave her *arniac* tea and would have forced it down her, but she gulped it hastily, the whites showing all round her tawny eyes. In a few minutes she fell into a semi-conscious state.

'What do you think you will see?' There was amusement in the old man's voice.

'Very little—but it will convince *t'an* Evalen.'

They took Havoth-jair and laid her in the slick coffin of a machine. There was little enough to see. One part of me shuddered at the thought that I had been where she was now. But willingly, I thought. That makes the difference, doesn't it?

And one part of me knows the technique, its limitations and its dangers, knowing that to rip the unwilling mind apart in search of memory is possible, but its effects are unmistakable. Which would have been more reassuring if my knowledge hadn't come to me through the technique itself. But that way paranoia lies.

'You're going to hurt her,' I said.

'It will not be painful.'

Aphasia, amnesia, blackouts, idiocy: and all the possible symptoms of brain damage.

'Suppose she's innocent?'

'Then I am sorry for her.'

Before second twilight we returned to the meeting hall, brown-robes leading the quiescent Desert woman.

'Havoth-jair.' Evalen stood, watching her. 'Of what city?'

'Kel Harantish.'

Evalen blinked, looked at the Hexenmeister, then returned her attention to Havoth-jair.

'You admit to the attack.'

'I was sent to kill the Orhlandis woman and the envoy.' Her eyes, half-veiled, were calm. So was the voice. Peaceful. Not angry, not afraid; as if nothing could touch her now.

'Tell me,' Evalen said.

'The Emperor-in-Exile had me sent to the Southland, me being of his household and having visited it before. I've sailed before, so it wasn't hard to gain a place on the *Methemna.* I knew I should be taken if I attacked the Orhlandis on the ship, so I waited until we reached the city and I could hire mercenaries to help me. Then I waited until she and the envoy met.' Calm, rational speech.

'Are you the only one sent out from Kel Harantish?'

'That wasn't told to me.'

'Why were you to do this thing?'

'That, also, I wasn't told.'

I shifted, easing one bruised leg. It was strange, the woman had attacked me, it was probably me who'd struck her with the *jayante;* and yet because I didn't recognize her face I couldn't connect her with the attack. Reason told me she'd done it, but I had no gut hate-reaction.

'She should testify to this,' Evalen said thoughtfully. 'In Tathcaer, master. *T'an* Rodion, *t'an* envoy, it were better for you if justice on this should be seen in that city.'

'Would she be safe in Tathcaer?' It was a little late to worry about 'safe', I thought guiltily.

'You!' Evalen demanded, 'is your face known in Tathcaer? Would any recognize you in the Southland?'

'I've been to Tathcaer before.' Havoth-jair's tongue ran on easily. 'And to another Southland city, Ales-Kadareth. Three times in the last two years we took ships to Melkathi, ships ballasted with gold; that was a gift from the Emperor-in-Exile. What he had in return for his gift, I know not. Harantish gold goes to the Hundred Thousand; it was on such a ship that I came to the Southland this spring.'

'*This* spring?' I said involuntarily.

'Gold for which *telestre?*' Evalen demanded, but the Desert Coast woman only shook her head. Her face was untroubled. 'Well, they would not tell her, I suppose.'

I said, 'That should have stopped when SuBannasen died. Haltern thought it didn't. Someone has taken over from Sulis.'

'The *T'An Suthai-Telestre* should know this,' the Hexenmeister advised. 'And, if *t'an* Evalen's wise, she'll take this woman to Tathcaer and guard her as if she were her own *ashiren.*'

Excited argument broke out among the Southlanders, each trying to shout over the other voices.

'Stay for this,' the old man said, laying his clawed fingers on my arm, 'and then come to me again. I must speak with someone, and the envoy should be present.'

29

The Emperor-in-Exile

The sunset gongs sounded distantly from the trade city. The gates were closing. The evening air was motionless, soaked with heat. I stood in the Tower's roof garden, watching the sun go down in a welter of silver and lilac. There are no long twilights on the Desert Coast. It was the kind of sky that makes you look for a thin new moon in the west, but here there was nothing but the white dots of stars. *Arniac* and rockmoss sent their night perfumes into the dusty air.

I had to get out in the open; the Tower was making me claustrophobic as any Southlander. And Evalen's methods of questioning Havoth-jair were more openly violent than the Hexenmeister's, and not something I wanted to watch.

The lift-dome slid open and the fenborn stepped out onto the roof.

'He wants me down there.'

'If you will,' Tethmet said distantly.

The city lay silent, domes catching the sun's last glow. I crossed to the lift, and the fenborn stood aside for me to enter.

'You live here,' I said as the halves of the dome slid up and shut out the evening. 'Do you like it, Tethmet?'

His webbed hand touched the switch and the lift began to glide down. The timeless, sourceless Tower light illuminated his masked face. At last he said, 'I don't remember the Great Fens now, except in past-dreams. He's here, and never leaves. What else can I do?'

Just as the lift stopped, far below ground level, he said, 'Are they still the same? He said you crossed the Fens. Have they changed?'

His thin body was tense. Muscles moved along his pointed jaw.

'How would I know?' That was a lie. His urgency impressed me. 'They haven't changed. Don't ask me how I know. They're the way they have been for thousands of years.'

Not until the tension left him did I realize how long he'd been waiting to ask that question. The lines round his eyes relaxed, and for the first time I saw a fenborn smile. It was fierce, a predator's joy.

He said nothing more, but led me through the maze of corridors until we came to a closed door. I heard voices, and a continuous sound under them that puzzled me. As the doors slid open I recognized it as running water. Tethmet followed me in.

It was a large room, pale-coloured, with a multitude of pelts and tapestries thrown down to cover the floor. The Hexenmeister sat hunched up on a low chair, with Evalen and Haltern on a couch beside him. Rodion sat cradling her arm, white-eyed with the effort of keeping awake; and Blaize stood behind her with his hands on the back of her chair. A vociferous argument was taking place.

I went down the steps between two crystal tanks, where blue and crimson fish swam. Another tank took up the far wall; there was a cascade-fountain running noisily. The air was cool, damp in comparison with the city, and the light shaded into green over the pools.

'Envoy,' Evalen called, 'let's hear your opinion on this. I say we must return to Tathcaer as soon as we get a wind and can sail. You'll come with us, and Rodion Orhlandis, and the woman Havoth-jair: and all shall be told to the *T'An Suthai-Telestre.*'

'That were best done soon,' Haltern said as I came over. 'You're rumoured to be dead, Christie, you and the Orhlandis here. If we don't stop that story it'll spread as far as Tathcaer, and then it must be denied before they'll hear you.'

'Dead?'

'In the attack. They have the Orhlandis carried bloody into the Tower and dying of her wounds—' he looked at Rodion, who grinned back at him '—and as for her companions, they were slain by an assassin in the Tower itself. Someone's heard of the woman Havoth-jair being brought here, I think, that's where that began.'

'And if it ends in the Southland—'

Evalen was interrupted gently by the Hexenmeister. He turned his gaze on me, veiling humour. 'There is the matter of getting to Tathcaer.'

'One way or another,' I said, pulling up a stool and sitting beside Rodion. 'I don't care how, I'm going back. With all due respect, I can't function as Dominion envoy while I'm under suspicion of murder. Rodion's evidence against Brodin n'ri n'suth Charain should be presented as soon as possible, and I think I should be there.'

The Hexenmeister inclined his head. 'And if Brodin n'ri n'suth Charain has taken bribes from Kel Harantish?'

'That evidence should also be presented to the Crown.'

'He would not be the only one who has done so, I think,' Evalen said soberly, 'but this may serve to drive such traitors underground, or —if he speaks—condemn more with him.'

'You miss my point,' the old man said. 'All this has its head in Kel Harantish. The Emperor-in-Exile knows you're in Kasabaarde. Indeed, the Desert Coast being what it is, he likely knows all the city's rumours as soon as I do. I mean that you may have an unchancy voyage to Tathcaer, and a grim welcome if you arrive.'

The cascade of the fountain was clearly audible in the quiet.

'I have a small company of guards,' Evalen said. 'We hoped to travel unnoticed. They won't send ships against us—Kel Harantish remembers the last time Southland warships went up against that city—but I'd be surprised now if there were no hired assassins. Those we can defeat if we take care, master.'

He didn't comment, only looking at her doubtfully.

'I don't like the idea of making myself a target,' I said.

'I assure you, envoy, I'll bring you safe to Tathcaer.' Evalen was determined. 'We've talked all this out, what else is there to say?'

'How safe will we be after we arrive in Tathcaer?' I asked Haltern. 'And how long will it take to bring Brodin to trial? Once this is known there'll be no point in anyone trying to kill us, but how long before it *is* known?'

He spread his hands. 'Who can tell?'

Blaize leaned down to hear something that Rodion said, then straightened. *'T'an,* suppose we didn't return on the *Methemna?* Suppose we travelled on another ship and kept our arrival at Tathcaer secret?'

'Good enough if it could be done,' the Hexenmeister said doubtfully, 'but with Harantish agents searching for you?'

No one else is going to suggest it, I thought, so it's going to have to be me.

'Suppose they weren't looking for us?'

Very sudden and shrewd, the old man said, 'How would you solve that?'

'It's happened to me once, more or less. Listen, if those rumours weren't stopped, but confirmed; if we're reported dead officially? That would stop anyone bothering about us. And then return to Tathcaer in secret, as Blaize says.'

Confusion broke out, all of them talking at once. The old man leaned back in his chair, eyes hooded. Clever as sin, I thought, he knows me, and he knows it sounds better coming from me.

'—hear about it in Tathcaer!' Rodion thumped her chair with her good arm, then looked shame-faced. 'Sorry, *t'an* Evalen; but if they hear we're dead, and believe it—my mother—'

'Some things must be endured,' Evalen was compassionate. *'T'an* envoy, I hear what you say. A good suggestion. And then we would take the woman Havoth-jair on the *Methemna*, as we should do if you had truly been killed? Yes . . .'

'They'll be looking out for her, unless she's thought dead too. She could travel with us, I suppose.' And just how did I propose to travel? I wondered.

'What, guard her all the way to Tathcaer?'

'Where's she going to escape to?' I was angry, a little disgusted. Nothing I could have done would have prevented the way they treated her, but I should have tried. 'Between us and Kel Harantish, we haven't left her anywhere to go. Didn't you promise her protection if she gave evidence in Tathcaer? Well, then.'

'If she comes with us, we can be sure at least one witness will get through. I'm not fool enough to have you travel all in the one party—'

'As Dominion envoy—'

'Peace!' the Hexenmeister said. We were quiet then as if we'd been children. He stood, and Tethmet-fenborn took his arm. Then the flare of anger faded and the sense of antiquity, and it was only an old Desert Coast man who smiled at us.

'This was a long day,' he said, 'and you, Orhlandis, are wounded; and the *t'an* Evalen has a company to care for—I will send brown-robes to let you through to the trade city, Evalen—and as for decisions, they can wait on the advent of a wind. No ship leaves Kasabaarde till then. And even I cannot call up a wind for you.'

Evalen chuckled aloud at that and Haltern smiled. Blaize gave Rodion his arm to grip as she rose.

'Say nothing,' the old man advised, 'and I will tell you what rumours go out of the city, and then we will talk again.'

I was about to follow the others out, when he signalled for me to stay.

'Have you eaten?' he asked when the room emptied, and when I said no, he sent the fenborn out for *arniac* tea and *del'ri* flourcakes. The water ran musically in the background, and the fish made constant slow sweeps through the tanks under the green and golden light.

We talked while we ate, mostly about Earth. Not the Dominion, not the governments, but how it feels to grow up under a different sun and a different sky, and how people get on with the business of living their own lives.

'I know so little,' he said at last, 'and I understand less.'

'All I can say to that is, what you've learned from my mind may not be true anyway.' I swallowed the last of the *arniac* tea, draining the bowl. 'I'm not a liar, master, but all you have is one person's view of Earth, and not even all of it, only the parts I know. If any of the xeno-team ever come here, they'd probably give you a completely different story. I don't understand Orthe, even with what you've told me, and you've seen more of your world than I ever will of mine.'

When he looked at me, I remembered he knew everything about me. That should have been frightening. The reason it wasn't, I think, is because not being human he couldn't judge humanity.

'Have you rested?' he asked. 'There is one more thing, as I told you, and you should be present. First, though, I ask you to undertake never to speak of what you see or hear.'

'That's not something I can promise. As envoy, I have to report fully.'

'Well then, say that you will report it only to your own people, and then only if you believe it to be necessary.'

That seemed fair enough. I agreed. He stood and gathered his robes round himself, and walked slowly to the fountain. There he thrust one arm under the surface of the water and remained that way for a minute. As he withdrew it, the far wall split soundlessly down the middle and the room opened to twice its size.

That part of the room was dark. I followed him into it, away from the underwater light, and a dim blue luminescence grew up round us. It centred on a great block of some transparent substance that stood on a dais. A golden light pulsed in its crystal depths.

His face was shadowed, the eye-sockets full of darkness. He said, 'That will call him out. I set it after I heard of the attack this noon. Now . . .'

His hands moved on a panel on the side of the dais. Then, as in the block that had shown me the view of his successor, the clear surface began to fill with images.

'Where—' my voice was husky.

'There are no others left but here,' he said, 'and in that ancient city, Kel Harantish. And this transmits nothing now but my voice, though perhaps that is as well: I keep my face hidden from him.'

The image was complete now, of a room very similar to the one we stood in. Three-dimensional, exact. Something bothered me. This degree of power—whatever the nature of the energy source—should have shown up like a beacon on the satellite survey of Carrick V. Had they missed it, skimped it, suffered a transmission failure? The atmosphere was badly suited to wave-transmission (or I should have been in contact with the xeno-team, legal or not). This shouldn't be here, I thought.

In that other room were geometrically-patterned carpets, and candle-stands whose holders were shaped like beast-skulls. Candlelight and the ruins of technology. An Orthean bent over the panel, so that at first I saw only his bleached loose-flowing mane. Then he straightened up and his face became visible. Narrow chin, broad forehead, and half-veiled eyes the colour of wet sand. And he was no more than nineteen or twenty.

'Dannor bel-Kurick,' the Hexenmeister said, 'you who call yourself Emperor-in-Exile, attend.'

The Orthean male glared at us—no, not at us, at what must be a blank: he looked clear through us. And he was beautiful. He had the presence, that quality the Goldens in my memory possessed. The ability to inspire fascination.

'Show yourself,' he demanded.

'I choose not.'

'Then I choose not to speak.'

'Your assassin,' the Hexenmeister said quickly, and the hand that bel-Kurick reached towards the controls hesitated. 'One of your spies. She had much to say before she eventually died.'

Dannor bel-Kurick laughed. His voice had a pure tone. He said, 'Is it war? I'll fight you, old man, I'll fight you gladly.'

With that I recalled the face of Santhendor'lin-sandru when the Golden woman brought the Empire down. Dannor bel-Kurick was a poor second to that, though he might pass now Sandor was forgotten.

This halfbreed, this Halfgold, I thought; this Witchbreed *boy*, is he the cause of all this?

'I make no quarrels with the Emperor-in-Exile,' the old man answered. 'But I remind him that his city Kel Harantish is a city of exile, and was no city before the Empire fell but only a desert garrison.'

The boy turned and seated himself, lounging back in his chair. Whether he knew he was seen, or whether his actions had that theatrical quality even when he was alone, I don't know.

'Well?' he said shortly.

'Only this: you survive on trade. Kel Harantish has always lived by it, and if I give the word you may die for lack of it. Can you eat rocks and sand?'

In the mind's eye I see shells of towers obscured by the dust of an arid land. The sea-like fragments of molten metal. And over the towers, blocking the sky, great whale-backed dunes, sharp-edged and shifting with the wind. Kel Harantish between two seas, the tideless salt water and the sand. Even water must be imported.

Bel-Kurick said measuredly, 'If you set foot on Harantish land I'll come west and burn your port, whether it costs me this city or not. I can still do that. I have allies in the south. I have my army, my ships.'

'I know. I know. Do you think I don't know the Golden Witchbreed?' The amusement was plain in the old man's voice. 'You're not Sandor, boy, whatever you think—'

'I am Golden!' He stood, staring with blind, uncanny accuracy at the Hexenmeister. 'I am of the line of Santhendor'lin-sandru, and I am Emperor! How many lies have you fed me, old man, telling me I'm nothing but a hollow man ruling a dying city? How many times have you tried to steal my throne? There's a price paid for power here that you never paid, old man, never in your lives. I know that.'

'That's true,' the Hexenmeister said, too quietly for the words to be transmitted. His face in the shadows showed pain, and a compassion I couldn't account for.

Dannor bel-Kurick sank back into the chair. 'One must be true Golden to gain the throne, and so I made myself as Goldens are. Anything else I crushed. Now will you tell me I did that only for northerners to call me Witchbreed? Emperor-in-Exile is Emperor still.'

Emperor of what? Kel Harantish with its empty name and halfbreed lineage, its power to inspire fear and contempt in equal measure? Emperor of craftsmen and mercenaries scattered across all the southern continent, simply because the city must trade to live. Dannor bel-Kurick: obsessed inheritor of a tawdry past and a tawdry future, ready to ally with anyone and anything promising him military aid—and to betray the rest of Orthe without a second thought. He was a little mad, even for an Orthean.

'What I have to say is simple.' The Hexenmeister paused. 'Will you hear me?'

'Will I ever not?'

'This, then. Your assassin who killed the envoy and the Orhlandis—she spoke of ships that went north to the Hundred Thousand, ships that carry gold.'

'What of it?' the boy asked tiredly.

'Nothing. But if I hear of any more ships from Kel Harantish in Tathcaer, then something.'

There was a pause. Without much hope the boy said, 'And perhaps they won't listen to you, Quarth and Psamnol and Saberon and the rest; perhaps they think it is time we joined together and broke your stranglehold on the Desert Coast!'

'And if I close the port to those who trade with Witchbreed? I ask again, Dannor bel-Kurick, can your people live on rock instead of bread?'

The cube faded to clarity.

'Let him have his temper,' the Hexenmeister said, 'he's stubborn, that one; cruel and wilful and cunning, but I could find it in my heart to be sorry for him. The Witchbreed glory is past, and he has the shadow of it only. Harantish is a desolate rock. He must take his hand from the Southland now for some years, now that they know he acts against them.'

'Will he stop the ships?' For a word, I thought, a threat?

'He has no choice. Kel Harantish is vulnerable, he can act only at second-hand; now that's finished.'

Does bel-Kurick fear the Brown Tower more than he hates the Southland, I wondered; and will he do more than hide his conspiracies with more care? As for allies in the south . . .

The Hexenmeister rested his hand on my shoulder as we went back into the brightly-lit part of the room, as if he were tired. I doubted it.

I said, 'I thought you weren't given to acting in other people's affairs?'

'That was the past,' he said, 'and this is the present, and now we have contact with your world. The first new thing that's come to me in centuries. Evalen is right, this affects all Orthe. And I believe, Christie, I am the only person who has the right to act for all of Orthe.'

Dim artificial illumination shone in the tiny room. I was far below ground here, down in the brown-robes' quarters, and I could have wished for a window open on the night.

I lay on a block that seemed a solid extension of the wall. Its surface gave under me, accommodating my weight. It should have been easy to sleep, but instead I was awake and restless. The light never changed. I had no idea how long until dawn. Time passed. A cool stream of air passed through the room but despite that the temperature was high.

They might just as well have buried me, I thought. And if I'm meant to be leaving Kasabaarde tomorrow, I need sleep. Damn.

Part of it was fear. The Tower was familiar to me only through false memories, which made it very easy to take it for granted. But the substance I lay on was not fibre or metal, nor did it have the tactile slickness of plastic. The light was sourceless to human eyes—though it seemed to me in memory that Orthean vision encompassed a greater range. Make a conscious effort of realization and it was frightening.

Because if the energy source here didn't register on a satellite survey, one possible conclusion was that it was something we hadn't programmed a satellite to recognize. Something we were entirely ignorant about.

There'd have to be a report made on that, and on everything I'd seen in the city. The department would take a keen interest. What kind of interest? I wondered. There was Witchbreed technology here, yes, outlasting its makers. But how much notice would the department take of the inner city, the Order houses of Kasabaarde?

I thought, I don't want to leave yet. If it was up to me, personally . . . but if I don't get back to envoy's duties soon, there won't be time to finish before I'm recalled to Earth.

Su'niar, Thelmithar . . . for all that they fed, clothed, and housed their Order, the only thing the Order houses really gave away was time. Time to sit under the street-awnings on the dusty steps, time to think, or time simply to exist. I had no illumination to match Beth'ru-elen or any of the mystics. Only I had learned to ask questions, and not to ask them, and to reach some kind of—is it balance I mean? And I would like to have known what happens to a human left in one of those Orthean sanctuaries.

I heard movement, and wondered if Rodion was awake. When I got up and went to see if her wounds bothered her, I found her room empty. I thought about that for a while. Then I went back to bed. She was safe enough.

'Havoth-jair is a witness for the Crown!' Evalen lowered her head, bull-stubborn. 'Also, she's one of my ship's crew. You say you can give us protection in your city, master. I'll undertake to protect Havoth-jair outside of it. I'm taking her to Tathcaer.'

The Hexenmeister was seated in the library, close by the open window. A breeze had come up with the dawn and not fallen yet.

'Perhaps it's better,' I said.

'She's a Southland sailor, but born on the Desert Coast—I cannot keep her in the Brown Tower either way. Very well, *t'an* Evalen.'

Blaize and Rodion stood together, talking quietly. Outside the *teles-*

tre Southlanders aren't demonstrative (inside the community is another matter) and their affection was low-key. Sometimes she touched his arm or his hand was on her shoulder. What was obvious was their closeness, eyes hardly leaving each other's faces, and the joy that came out in sudden muffled laughter.

'*T'an* Evalen,' Rodion said, becoming serious, 'may I ask you to do one thing? When you get to Tathcaer, tell my mother that I live. I know the lie's necessary but don't let her believe it longer than she has to.'

Evalen nodded. 'If necessary I'll ask *T'An* Ruric to keep the secret until you reach the city—but you may be there before we are, the winds are treacherous in spring.'

I would have asked her to inform the xeno-team I wasn't dead, but if they knew, pretty soon everybody else would. Huxton and Eliot and Adair . . . they hadn't developed the sheer paranoia necessary for Orthean affairs.

If I get back to Tathcaer, I thought. This won't be easy.

'As for leaving the city,' the Hexenmeister said, 'I can perhaps help you there, envoy, but we'll speak of it later. *T'an* Evalen, I release the woman Havoth-jair to you. My people will bring her secretly to your ship.'

Before they left, I spoke to Haltern.

'Take care,' he said. 'Sea travelling is an uncertain business at the best of time, and in Durestha. . . .'

Any journey on Orthe was a momentous undertaking, it was true. Less safe, less sure than on Earth. Natural hazards might be a bigger danger than conspiracy.

'I'll meet you in Tathcaer. We'll get this whole thing settled. Hal, watch out for yourself.'

The wind blew dust against the Tower's impervious walls. Clouds came over from the southwest, hiding the daystars. Evalen's people were arguing over something with the brown-robes.

'It's bad news to be taking home,' he said, 'and Charain's a south Dadeni *telestre,* and Brodin a good man. I know him, Christie. To go back and do this—it's hard.'

'You're Peir-Dadeni; what about Kanta Andrethe?'

'Yes,' he said. 'That demands justice. And for the envoy, too. God-dess give you a good journey, Christie.'

'My people have packed supplies for you,' the Hexenmeister said when I rejoined him in the library. Behind him, through the window, the shadows of clouds glided over the domes of the inner city. He was alone. Tea-bowls, scarlet with *arniac* dregs, cluttered the table. A forsaken atmosphere clung to the room.

'What ship do we take?'

'Yes, ships . . .' He coughed, pinched the bridge of his nose, and then sighed. With an old man's preoccupation with comfort, he tugged his dark robe more tightly round his shoulders. 'There is one way you can leave the city and be certain you're not seen, Christie, and that's to go by way of the Rasrhe-y-Meluur.'

I remembered the line of pylons that had followed us south, their great shadows distinct on the waves. 'Is it safe?'

'As far as the first waystation, Firerock, and you might take an island ship up the Archipelago from there.'

'Ask the others,' I said, thinking of Blaize's competence. 'If they'll agree, I will.'

They came back from saying their farewells, Tethmet with them; and, though dubious, they eventually agreed. The old man took us into the centre of the Brown Tower then, to a lift that went down for so long that I began to wonder just how far below ground we were going.

The light had a different quality where we disembarked, a harsh blue luminescence. Dry, cold air circulated. Rodion shivered, pulled Blaize's arm around her, and grinned toothily.

Doors opened into a small chamber containing only two benches. Brown-robes brought us packs and water bottles, which Blaize proceeded to check expertly. There was some discussion with the fenborn. Then we joined the old man, the doors slid shut, and what I realized now was a kind of monorail began to move forward. The acceleration was smooth. Blaize and Rodion both flinched, and I saw their hands link.

Beside me, the Hexenmeister said, 'What do you think, Christie, when you see this?'

He probably knew what I thought better than I did. 'That Orthe's is a very ancient civilization.'

He looked at me quizzically. 'Us, or the Hundred Thousand?'

'All of it. Odd to realize it now, after all this time. It isn't the popular idea of an advanced race.'

You could all but see him sorting through archetypes in borrowed memories: high technology, controlled emotions. His face furrowed, eyes veiling, then he nodded.

'They advance beyond the Witchbreed method. No one makes land yield like a Southlander.'

But you don't expect an ancient race to be dirty-handed, I wanted to protest. You don't expect them to kill—or if you do, it's with world-destroying weapons: nothing so simple and bloody as a yard of razor-edged metal. And yet they're not simple.

'It's their own choice,' he emphasized softly.

'I'm not arguing.'

The fenborn sat silent as ever, and I wondered if he was thinking of that flat, watery country in the north. Blaize and Rodion took no notice when the old man spoke. At first I thought they were too taken up with each other to notice, but then I realized the Hexenmeister was using a Desert tongue unintelligible to them. And I'd been able to answer. The implanted memories had gifted me one thing, then.

A long time later the car began to slow, and eventually it came to a halt. Then there was a jolt and it began to rise vertically, a car that became a lift.

Rodion flexed her arm, grinned ruefully, and allowed Blaize to help her strap the pack on her back. I watched them, the man and the young woman. Their reaction to attack was alien, Orthean: they picked themselves up like children after a scuffle. For a hired fighter I could understand it, but Rodion . . . yet she was alert, restless, eager to be on the move; and it wasn't a day ago that someone tried to kill her. While I—

The reason I remembered so little of the attack is that I was blind with terror. All my reactions had been instinctive, fear drove me to fight. Even now, with it safe in the past, images haunt me. Not Havoth-jair, or the way a *jayante* jars against bone. The man that I saw only for a second, the man Blaize killed. I still see him. On his back, dead arms raised stiffly over his face, specked all over with red. Fixed in that attitude of pain. Holding his arms up to ward off an injury that had already put him beyond hope.

'I wish you all well,' the Hexenmeister said as the car at last stopped. 'Leave the Rasrhe-y-Meluur before you come to Rimrock, at the latest, it isn't possible to keep the way safe any longer.'

'Orhlandis thanks you,' Rodion said formally. Blaize nodded stiffly, still not at ease with the old man.

The doors slid open and we stepped out onto a blue-grey fused surface. I thought, Kirriach's stone. Air buffeted my face. It was cold. A great high space opened round us. Thin sunlight speared down into the depths ahead. Echoes rustled, and somewhere water dripped into pools. There was a sharp, open-air smell.

Rasrhe-y-Meluur. Not below ground, then, but above it: the car had brought us up the pylon to the beginning of that great bridge.

'You will not need torches,' the Hexenmeister said, 'you can reach Firerock before nightfall.'

From where we stood, the fused stone floor curved out and into distance, and in the crepuscular light began at last to curve upwards. And that rising curve of stone soared up into the dimness, and up until it was lost in mist and distance. And to the other side, also, the stone ran out to the edge of vision and then swung up in a great curve to hidden heights.

Ahead, a vast shaft of light fell down into the darkness, hiding the view beyond. When I stepped forward my boots splashed in the edge of stagnant water. The air smelled suddenly of rot. The dripping water echoed. Then I felt a cold wind, and I stared up and saw the mist that moved in the heights of Rasrhe-y-Meluur. It was not mist. Across and up and through such a vast distance of space, I saw that what moved were clouds.

The shaft of light burned silver, then white; and I thought some part of the giant tunnel must have fallen in until I saw how straight-edged the shadows fell. And I saw then that there were apertures in the stone, high enough above our heads that they appeared mere slits, but in reality big enough to pilot a flyer through—high enough for the clouds to drift in.

Rodion, boots clopping through the water, took a few steps forward. It grew deeper, and I realized we would have to follow the sides of the Rasrhe-y-Meluur. Clouds obscured the light, and I saw what lay ahead. That great circular shaft, rank water flooding it like a sea; and the broken and time-worn stumps of buildings jutting out halfway down from the clouds . . .

The sheer size of an enclosed space has an effect of its own—witness any cathedral. But *this* . . . Something in the human mind feels that it's wrong for anything constructed to be so large. A cave, or a river canyon, or the pit of a volcano: they inspire awe. But something as large as the Rasrhe-y-Meluur inspires fear. For it to be man-made is wrong, and for it to be made by aliens is simply frightening.

I saw in memory more real than vision what had filled this shell. How the Rasrhe-y-Meluur had been divided into upper and lower hemispheres, where we stood now housing the hidden machinery, and the top segment housing the multiple rails of the transport systems and the great hexagonal towers of the Witchbreed. The apertures blocked by force-screens, the controlled indoor 'weather' . . .

Now only the tubular shell remained, scraps of stonework jutting out halfway up its height, and the lower level rotting in acidic water.

This that had been Rasrhe-y-Meluur, the city of the triumph of the Witchbreed, astounding in its ruin.

'Send no word to me,' the Hexenmeister said, 'I shall know whether you come safely to Tathcaer or not. Envoy, give my greetings to your people.'

The old man coughed, and Tethmet took his arm. The doors slid shut on them, the fenborn and the stooped man in brown robes. We were alone with echoes and chill twilight.

The three of us began walking. The perspective of the Rasrhe-y-Meluur moved with us, now dim, now sunlit; and it seemed that we walked a day and more than a day without moving at all. Only the floodwater grew deeper, and the stone slick with lichen and treacherous, and the seabirds called and called.

It was only then that I wished I'd thanked him properly, that old man, thought of things I should have said, because I was unlikely ever to see him again. But much of me remains in the Brown Tower, and much of the Hexenmeister travels with me still.

PART
EIGHT

30

The Edge of Summer

More than three weeks travelling: thirty days from Kasabaarde.

Storms kept us on Firerock for a time. Then by island ships up the Archipelago, never out of sight of land; and after that the long run out to Lone Isle. I hoped for news of Evalen's ship there, but no one had seen it. A calm kept us fifteen days. And then the *Ahrentine Star* took us to Perniesse, first and southernmost of the Sisters Islands. From there we island-hopped, mostly on fishing boats: Perniesse, Valerah, Iraine's Grave, Little Sister, Ahrentine itself; and then across the last strip of water to a bay between the white headlands of Rimon. Blaize, being a Rimon man, judged us only a few *seri* then from the estuary of the Oranon.

Riders passed us towards noon, as we sat up on the hillside away from the road. Blaize paused, unwrapping provisions.

'That's a Rimon *telestre.*' He gazed down at the *marhaz* and the cloaked riders. 'Hezreth or Makhir, I'd say.'

Rodion took two of the bread-fungus loaves and passed one over to me. 'At least we know we're on the right road for Tathcaer.'

The bronze riderbeasts were bright against the mossgrass of the valley. Their feathered hooves were clogged with yellow mud, and they plodded on until a turn in the road took them out of sight. The air was humid, and the blue mossgrass—still damp from the night's rain—gave a wet scent to the day. Carrick's Star was bright as glass.

I chewed the tough bread-fungus slowly. It had the smell of seamammal clinging to it, having come from the boat that brought us from the Sisters Islands.

The other two fell silent. He sat against the bole of a *ziku,* resting his head back against it. Small muscles bunched in his jaw, the milky nictitating membrane slid across his eyes: he was chewing *ataile*. She gave him a slanting look but kept quiet. It was a point of argument between them. Her brown-dyed mane flopped over her forehead as she bent down to reach inside the pack. Once she stopped and gazed at him with an expression I couldn't identify. She sat beside him, close but not touching, and drew her knife and began to trim her nails. Without opening his eyes, he put his arm round her.

What am I to make of them: Aluys Blaize n'ri n'suth Meduenin, Ruric Rodion Orhlandis? One minute close to me as brother and sister, the next removing themselves lightyears into an alien humanity. The eternal problem of the empath—however close you come to a world, it's never as close as the native-born; but it's possible to draw so far from your own society that you strand yourself between the two. Out of that tension comes the work of envoy, diplomat, xeno-team. And I am Christie *S'aranth* more than Lynne de Lisle Christie.

'There's more of them.' Rodion pointed down at the road. 'All the *s'ans* going to Tathcaer . . . I don't remember the last naming, I was too young.'

'You'll remember this one.'

She laughed. A brisk wind came up the valley between the Rimon Downs, and the smell of rain came with it. She reached up and pulled down the new, seamless leaves of the *ziku*, rubbing the scarlet buds between her fingers.

'The edge of summer,' she said dreamily, 'when everything grows. That's what we used to call it in Peir-Dadeni, the last few weeks of Durestha. Spring's earlier here. It must be getting on towards the end of Seventhweek . . . It's good that we're home.'

'Will we get to Tathcaer before night?' I asked Blaize.

'Not if we don't start now.' He stood up, spat *ataile* juice behind him, and picked up his pack. Rodion sheathed her knife. She looked troubled.

'I wonder what news they've heard.' She frowned. 'If my mother—I don't know what I'm going to say to her.'

Getting here had taken all my attention. It was only now, a few *seri* from the city, that I also began to wonder what I was going to say.

Cold mist drifted up from the river, blotting out the fierce light of the stars. The pitch-torches on the slipway flared yellow and black. We kept on the edge of the crowd. *Marhaz* bugled and hissed, shuffling their hooves while they waited, and their riders shouted noisily to each other. Every second or third person wore the gold circle of a *s'an telestre*. Over the light-streaked water a darkness rose, massive as the hills, speckled here and there with lanterns: Tathcaer, the city, at last.

A team of *skurrai* dragged a creaking wheel round, and out on the water the torches of the ferry-platform were visible. Chains lifted taut from the river, dripping water that flared orange.

An ancient woman collected the ferry tolls. She was brown-skinned, with only a thread of mane left on her head, her face as whorled as a fingerprint. I unknotted a cord and slid off a silver piece, all the time staring at her familiar features.

'Salathiel *telestre!*'

'What?' Rodion said. Blaize lifted his head, then nodded sharply. I went after the old woman.

'Excuse me.' I caught her up close to the boat-sheds. 'Is there an *ashiren* here, Maric Salathiel?'

'Oh, yes. Yes. Maric!' she called, then added, 'not an *ashiren,* not since Orventa. Maric—someone to see you!' She sniffed disapprovingly. 'One of your Outland friends.'

'Who is it?' A figure came out of the sheds into the torchlight: I recognized the voice.

'Me, Christie, but keep quiet—' I stopped.

With that part of me that was Orthean, I expected it; recognized in retrospect those subtle changes that take place before the end of *ashiren.*

The voice was the same, and the face was Maric's, brown-skinned and black-maned with the old sullen expression giving way to a grin. But—and I could recognize it now—Maric was no longer *ashiren.* A patched tunic pulled tight over small breasts, she was broad across the hips where, at her belt, hung the paired *harur* blades of Theluk's that I'd given him—*her*—before Kirriach. It's hard enough to tell any Orthean's gender, but Maric had come out of *ashiren* a young woman.

'I knew you'd come back! Are you going to the city?' she said. 'Christie, I'll come with you; just let me tell Everil I'm leaving.'

'No, wait, not tonight. I'll send word—' I'd been prepared for a mental shift, to think of Maric as female if need be; what was much harder now was to think of her as adult. '—I'll send word from the city. That is, if you decide you still want to act as my *l'ri-an.*'

'Yes, of course.'

That sounded determined. Salathiel didn't approve of the envoy, I guessed. And Maric was still a very junior adult in her *telestre.*

'You got back from Shiriya-Shenin all right?'

'Yes. I've got your *marhaz* here, shall I bring *ke* with me when I come?'

'Good idea, yes.' The ferry was coming in to shore, and the crowd beginning to press forward.

'I told them you didn't do it,' she said. 'Why should you harm Kanta Andrethe? I told them.'

Her tone demanded reassurance. I gripped her shoulder. 'Keep telling them—but not that you've seen me here. I've got to go. Take care.'

'I will.' She grinned as I left. 'They said you were dead. I never believed that either.'

It was a cold crossing.

The river ran fast and deep and the ferry inched through the water, Ortheans calming nervous *marhaz*. I stood between Rodion and Blaize at the crowded rail. The city loomed above us. As white as spectres, *rashaku-bazur* flew silently overhead.

'What will you do?' Blaize asked. 'I should take the Orhlandis to her mother, if the *T'An* Melkathi's in the city. That's safe enough for a Crown witness: besides, it's what I was hired for.'

Silvered water gurgled where it sucked round the piers of the dock. A warm wind came from the city, and the smell of frying oil, fish, and dung. The ferry rocked.

'The island's subject only to Crown law—that still means I'll be arrested the minute I present myself to Suthafiori, there's nothing else she can do. It may well be the safest place, but I can't say I like the idea.' Corbek was in my mind then. 'Anyway, it's too late to do anything tonight.'

'Come up to the Hill,' Rodion asked. 'I want to see my mother. She'll advise us. We can go to the Citadel in the morning.'

Has anyone seen us arrive? I thought. Who knows we're in Tathcaer? No, it's a very small chance that we've been seen.

The ferry shuddered, halted, and I saw the front ramp lowered. The crowd pressed forward. It was difficult to keep together. The stones of the dock were hard, uneven, slick with river-moisture. Light dazzled from the open doors of the companion-houses. Ortheans shoved past us, shouting; and I was for a moment separated from Rodion by the cold shaggy flank of a *marhaz*.

'If you're going to the Hill, be careful,' I said when I got back to her. 'First thing in the morning I'm going up to the Citadel. You be there. I think the sooner we see the Crown, the better.'

'Where—' she stopped. 'Yes, I agree.'

If Blaize had any doubts, he was keeping them to himself. He said, 'This isn't the safest city for Outworlders. Be careful who you trust.'

It hurt to be called an Outworlder in a city and among people so familiar to me.

We parted there, they heading along the western shore of the island towards the Hill district. I went in towards the heart of the city. It was late, but the streets were still full of people. Companion-houses stood open, light from the courtyards spilling into the gaps between *telestre*-houses. The atmosphere was carnival. But as I went on, *telestre*-house walls rose up and all I had to see by were the stars. A thin river of light showed between the rooftops and I fumbled on. The passages stank of riderbeasts and sewage.

Midnight bells chimed. Cold, tired, I stood in the darkness and listened, eyes stinging. Tathcaer. It felt like coming home. Hadn't Ruric said it was the heart of the Southland?

Coming home to be lost, I thought sourly, having come two or three *seri* from Westbank. How can you cross half a world and then get lost trying to cross a city? Hell, have they never heard of street-lights?

Eventually I saw torches and headed for them, and came out on the quay with the harbour in front of me and Easthill and Westhill rising against the stars. That enabled me to find Eastharbour, and I wandered the narrow passages searching for Eastharbour-Salmeth. All the blank walls and bolted archway gates looked the same.

How long am I going to go stumbling round in the pitch-dark? I wondered; and then at last recognized where I was. It wasn't the *telestre*-house I'd been looking for. I couldn't care less.

I slipped the *jayante* out of its strap and hammered it on the gate of Eastharbour-Kumiel. The banging echoed hollowly. After I'd been pounding for some time—and it was bitter cold by then—there was a flicker of lantern-light behind the gate.

A very badly accented Ymirian voice shouted, 'I've told you I won't be called out at this hour of the night! You'll have the door down—'

I heard the bolts being undone. I tried to brush some of the mud and dust off my cloak and boots, without success. One half of the gate opened. Was I recognizable? I wondered wryly.

'Doctor Adair,' I said, and he lifted the lantern up and hung it on the bracket beside the gate. He had an old *becamil* cloak flung over sleeping robes, and he blinked at me for several long seconds.

'Good God!' he said at last. 'Lynne Christie?'

Outside the windows of Adair's cluttered room, the sky began to lighten. The end of first twilight: soon they'd sound the dawn bells. I rubbed my eyes, wishing I'd had more sleep. Adair had insisted on an

immediate medical examination. He—or rather, his Orthean *l'ri-an*—
loaned me clean clothes. I'd washed, and eaten, I should be fit. And it
was all wrong to me: to travel all this way and come home a stranger.

'Well?' Huxton repeated. He drew a breath and yelled, 'What the
fuck do you think you've been *doing?*'

'You got my reports.'

'Reports? Oh, that's what they were meant to be: reports?'

His voice was harsh, blaring. Getting my mind round English again
after so long was hard enough. Seeing the two of them was strange:
hard-eyed and hard-voiced people with squat hands and sleek caps of
hair; towering giants.

'You realize you put a stop to any chance the team had of getting
outside this settlement?'

'That's debatable,' Adair interrupted.

'Debatable, shit!' Huxton didn't sound as if he'd been awake long.
'Where do you think we've been this past year?'

I said, 'The *T'An Suthai-Telestre*—'

'It's your business to deal with the native authorities,' Huxton said
flatly. 'If you can't do it, they should have sent someone who can.'

'Screw you!' I said. 'Don't talk to me about natives—go out there
and talk to them! And when you do, mind your back, you're very likely
to find a knife in it!'

He glared at me, and then sighed. 'Well—I had two reports of your
death—'

I said, 'We're not easy for them to assimilate, Mr Huxton.'

'No? They seem to have assimilated you without much difficulty.'

'Meaning?'

He looked at me. 'Meaning whose side are you on, Ms Christie?'

'*Really,* Sam!' Adair slammed his hand down on the table.

I grinned. 'Do you know how much like paranoia that sounds? I
think you're learning—you'll understand Orthe yet!'

He ignored the second comment, but the first cooled him down.
Almost apologetically he said, 'You've changed. I wouldn't have known
you.'

Huxton would calm down, I thought; he would probably even work
with me in the future, but he was never going to regard me as trustworthy. It wasn't something I had the time or inclination to worry about.

Dawn bells shocked the *rashaku-bazur* off the dockside roofs.

'I must be going,' I said.

'You *can't* go to the native authorities,' Huxton protested. 'It's nothing more than lunacy! Stay here with the team, Ms Christie, and present

your evidence in writing. Going to court in person would be extremely ill-advised.'

'I'd sooner go than be fetched,' I said. The thought of Sam Huxton repelling a troop of Crown Guard on my behalf was engaging, if impractical. 'Besides, it demonstrates goodwill.'

'It isn't long to the recall date,' Huxton added. His chin was rough with stubble. A much-worn one piece suit covered his burly frame. All his movements were jerky; he hadn't the cat-glide that Ortheans pick up in weapons training. 'Don't risk your freedom of movement.'

'You can testify you've seen me,' I said. 'You've got my report, you know where I'm going, and if you don't hear from me soon then kick up a fuss, I'll need all the help I can get.'

The cords of money were light now. I slipped them round my neck, under my tunic. Should I take the *jayante?* No, though I felt odd to be separated from it. I straightened my knife-belt and picked up my cloak. The light at the window was brighter.

'We'll get it settled,' Huxton said. 'Don't worry.'

He was under strain, carrying responsibility for the team for all this time, and he looked tired. A year ago there hadn't been that weariness.

'There's a *skurrai-jasin* here,' Adair said from the open doorway. 'Though where my *l'ri-an* found it at this unearthly hour, I'll never know. I've made this up for you, by the way. Medical supplies. Take the capsules with meals, they should help combat allergy and fatigue.'

'Thanks.' I took the leather wallet he held out. 'I should see you pretty soon, I think.'

Crossing the courtyard I thought, you should have said something to reassure them. Their job's hard enough without the envoy making trouble.

The relief I felt at leaving their presence was frightening. Decent enough people, but I wasn't comfortable with them. Other worlds mark you: not all the scars are visible.

Despite the early hour the *skurrai-jasin* had difficulty getting up Crown Way through the crowds. *Rashaku-bazur* yawped in the high air. Blue haze rimmed the buildings, yellowed on their sunward side. The wind was fresh. On its crag, the Citadel rose out of rivermist as if out of cotton-wool. High windows flashed back the sunrise. In the great square below the crag the mist billowed and curled, shot through with sunlight.

Sudden fear touched me. Something must go wrong now, now that I'd come so far, and with so much luck on my side.

I paid off the *skurrai-jasin* and began walking across the square.

Morning noises jarred: *marhaz* hissing, *rashaku-bazur*, shouts from the barracks nearby. There were fewer people here. The gates of the great Wellhouse stood open, and fountains sparkled in the courtyards beyond. I walked past, towards the bottom of the zig-zag way and the guarded gate-arch. Remembering: here is where it began, in the common audience. To see and be seen . . .

Three or four Crown Guard stood in the shadow of the gateway; one looked up as I came closer, a woman with troopmaster's badges on her belt. She called something over her shoulder, and Blaize n'ri n'suth Meduenin came out of the gatehouse.

'That's her,' he said. 'Hello, Christie. Rodion's just gone on up, I said I'd wait for you.'

'Sure. Let's go.'

The troopmaster detailed off another four of the Guard to accompany us. Protection or arrest? I wondered. We went up the zig-zag way, from mist into sunlight.

'How'd it go?' I asked.

'We found the *T'An* Melkathi's place on the Hill. The *T'An* Ruric wasn't there—I don't know where she is at the moment—but we stayed there overnight, and then came along here.'

The city and the estuary lay below us, and the sun dazzled off the morning sea. Our shadows went long into the west. The Guard took us into the Citadel by a different gate than I'd used before.

Ortheans, I thought. Immediately after meeting Adair and Huxton, Ortheans had seemed the small lithe people I'd first seen: cropped manes, claw-nailed hands, and whiteless animal eyes. Now I saw them as familiar, with memories that weren't entirely mine.

We came by various ante-rooms into a high-roofed chamber, where tall slit windows let light in from an inner courtyard. A group of people stood arguing with such vehemence that they didn't notice our arrival.

'She's here!' Rodion said, her arm linked round a dark-skinned woman; and the woman turned and pushed her black mane back from her face with her single hand.

'Sunmother!' Ruric exclaimed, 'the only time I'll believe you dead is if I see the body burned! Christie, what's this about Dadeni—'

'And the ship,' a man rumbled. Ramrod-straight back, white crest: I recognized old Hellel Hanathra, Ymir's First Minister. 'The *t'an* Evalen's company?'

'They haven't reached here yet?'

'We were delayed,' Rodion interrupted, 'maybe they were too.'

'With your permission,' Ruric said perfunctorily to Hellel. 'Clear the hall—Romare, take word to the *T'An Suthai-Telestre.* Troopmaster, guard the entrances here.'

She sat back against the table, fingers knotting up the empty sleeve of her shirt that had come unpinned. 'We've been up all night, Suthafiori and I—this naming's an unchancy business. My sire and dam! Then you turn up.' Ruric's eyes strayed to Rodion, who was talking to Blaize. Her brown-dyed mane showed silver at the roots. 'I hardly knew her when I saw her, Christie.'

Hellel Hanathra stayed, but the other members of the *takshiriye* left the hall. Crown Guard stood at the doors, *harur* blades drawn. Then a woman came in, and Rodion and Blaize made formal bows, and I followed.

She looked older, mane more silver than gilt, lines scored heavily into her face, translucent, diamond-patterned skin stretched over hard bone. Her whiteless blue eyes were keen as ever, and quietly amused.

'Has the Mother given you back to us?' Suthafiori said, 'or is there a simpler explanation?'

'There's an explanation, *T'An,* but it isn't simple.'

She laughed briefly, and settled herself in the great carved chair at the head of the table. Ruric said, 'There's something you ought to hear, Dalzielle. About Peir-Dadeni.'

Rodion and I told it between us. What sounded plausible in Kasabaarde had a hollowness about it in Tathcaer. I was aware of the growing silence. But when I'd finished I knew there was still, in all the uncertainty, that one fact: that Brodin spoke to Rodion Orhlandis outside the Crystal Hall. That remained, and demanded explanation.

Suthafiori said, 'This is that Brodin n'ri n'suth Charain who is now first minister for Turi Andrethe?'

'That's the man,' Ruric confirmed. 'He was intelligencer, if you recall, for Kanta. Well. . . .'

'Well, we have suspected her intelligencers.' Suthafiori linked her fingers and leaned back. 'Albeit without proof, but that in the main because of the supposed guilt of the envoy—I must hold you under Crown arrest, Christie, but I think you know that.'

I nodded. She continued, 'This must be investigated, this and that other matter of Kel Harantish, which must wait on the *Child of Methemna's* return. *T'An* Hellel, be good enough to take the Guard to the Andrethe's apartments in this Citadel: bring Brodin n'ri n'suth Charain here to me.'

Hellel bowed and left. We were all silent. My stomach was tight. Rodion, one hand on Blaize's arm, sat between him and her mother.

She wouldn't look directly at anyone. Ruric's narrow dark face showed nothing at all: she must be working out the implications.

'Would that you'd come sooner,' Suthafiori mused. 'Seventhweek Eightday . . . and the solstice and the naming only twelve days away. Still, that may be to the good. If a trial's held, the news need go nowhere but across the island, every *s'an* of the Hundred Thousand must be here by now.'

'Will you try him?' Ruric asked.

'Both of them,' Suthafiori said. 'If nothing else, the envoy's innocence can be established. The word from the Brown Tower has weight. And if the man's guilty, then well and good; and if not, the murderer's still to find. But there's little time for any of it.'

There were footsteps outside. The double doors opened. The acting first minister of Peir-Dadeni came in flanked by four of the Crown Guard, Hellel Hanathra behind them. Brodin wore no *harur* blades, nothing but a richly-embroidered *chirith-goyen* robe, and his sharp face was dazzled with sleep.

'*T'An,*' he began, and then his eyes went to Rodion and to me, and he was silent.

I saw his lean face and I knew I was right, Rodion was right, the Brown Tower had the truth of it. His eyes were feverishly bright as he faced Suthafiori. His hands gripped the back of the chair, knuckles jutting whitely. I have never seen a face so ravaged by grief and guilt.

As it dawned on him what was happening, the strain left him. He seemed to be welcoming what was happening to him. I thought, Yes, you want to be caught. You killed her. And you can't live with it.

'You are held under arrest,' Suthafiori said, anger tempered by his obvious suffering. 'The charge to be answered is the murder of Kanta Andrethe, how say you?'

'Yes,' he was dazed. 'She—my *arykei*, I—'

'Do you confess it?' Ruric was sharp.

'I did it from my own ambition.' That was a mumble. He breathed deeply and raised his head, his eyes on Suthafiori. 'I killed her and I'm sorry for it—more than you could ever know. I killed myself with her.'

'So, and did you also attack Orhlandis?' Ruric was on her feet, hand clamped on Rodion's shoulder.

'Peace, *T'An* Melkathi. That can wait.' When Ruric resumed her seat, the Crown continued. 'Brodin n'ri n'suth Charain, you may have what aid from advocates or Wellhouse that you desire. You will be confined in the Citadel until Durestha Eighthweek Firstday: that day the trial begins.'

'Yes,' he said, and after that nothing more, standing still and quiet as if he might shatter at a touch.

'Remove him,' Suthafiori said, and as he went out added to Ruric, 'A full trial in the presence of all the *T'Ans* of the provinces—then let them say what they like, they have no excuse against my Outworlders now.'

'And if he didn't work alone, if Kel Harantish gold is at the back of it, and others like SuBannasen?' Ruric demanded.

'We'll see what else he'll confess to,' Suthafiori said, then turned to listen to a man who'd just entered. Her intent expression lightened.

'Here's good news,' she said, 'Romare brings word: the *Child of Methemna* is sighted at the Sisters Islands.'

31

Brodin n'ri n'suth Charain

A short time later Romare brought another man in. He was elderly, brown-skinned, his mane shaven down to black fur: I knew him from somewhere. He wore the skirt of an Earthspeaker.

'There must be no suspicion of my hand in this,' Suthafiori addressed us generally, 'or else I'd keep you in the Tathcaer prison under Crown law. Earthspeaker Tirzael, will you consent to take all witnesses in this matter into the Wellhouse?'

'If it be all of them,' he said. 'I've heard the Charain man has to do with this: him too. And they must live by custom, no weapons, no word, no contact outside the House.'

'May I send word to my people, if that's the case?' I saw Suthafiori hesitate before she agreed.

'Yes . . . yes, they should know where you are.' Her irritation with Tirzael faded as she spoke to the Orhlandis woman. 'Ruric, Rodion, I'm sorry to part you again so soon.'

'At least I'll know where she is,' Ruric said drily, and a little unsteadily. 'There's no safer place than the House of the Goddess.'

'What of your hired sword?'

'I'm witness to the attacks on Orhlandis,' Blaize said. 'Make what you will of that, *T'An.'*

'Confine them all,' she said to Tirzael, and then to us: 'It's for three days only, you'll be free after the trial—all of you who are innocent.'

They took us down from the Citadel to the square, and to the Wellhouse.

Passing through the archway into the courtyard, I managed to pin down the sense of déjà vu. There was the same atmosphere as in

Su'niar, Gethfirle, Cir-nanth, any of the Order houses of Kasabaarde's inner city.

Tirzael dismissed the Guard peremptorily. To us he said, 'Now I must take your weapons.'

Blaize slipped the buckles of his sword-belt, giving *harur-nilgiri* and *harur-nazari* to a young woman beside Tirzael. Rodion bristled, but took off her blades. I'd left the stunner with Adair.

'And your knife,' the Earthspeaker said to me.

'It isn't a weapon.'

'All the same.'

I felt naked without it.

'Now you are free within the walls,' he said. Brodin, who had stood silently by, followed him as he walked off, and I saw them enter the great central dome of the Wellhouse.

Blaize saw me watching. 'They can't deny it to him. Let's find the kitchens—I haven't eaten since last night.'

Is he afraid of us? I wondered, looking after Brodin. It might be doing him an injustice. He was south Dadeni, and as likely to be a religious man in search of temporary peace or consolation.

Like Hill-Damarie the place had kitchens, stables, and smithy all within its walls. Gardens and courtyards extended for a considerable distance, and bird's-wing bushes grew, and tall feathery *lapuur*.

Late in the morning I went back to the courtyard close to the gate, restless and curious. There was nothing to do but wait, and the very waiting ruled out the possibility of a serenity like Kasabaarde's.

Many of the Goddess's people were there, barefoot, shavemaned, and wearing priest's skirts: a length of brown cloth wrapped round the waist and knotted over one hip. The ancient tiles were tracked over with muddy footprints. None of the Earthspeakers or Wellkeepers spoke, though some stared curiously.

So I was there when another party came, the Crown Guard and some others in sailor's dress, and I recognised *t'an* Evalen at their head. She had the Desert Coast woman Havoth-jair with her, and Haltern. I saw Tirzael coming, and went over.

'How's it going?' I asked Haltern.

'Seas like mountains,' he said palely, 'I've not recovered yet. We were two weeks in Quarth harbour waiting out storms, or we'd have been here before you. Christie, is there anything you need?'

'If you're doing favours, you can keep Sam Huxton up to date about what goes on—' I was interrupted by Tirzael, who parted us fiercely. He took Havoth-jair from Evalen, and hustled the others out.

'You,' he said when they'd gone, 'make no sacrilege in Her house.'

'I was marked for Her once,' I said, with a sneaking satisfaction at the amazement on his face. 'In Corbek, in a Wellhouse.'

And there was that other Wellhouse in Corbek, and Arad's mockery of a trial, and nights in cells that I didn't want to remember. I wondered then how Crown law would differ from Wellhouse justice.

Nothing in the House of the Goddess changed except the light: white sun in the day, fierce stars the next night. Blaize retreated into silent watchfulness. Rodion fretted like a *kazza* in a cage. Havoth-jair kept herself apart, too untouched by the world to be normal.

My one attempt to talk to her that day failed. When I finally did get her to respond:

'I don't want to know,' she said in thickly-accented Ymirian. Though it was a warm day she was shivering. 'What's one stranger more or less to me? If I'd killed you, at least I'd be able to go home to Kel Harantish.'

'You want to?' With all I'd heard, that astonished me.

'It's what I knew.' She had her back to the courtyard wall, sitting and staring up at the intense sky. 'What do I know about conspiracies, other worlds? Nothing. What do I want to know? Even less. And now I'll never—'

She trailed off, and went back to stirring patterns in the mud on the ancient cracked tiles. I left her. The hostility was plain. Sometimes she had a bewildered look, as if she knew something was wrong but not what it was. I knew she blamed me. I should have been obliging and died in Kasabaarde . . .

I took care never to turn my back on her.

'Tomorrow,' Rodion said, kicking her bootheel against the leg of the table. 'Tomorrow. Land's destruction! how can you just *sit* there?'

Only we three were left in the kitchens. The Goddess's people had eaten, and gone about their business. Afternoon light slanted through the slit windows, gilding the brown bricks and tiled floor.

'You got a better idea, I'll hear it.'

She glared at Blaize. The brown dye had washed out and left her mane a sepia colour, pale against her gold-dust skin. 'There's got to be something we can do!'

'Waiting's a talent. Develop it. No,' he said, 'sorry, *arykei-te.*'

She stood up. Her hand brushed back, the automatic Southland gesture to check the presence of a *harur* blade. Their absence irritated her.

'Sit there until you turn to stone,' she said, 'much good may it do you.'

Her shadow blocked the door for a second, then I heard her heels rap across the court. Someone spoke to her, and I heard her snarled reply.

'Well, kinsister,' Blaize said wryly, 'what do you make of that?'

'I think she's very nearly as nervous as I am.'

He smiled briefly. 'There's no point raising dust when all you can do is wait. I learned that a long time ago. Christie, you don't think it's something else wrong with her?'

'Like what?'

He searched for words, then said, 'Maybe it looks different to her now, in Tathcaer. Not the way it did on the road and in Kasabaarde.'

His unscarred profile towards me, he looked younger; but under the vulnerability there was more than just physical strength.

'I thought you and she were good *arykei.*'

'We quarrel sometimes. It's the way of things. I thought, I hoped . . .' On the table, his hand closed into a fist. 'We should be *n'ri n'suth.* Meduenin, Orhlandis, doesn't matter. Christie, she's young. She wants to do all the travelling and fighting and having *arykei* that you do when you've changed from *ashiren.* Where does that leave me? I've hired out over half Orthe, and there isn't one place I'd go back to.'

After some time he said, 'Well?'

'Mmm? I was thinking about Hakataku. Where I was last; that's a world that's mostly agricultural,' I explained. 'Dirty, and the food was rotten, and you had to walk everywhere. Only what I was thinking: when I got back to Earth I swore that's it, no more, that's the last time I ever go off-world. Ever. Then Carrick V came up, and you wouldn't believe how fast I jumped at the chance. Incredible, it was, for someone who was never in her life going off-planet again.'

'I've been doing this longer than you.'

'Not much longer, I shouldn't think; and what's that got to do with it?'

His head went back and he laughed, tendons cording his throat. 'Ahh, you may be right, at that. And there's nothing to be done until this trial's over. I'll take my own counsel: patience.'

I want patience, I thought. But I want it *now.*

Rodion was sitting on the edge of the great fountain, looking out through the main gate. The Goddess's people wouldn't interfere unless we attempted to leave. I sat down beside her, trailing a hand in the chill water. Many people were visible in the great square; there was much coming and going, and what looked like tents or booths being set up. It was no cure for impatience, to sit there and be aware of being in a backwater.

Rodion flicked her claw-nail thumb on the water's surface. Crimson fish scattered. She said, 'I wish I was back in Shiriya-Shenin.'

That was unexpected. 'Why?'

'Oh, I don't know . . . I was there four years, you know. A lot of the time I liked it. Even being called Halfgold, that was only a few people.' She shrugged. 'I suppose I'll get used to this place, and Orhlandis.'

Something in her attitude was at odds with her speech. She was holding down joy, excitement, surprise. What fear made her conceal it? I asked myself.

'What will you do, now you're not *ashiren?*'

'Learn policy,' she was succinct. 'With an Orhlandis as *T'An* Melkathi, what else? If I stay Orhlandis.'

Under short pale lashes, her eyes glanced up.

'And Meduenin?'

She sighed, stretching her wiry body. Reflectively she said, 'Yes. Meduenin. I don't know the Rimon *telestres.* . . .'

'Does it have to be one or the other, and no alternative? No, don't tell me: it does. I know the Southland. But you'll travel, won't you?'

'Where I come back to is important too.'

'And Blaize?'

'Is important, yes. Yes. I have to make a decision soon, Christie.'

She seemed more adult as the days passed now, not just in body but in mind and thought and gesture. I said, 'Should you hurry it?'

'It's later than you think,' she said, exuberance surfacing in her eyes. With a mixture of joy and concern that was wholly Orthean, she added, 'I have to decide which *telestre's* best suited to bring up *ashiren.'*

'What—soon? *Now?'*

She laughed. 'I knew since Ahrentine, I'm carrying children. Christie, keep it silent until I decide—it isn't fair to say until I know what I'm going to do. The *ashiren* belong to Orhlandis. They might not permit me to be *n'ri n'suth* Meduenin—if that's what I decide to do.'

'You'll tell Blaize.'

'Yes, if Meduenin's to be involved . . . *S'aranth,* what are you thinking?'

The child, or children, would belong not to the father, not even to the mother, but to the entire *telestre:* I had seen that at Beth'ru-elen.

'I won't tell anyone before you do,' I said. 'You're a Southlander, you'd better solve this one yourself.'

Eighthweek Firstday, the day of the trial. I was awake long before first twilight, and heard an escort arrive. They'd gone again before I'd dressed, and I realized Brodin had gone with them, taken to the Hall of Justice before dawn.

At midmorning-bell they came for Rodion, and then shortly before the noon-bell took Blaize; and I was left to wait.

Clouds drifted over, solid as castles, and the sky was pale and starfreckled. Noon passed. Nothing moved in the Wellhouse grounds but shadow and sunlight. A sea-wind was stifled between the buildings. I thought, Are they going to call me today? Because if not—

I saw a stir at the gate, Crown Guard uniforms, and went over before Tirzael sent for me. There were eight Guard beside the troopmaster. How much trouble are they expecting? I thought. And realized I wasn't even certain where the Hall was.

We left by another gate, passing into the narrow passages between *telestre*-houses that clung to the foot of the Citadel crag. Twists and turns confused me. Then, before the Hall was even in sight, we hit the crowds. Native Ymirians, Melkathians with sari-robes and serrated knives, Roehmonders hot in high-necked tunics; all rubbed shoulders with Rimon men and women, robed Dadeni, Freeporters, and even Ortheans from the Kyre. The Crown Guard formed a wedge with me in the centre, and we pushed on through.

Over the heads of the crowd I saw a sprawling building, ancient and familiar. Brown brick walls followed a succession of curves, and above the first six or eight feet swelled up into an egg-basket of domes. Old, this Hall of Justice, old as Terison.

The crowd didn't lessen as we went in under the round archway. A passage opened for us. Many there were *s'an telestres,* I saw, and many were children. A surprising number were just past being *ashiren,* in their sixteenth or seventeenth year.

Beyond the antechamber, the Ortheans were sitting packed together on the tiled floor. An unexpectedly wide space opened up: the multiple domes were supported on brick pillars and the building was one great hall. It was loud with conversation, restless with the vivid gestures of Southland argument, and as the Guard brought me through towards the centre of the hall, many of the *ashiren* and young adults began that

sibilant hissing and beating of hands against the floor that signifies
Orthean applause.

The troopmaster, a small dark man, observed, 'You have a following
with the young ones, *t'an.*'

'I didn't know.' I had no time to think about it.

Under the central dome, eight thrones stood in a semi-circle, hacked
out of black rock and covered with pelts and cushions. Between the
arms of the horseshoe was a stone block, only a few inches higher than
floor-level. All but one of the thrones were occupied: Suthafiori leaning
over to talk with Ruric, Hellel Hanathra listening to a man in the
brilliant sashed robes of the Kyre, sleek and bright-eyed Howice Talkul
T'An Roehmonde deep in conversation with a man and woman I didn't
recognize. Facing the thrones and completing the circle was a horse-
shoe-shaped stone bench: the Ortheans here had divided into two seated
groups, some talking, some consulting books and parchments.

Haltern n'ri n'suth Beth'ru-elen beckoned me to sit beside him on
the bench.

'How's it going?'

'They're still hearing the Andrethe *telestre*. Turi's doing most of the
talking.' He indicated a brown-skinned woman close by me on the
bench. 'Charain *telestre* aren't pleased, but what can they say: the man's
guilty.'

In Haltern's eyes Brodin was already condemned. I saw him then,
on the far end of the bench, flanked by Crown Guard. His hands moved
like restless, independent animals. His face was motionless, the pale
marks of dried tears streaking his skin; and he seemed oblivious of the
moisture that from time to time seeped from his eyes.

A bell chimed. The talking died, silence spreading through the Hall
until the only sound came from the street crowds. Suthafiori leaned
back, steepled her six-fingered hands, and nodded to Haltern.

'We'll hear the Dominion envoy next.'

'Pardon, *T'An Suthai-Telestre.*' The big man next to Howice spoke.
He was a giant by Orthean standards, something over six feet tall and
bulky with it. His mane had a long crop.

'Thu'ell *T'An* Rimon, I hear you.'

'This, then: the woman here—the envoy—was accused of this same
murder. What chance that her evidence will not be false?'

The woman pointed out to me as Turi Andrethe stood, answering
from the bench. 'For this reason we do not, ourselves, accept *t'an*
Brodin's confession of guilt on its own: we bring evidence from the
tha'adur of Shiriya-Shenin. If you and these others assembled decide

that despite motive, despite confession, *t'an* Brodin is not guilty—then is the time to look again at the envoy's evidence.'

Thu'ell subsided, rumbling inaudible comments.

I went to the stand and told of events in Shiriya-Shenin, sometimes being questioned by Turi Andrethe and sometimes by the Charain people. Towards the end of it I mentioned Morvren and the Freeport. The woman next to Howice leaned forward. She was pale-skinned, with a great unbound mane flaring crimson over her blue robe. A small child sat between her feet, playing with the ship-embroidered hem.

'And from Freeport you went—where?'

Accent, dress, and position: she must be Seamarshal of that port, I realized. 'To Kasabaarde, *T'An.*'

Voices died, Ortheans exchanged troubled glances. Turi Andrethe stood.

'Envoy, will you tell us what took place at the Brown Tower.'

In the silence I heard *ashiren* fidgeting, a baby whining.

'Much took place there, *t'an,* but as to this matter: the Hexenmeister declared himself satisfied of my innocence—the *t'an* Evalen Kerys-Andrethe will confirm that.' It was a strange thing to carry weight in a court of law, I reflected. 'I may add, it was the Hexenmeister whose aid helped uncover the evidence you hear.'

That more or less ended it, though Charain made a desultory attempt to trip me up on small details. They weren't too interested in the Dominion envoy, either as envoy or as murder suspect. Being dismissed, I returned to the bench; and then saw Blaize and Rodion seated on the floor in the front of the crowd, and joined them.

'We will hear the *t'an* Brodin,' Suthafiori said to the Charain.

There was some hesitation, the man not being able to stand, while they brought a chair to place in front of the *T'Ans.*

'We judge the dispute between Andrethe and Charain,' Suthafiori said formally. 'You are accused of killing Kanta Andrethe, third of that name, in her city of Shiriya-Shenin. Do you understand?'

'I hear you,' he said quietly, rationally.

'What say you?'

'Yes,' he said. 'I killed her. You've heard the truth.'

The man in Kyre robes signalled, and Suthafiori nodded. In badly-accented formal Peir-Dadeni he said, 'Even in the mountains it was known, *T'An* Andrethe had her *arykei* among the *tha'adur:* why would you kill her?'

Brodin nodded to himself. 'Kelveric *T'An* Kyre, you have known ambitious men. She—knew certain things of me. *Arykei,* intelligencer

. . . with her gone, there are ways for a clever man to become minister, perhaps even First Minister.'

'And for that you murdered her?'

'I have said so.'

One of the Charain woman stood, saying *T'Ans,* our brother is sick—'

Ruric asked recognition from Suthafiori, then said, 'If you would have become powerful in Shiriya-Shenin, would it not have suited you better to remain the Andrethe's *arykei?'*

Brodin shifted uneasily. 'She knew—my life wasn't always guiltless.'

Dark-skinned, pale-eyed; Turi Andrethe came forward again.

'I will ask *t'an* Brodin to listen to this and account for it. The body of Kanta Andrethe, when discovered, showed marks of having fought against an attacker. Not only that, she was struck first with the intention of stunning her.'

'She had been a trained fighter,' Brodin interrupted, highly agitated. 'I knew it would be difficult. I killed her. Why else would I kill her?'

'Why? Yes: why?' Turi surveyed the seven *T'Ans.* 'In Shiriya-Shenin last Orventa we heard Sulis n'ri n'suth SuBannasen, we heard of her guilt; taking gold from Kel Harantish. What more likely than, before she died, she used that gold to good effect—good for the Emperor-in-Exile? I say that Brodin n'ri n'suth Charain killed Kanta Andrethe not for his own advancement, but solely and simply because he was paid to do so.'

Brodin shook his head rapidly. 'I swear by the Goddess, by my hope of Her—SuBannasen paid me for nothing, not for murder, not for any intelligence: I never took gold from her!'

Haltern stood up beside Turi. *'T'Ans,* there is another witness you should hear, it touches closely on this matter.'

'Call your witness,' Suthafiori said. 'Charain, look to the *t'an* Brodin.'

They surrounded the hawk-faced man. I saw one of them offer a wine-flask.

Haltern's witness was Havoth-jair. The Desert woman spoke of gold ships from Kel Harantish; those that had gone to Sulis n'ri n'suth SuBannasen, and those that sailed for the Hundred Thousand long after she was known to be dead. It seemed that the half-idiot stare, coupled with the knowledge she had been in the Brown Tower, profoundly affected the Southlanders.

'Sulis was not the Hundred Thousand's only traitor,' Haltern said. You could sense the disapproval radiated by the crowd.

'I'm no traitor, I'm no SuBannasen either.' His voice barely under control, Brodin rapped out: 'I've told you I killed her, what more do you want of me?'

'You have never taken Kel Harantish gold?'

'I received no gold ships from the Emperor-in-Exile.'

It was an evasion. Watching Brodin, I realized he wasn't far off total mental collapse.

'Nevertheless, there is a conspiracy, there are traitors to the Hundred Thousand.' Haltern's certainty echoed in the Hall. I'd never seen him so positive. 'You are a confessed killer. Now confess why it was done.'

'I've told you! How many more times?'

'It was unplanned, no other person had a hand in it?'

Brodin's eyes went to Suthafiori. *T'An,* how often must I say it?'

Sudden and shrewd, Haltern added, 'And will you swear, in the name of the Goddess, that you have never been paid in Kel Harantish gold?'

Brodin shrugged. 'What need to swear?'

'A great need. Swear that oath: you never took the Emperor's gold, you were never part of a conspiracy to blame the Andrethe's murder on another—let us hear, *t'an.*'

A long silence. Brodin looked this way and that, from the *T'Ans* to Turi Andrethe to Charain *telestre.* I remembered him sequestered in the Wellhouse. The silence lasted. It became obvious he would say nothing. You could feel the crowd turning against him, without a word being said.

'You will not swear?' Haltern persisted.

Brodin at last looked up and said, 'I've said all I have to say here, I'll take no oaths for your pleasure.'

Haltern resumed his seat. Turi Andrethe said, 'There is nothing else we can ask him.'

Eighthweek Twoday I spent in the Wellhouse, with Rodion and Blaize and the Desert woman, while the *T'Ans* debated the case between themselves. Tirzael Earthspeaker had charge of Brodin. He never spoke after his final words in the Hall of Justice. And the next day we were called back to the Hall again.

'Hear me,' Suthafiori said. The crowd's noise died. If anything, there were more people packed in than there had been on the first day. 'Hear the word of Thu'ell *T'An* Rimon, Ruric *T'An* Melkathi, Hellel

Hanathra, First Minister of Ymir; hear the word of Howice *T'An* Roehmonde, Emberen Seamarshal, and Kelveric *T'An* Kyre.'

Brodin sat with the Charain *telestre*. One of the men put a hand on his shoulder. Brodin never moved. His eyes were bright, showing their whites.

'For the first accusation, of the murder of Kanta Andrethe, Brodin n'ri n'suth Charain is confessed and proved guilty.' She hesitated. I saw she disliked the whole affair. 'That has the lesser penalty, death. For the second accusation, of a conspiracy with agents of the Emperor-in-Exile, we can reach no decision. By ancient custom we have a season of time before the penalty is carried out. Our word is this: Brodin n'ri n'suth Charain, being condemned to die for Kanta Andrethe's murder, shall be held and put to the question on this matter of conspiracy. Sentence of death will be carried out publicly in the season of Merrum.'

Brodin's face looked as though someone had blown chalk-dust over it. The Charain *telestre* were arguing with the Crown Guard surrounding them, and the hubbub as the crowd spread the news made speech impossible.

I suppose I'd been deceived by the way Southlanders spoke of their Goddess into thinking it wasn't something they took seriously. But here was Brodin n'ri n'suth Charain, already a dead man for the Andrethe's murder, who would not excuse himself under oath to Her. And what he risked by it wasn't simple execution, but being tortured until he broke and confessed.

Confessed to what? I wondered as the Hall emptied. Whatever it pleased the *T'Ans* he should confess to?

Death and pain to an Orthean are lesser penalties, that's a difference in species and culture. But what I thought after Brodin's trial was that there was no more justice in it than in that travesty of a hearing I'd undergone in the Corbek Wellhouse.

32

S'aranth

'It's not finished,' Haltern predicted, 'no matter what that thing says.'

The Fiveday broadsheet ran to three pages, most of it devoted to Brodin's trial. I spread the second sheet out on the courtyard tiles. Maric came out of the kitchen with another jug of herb-tea, and put it down on the table beside Haltern. He—she—had come back to Easthill Malk'ys after I sent her a message on Fourday.

'Listen to this,' I said. ' "We anticipate also the early confession of Brodin n'ri n'suth Charain to a like charge with Sulis n'ri n'suth SuBannasen, namely, trafficking with the Emperor-in-Exile and receiving bribes direct from Kel Harantish." '

'But did he?' Haltern drained his tea-bowl, wiping his mouth fastidiously. 'I know—I thought I knew the man. I worked with him. He hadn't the mind of a planner. He's a follower, not a leader.'

'Meaning there's someone who was behind him, someone still at large.' It hadn't taken much thinking to reach that conclusion. I weighted a corner of the large, unwieldy broadsheet with a rock. 'Hal, tell me if this makes sense. SuBannasen's intention was always to have the envoy killed, therefore that was the Harantish Witchbreed's intention also. That accounts for the poison, for assassins, maybe even for Corbek. But the Andrethe . . . that's different. That wasn't designed to have me killed, that was done to discredit me, and therefore the Dominion. That was done to break down relationships between the worlds.'

Haltern nodded. He had the distracted look that meant he wanted to conceal what he was thinking. 'So?'

'So whoever took over from SuBannasen has ideas of their own—

and I can't see it being Brodin, that's all. It doesn't fit, not with that kind of man, you're right.'

'Mmm.' He reached down and snared one sheet, shaking it out and studying it. 'You may be right, I couldn't say . . . are you going to the ceremony?'

'When is it?'

'Noon.'

'I don't know if I'll have the time. Every *s'an telestre* in Tathcaer seems to want to meet the envoy, and I've got to see as many of them as I can. I'll try and make it.'

'There's not too much to this one—just the *T'Ans* giving up their offices, and the *T'An Suthai-Telestre* giving authority for Tathcaer over to the *T'An* Commander. You've met Asshe?'

'When he took over from Ruric, yes.' I turned the broadsheet again. It was cool now, just after dawn; later in the day it would be uncomfortably hot. Easthill Malk'ys was small, cramped, and dark—or so I thought, after my travels. The city was bursting full. Streets were mired with dung, and the stench of the drainage channels was unbelievable. The most common overheard remark in Tathcaer was, No wonder it only happens once in ten years.

'At least the press supports us,' I said. 'Looks like Earth's in favour, for once—what are you grinning at?'

His eyes veiled, amused. The mask of innocence slipped from time to time. 'What the press supports isn't the Dominion, but *S'aranth*. Those schemes against the envoy rebounded when you were proclaimed innocent—for the moment, anyway, Christie *S'aranth* can do no wrong.'

'Bloody hell! My god, Hal—'

He wheezed with laughter. 'If you could see your face! Don't argue with it, Christie. It won't last long, but it'll help you while it does.'

They don't have the exact term, but Crown Messengers know all about public relations.

'I'll talk to the xeno-team,' I decided, 'see if I can't rope some of them in and take the heat off. It's only simple questions need answering.'

Shadows were shortening, the sun that touched Easthill and Westhill now descending into the city. *Rashaku-dya* flashed black and bronze, their chirruping clear in the high air. I heard Oru shift in the stables, scuffing the straw and hissing softly. Scents were clear after the dampness of the night, musky dung and fading *kazsis* nightflower and the sharp tang of herb-tea.

'Has Ruric seen this?'

He peered over my shoulder. Tucked in a corner, the name had caught my eye:

'News from the Lu'Nathe: Southland ship *Hanathra*, shipmaster Sadri Geren Hanathra, wintered over in L'Dui; reprovisioned and departed Hanys Firstweek on second attempt at Western voyage.'

'That, yes. It didn't please her.' He stood, brushing his close-cropped fair mane into some semblance of order. He was as shabby as ever, unlikely to be noticed in the busy city.

'I must get back to the Citadel. Christie, I don't have to tell you, do I? Whoever's behind Brodin has lost their gold-supply, their freedom of action, and they won't look far to blame it on someone. Be careful.'

'I will,' I said. I meant it.

Noon announced itself from the bell-towers. There was no time to attend ceremonies. I managed to get down through the crowds to Eastharbour-Salmeth and see Sam Huxton, who turned out to be nearly as busy as me.

'Do you realize—' he reached over and flicked the recorder off. 'Do you realize we've got slightly over four weeks to the recall date? And I have to have everything up to date and collated—'

'So do I, Mr Huxton, and for various reasons I'm having to do half a year's work before Merrum Forthweek.'

'Various reasons?' He rubbed the bridge of his nose. He was trying not to smile. 'Yes, you could put it that way. Well, what can I do for you?'

'You can lend me anyone in the team that you don't need for a few days. Let them come up to Easthill Malk'ys and handle some of the simpler interviews.' Best to be direct, I thought. The very fact that I had to come to him for help would make him amiable.

'Anyone I don't need—!' He made an incomplete gesture at the pile of tapes scattered over the table. 'In bio-readings alone . . . never mind. All right, Lynne. Carrie Thomas is pretty well finished, I think, and so is John Lalkaka; tell those two I said they should help you.'

'I'll do the same for you someday.' I got up to go. The pseudo-Earth decor of Eastharbour-Salmeth made me uneasy.

'Not me,' he said as I left, 'this is the last time I'm going off-world. Aboriginal pest-holes.'

I walked down with John and Carrie when we finally closed Easthill Malk'ys for the day. Down the narrow passages between overflowing *telestre*-houses, walking in the long golden evening. The companion-houses were open, and we stopped to drink pale wine in a dusty courtyard, John's thin brown fingers darting to emphasize a point as he spoke, Carrie sprawling her elbows on the table and grinning.

'Four weeks,' she said. 'Thirty six days. Then home.'

'If you don't count three months FTL.'

'The first thing I'm going to do when I'm back on Earth—'

I stood. They looked up, barely noticing the interruption.

'I've got to get back. You'll come along again tomorrow?'

'Sure,' Carrie agreed. 'Anything's better than listening to Sam bitch at us. We'll be there.'

I began elbowing my way through the crowds. Occasionally someone spoke to me, and I acknowledged it. I didn't know them, but after the trial the envoy's face was familiar to many.

Ortheans crowded the *telestre*-houses, slept in courtyards and roof-gardens and public parks. An encampment of tents had sprung up on the east bank of the Oranon river and when the wind came from Beriah's Bridge you could smell them. Tradition kept the city from total breakdown, the *telestre* tradition that guests should do their share of the work, so that the *s'ans* cooked and served food, unloaded ships, cared for *ashiren*, drove *skurrai-jasin*, cleaned the passages—did anything that required their labour.

Crowding doesn't suit Ortheans, not in a city. There were few killings but many fights. I witnessed some: the brief vicious scuffles that by tradition end at first blood-letting. Thieving went on without much notice being taken of it, Ortheans not regarding it as serious. I had to keep a close eye on Easthill Malk'ys to prevent them walking off with souvenirs. In the streets I was aware of *T'An* Commander Asshe's troops, but their presence wasn't obtrusive. The atmosphere was festive.

The companion-houses overflowed with custom. Warehouses, previously stored full to bursting, emptied in a rush. Ships in the harbour lightened as their loads poured onto the island. The Guild-Ring stayed open for business from the dawn bell until midnight.

It being a naming, I'd expected the general talk to be of *T'Ans* and the Crown. But these were *s'an telestres*. What I heard as I passed groups in conversation was: the drought in southern Melkathi (dry spring succeeding dry winter), new varieties of grain, Rimon's schemes to make the Oranon a passable waterway above Damory, Morvren's coastal trade, the Peir-Dadeni programme for breeding *skurrai*, *zilmei* hunts in the Roehmonde forest . . .

Almost as an afterthought, they each made their way up to the booths in Citadel Square to name their choice of *T'An.*

That's the split, I thought as I climbed the last hill slope to Malk'ys. *S'ans* and *telestres* on the one hand, and cities and conspiracies—the game—on the other. And yet they're both integral to the Hundred Thousand . . .

The climb left me breathless. Second twilight was coming on, the shutters in the courtyard closed, and I could see Maric had lit the oil lamps. She came out of the archway to greet me.

'There's someone waiting to see you.'

'Good grief, not another one! Didn't you say to come back tomorrow?'

'No, I didn't think I should.'

I followed her into the *telestre*-house, decided we'd better have herb-tea and be social, and went into the room I was using as an office. A small woman in a light *chirith-goyen* cloak stood at the window. She turned. Dalzielle Kerys-Andrethe, Suthafiori.

'Ah, Christie.' She shed her cloak, taking a seat by the hearth. There was no fire, the evening being mild. Maric brought herb-tea, grinned at me, and retired.

'*T'An Suthai-Telestre.*' To cover my surprise, I began to serve tea.

'Oh, there is no *T'An Suthai-Telestre*—not until the solstice,' she said, smiling. 'And any Orthean may call on the Dominion envoy, yes?'

'Yes, of course.' Fencing, guessing: why was she here?

'Yes . . .' Her fingers hooked in her belt, she gazed up from under fair lashes. There was still a hint of winter scale-pattern in her skin. She gestured for me to sit down.

'There are ships newly into harbour,' she said. 'Some Desert Coast, some Rainbow Cities, Saberonisi and the like. You will see them, will you, if they visit the envoy?'

'Naturally, *t'an.*'

Membrane clouded her eyes. 'You favour a slow contact between our worlds—what did Evalen call it? Restricted, yes.'

'There's a danger of infection.' She took that at more than face value, I saw. 'If you're asking me what my recommendation will be, I'll have to say I think this should be a restricted world with a small permanent station of Dominion people.'

'That's wise, yes. I hope your *t'ans* agree.'

'I can't tell you what the final decision will be.'

'No.' She watched me with all the unconscious authority of the *T'An Suthai-Telestre.* Abruptly she said, 'There's another vessel in harbour, one from Kel Harantish. Ambassadors—or so claimed—from the Emperor-in-Exile. Asshe thinks one ship's crew is no hazard to the city. But likely they'll ask to see the Dominion envoy. Were I you, I'd be too busy.'

'If they come, I'll see them. Taking all precautions.' It might do to have company, I thought, Lalkaka and Thomas, and perhaps Maric and Blaize. Facing witnesses, what else could the Harantish do but talk?

'It would be better if you didn't see them,' she stated.

'*T'an*, I think I should make something clear. Any conditions of contact with this world—however restricted or quarantined—apply to the whole of Orthe. Southland, Desert Coast, the Barrens, whoever.'

'Kel Harantish too?' She was grim.

'We can't be partisan,' I said, seeing the anger she was holding in.

'Harantish Witchbreed! Give them technology, and then—and then beware.' Her gaze held mine.

'If Carrick V's restricted, that means no importing high technology.'

'Laws, rules, I've heard that before—and you,' she said, 'are not the only Outworlder we'll have contact with.'

'Anyone else will say the same.' It took a very short time for me to realize that this was the *T'An* Dalzielle Kerys-Andrethe, Flower of the South, probable next holder of the Crown, and some thirty years my senior; and that I was a junior representative of a very distant world.

The tension broke when she laughed. 'You stiff-necked woman, you're as like Ruric as if one mother bore you. The times I've had that same stubborn look from her . . . ! well, let be, let be; we'll speak of it again after midsummer.'

When she'd gone, I sat shaking for a few moments. The woman was a pussycat on the surface, but underneath—it wasn't to be wondered at, hadn't she been *T'An Suthai-Telestre* for twenty years?

The courtyard of the Mercenaries' Guildhouse was all but empty. Two women spun the double-bladed pikes of south Melkathi, hugging the scant midday shadow. Blaize n'ri n'suth Meduenin, in britches and an old leather vest, circled with a younger man. *Harur-nilgiri* and *harur-nazari* caught the sun. Bare feet scuffed the tiles.

'Peace!' he said, breaking off when he saw me. The younger man bowed. Blaize came across, sheathing paired blades.

'Are you free for an afternoon?'

'Usual rates.' There was nothing sardonic in his tone; he was serious about his business.

'Sure. You might not have to do anything. I just want you looking as though you might.' When he consented, I said, 'You're not up at the Hill with Rodion?'

'She asked me to give her time to make a decision.' Under his scale-pattern skin, alien musculature shifted. 'Let her decide soon—there's enough offers going in this city now to keep the whole Guild working for a year. Ahh, what am I saying?' His glance held complicity, humorous resignation.

'Don't be in a hurry,' I said. It was as much of a warning as I could give.

'That seems satisfactory.' The Harantish ambassador leaned back in her chair. Her gold eyes surveyed the room without ever seeming to watch any of us. 'But this trafficking with your Otherworld—comes through the Southlanders, eh, their island here?'

'At the moment, yes, but not necessarily in the future.' I went through the usual explanations about restricted contact between the Dominion worlds.

Blaize stood at the door, relaxed and expressionless, hands clasped on the hilt of his drawn *harur-nilgiri*. The ambassador's gaze took in his mottled half-face, the worn leathers of the Mercenaries Guild. She was not surprised by his presence. John and Carrie shared a desk over the far side of the room, working on some of the tapes and talking quietly. Maric managed to find some of the *arniac* tea popular along the Desert Coast, and when she brought it in I saw she wore Theluk's blades.

'Not impossible you'd trade with us, then?' the ambassador demanded.

'Trade? I can't answer that at the moment, ambassador, not until my government finalizes its decision. But certainly there can be contact between our two cultures. If the Emperor wishes—'

'Ach!' She scowled. Her dark robe shifted, and under it was the glint of scaled bronze mail. The face under the unbound white mane was not young, though with the snake-gold of the Witchbreed skin it was difficult to tell. 'Dannor bel-Kurick is a fool, I'm sorry I ever bore him. When you have your answer, *S'aranth*-envoy, send it to Kurick bel-Olinyi; I will see it is heard.'

'Ambassador, you realize I'm unable to give guarantees—'

'Yes,' she said, and to Maric: 'My carriage is outside? Good. *S'aranth*-envoy, one word to you.'

Whether she was deliberately uncivil or whether it was Harantish custom, I didn't know. I stood, giving her a formal bow. 'Ambassador?'

'There's a certain Tower,' she said, for the first time in that long afternoon sounding neither threatening nor evasive. 'Only this, *S'aranth*-envoy: do not believe all you hear in that Tower. Nor all you hear of us.'

She left, going down towards the harbour in a closed *skurrai-jasin*. Blaize followed me out into the steep hill passage.

'I'm glad to see the back of that one,' he commented. 'Kinsister, you're well-spoken in the Desert tongues, did you learn them in Kasabaarde?'

'In a way,' I said, and wondered for a minute what else I'd learned in Kasabaarde, and what price I'd paid for it.

Sixday passed, and Sevenday, and the naming went on. I was seeing no one except *s'an telestres*. On the evening of Eightday Haltern called, walking up to Easthill Malk'ys as second twilight gave way to starlight.

'They want an official Dominion representative there on solstice day,' he said as he sat down beside Maric. 'The *t'an* Suthafiori suggested you, but I can ask Huxton if you're too busy.'

'I'll take a day off.' I wouldn't miss it for a gold clock; certainly I wasn't about to let Sam Huxton oil his way into my place. 'What's going on up there? I haven't had time to ask anyone.'

He picked among the remains of the evening meal, helping himself to a crust of the dark bread. 'It all waits on the naming.'

There was a question I didn't want to ask, but I asked it anyway. 'And Brodin, what about him?'

'He said nothing, nor ever will.' He chewed bread, swallowed; then glanced at me. 'No, you won't have heard, will you? It was only discovered at noon. Brodin took the *T'An Suthai-Telestre's* verdict on himself. He poisoned himself in his cell. He's dead.'

33

Midsummer-Tenyear

Solstice day:

'You're *late, S'aranth.*' Maric paused. 'Is that what they wear on Earth?'

'Yes—but it doesn't look like this.'

The clothes, having been in a chest for the better part of a year, smelled of preserving-herbs. I stood while Maric tilted the mirror, and looked at my remaining formal gear. The skirt hung loose at the waist, the jacket was tight enough across the shoulders to split the seams.

'Oh god. So much for the Dominion representative.' I stripped off. A loud hail came from the archway below.

'I'll get it.' Maric ran; I heard her clatter downstairs.

I dressed again. *Chirith-goyen* shirts were fuller in the sleeve than when I'd last ordered clothes in Tathcaer. Nearly a year? Yes. Clip-fitting britches tucked into soft leather half-boots, laced up the calf. A brown *becamil* tunic over that enabled me to wear the recharged stunner holstered at the small of my back. I didn't trust bel-Olinyi and her ship from Kel Harantish. And there was the unknown person—perhaps to remain unknown now Brodin was dead—with every motive to resent the Dominion envoy.

Maric came back in as I was buckling the knife-belt.

'Message from *t'an* Carrie,' she waved a folded sheet of paper, 'and the *skurrai-jasin* is here to take you up to the Square.'

'Already?' I stuffed the paper into the sleeveless tunic's inner pocket. 'Let's go, then.'

A black, crop-horned *skurrai* pulled the open carriage down into the city centre. The driver was a young shaven Earthspeaker; she said little, concentrating on bringing us through the crowds. All the *telestre*-houses we passed had their gates wide open, and Ortheans in festival dress thronged the courtyards. A sea-wind cleared the stench of dung and drains. Towering cumulus glided overhead.

Avoiding Crown Way—too crowded to pass—we came among the narrow passages and multiple junctions of the Eastside. A ribbon of blue sky was visible between the high *telestre*-house walls, pricked with daystars. The closer we got to Citadel Square, the more dense were the crowds. To my surprise I saw the brown-skirted priests directing the flow of people. Only a few of Asshe's guard were present. The *skurrai-jasin* approached the Square from the Wellhouse side, and Earth-speakers directed Maric and myself along to the front Wellhouse steps.

'Christie—over here!'

Ruric stood under one of the awnings that shaded both steps and Square. As she stepped into the sunlight, her cropped mane glittered like a starling's wing. In the shade, Rodion's silver mane gleamed. Blaize, back in the shadow, signalled a greeting.

'Thought you weren't going to get here.' Ruric gripped my hand. She looked tired but happy.

'Have I missed anything?'

'No. It's just beginning.'

Unbleached cloth cast a sepia shade under the awning. The Saber-onisi flanked us on one side, and the Seamarshal's guard on the other. Maric elbowed in next to Blaize, said something inaudible but cheeky, and the scarred man gave her a short answer. Knowing him as I did, I could see he was holding back laughter. Was that some memory of Kirriach?

'I can't find—ah, you're here.' Haltern, harassed as ever, joined me on the steps. Still sheep-dogging the envoy, I thought, privately amused.

Horns blared, drum-frames banged.

Citadel Square quietened, the crowd focussing its attention on the House of the Goddess. Crown Guard stood by the closed gates, feather-crests and belt-badges glittering. At that signal they turned and began to push the double gates back.

Thin pennants hung from the awning-supports, unrolling on rare gusts of wind. I could see the whole Square from where I stood. The entrance to Crown Way was choked. The Citadel gate was barred and guarded. Under the awnings, the crowd was at first glance a blur of colour: green, scarlet, blue, gold, white and earth-brown. Resolving it I saw *s'ans* in robes and bright tunics, *harur*-blade hilts shining, some with young *ashiren* sat up on their shoulders. Near me were a scatter of city tradesmen and merchants and young adults from the Artisan's Quarter. A woman in Mercenaries' Guild leathers and another with the plume-mane of a Dadeni rider shared a flask with one of the Quarth ambassadors.

'Now we'll see,' Haltern said quietly.

Sun glared back from the windowless white masonry. Through the open gates of the House I saw cool fountains, the great dome. A party of Earthspeakers came out onto the steps. A grey-maned Orthean in Guard uniform accompanied them: *T'An* Commander Asshe.

The priests beat a rapid tattoo on metallic drum-frames. A horn blared. No melodic fanfare, but a call as raucous and raw-edged as a hunting horn. An immediate silence fell.

'All hear, all hear!' Asshe's hoarse voice penetrated to the far corners of Citadel Square. 'Let all who hold land by the gift of the Goddess hear this!'

One of the priests—Tirzael? yes—came forward, holding a sheaf of parchments. The sun shone under the high edge of the awning, illuminating him. Midmorning bells sounded, and he waited out their chimes before he spoke.

'Listen and hear. These are the *T'Ans* of the Hundred Thousand, called to their offices by gift and desire of the people, called to be crowned this day in the House of the Goddess.'

At first I took it for an echo, then I realized that priests stationed at the edges of the Square were relaying his words out to the city.

'Called for the Kyre,' he announced, 'Arlyn Bethan n'ri n'suth Ivris!'

A growl of approval went up from the Kyre men and women scattered through the crowd. A surprisingly large number of those insular *telestres* were represented. I saw a plump pale-skinned Orthean woman go striding up the steps, bow to Tirzael, and sign herself with the circle of the Goddess.

'Called for Morvren and the Freeport—Zannil Emberen n'ri n'suth Telerion.'

A louder cheer for the flame-maned Seamarshal, and a buzz of speculation; the Seamarshal's guard near me seemed resigned rather than enthusiastic.

'How do they know to come?' Maric said, leaning between me and Haltern. Her young face was flushed, her dark eyes glittered. 'How do they know who'll be chosen?'

'Technically I suppose it could be any one *s'an* of the Hundred Thousand. Practically . . .' Haltern shrugged. 'I don't suppose there are more than two or three dozen likely names.'

'He's a cynic,' Maric objected, grinning at me.

'What game do you think they've been playing for the last half year?' It was an irritated question. Haltern's eyes were fixed on the priests at the Wellhouse gate, as if he could force them to announce the names he wanted to hear. 'I have a feeling, Christie, this is the most important Midsummer-Tenyear we'll see in a long time. Maybe the most important in my lifetime. I hope they know why . . . We can't afford to ignore the Dominion. Not now.'

'Called for Peir-Dadeni,' Tirzael continued, 'Cethelen Khassiye Reihalyn.'

Pale-skinned, gold-maned; as he went up the steps in his rich robes, gold flashed from his studded hands. Shiriya-Shenin: Fifthwall. Beside me, Maric grunted in disgust. She remembered Kanta's first minister.

'My sire and dam!' The Dadeni rider near me froze, flask halfway to her mouth, her face a mask of astonishment. 'Khassiye? The man's nothing but an upstart river-man—'

Ruric's narrow features creased into a smile. 'And I dare say he'll be *n'ri n'suth* Andrethe before the season's end.'

'Called for Roehmonde—Verek Howice Talkul!'

'Oh ho,' said Ruric sardonically, *'there* goes a man who expected the *s'ans'* call.'

The crowd parted to let him out on the steps. Howice, hot in gem-studded tunic, loose trousers tucked into *kuru*-leather boots. After the new Roehmonder fashion, he wore *harur* blades cross-strapped across his back. Rings gleamed on his fingers. If there was any Orthean I distrusted and thought dangerous—and perhaps more than dangerous —it was that sleek, plump Roehmonder.

Ruric's thin fingers worked, knotting the loose sleeve of her shirt. She dusted her plain britches. Wryly she said, 'And now we find out what Melkathi thinks of my work this past season.'

'Or how clever Hana Oreyn Orhlandis is.'

Her gaze met Haltern's, and she nodded, 'Oh yes, he'd like my place, I know that.'

There was some delay, the priests conferring in a group; and then Tirzael stepped forward again into the sunlight. 'Called for Melkathi—*amari* Ruric Orhlandis!'

Loud cheers and hissing applause came from the people round us. Ruric shoved her fingers through her mane, tugged her sword-belt straight, and strode down towards the steps. The applause followed her.

Rodion pushed past me, ran after the dark woman, and caught her arm. Ruric stared, listened, then pulled the girl into a hard single-armed embrace. A roar went up. Rodion came back flushed and grinning, as Ruric mounted the steps to the Wellhouse gate.

'What was all that about?' I asked.

'*S'aranth,* I said I'd tell her.' She took Blaize's hand, as he stared bemusedly at her, and announced loudly, 'I'm carrying your children.'

He snatched her up with a whoop. The Ortheans nearest to us crowded round and congratulations were offered to her, and wine-flasks. Another very pregnant woman hugged her. The rowdy celebration was hushed by the Saberonisi, who regarded everyone with disdain. Quiet came, not in time for the next announcement, but I recognized the Rimon man from the trial: Jacan Thu'ell Sethur.

Haltern's hand closed over my shoulder, tightened. His face was tense. The mask of bewilderment slipped; I saw him then as a clever man bitterly concerned for his world.

'Now,' he repeated.

'Called for Ymir,' Tirzael bellowed. Heads turned, talk stopped. 'Called for Ymir—the *t'an* Dalzielle Kerys-Andrethe!'

The sound was frightening. Spontaneous, raw, wordless: a mob-roar from thousands of throats. Wrenching breath from the lungs, vibrating in the air: I stood deafened for long seconds before I knew it was a massive roar of approval. Haltern stood shaking his head and laughing, as unrestrained as Maric who was jumping up and down. Blaize and Rodion tightened their embrace.

Six of them stood on the Wellhouse steps. Dalzielle Kerys-Andrethe walked to join them, across the dusty square between the awnings. The sun put the awnings' shadow across her path, so that she was one minute a woman in cloak and mail, the next a flare of silver. A short stocky Orthean in her fifties, moving easily, *harur* blades jangling in the quiet. She climbed the steps and the cheering broke out again: Suthafi-ori, Flower of the South.

Small bright figures surrounded by brown-skirted priests, they stood for a while to acknowledge the crowd, and then went into the Well-house. The bells chimed for noon: I hadn't realized how much time had passed.

An immense relaxation went through the crowd, and the noise-level fell to conversational. I saw blankets spread on the flagstones in the sepia shadows. Flasks were opened, food-packs unwrapped. Ortheans sat in groups, talking, eating and drinking, some playing *ochmir.* The celebration that had begun round Rodion started again, she and Blaize becoming the centre of much attention. I sat down on the steps beside Haltern.

'That's it,' he said, 'it's up to Her now.'

'I'd have thought this was the time you'd be worrying. You've no proof they'll choose the *T'An* Ymir as Crown, have you?'

'Nobody chooses.' Seeing me puzzled, he said, 'You remember how it was with the Earthspeakers at Beth'ru-elen? That's how it is now. All seven of them will talk with the Earthspeakers and Wellkeepers, and in time one of the seven will know who is fittest to be *T'An Suthai-Telestre*. Yes, I hope it's her, I believe it must be, but. . . .'

But these are Ortheans, I reminded myself. And psychology has a home in the theocratic houses, if not under that name.

'It's not a matter of ambition now. To be chosen *T'An*, yes, that's in the game.' His inflection gave it every connotation of intrigue, cabal, influence. 'But to be *T'An Suthai-Telestre* . . . you must know yourself well enough to name yourself.'

'How long do we wait?'

'We'll know well before evening.'

A *rashaku-bazur* sailed across the square, swooped and clung to the top of an awning-pole. Its wings beat wildly for balance. Sunlight shone through the white feathers. Double tail-plumes flailed, the scaled breast gleamed. Harsh cries echoed back from the high walls.

Looking round, I saw bel-Olinyi and the Harantish delegation and, on the other side of them, John Lalkaka and Adair. The rest of the xeno-team had got there—I saw a bewildered Tim Eliot trying to understand bel-Olinyi's remarks—with the exception of Sam Huxton.

'Oh god.' I fished Carrie's crumpled message out of my pocket and unfolded it. It read:

> Tathcaer, dawn.
> Lynne—
> Just heard there's a ship called in from the pick-up point, with someone from the department on it. Sam's with him now. Think maybe he's a replacement; guess the report that you were dead got home before the message cancelling it.
> —Carrie
> PS: His name is David Meredith—mean anything?

'What's the matter?' Haltern asked.

'As if I didn't have enough trouble.' I gave him the paper, then realized I'd have to translate it—but he was following the mechotype print with one clawed finger, translating under his breath. It didn't pay to underestimate him.

'If he hasn't got up to the Square by now, he's not coming,' I guessed. 'Well, I can wait.'

'I hadn't thought your people would send a ship so soon.'

'They'll have detoured him off some other route, I expect.' I managed to catch Carrie Thomas's eye and signalled, message received. She nodded. 'We'll both go back on the xeno-team pickup, Fourthweek.'

'Fourthweek? Yes, of course. I hadn't realized it was so soon.' He handed the message back. Eyes veiled, cleared; his smile held less irony than affection. 'I'm sorry you're going.'

'I'm sorry too.'

'If your people are going to have a station here—'

Rodion, leaning back from a lower step, interrupted. '*S'aranth*, you're not leaving already?'

'Not for four weeks.'

'We'll be back from Meduenin before that,' Blaize said.

'Are you coming back?' the silver-maned young woman asked. Her face was concerned, uncomplicated. '*S'aranth?*'

'If I can—yes, I will.'

'It would be best,' Haltern mused; then spreading his hands, shame-faced, said, 'Yes, but it's not simply policy, Christie.'

'All right, I believe you.'

And will I be back? I wondered. Permanent station, that needs a promotion, but I may be in line for one anyway now. It's not what I'd visualized, but . . .

You start off and you think you're going to do the big things, the spectacular alien worlds, the big embassies. Maybe you do. Then you get caught up in some little detail—and it turns out it's not little. It might not be that grand, but it's going to take you the rest of your life to sort it out.

Carrick V: Orthe. Barbaric, yes, complicated too: a post-technological world. All I'd learned about it only emphasized how ignorant I still was. But the people . . .

'Christie.'

I snapped out of thought, saw Blaize on the step below. Maric and Rodion were further down in the crowd, Maric introducing her to a group from Salathiel *telestre*. They shone and glittered, that company, with gems and *harur* blades, looking like something between a festival and an armed camp.

'You want to play *ochmir* while we're waiting?' Blaize had the battered old set we'd used in Kirriach, still with him. Ruined flesh made his face impassive as he glanced at Haltern. 'You too?'

Haltern gave him a look that was all Crown Messenger, then shrugged. 'Yes, why not.'

We played three-handed *ochmir* on the steps of the theocratic house. For that game the counters' permutation is between white, blue, and brown; the winner being the first to get all 144 faces up. I turned a *leremoc* up early in the game, lost it to Haltern, but remembered where it was and forced a reversal on him. The three-handed game moves quicker—instead of a four or five-counter majority in a minor hexagon, a three will serve to force reversal—but if anything takes longer, because of the shifting alliances between the players. I gained a notable advantage when, a nearby scuffle distracting Blaize and Haltern, I took the opportunity to flip over a number of counters to show my colour (including three *thurin* and another *leremoc*). The game went in my favour after that.

The afternoon lengthened. Rodion took us up past Hill-Damarie to Hill-Melkathi for a late meal, and we returned to find nothing changed. By the time the midafternoon bells rang the crowd had swollen again, filling Citadel Square to overflowing and blocking the wider passages of the Hill, and the narrow alleys behind the Wellhouse.

'*T'ans,* Outlanders.' A young Earthspeaker came along the steps to us. 'Will you come to the gate, please.'

We reached the gates as they swung open, passing through into the great courtyard where the fountains sparkled in the sun. Saberonisi, the ambassadors from Quarth and Kel Harantish and Kasabaarde, the xeno-team, the *telestres* of those chosen *T'An,* their *l'ri-an* and *ashiren;* and after us all the Ortheans from the Square. The great dome rose up white against a star-specked sky, a sky that glimmered with *rashaku* on a high wind. I saw Blaize's face, scarred and sardonic, and wondered if he too was thinking of Brodin n'ri n'suth Charain. A year is a long time: what would Brodin have done in Hill-Damarie if he'd known he had only a year to live?

Earthspeakers ushered us through the archway and into the dome.

My eyes had difficulty adjusting from the brilliant sunlight to the dim interior of the dome. Half-blind, I made for a seat, and found myself between Rodion and one of bel-Olinyi's Harantish Witchbreed.

Vast iron trees of candles stood at intervals, the myriad white flames illuminating packed tiers of people. The light was mist-pearl. The dome soared up, alabaster-pale. A column of sunlight fell from the roof-opening like molten metal on the polished rock floor.

All the foundations of the dome had been hollowed out, so that people entered at ground-level and went down the carved tiers of rock on ancient worn steps. It was amphitheatre-shaped: here on the top tiers we looked across vast space to Ortheans entering from the archway. Below, in a carved circular space some thirty feet across, the black well-mouth opened. The afternoon sun illuminated a few yards of the shaft and a wide area of the floor.

I saw the seven of them, bright among the Earthspeakers and the Wellkeepers: Emberen and Thu'ell laughing at something Howice said, the Kyre woman talking with Khassiye Reihalyn, Ruric absently massaging the stump of her arm while she listened to Tirzael and Suthafiori. The acoustics were good enough to hear them speak; if not for the clatter of people coming in, every word would have been clear.

Rodion leaned forward, tense. Her thin fingers interlocked. 'She must know. She's the only one that can do it.'

'Suthafiori?'

She nodded. I saw her swallow. It suddenly seemed a remote chance. How many of the seven favoured contact with the Dominion? Not more than two, perhaps three. One firmly against: Howice wouldn't have changed. The others? Ortheans like generations to come to a decision.

The Harantish man beside me shifted position, with a brief comment to bel-Olinyi. His mane showed black roots, his unveiled eyes were a warm brown. Witchbreed? I thought. Rodion, her gold eyes intent on the wellmouth, was a closer image.

Metallic drumbeats left silence in their wake.

'Let the Hundred Thousand hear.' The old Earthspeaker pitched his voice to carry. 'These are called to the office of *T'An* in Her sight and in yours. Bethan n'ri n'suth Ivris, do you accept the office named?'

'Laying down all offices I now hold,' the Kyre woman said, 'I do.'

As each was named and swore the Goddess's oath at the well, a priest brought forward the silver circlet that was their outward symbol of rule. Now there was no applause, no cheers, no noise; only an exhalation of breath at each oath.

'You hold the provinces,' the old priest said at last. 'Their kin are your kin, their desires your desires, their welfare your own. Listen and hear! Older than the provinces are the *telestres:* the Hundred Thousand.'

Tirzael came forward to stand by the old man. In his hands he carried a plain circlet of gold. Unadorned, undecorated, seeming to draw into itself the light of sun and candles.

'It is no light thing to wear it,' the old man said. 'The Crown of the

Southland. Who trusts the Goddess for strength to bear it? Who will name themselves *T'An Suthai-Telestre?'*

No sound in all that space: all attention focused down on the loose grouping of people at the wellmouth.

What holds them back? I thought. Howice stirred, one gold-heavy hand loosening the neck of his tunic, but didn't speak. What stopped his ambition? The silence lengthened. The priests waited. Tirzael held the Crown between his palms.

Brodin came into my mind again. The hawk-faced man, murderer, who would not lie under the Goddess's oath. There was the dichotomy: between intrigue and philosophy. So that at the heart of Southland government there is this public honesty.

'Will none of you speak?'

Two shook their heads briefly, an involuntary gesture: Ruric and Emberen.

At last a voice:

'I speak. It is no light thing, to be the hand of the Goddess on earth; but with Her power it becomes possible to endure and enjoy. Unless Her *s'an telestres,* Her Earthspeakers and Wellkeepers, revoke it: I will hold the Southland's Crown.'

Her gilt-maned head came up to survey the tiers of people. A stocky aging woman, the badges of Kerys-Andrethe gleaming at her belt; the black mouth of the well behind her.

'By your will,' Dalzielle Kerys-Andrethe said.

Tirzael stepped forward and placed the gold circlet on her head. A single voice broke the silence:

'Flower of the South!'

Against all precedent, but others took it up; her oath-taking was not audible for the shouting. It spread out from the Wellhouse, out to the courtyard and the Citadel Square. A great bell pealed out.

Out of time, spreading from the Wellhouse out to the farthest parts of the island, out of rhythm, wildly and joyously, all the bells of the city rang.

34

Night Conference
at the Citadel

Celebrations continued well into the night.

From the Stone Garden you can see all the land north of the island, and the lazy curves of the Oranon-like plate-silver under the stars. Flat water-meadows stretch away, only at the horizon is there a hint of hills.

The talk stilled for a moment, I heard the sound of broken water at the foot of the Citadel crag. A cry of nightbirds came from the garden, cool in these hours after second twilight, and the scent of *kazsis* nightflower was persuasive. The Citadel itself—towered, windowless, rearing up into blank domes—blocked any view of the lower city. But Tathcaer would not sleep: the alien city was noisy with shouting and singing, the Ortheans feasted and danced and made love; all the *telestre*-houses kept their doors open.

Rodion and Blaize sat at a table with some of the Shiriya-Shenin *tha'adur*. She brushed her silver mane back, laughing. He sat farthest from the lantern, his face in shadow.

'Will she stay Orhlandis?'

Ruric gave her crook-shouldered shrug. 'Who knows? I've told her to visit Meduenin—she might as well see his *telestre*. I won't keep anyone Orhlandis who wants to change.'

We passed them by, walking on down a narrow flight of steps towards other tables.

In the Stone Garden the natural rock of the crag is shaped into steps and platforms, into screens and pillars. Hollowed out into dew-ponds full of sparkfish, polished into domes that are grown over with thousand-flower and mossgrass, the Stone Garden of Galen Honeymouth stands at the northernmost point of Tathcaer.

The silhouettes of domes and archways were fringed with stars, with clouds of light. Tables and couches were set up on the platforms, under coloured lanterns that were no more than decoration in the starlight; and there was a profusion of food and drink. The Ortheans, according to custom, moved from table to table during the festivities. Haltern said a night's observation of the shifting groups gave a clearer picture of the Hundred Thousand's policies than anything else. I remember someone once told me that *ochmir* originated in the cities.

'That's the new one, isn't it?' Ruric hesitated, looking towards a table below us. 'What's the name—'

'Meredith,' I supplied. Sam Huxton was introducing him to Suthafi-ori. I heard his accent, the way his inflection altered in the course of a single phrase. 'Was I ever as bad as that?'

'Until you came back from the Desert Coast.' Ruric grinned widely.

'Thanks a lot, *T'An.*'

'Maybe not *that* bad, then.' She laughed.

'I guess I'd better go down and meet him.'

'I'll be with the Melkathi *s'ans,*' she said. 'Good luck.'

Mosses covered the stone screen, their colours visible in star and lamp light. Blue, scarlet, yellow and green. Dew-ponds glittered. I went down the steps, past grey rock polished, faceted, cut away to show seams of white marble and black basalt. The garden was loud with talk and laughter, with the atonal songs of Peir-Dadeni and the Kyre. The scent of crushed mossgrass rose from underfoot.

'Mr Meredith? I'm Christie.'

I'd caught him leaving Suthafiori's table. He paused, the lantern light falling on him. A broad man, darkhaired, somewhere in his late thirties or early forties. Like most Offworlders he struck me as slightly absurd. He shook hands: at first I didn't realize what he intended. He had a strong grip.

'Pleased to meet you,' he said, 'though I admit it's a somewhat unexpected pleasure.'

'I'm not as dead as I'm reported to be, you mean?'

'Something like that, yes.' Impatience underlay his good humour. 'The department diverted me here from the Parmiter's Star system— now I find it's not necessary.'

'Communications aren't the most reliable thing round here. But I wouldn't say it wasn't necessary.' I steered him towards a deserted table on the edge of the Stone Garden. We sat down. 'At the moment I've got a workload that means I'm having to second personnel from Sam's—

from Mr Huxton's team. If you can handle some interviews, we might get a report finished before recall date.'

He nodded. I poured bowls of herb-tea, the scarlet *arniac* of the Desert Coast. It wasn't until then that I noticed the odd look he gave me.

He said, 'You seem to have fitted in remarkably well, Ms Christie.'

'Call me Lynne, please.' It wasn't politeness. Lynne Christie and Christie *S'aranth* were two different people in my mind, I wanted to keep them that way. 'Yes, I suppose you're right, Mr Meredith.'

'David,' he said. There was a remnant of Welsh in his accent. He sipped the *arniac*, and looked at it unbelievingly. 'I've seen some of your reports.'

'There's another, but it's not complete. You can play it through.'

No one was in earshot, but I was aware we were watched. *S'ans* passed at a distance. The stars blazed over the Citadel. A faint mist rose: river-fog forming below the crag. The lanterns were haloed.

'They read like the worst kind of microfiche novels,' Meredith said. I realized he meant the reports.

'Life's like that—at least, it is here, David.'

'Yes.' He eyed me thoughtfully. The team would have given a fairly strange picture of Lynne Christie, I guessed, since they took me for a lunatic or worse. Meredith was old enough to have been born before the FTL discovery, to have come to this career late. A grade 6 envoy, Huxton said: that meant capable of dealing with high-tech worlds.

'Carrick V's more a post-holocaust rather than a pre-tech world.' He cupped the bowl between his palms, swirling the liquid. 'Not that you can be blamed for that of course, Lynne, just another example of the department acting on insufficient fieldwork.'

What about Kasabaarde? I thought. No, that wasn't in the report yet. Time enough later to tell David Meredith about that.

'When you're de-briefed—'

'The exposure principle, we used to call it on the training courses.' I grinned at him. 'Like, you expose someone to a culture same way as you expose film to the light—bring them back and develop them and there's your world.'

Meredith laughed. 'There's truth in that. Some.'

'Sam will have given you the details of this society?'

'As far as that goes, yes.' Some obscure emotion crossed his face when he looked at the nearby Ortheans. 'Obviously there's classification to be considered. I don't know if you've decided on your recommendation?'

'Restricted.' I elaborated, 'There has to be quarantine—what we have here is practically zero population growth, and an unknown degree of susceptibility to Earth diseases—'

'I'd have thought that a good reason for a medical aid programme.'

'Which brings me to the other reason.' I hesitated. How to put it simply? 'We have an extremely narrow margin of acceptance here. It's a cultural thing, they like to take decisions slowly, over a period of years. If the world's restricted to minimum contact it gives them time to adjust to the Dominion.'

'To grow until they have that capacity?' Meredith's prejudices were showing. 'I admit, at first glance it doesn't seem this world has much to offer the Dominion.'

'I'd've put it the other way myself—the Dominion doesn't have much to offer Orthe. Except medical technology, of course, and that comes within the terms of a Restricted classification.'

His eyebrows quirked up. 'You'll report to the Classifications Board, of course.'

'What's policy these days?' I felt uneasy. 'Remember, David, I've been off-Earth for eighteen months.'

'I think you'll get your classification,' he said. 'There was a spate of Open classifications—someone got it into their heads we were discriminating against non-tech worlds—but that died down when they saw what cultural damage was being done. Carrick V will count as non-tech, because of this anti-science religion and elite that's in power.'

One thing bothered me (and it didn't bother me as much as it should). In my reports on Witchbreed technology I'd gone fully into their past achievements, mentioned what remained in Kirriach, and the communications devices in use in Kel Harantish. What I never reported fully were the devices used by the Hexenmeister of Kasabaarde.

It's unimportant, not worth mentioning, it doesn't worry me—

And it should do.

Kasabaarde has left dreams in my head, visions of Orthe's past that come back with all the force of reality. Sometimes I wonder if that's all the effect it had. That's an old city: unchancy, as the Southlanders would say. Kasabaarde and Kel Harantish using the Hundred Thousand, perhaps, as an arena for the continuing battles of the Golden Witchbreed . . . How widely might that conflict spread?

'*T'an* envoy.' Emberen Seamarshal nodded as she passed us, arm in arm with one of the Earthspeakers. I acknowledged her absently.

'I don't like to see it myself,' Meredith added, 'I believe a world should be allowed to progress. But with the current hands-off attitude no one will interfere.'

I wanted to deny what he said, and yet from his point of view it was true. Even the remnants of technology in Kasabaarde and Kel Harantish didn't alter that. What did, what made him in error, was the mental attitude behind Orthean custom—and that I didn't have the right to explain. For that he would have to speak to an Orthean.

The scent of *kazsis* nightflower and mossgrass was overlaid by the cool smell of the river. It was chill. The Orthean festival would continue, they weren't so affected by cold. And overhead the summer stars were fierce.

Remembering Eastharbour-Salmeth, so long ago, I said, 'So tell me —what's the news from Britain?'

The first few weeks of Merrum stayed fine: long sunny days cooled by a sea-wind. Huxton's team were bringing their work to a close, and John and Carrie came up to Easthill Malk'ys as often as they could. Meredith's presence meant we weren't as overworked as before, and we worked quietly towards the recall date. *S'ans* came, and—now that the naming was over—Earthspeakers and Wellkeepers too, all wanting to hear about the Dominion.

If I had doubts (and it may be only hindsight to think that I did), I ignored them.

Because there was Tathcaer: the White City, in summer. Waking at first twilight and hearing the water-carts come down Easthill, the clopping hooves of *skurrai,* the water sluicing down the steep paved ways. Dawn on the roofs, then, flaring into gold and drying the passages, shining on the blank walls of *telestre*-houses. Even at that hour there was no need to wear a cloak as I walked barefoot down to the fishmarket at the quay for breakfast. Feastdays, fast-days, holidays: it was no hardship to work. Meredith, like the Eliots with whom he was staying, adopted the custom of a midday siesta. I liked to spend mine on the flat roof of Easthill Malk'ys, among the tubs of *kazsis* and *sidimaat,* dozing under an awning and looking down at Tathcaer. And the long afternoons blazed on, rung in by bells, and Carrick's Star went down over Rimon and gilded the sea out to the Sisters Islands, and the city rang with bells at second twilight. And then there were the stars.

So for that time I managed to dismiss the thought of Brodin, of SuBannasen, and of their living successor. To forget *saryl-kabriz,* the Wellhouse at Corbek, the death of Kanta Andrethe. The malice that prompted that was only hidden, not destroyed. I saw bel-Olinyi still in

the city, her ship docked under the shadow of Easthill, and wondered
which *s'an* it was that Kel Harantish had sent gold-ships to in the
spring. Kel Harantish and the Golden Witchbreed: they were at the
back of everything.

I should have known the game wasn't over yet.

Blaize and Rodion arrived back from Medued-in-Rimon towards the
beginning of Merrum Thirdweek. I was at the *T'An* Melkathi's house
on the Hill when they got there.

Rodion was astride a copper-striped *marhaz*. She wore loose white
robes, and over that one of Blaize's leather vests, the top few holes
laced. Her belly was round, already protruding.

She grinned at me. 'There must be at least four, don't you think?
Hello, Christie.'

Blaize caught her as she slid down in a jingle of Rimon bracelets and
coin-cords. Her *harur* blades were slung across her back, as the custom
is for pregnant Southland women. Two others rode with them: a merry
woman with a straggling blonde mane, and a man whose unblemished
face was startlingly familiar.

'Aluys Feryn, Aluys Ryloth.' Blaize introduced the other two members of his three-birth.

'Come inside.' Ruric linked her single arm with Rodion's. 'You'll
guest here, I hope, Meduenin?'

Feryn and Ryloth both dismounted and bowed. We went back into
the house. Maric was there, and I saw Haltern had arrived; there would
be others coming as the long evening continued. John Lalkaka, and
Carrie, and maybe Adair.

We drew together as the recall date approached, wary of wasting
time now that we had so little of it.

Shadows flickered in the wide hall. Ruric and I sprawled by the fire,
distant from the others; she with her booted feet extended to the flames,
slumped low in her chair.

'Ah, Goddess!' she said. Her eyes were half-hooded, her chin rested
on her breast; only the curve of her lips showed amusement. 'What a
year, what a Shadow-haunted year . . . a few more weeks and I'll have
to go back down to Ales-Kadareth, be *T'An* Melkathi. . . .'

'You're complaining?' I heard laughter from the other hearth, where
Rodion was holding forth to Blaize's brother and sister.

'Complain?' She chuckled. 'Well, maybe I was getting too fond of
the game to be *T'An* Commander of the army . . . but Melkathi! Now

that's a game worth playing. Between the *s'ans* that support Orhlandis, and those that hate it, and the SuBannasen and their supporters . . . Knife-edge work, that. You'll have to come down and stay in 'Kadareth sometime. In Orh—' she yawned massively, arching her back, stretching her arm '—in Orhlandis too, if you feel brave enough. Strange place, Melkathi.'

'That's because it's run by strange people.'

'I sometimes think you Outworlders have a very obscure sense of humour.' Her expression struggled for solemnity. 'Me, I don't see the joke.'

'That's because you're a savage living in the ruins of a once-great technological society.'

She laughed uproariously. 'That Meredith!' she said at last. 'He should remember his tongue's not unknown here, before he calls us that! Another of Huxton's breed, that one.'

'He's OK.'

'I can't say I—oh, are you going?' she hitched herself up as Haltern came over.

'I have to go to the Citadel.' He glanced at me. 'If I can borrow your *l'ri-an*, Christie? I may want to send you word later.'

'If it's agreeable to Maric, sure.' Now is that further business with Suthafiori? I wondered. I was expecting to meet with the *T'An Suthai-Telestre* again before I left Orthe.

Ruric saw him to the door, and on her way back spoke to Rodion. She and the Meduenin went off to see to their quarters. Ruric dropped back into her chair beside me.

'It may be court business,' she said, using the inflection that makes *takshiriye* mean government. 'There'll be more of that before you go—when is it, now?'

'End of Fourthweek.'

The nictitating membrane slid back from her yellow eyes. 'Christie, will you be coming back?'

'If my people send me here. They'll want some representation on Orthe.'

'Don't avoid the issue. Will *you* be back?'

Lapuur wood burned steadily in the hearth, warming the stone walls that were cold even in summer. Outside, muffled, I heard the sunset bell.

'I can ask you this,' I said. 'Maybe I couldn't ask anyone else. Is it ever possible for an Outlander to fit into the Hundred Thousand?'

'You're asking me because I was born Outland?' She was thoughtful.

'It's true I'm careless of Orhlandis, more than a Southlander should be, but that doesn't mean I don't have the affinity. Truthfully, I think this is my *telestre*—Tathcaer. I've been coming here since I was *ashiren* and I always end up coming back. But am I a Southlander or an Outlander? I don't think I know.'

She pulled herself up, stood and stretched in front of the fire. Yellow light danced on her obsidian skin. The shadowed angles of her bones were wrong, humanoid more than human.

She said, 'Meredith calls us a backwater world—no, quiet, who's complaining? For him it may be true. Not for us. But you, is this where you want your career to be?'

'I can do it. Liaise between Orthe and the Dominion.' I watched her: the narrow-chinned face intent, the animal whiteless eyes veiled. 'Maybe I can do it better than a lot of people could.'

'Yes, to be *S'aranth* is a happy accident here and now: good for both worlds. But that isn't what I asked, Christie. Is this where you want to spend your life?'

Here? I thought. Here is a long cold way from Earth, from home.

'Orthe means a lot to me—and I don't know more than a fraction of it. I think the place suits my temperament.' I shrugged. 'And you mean a lot to me, I think you're my closest friend here. And there's Hal, and Blaize; and Rodion and Maric—I've been lucky, very lucky. I just don't know . . . an Earthspeaker told me once that what I really wanted was to have been born here.'

'Oh yes,' she said, and nodded, and looked down at me with veiled eyes. 'I know how that feels. But you're *S'aranth* and I'm Yelloweyes, we're known now. Someone should have warned you, Christie, you come here and the place changes you; something of you always stays behind when you leave.'

Rodion called her then, and she smiled and went to see what the woman wanted. I watched the flames, the shadows.

The ship would leave for the Eastern Isles at the end of Fourthweek, the uncertain sea-voyage from Tathcaer. And then by shuttle to the waiting craft, ninety days standard-time to Earth. Classification is always a slow business, and there was no certainty they'd send me to a manned station on Carrick V. Possible, yes; certain, no. If they did, it was a long time coming back . . .

A tempting voice in the back of my mind said: let David Meredith go back and deal with diplomatic bureaucracy. Surely I can trust him to do it right. Can't I? Wouldn't it be better if there was a continuous

Dominion presence on Carrick Five? And who better than Christie *S'aranth?*

Voices echoed in the *T'An* Melkathi's house. The *l'ri-an* came to light the oil lamps and refuel the fire. From the arched windows I could see across the courtyard, through the gates to Tathcaer down the Hill, dark under the rising stars.

I thought, Yes, I'll stay.

Shortly after the midnight bell, when Ruric and I were still talking, there was a hammering on the outer door. The *l'ri-an* admitted Maric. She bowed hurriedly.

'Talmar Haltern n'ri n'suth Beth'ru-elen requests that you come to the Citadel,' she said.

'Now?' Ruric looked surprised.

'Yes, *T'An,* if you will.' She glanced at me. 'He said also, Christie should come if she desires to.'

Ruric scratched the roots of her mane, pulled the laces on her shirt. 'Damn intelligencers can't conduct their business at a reasonable hour . . . Yes, I'm coming.'

I pulled on my boots, Ruric grabbed a blue and silver *chirith-goyen* cloak against the night's chill, and we went out into Tathcaer, under the brilliant Orthean stars.

Maric led us past the Crown Guard, up into the Citadel, up through innumerable passages and galleries into the new wing and past more guards to a small richly-furnished chamber in a southern tower.

There was Haltern, harassed-looking as ever, deep in conversation with Suthafiori; and Evalen Kerys-Andrethe with the scribe Romare, and a dark man from Melkathi who I remembered to be Nelum Santhil, Portmaster of Ales-Kadareth. Ruric frowned when she saw him there.

'So: you're here.' Suthafiori glanced at us, and we took seats round the table by the candle-stands. Haltern spoke quietly to Maric, who left. As she closed the door, I saw there were Crown Guard outside.

I sat between Evalen and Ruric. Haltern stood at the opposite side of the table, shuffling papers.

'Haltern, this is your doing?' Suthafiori said.

'*T'ans, s'ans,* I beg your pardon for the suddenness of the call, and for the lateness of the hour. Nevertheless, I have urgent news.'

He seemed reluctant to continue. Evalen and Santhil looked intently at him, Suthafiori frowned. Ruric rubbed at her forehead with slender fingers.

'There is this to be said,' Haltern went on, 'we have not reached the end of conspiracy.'

Suthafiori nodded. 'We never imagined Brodin n'ri n'suth Charain acted solely for himself, but he—wisely, perhaps—went beyond reach of our questioning.'

Haltern's veiled eyes watched us. This is bad, some instinct told me.

'And the Witchbreed,' he said, 'there was a discrepancy there: gold was still being taken from Harantish agents long after Sulis n'ri n'suth SuBannasen's death.'

'That's true,' Ruric said, 'what's the connection?'

Evalen cleared her throat. 'He means we have a traitor among the s'ans. It may be so. But there's no proof, Haltern, is there? The dead cannot accuse.'

'They can speak, t'an, if they are given time.' Again he hefted the papers, as if weighing something less material than parchment. 'This came to me tonight by way of informers. It seems there were other copies, but those miscarried or were prevented, I don't know. But what is addressed to me commonly comes to me—sooner or later. Will you let the dead be heard?'

I saw Evalen and Suthafiori and Ruric look at each other. Then Suthafiori nodded consent.

' "Confession of Brodin n'ri n'suth Charain," ' Haltern read, with no trace of the dramatic. ' "Given this day Durestha Seventhweek Sixday in the Crown prison of Tathcaer, and made because I fear for my life, not from Crown or church, but from another who I will later name." ' Here Haltern looked up and said, 'The details you may study later, they are much as we supposed; he was employed first by SuBannasen and then—but if I may I'll pass to where he names the traitor.'

'Read,' Suthafiori said harshly.

Haltern thumbed and folded papers. 'Here . . . "On my return to Shiriya-Shenin I was again directed to endanger the life of the Offworlder envoy, this time by a mock attempt on the life of Kanta Andrethe. This is the worst that ever befell me: that I was recognized in the attempt, and so to save myself must turn pretended murder into reality. After this I quarrelled with my employer, but confess I was cowed by threats. Also, gold was given me, which I believe had its origin in Kel Harantish. Now I am justly accused of murder, to which I confess; and of conspiracy, of which I am also guilty." '

Haltern read quietly, in the formal phrasing of the Peir-Dadeni tongue.

' "And I do here affirm and swear by the name of the Goddess that all I have done, I have done on the express orders of the *T'An amari* Ruric Orhlandis, once *T'An* Commander and now *T'An* Melkathi, first named Onehand and Yelloweyes, and now and forever after to be named murderer, conspirator, and paid traitor to the Hundred Thousand." '

Suthafiori laughed shortly, incredulously. Nelum Santhil bowed his head. I think it was a full minute before any of us looked at Ruric.

'Deny it,' Suthafiori said, 'I believe you, Ruric, I'll have this liar killed—'

The woman eased back in her chair, smiling sardonically. Her bright eyes glanced round the circle of faces.

'I've evidence,' Haltern said, 'or I'd not bother to make the accusation. There is Santhil Portmaster of Ales-Kadareth, who received and passed on to you gold from the Emperor-in-Exile; there are the Crown Guards Ty Damory and Ceran Gabril who let their old *T'An* Commander visit Brodin in his cell shortly before his . . . suicide. And there are those who saw you in Shiriya-Shenin, I think, *T'An*. Do you deny it?'

'No,' Ruric said, 'I do not.'

She was within a foot of me, the vibrant breathing warmth of her body, the energy of her eyes. She kept her hand flat on the table and made no move towards her sword.

'You?' I felt dazed. 'That was you?'

Evalen stood and made a sign. Four Crown Guard entered and stood by the door, out of earshot.

'Now let us talk,' she said grimly.

Ruric, with all the calm of the professional soldier, reached out and flicked through Brodin's confession.

'That, I didn't expect,' she said idly. 'You understand he was not such an innocent as he would have you believe?'

'Innocence!' Suthafiori said tautly. 'You speak of innocence!'

'But it is true in most of its particulars.' Ruric let the parchments fall. 'Well, what now?'

'I don't believe it.' Evalen stared at her.

'I'd deny it, but I know my friend's efficiency too well.' Here she inclined her head ironically to Haltern.

'Then let us hear the evidence.'

I sat stunned. Santhil spoke, and the Guard were called to testify. I don't know if I listened. No one was going to dismiss the incredible reality of her guilt.

In one of the pauses Suthafiori said, 'Ruric—how could you do it?'

It was naked hurt, what we all felt: this was personal betrayal. Ruric did not reply.

I thought about Orthe, what had happened to me: the murder, the long pursuit across wild country, across the sea . . . because of this woman I trusted. This woman I'd believed was one of the friends that only come once in a lifetime.

'You lied to me,' I said. 'Everything you did was a lie.'

'Ruric,' Suthafiori broke in harshly. 'In the Goddess's name, I have a right to demand your reasons! *Why?*'

'I suppose it started in Roehmonde . . . no, it was longer ago than that.' The dark woman shook her head, looked suddenly tired. Her eyes sought Suthafiori's face. 'You know I've been against this Offworld presence from the beginning, since I met the *t'an* Huxton and his people. Then I went north in Christie's company—I knew SuBannasen and Howice planned something, but I didn't interfere. When I came back and saw what an effect one Earth woman had on that province. . . .'

'Roehmonde,' I said bitterly, 'was that you, too?'

'No, that you may leave at SuBannasen's door, and Howice's. After that—and you must remember, Christie, I thought you were dead— after that, I joined in with the anti-Dominion faction who supported SuBannasen, and I met Harantish agents in Tathcaer that autumn. And in Shiriya-Shenin . . .' she shrugged, not looking at me; arrogance kept her gaze on the Kerys-Andrethe woman. 'Christie being alive, I saw SuBannasen brought to trial. Orthe couldn't defend her own. So I took over SuBannasen's contact with Kel Harantish, and determined to have the Dominion envoy disgraced.'

'Kanta's death, *was* it a mistake?' Evalen demanded.

Ruric ignored her. 'You know how that ended. Brodin and I fell out when he sent assassins against my *ashiren* Rodion, so I saw no need to defend him. But he might have betrayed me.'

'You killed him,' Haltern said.

Suthafiori bowed her head for a moment. When her voice was steady she said, 'You were *T'An* Melkathi, you could have named yourself Crown . . . grief of the Goddess, a Witchbreed agent Crown of the Southland!'

Ruric smiled. Regretfully, as if at lost opportunities.

'And had you done with them, or are you still their agent?' Suthafiori shook her head. 'Ah, no, why? Why, Ruric? It's senseless!'

'Senseless? No.' At last she looked at me. Our eyes met, and I looked away. She stood, in blue and silver, the candlelight like honey on

her black skin. She was tall, gaunt, an ageing woman carrying herself
with crook-shouldered balance.

'What happened, happened as I've told you. The reasons—' she
looked at me again. 'Christie, if you'd been scared off by poison or by
prison . . . no, but we'll speak of what occurred. My intention was to
discredit the Earth envoy, and the Dominion—'

'Why not kill me?' I asked bleakly.

'What use would that be? They'd send another. I wanted us rid of
you and your world.'

Slow, amazed, Suthafiori said, 'You never agreed with me on that,
but I didn't imagine you traitor because of it.'

'I'm no traitor!' Ruric flared. 'All I've done, even to murder, I've
done for the Southland.'

'Even to taking Harantish gold?' That was Haltern's barb.

'I see no reason not to take my enemies' gold, if I can use it for my
friends' good.'

That coolness silenced everyone.

'If you'll have reasons,' Ruric said simply, 'they are these. Earth will
destroy us. Either it will change us out of all recognition, or it will
destroy the land itself. We've all heard of the Dominion's fireweapons.
T'ans, there has never been a weapon in history too terrible for use. No
matter how awesome, they have been used. We have for witness the
Glittering Plain, the deserts of the Elansiir. Do you think Earth will
hesitate to use her weapons on us? As I love the South—I love it more
than life—so I have tried to protect it.'

Stubbornly, Suthafiori said, 'You can't turn back time.'

'Can you not?' Ruric shrugged. 'But it seems we have the Golden
Witchbreed come again. Oh, not that poor remnant walled up in Kel
Harantish. But you star-travelling, land-owning, fire-weaponed Earth
people—are you not the same breed as Golden?'

There was silence.

'*S'aranth?*' Evalen prompted.

'There are superficial similarities between that civilization and
Earth,' I said carefully, 'and I can't deny that we have terrible weapons.
I *do* deny that we would ever use them—least of all on a world with
which we have such friendly alliances—'

'Oh, you are different,' Ruric said regretfully, 'not all your people
are Christies, though. I've studied your people who studied us, I begin
to know the Dominion by its kinfolk.'

'We'd never do it.'

'Never is a long time,' she said, 'and while we're a backwater world with nothing desired from us, perhaps we're safe from war. But even then, not from change. You are utterly unlike us, and when you come here we can't help but alter. And if we're ever found to have something that Earth requires—why then Goddess help us, Christie, because no one else will!'

I couldn't answer her.

Ruric said, 'I'm a soldier. I know the odds. The Southland can't *fight* Earth. I saw that a long while back. I thought that an envoy disgraced as a murderer might hold back the tide—might even give us an excuse to break off relations with the Dominion. But you've a gift for survival, Christie.'

'Do you excuse yourself?' Evalen asked. 'You've broken every law and custom in the Southland, there *is* no excuse!'

'I'm right,' Ruric said, 'but yes, there's no excuse for failure.'

Suthafiori called the guards. 'Confine her in the outer chamber. Let none come to her, and let her speak to no one.'

Ruric walked out untouched between the soldiers, leaving silence in her wake.

'Goddess!' Suthafiori said at last. *'T'an,* she may yet spoil things between our worlds.'

'Worlds? No.' At that moment I wasn't fond of anybody there. 'She forgets one thing: the Southland isn't all of Orthe. We'll deal with others if we have to.'

'I don't think she cares, so long as you touch no part of the Hundred Thousand. And yet it would come to that in the end. We are one world.' She put her hands to her temples, rubbing six-fingered hands through her sandy-white mane. 'Excuse me—I'll call for refreshment, *t'ans,* we have work to do. There's much we must discuss and decide before the morning.'

35

The Legacy of Kel Harantish

'You cannot keep it from them!' Asshe stopped his pacing, turned and faced the *T'An Suthai-Telestre*. The grey-maned Orthean was edgy, claw-nailed hand resting on his *harur-nazari* hilt.

'What good will it do my *T'Ans* to know they have a traitor among them? After such a year as we have just had?' Suthafiori sighed. 'No, Melkathi must have a new *T'An*, but the fewer who know why, the better.'

The *T'An* Commander shook his head. 'And the Orhlandis?'

'Yes, the Orhlandis . . . Haltern, I think you had better find Hana Oreyn Orhlandis for me.'

Haltern left the chamber. Candles and oil lamps guttered unnoticed in first twilight. Dawn was lightening over Ymir, lost in river-mist.

I still couldn't believe it. It was a fiction, a bad joke—but it was true, and I might have suspected it long ago. I trusted her. The betrayal hurt.

Evalen was talking to Asshe, trying to persuade him. Suthafiori stood and walked to stand beside me at the window. The courtyard was grey below us.

'I'm sorry you should witness this,' she said, 'though I agree with Haltern, it's your right. You've suffered from her conspiracies.'

'She shouldn't have done it.' Not to us, I meant. She had lied, killed, but most of all betrayed the trust put in her.

'You look on the game differently.' The pale eyes veiled. 'But I agree. Melkathi may be a poor province—but she should not have gone to the Witchbreed for help.'

'What do you expect from an *amari* and a golden-eyes?' Evalen was bitter. She and Asshe began arguing again.

'No, that's not it . . .' As a thought struck her, Suthafiori called the scribe. 'Romare, send word for the Harbourmaster to come to the Citadel. Tell him I want the Harantish ship kept in port.'

Now the dawn brightened, so brilliant a silver as to bring tears to the eyes. Carrick's Star was fiercely white. Daystars peppered the arch of the sky. The city came clear of the shadow.

Amari Ruric Orhlandis . . . living in a world that was violent, precarious, unpredictable, herself marked and crippled. After that illness at Path-of-Skulls, she must have come back to Corbek feeling she was running out of time. Seeing the chaos those *telestres* were in, and all that change caused by one Earthwoman. Could I understand Ruric?

I felt close to her because she was the most 'human' of the Ortheans. That in itself was wrong. Did she fall prey to an Earth disease that most Ortheans are immune to—impatience? The Golden race never dreamed past-dreams, did the golden-eyed woman never dream them either? Did she believe that this is the only life there is, the only chance to act? Maybe that's what we had in common, the alien woman and I.

I must understand her, I thought. Nobody does anything like this without a reason. I must try to understand why.

A short time later, Haltern returned.

'Oreyn Orhlandis is not in the *T'An* Melkathi's house,' he said, 'nor are any of the Orhlandis *telestre.* I've begun a search.'

'None of them?' Suthafiori took her seat at table again, thin fingers resting on Brodin's confession. '*T'An* Commander, tell your guard to bring in Ruric Orhlandis, I will question her.'

He left. Shall I go? I wondered. I knew I didn't want to see her again. But I shouldn't go until the *T'An Suthai-Telestre* dismissed me. I rubbed my eyes, shook my head to clear it. I'd been awake all night; the last sleep I'd had was yesterday noon.

The waiting continued. Suthafiori, growing impatient, sent one of her *l'ri-an* after Asshe. Gradually, talk died down. Then Romare entered the chamber.

'The Harbourmaster attends you, *T'An,* and sends a message: the Witchbreed ship sailed at first light this morning.'

'Shadow take it!' Her fist crashed on the table. 'Have they heard— Haltern, find Asshe, find the Orhlandis woman; I want to know just how many Harantish agents there are in this city!'

At that moment the door opened, admitting Asshe. For once the arrogance had gone out of him.

'She's gone,' he said without ceremony. 'And half an army detachment with her. I've questioned the nightwatch. They say she left before first light. They had no orders to prevent her going. She went down Crown Way to the docks.'

The small woman covered her eyes for a moment, then looked up. 'She was their *T'An* Commander . . . I should have left her with the Crown Guard. Romare! Bring the Harbourmaster in. I want to know what ships are ready to sail. Asshe, bring the Guard—she's gone with bel-Olinyi.'

Then, incredibly, she laughed. Laughed bitterly and shook her head. 'Only she could do it. Only Ruric.'

In the frenzied activity that followed, I didn't wait to be dismissed. I found Maric, borrowed Oru, and rode the *marhaz* as fast as I could towards Easthill Malk'ys.

'Morning, Lynne—' Meredith hesitated, then shut the office door behind him. 'What's the crisis?'

'Is it that obvious? Hold on.' I finished what I was writing. I could have made a tape, but tapes can be wiped. David Meredith sat down, watching me. I said, 'You're early.'

'I'm getting used to the time-scheme.' He was keenly aware that something was wrong.

I finished writing and glanced round the office. It was as informal now as any Orthean place of work, the tables piled with papers and broadsheets as well as tapes, graphs pinned to the wall-hangings beside old illuminated maps, haphazard cartography beside satellite-survey prints. Stained tea bowls were piled on a chair, from when the last *s'an* had visited me. I was going to miss the work I'd been doing here.

'I haven't got much time,' I said, 'so here's the way it is. This is my resignation from the post of envoy—'

Meredith protested, but I overrode him. '—and as you're here, that means you're now the official envoy for Carrick V. I'm just a private citizen, as of now. What I do is my own affair, and doesn't reflect on the Dominion.'

As I moved towards the door, he stepped in front of it.

'I don't know what you're getting mixed up in, Lynne, I don't want to know. But I'll say this. Don't. It won't help this world, it won't help Earth, and it certainly won't help you. Don't be a bloody idiot.'

'You're right. Don't think I don't realize that.'

He relaxed fractionally. 'Now will you tell me what's going on?'

'You'll hear. I'm leaving Tathcaer. I don't know when I'm coming back. What I do know is, I won't be able to go as envoy. And I have to go.'

'What about the recall date?'

'What about it?'

He read the paper, looking for a moment as if he didn't intend to move. Then he folded it, put it in his pocket, and stepped aside.

'I'll make this public if it's necessary.' There was a faint emphasis on the last word.

'Thanks.' I stopped. 'Thank you, David.'

He said something as I went out. It might have been, *good luck.*

Down on the quay, at this early hour still in shadow from the Easthill, I found Asshe's men embarking on a Morvren trader. It was a broad-hulled *jath-rai* ship, nothing more than a coaster. Pushing through the crowd, I at last found someone I knew: Evalen Kerys-Andrethe.

'What do you want, *S'aranth?*' She was busy with messengers from the Harbourmaster and the Crown.

'Permission to sail with you.'

She frowned. The stolid face showed indecision. I should have asked Haltern, I thought, or even Suthafiori, they'd understand.

'I can't take a foreign envoy,' she said.

'David Meredith isn't asking to come.'

There was the subtle flick of nictitating membrane that might mean amusement. She was not as slow as I'd taken her for, this Kerys-Andrethe woman.

'Find the *t'an* Haltern,' she said, 'he's somewhere aboard. But take care, we sail as soon as possible, and can't turn back to land passengers.'

I went aboard, dodging the crowd: ship's crew and Asshe's soldiery settling down together. The harbour smelled dank and salty, fish-heads floating in the green water. Scavenger *rashaku-bazur* dipped and wheeled in the cool air, riding the wind.

The sails of bel-Olinyi's ship were still visible on the horizon when we put out from Tathcaer. Behind us, from the fortresses on Easthill and Westhill, the heliograph flashed warning messages towards the Sisters Islands and the south.

'This wind won't last,' a voice was saying. 'There's a calm coming.'

'When?' Haltern answering, frustration in his tone. The inflections of Ymirian, alien, liquid, but nevertheless respectful. When I opened my eyes I saw he was talking to an Earthspeaker.

I'd reached the state beyond tiredness that morning and found the light too bright. My voice was high and hoarse from talking through the night, and the skin across my forehead tight with a semi-permanent headache. My concentration had odd lapses in it.

Must have lapsed now, I thought, sitting up on the hold-cover. But the white sun was high, it was past noon. I'd slept.

'Where are they?' I went forward to stand beside Haltern at the rail. The rhythm made me stagger, hesitate as the deck swayed. With a firm grip on the rail it was better, I could watch the bows cut the swelling water, see the fans of rainbow spray.

'There,' Haltern pointed. It was a speck against the sunlight and the rolling water, barely visible to a human eye. We were no closer.

'Damn it, can't we go faster?'

'You can't hurry the sea.' His voice was quiet under the creaking of wood, the belling of sails.

A faint coastline was visible to the north. The sun's light, dipping on the water, flashed and dazzled me. I thought, not for the first time on Orthe, What am I doing here?

'Come below and eat.' Haltern's clawed hand rested on my shoulder for a minute. Wind ruffled his sparse mane. He was still the same secretive man, but even he couldn't conceal how this had shaken him.

'Hal—what will happen to her?'

'Let the Mother judge her,' he said, 'I can't.'

We ate sparsely, with Asshe and the shipmaster and *t'an* Evalen, to whom Suthafiori had given command of this makeshift expedition. There was little talk. The day wore on.

The turning-point came in the late afternoon, out of sight of land. I wouldn't have realized if Haltern hadn't told me.

Bel-Olinyi's ship lost a little time, or else the shipmaster managed to coax more speed out of the Morvren *jath-rai.* The sails were visible and the dark spot that was the hull. Only the two ships, under a stainless sky, daystars masked by high haze. Then the lookout shouted.

Two other specks were visible ahead of the Kel Harantish ship, and then I saw another off to the south, and what might have been a fourth. Ships that scarcely appeared to be moving, answering the heliograph messages, cutting off the way to the south. Ruric's bad luck that there were ships in sight of that call.

After a little while it became apparent that bel-Olinyi's ship was changing course, and that we were drawing closer to her. But not close enough.

The Harantish ship fled north and east towards the Melkathi coast, and we followed.

The ship's boat grounded and the crew shipped oars. I went over the side after Evalen and Asshe, splashing through shallow water. The flat sands stretched out, lapped by thin waves and ripples, silvered in the west as sunset approached. The sand sucked at my boots. A failing wind feathered the water, and brought from somewhere the smell of burning.

Another boat lay beached a hundred yards away, now empty and abandoned. Far out, where the shallow water shelved, bel-Olinyi's ship was anchored close to the Morvren *jath-rai.* And, walking towards us across the deserted beach, came an Orthean woman I recognized as bel-Olinyi herself.

Asshe gave orders to the Guard with him. Another boat was rowing the long way towards us from the Morvren craft, presumably reinforcements. He ordered the winch-bow holders to cover the woman's approach.

Haltern came up, eyes veiled against the light. 'Don't trust her, *t'an.'*

Evalen's eyes were turned inland, towards the low dunes and flat expanses of yellow mossgrass. A mist was coming up, so that it was not possible to see for any great distance.

'We must be east of Rynnal Sands . . .' she mused. 'The 'Breed doesn't matter, it's obvious the Orhlandis has gone inland. *T'An* Commander! Send your scouts to track their party. Be wary of ambush.'

Asshe nodded curtly. 'They may make speed, *t'an,* and not be concerned about us. If we've passed Rynnal, we're not far from Orhlandis itself.'

A look passed between them. Evalen said, 'Try and stop them reaching it. We'll follow you.'

Two of the Crown Guard brought bel-Olinyi forward. One carried the spear and knife that she surrendered without argument. She loosened the scarf at her throat, pulling it free of the laces of her bronze scaled mail, and surveyed us with composure.

'*T'an.*' She inclined her head to Evalen, then to me, speaking in her gutturally-accented Ymirian. '*S'aranth.*'

Evalen said bluntly, 'Where is she?'

'Your countrywoman? I wish I knew.' Her mouth tightened. 'I think I must speak to your *T'An Suthai-Telestre* when I reach Tathcaer again. It is not fitting for an ambassador to be kidnapped at sword-point—'

Haltern swore. Evalen continued stolidly, 'You claim that you were forced?'

'The woman comes aboard, her people are armed—what am I to do when my life is threatened? I did what she told me. But rest assured, the Emperor-in-Exile shall hear of this.'

'Oh yes,' Haltern said softly, temper for once uncontrolled. 'He surely will! So the traitor is betrayed, and you have clean hands, do you, Witchbreed?'

'Quiet.' Evalen's eyes hooded and narrowed, her six-fingered hands clenched into fists. 'You—troopmaster—take this woman to the ship, tell the shipmaster she is under my protection. And do you tell your own people, bel-Olinyi of Kel Harantish, that you will indeed return to Tathcaer. As soon as I have finished my business with Melkathi.'

'We'll never do it.' Haltern sounded depressed, as if he were still ashamed of his outburst before bel-Olinyi. 'Not in these mudflats, when we don't know the land; we won't come up with Ruric Orhlandis.'

'There'll be light for a while yet,' I said.

The long hot dusk of Merrum wore on towards sunset. What I took to be yellow mossgrass was the ordinary variety half-killed by drought. Light gleamed on ridged expanses of silt, dried waterways, and sand-marsh. Lizardbirds spiralled down, shrieking like rusty metal, settling into dry reedbeds that rattled like bones. The desolate coast stretched out to either side, losing itself inland in dunes and hillocks.

Evalen had brought her people to order, adding those men and women who had come ashore from the other ships. About three hundred, I estimated. Now she was sending scouts ahead of us, so that she would be informed where Asshe and Orhlandis were.

'The night should be clear,' the brown-robed Earthspeaker with her said as we approached. 'Wait out the second twilight, and travel on; I can give some aid to guide you.'

'Go at the front, Lishaan; we'll start now.' Evalen spoke with the formal inflection. Seeing us, she added, 'Keep with the main body. It's possible we'll be attacked.'

Sand stuck to wet boots, clouds of insects followed us as we trudged through the mossgrass-covered dunes. The marsh *rashaku-nai* began to roost. Walking was tiring, irritating. Haltern gazed, pale eyes unveiled, as we faced the flat land that lay back of the shore.

'Those might be Eirye Hills . . . or Vincor, if we're further south-east. *T'an,*' he said to Evalen, 'she may not stop at Orhlandis.'

'Why not?'

'Her *telestre* may furnish her with a guard and with *marhaz,* and it's not impossible to get down the coast from here to Ales-Kadareth. *T'an,* a person might lie concealed in that port for some time, and perhaps take ship—'

'To Kel Harantish?' Evalen shook her fair-maned head. 'It must not be allowed.'

Haltern caught her arm. 'She is Ruric Onehand, Yelloweyes of Melkathi, she has friends. If the *T'An Suthai-Telestre* were to judge in haste, and regret that later—'

'No,' Evalen said. 'I won't let her go. She must be judged. If it were my decision—she was my friend also, Haltern, but I'll bring her back to Tathcaer. Excuse me: I must send messengers ahead to warn Asshe of this.'

They're ambiguous, I thought, in their loves and in their hates. But not me—no, not me, I want to see her answer for what she's done.

Threading a way between bogs and mudflats, we came at second twilight to a *telestre*-house on higher ground. Torches set by the open gates illuminated the ancient, mortared stone walls.

'It is Vincor,' Haltern said, as we ate. Evalen was conferring with Asshe's scouts, and the sullen men and women of the *telestre*. 'We'll wait out second twilight here.'

The dusk was warm, and I fell asleep where I sat in the courtyard; not waking until the bustle of Evalen's leaving disturbed me. She and the Earthspeaker Lishaan took those men and women who were able to travel quicker, leaving her Second—a dark Peir-Dadeni man—to bring the rest on later.

'She'll try and keep Orhlandis from the Ales-Kadareth road.' Haltern eased down beside me. 'Rest now, there won't be time later.'

As when I'd first come to Orthe, I was getting used to catnapping wherever and whenever I could. So the next time I woke, insect-bitten and with aching legs, it was in full starlight. Two men were speaking with Evalen's Second. One had an arm roughly bandaged, seeping blackly.

'We'll take the border-path to Orhlandis,' the Peir-Dadeni man said. 'The *T'An* Commander Asshe was ambushed, but *t'an* Evalen's people came up with the Orhlandis company and turned them from the 'Kadareth road; now we are to make all speed to Orhlandis *telestre.*'

Starlight leached the colour from the land, from the stunted *lapuur* that edged the water channels, from the mossgrass that crumbled like ash underfoot. The way was winding, difficult to follow, crossing channels by plank-bridges. After the first we found broken down, the Ortheans carried a set with them. Orhlandis had tried to delay Asshe and Evalen, I thought.

The warm night at last grew chill as the stars faded to first twilight, and we waited out that time until dawn. So light came and showed us still in the flat water meadows, seemingly no closer to the distant high ground that didn't deserve the name of hills.

We came up on higher ground, following tracks through meadows where mossgrass was dying on acres of cracked mud. *Skurrai* raised their heads as we passed, all hide and bone under shaggy pelts. Stunted *lapuur* clung to the borders of the dikes, where *kekri* and *siriye* hovered in clouds over the mud. The pale sun rose from the haze, the air already warm. Then we came up on the spine of a ridge and I saw another high-walled *telestre*-house ahead. Two of Asshe's men appeared out of no-where with drawn *harur* blades, and led us on to where Evalen was camped.

'*S'aranth.*' She was civil but preoccupied. 'Haltern, good. I'm going to speak with Orhlandis; you as Crown Messenger should come with me.'

'She's under siege?' Haltern glanced at the distant *telestre*-house. He brushed futilely at the mud that spattered him. None of us, after the night's travelling, were in a better state. 'Christie, you speak with her as well, we might still end this without fighting.'

'I'd as soon do it with words. These *telestres* were built to stand against the sea-raiders, it will be bloody work to bring her out of there.' Evalen looked at me. 'She may hear you.'

'I doubt it. But I'll come.'

It was an effort to begin walking again. The hot air was motionless. I followed Evalen and Haltern. The tracks were dusty, winding through stands of *lapuur* and *saryl-kiez* bushes, crossing wide dikes. When I looked behind, the landscape seemed empty. Yet there were two or three hundred armed men and women there. As we came closer, we were softly challenged.

'Go forward,' Evalen told one of Asshe's people. 'Say we'd speak with them.'

The woman laid down her swords and walked towards the *telestre*-house, holding up empty hands. There were none of Evalen's company closer than this, bowshot-length.

Sun cast the shadow of the walls towards us. It was not a large building—it was so small that it surprised me, no more than high walls and a squat tower at one of the obtuse-angled corners. I made out stout gates barring the entrance under the tower. Surrounding the walls was a moat all of thirty foot wide. A single causeway led to the gate.

'There's the obstacle,' Evalen said. 'This Shadow-sent drought has left only mud; Asshe had a man near sucked down trying to spy out a place to attack. You've to cross that in the open, no way to surprise the defenders; and then with no scaling ladders, you've to attack the gates direct—we'd take it by weight of numbers, but not easily.'

'She was *T'An* Commander,' Haltern said, 'and knows all about sieges in Melkathi, *t'an.*'

The messenger's shouting brought movement on the walls, but little answer. Eventually a winchbow-bolt buried itself in the dry earth at her feet, and Evalen called her back.

'Why should she speak with us, *t'an?*' Asshe appeared, cat-silently. 'I've posted the Guard at all points now, she's surrounded.'

A frown settled on the woman's high forehead. 'We'll wait. She may try to break out. And she may be more willing to speak when she realizes she can't escape.'

They set up tents back where the cover of *lapuur* was thicker, and I shared rations with Asshe's company. The day grew hotter. Evalen and Asshe spent much time with their heads together, planning attack. My stomach went cold when I thought that might happen. Haltern was restless, and we made one wide circuit of the country round the *telestre*-house, from the marshes to the *lapuur*-choked low hillocks inland. He spoke little. The sun blazed down and the daystars gleamed, and we went back to the shade of the tents. A tense atmosphere kept us from resting. A *rashaku-nai* that flew up suddenly in the noon silence fell with four winchbow bolts in it.

Towards evening Evalen sent another messenger to the gates, but with no result.

We waited. Asshe set the night guard-posts. Tension rose: I could see they expected a night attack. But the night was clear, the starlight made everything visible, and Orhlandis remained blank-walled and quiet.

We waited.

'Who's that?' I indicated the group of Ortheans in drab robes who were speaking to Evalen.

'People from the nearby *telestres.*' Haltern eased into the shade of the *saryl-kiez.* If anything, this second day was hotter than the first. 'They want to know what the *t'an* Evalen's doing.'

'Will they help?'

'In Melkathi?' His eyes blurred. 'At best we'll get indifference, at worst—well, Orhlandis is a Melkathi *telestre.*'

Fear transmuted into resentment, into hate. The blank walls of the *telestre*-house shimmered in the heat, mocking me.

'Why doesn't she *do* something?' I demanded savagely.

Haltern had no anger in his voice. 'What can she do?'

Twilight came on the second day, and we waited.

Dreams merged with waking: shouts, darkness, and confusion. *Becamil* cloth flapped in my face, I was out of the tent and into the warm air. Yellow sparks flared across my vision.

'—*fire!*'

Another flight of sparks: I stood, head back, watching with all the concentration of a child at a firework display. Sleep blurred the image of rockets trailing down, sinking down and still burning—

Flame ran through the dry mossgrass and *lapuur,* red sparks went up into the windless night.

'Fire-arrows!' a man beside me shouted. I was at the centre of a group of robed Ortheans—the other *telestres,* it must be—chattering questions, wiping sleep off their faces, buckling on swordbelts and lacing robes. Evalen had been trying to gain their aid.

A company of Guard ran past. The camp was in uproar, like an over-turned *becamil* hive; frantic, shouting, panic controlled but present. I blinked in the flickering light. One of the tents hissed up in flame.

'You!' I grabbed the arm of a middle-aged Orthean woman. 'How close is your *telestre?*'

'A few *seri* north—'

'Get your people, bring them here. Now! Help fight the fire.' She stared blankly at me, and I shook her. 'Don't you realize how dry it is— the whole countryside could go up in flames!'

She was silent for a few heartbeats. Then as the din and shouting came closer, and I heard the crackle of burning wood, she gave a quick nod and ran off towards the back of the encampment. I saw her mount one of the scrawny *skurrai* there, kick bare heels to its flanks and ride off at breakneck speed. Starlight showed her the trail.

When I turned back, half the sky glared red.

The speed of it shocked me. I saw silhouettes of tents, then they blackened, crisped, curled—nothing but leaping flames. Showers of gold sparks went up. *Saryl-kiez* underbrush snapped as it burned. Dark shapes of men and women tried to beat out the fire, but as I watched they abandoned the effort. Another flight of fire-arrows soared from the *telestre*-house, then rolling smoke hid it.

Ruric?

Who couldn't take a siege, who was going to burn us out—

I scouted back, trying to circle round the fires. The *lapuur* was dry as tinder. Shouts faded. The fire was a dull roar. I was running, eyes dazzled, night-vision lost, finding the trail by luck and starlight; running as if I wasn't tired, as if I could run all night.

A dike blocked my way. I ran frantically along the edge and across a plank-bridge. Shallow water gleamed in the middle of the silt. Once across, I could turn and look back.

There is fear, and then there's terror. Standing there, heaving air back into my lungs, I knew the difference. With terror there is no fear, because there's no possibility of facing (say) the fire. There's no decision to make. You run, that's all.

A few moments later I came to a group of soldiers, and stumbled to a halt. I was about to ask them where Evalen was, when I saw Haltern there.

'You're all right?' He broke away, facing me.

I had no breath to speak, and could only nod.

Blackness blotted out the stars, darkness with a flaring red curtain at the foot of it. The smell of burning drifted to us. The air was no longer still, an intermittent wind fanned the flames.

'Move out!' Haltern ordered. 'We'll join the *t'an* Evalen at Rimnith.'

Within a surprisingly short time the soldiers were making an orderly way along the trail. I looked back. Flames crackled, rolled twenty foot into the night air, seething in smoke, orange and gold fire.

'She's broken siege,' Haltern muttered as we went, 'she's got her distraction, we can't stop her now—I hope the fire traps her and all her Shadow-haunted *telestre!* Just let her try and seek refuge anywhere in the Southland—'

He had no more breath to speak. We were running now. Behind us, the fire spread as fast as water flows.

Fine black ash-flakes drifted in the air. I coughed, throat raw, the breath rasping in and out of my lungs. The ground in front of me was soft and black and hot. Charred stumps of *lapuur* jutted up. Wisps of grey smoke still issued from the ground. The ashes were too hot to step on, even in stout boots.

I walked back across the dried watercourse and the turned earth, came to a knoll and sat down. My palms were blistered with shovelling and digging. From here I could see the line of dikes that had been turned into firebreaks. Ortheans were scattered along the edge of the burnt earth, sitting, or standing and talking, or just staring at the noon sun. The smoke that had mushroomed up to cover the coast was dispersing. Carrick's Star was a sepia disc, seen through the acrid pall.

They had it worse on the higher ground, I thought. Weariness blurred my eyesight, but I could see the stands of *lapuur* and *saryl-kiez* that grew there, some still sending up plumes of black smoke. I meant to go and look for the people I knew, but thought I'd sit a while longer.

The distant *telestre*-house of Orhlandis stood, a blackened stump, stones brought down by the heat. Gutted. Ash and desolation surrounded it. There'd been no way to put out the fire, it had barely been contained. Only the dikes and lack of vegetation made that possible. Evalen's people and the nearby *telestres* had thrown all their effort into fire-fighting.

Where's Ruric? I wondered. I was too tired to lie to myself now. No, I didn't hate her. I might hate what she'd done, but not her. If she'd managed to get away, if she sailed overseas from Ales-Kadareth. . . .

I got up and walked slowly back towards Rimnith, another small *telestre* on the edge of the blackened acres. Ortheans passed me, giving tired greetings. They were dirty and exhausted. I joined those in the courtyard, taking drinks from the well there.

Haltern found me while I was washing my face in a bucket.

'What do you think?' His gaze went through the archway to the burned land.

'It should be watched. It might still be burning underneath.'

He grunted assent. I wondered what was the matter with him. But it was the general atmosphere, there was more depression than could be accounted for by a fire, especially one that had been successfully contained.

'Hal, what is it?'

'Evalen's sending parties out to search.' He sounded as though he hadn't heard me. Then: 'She fired her own land. Burned her *telestre*. The stinking golden-eyed—'

'Hal.'

'You can't know,' he said. 'What it means. To do that—the 'Breed are land-destroyers, the Golden Witchbreed, and she—'

'When we came here, you were all for letting her escape to the port.'

He was silent. Then he said, 'The *T'An* Commander's found a *telestre* willing to sell us *marhaz*. You'd rather ride back to the ships?'

'Given the choice, yes. Let's go and see about it.'

I didn't mention Ruric again. Empathy and memories: yes, I could sympathize with what he felt. But then . . . Ruric. I heard enough talk from the Ortheans to know that Haltern's opinion was general.

Evalen was in Rimnith's small main hall, and as the members of her company straggled in she arranged for them to eat and then go out on patrol.

'She may be making for the coast again.' Asshe's grey-maned head was bent over a map. 'Or inland, hoping to hide.'

'You!' Evalen leaned back in her chair, shouting at a man who stood in the corner of the hall. 'Where did she go?'

'I don't know.' The man was sullen. It took a minute for me to see past the dirt and recognize the praying-mantis face of Hana Oreyn Orhlandis. 'I'd tell you if I knew—believe that, t'an.'

Evalen grunted. There were others under guard there, some with the Orhlandis face, and some in army gear. I recognized faces from my trip to Roehmonde: Ho-Telerit, and a red-maned male. So they'd abandoned Ruric, or she'd abandoned them. . . .

'Have you messages for the Crown?' Haltern took the papers Evalen indicated. 'How long will you stay in Melkathi?'

'Until I've made a thorough search. Let the other ships escort bel-Olinyi's ship back to Tathcaer with you, the Harantish woman has many questions to answer.' She raised her head and saw me. 'S'aranth, I'm glad to see you safe. Will you stay here, or return with the ships?'

I felt bitterly tired. Nothing had been accomplished by my coming to Melkathi, and as for Ruric . . . Patrols were already skirting the edges of the fire. I thought it likely they'd find her in there. If she'd got out, I thought, they'd have found her by now.

'I'll go back with Hal,' I said.

In the event they found me a copper-coloured *marhaz*, very docile, and I joined Haltern's small party. It was mid-afternoon by then. The rocking gait of the *marhaz* was oddly soothing. I trailed along behind, the sun hot on my head, half asleep. The sky was powderblue, dust from the earth track mixed with floating ashes . . . the smooth dry meadows, broken by muddy dikes . . . beyond that, beyond the *rashaku* that wheeled over the sandflats, the soft-edged blueness of the sea. . . .

The *marhaz* stopped. I jolted awake.

Hooves rang on the hard earth. There was a scuffle. I saw the half-dozen Guard vanish into a thick copse of *lapuur*. Haltern rode to the edge of the dike, by the plank-bridge. Sunlight shone on his drawn *harur* blades. I kicked the *marhaz* and it lumbered into a trot.

The feathery *lapuur* fronds blocked my vision. I swung down from the saddle and plunged into the copse. I was aware that Haltern followed me. I heard cries from deeper in.

'Landwaster! *Amari*—'

'—fired her own land—'

'—against the Goddess!'

Haltern shouldered past me into a clearing. 'All right, all right, *leave* her! I said leave her, Goddess rot your guts!'

There was a *skurrai* standing with its head down, cropping at the mossgrass that grew between *lapuur* and watercourse. Beside it, anonymous in shirt and britches, stood Ruric Orhlandis. Her clothes were smeared with ash, only the *harur-nilgiri* she held was bright. The dark mane fell over her high forehead, the narrow-chinned face was watchful. Her eyes glinted.

The Guard spread out, giving each other room, drawn *harur-nilgiri* and *harur-nazari* in their hands. Violence ran like an electric current, sparking in the air. Four men, two women, each face distinct, then merging into an animal gestalt. Ruric half-crouched, eyes flicking towards the dike. No way out. She was *s'an:* they hesitated. But she destroyed the land . . . The possibility almost realized: the unspoken desire to attack—

'No,' Haltern said quietly, his voice shattering a silence like glass. 'You there! Disarm her. If any of you touches her, I'll have your guts! She's going to Tathcaer, to the *T'An Suthai-Telestre.* Now *move!*'

Then he looked Ruric in the face. Something unspoken passed between them. Her thin lips parted, showing white teeth in a curious smile. The tension went out of her crook-shouldered balance. Sunlight flashed as she opened her six-fingered hand, letting the blade fall.

They hustled her off roughly, binding her arm behind her back and drawing blood cruelly. Haltern took no notice of that. I went back to find the *marhaz,* leading them after the party.

'I thought she might . . .' Haltern glanced at me, then ahead. 'She had that last escape, to make them kill her.'

'Not Ruric.' Perhaps if she'd been ordinary Orthean, not golden-eyed; if she'd had faith in more than one life—then she might have done that.

A wind feathered ashes from the burnt land. The heat of the sun was like a blow. We went on, taking Ruric Orhlandis back to Evalen, back to Tathcaer, back to whatever justice there might be for an ally of the Golden Witchbreed.

36

Exiles

Tacking back up along the coast of Melkathi, it was not until the dawn of Fiveday that we docked in Tathcaer. Westhill's fortress windows glittered in the sun, Easthill was still in shadow. I stood on the dock while the ferries brought Evalen's company from the ship. The solid earth swayed. I'd got accustomed to the sea's motion again.

'They're sending the Witchbreed,' Haltern observed, watching the Kel Harantish ship's boat approach. Then, turning away, made a formal bow. *'T'An Suthai-Telestre.'*

Suthafiori, dismounting from a *skurrai-jasin,* nodded briefly. 'Is the *t'an* Evalen here?'

'She's bringing the Orhlandis.' Haltern pointed.

'I've heard—' the small woman hesitated. 'Rumours out of Melkathi, the city's full of them. A burning. Is it true?'

'It's true.'

Her eyes narrowed, anger snarled across her face. 'Was it her? Was it Ruric?'

'She's said as much: her people confirm it.'

'The fool, the yellow-eyed freak—' fist hit palm, then she was calm with an effort. 'So that's the truth of it. Send Evalen to me.'

Suthafiori went back to sit in the *skurrai-jasin.*

'The way she says it, you'd think it was the worst thing Ruric did.'

Haltern shook his head. 'You're Outworlder, Christie. To intrigue is one thing, but to desecrate the earth . . . The Orhlandis was my friend. But you can't expect a Beth'ru-elen to approve of a *s'an* destroying her own *telestre.'*

'It's not destroyed.'

'The land will grow again, eventually, but the continuity's gone. A *telestre* can't live if its *s'an* betrays it.'

He went to meet Evalen. I watched him go. No, he couldn't feel any other way than he did. Land, history: more important to Ortheans than any individual person. I could feel it in me too: empathy with the earth.

Evalen spoke to Suthafiori, calling Asshe to her; and the Guard brought the Orhlandis *telestre* on to the quay, with Kurick bel-Olinyi and two other Kel Harantish Witchbreed. After a short discussion, Suthafiori drove off; and the company followed her on foot.

We went between the Guildhouse and Harbourmaster's office, under the great arch and up Crown Way. The city was empty in the half-light. The paved way went in a straight line, over the saddle between Easthill and Westhill, down into the city itself, then rising up until I saw the Citadel itself, catching early light. I imagined that our destination, but Evalen directed the company through the open gates of the House of the Goddess.

The great courtyard was empty, the fountain echoing loudly in the desolation. A warm wind lifted my hair, brushed my skin, brought for a moment the scent of cut mossgrass and a lifting of the heart. Then, as the company entered the Wellhouse dome, I saw Blaize n'ri n'suth Meduenin. Only a sick resentment stayed with me, that such things as the Orhlandis betrayal should happen.

'Christie,' he caught my arm as we went down to the lower seats, 'they've taken Rodion. Goddess! she's hardly more than *ashiren*, she knew nothing of this—'

'How did it happen?'

'She had a message from Ruric—a few days back, this was—telling her to leave the *T'An* Melkathi's house; being her *s'an*, what else could she do but obey? We'd planned to visit Meduenin again, but they took us on the road there. Christie—'

'Wait,' I said. 'It'll work out. They can't blame a kid like her.'

I took a seat down at the front, close to Haltern, Blaize with me. I saw the *t'an* Evalen frown. There were few enough people in the space under the dome, and most were Earthspeakers and Wellkeepers. Some of Asshe's soldiers guarded about thirty men and women in the sari-robes of Melkathi, and there were other soldiers with them.

Maric reappeared. 'Christie, the *t'an* Evalen asks if you aren't fatigued, and wish to return to Easthill Malk'ys to rest.'

I wiped blistered hands on ash-stained britches, amused. 'Tell the *t'an* I'm grateful for the thought, but my duties as observer compel me to remain and witness this.'

The brown girl smiled. 'I'll tell her.'

Evalen might appeal to Suthafiori to have me thrown out, but I didn't think so. All there was to know about this affair, I already knew.

Seats round the edge of the floor were crowded. I recognized Hana Oreyn Orhlandis, then silver-maned Rodion—her head bowed, her six-fingered hands clasped over her swollen body—and Tirzael Earth-speaker among a group of brown-skirted priests, and Evalen and Romare with Suthafiori herself.

Their bright clothes and sheathed blades shone in the gloom. The long shaft of morning sunlight fell from the roof-slot, illuminating vast spaces of dusty air, leaving the upper tiers of seats in half-light; then shone on dark skin, fair manes, complex braids, on sharply-angled ribs, brilliant eyes, scuffed robes and quick-gesturing hands.

The black mouth of the Well drew my eyes, and it was across that void that I found myself staring directly at Ruric Orhlandis.

She inclined her head.

They had not handled her gently. Her mouth was swollen and crusted. The filthy shirt was torn, so that you could see the black mane rooting down her spine. They'd left her arm free, and she picked uncon-sciously at the knotted empty sleeve, massaging the stump of her right arm; but a chain hobbled her ankles. Lines were incised in the reptilian skin of her face, drawn lines of tension.

Evalen spoke first, then Asshe; and Suthafiori and the priests lis-tened in silence to their recounting of events in Melkathi. As always, it was the skirted priests that impressed me as alien: ribs sharp as a ship's hull, paired nipples, cropped and shaven manes. The Orhlandis *telestre*, when they spoke, could have been taken for human. It was the old deception of Carrick V.

Of the soldiers that fled with Ruric, only Ho-Telerit spoke. She faced Suthafiori, broad hands tucked in the belt that strained round her waist.

'Conspiracy's one thing. I'm a soldier, and when Onehand—when Ruric Orhlandis was *T'An* Commander I was content to follow her. So also when she left Tathcaer.' The woman shifted her feet. 'But I'm no destroyer of the land, *T'An Suthai-Telestre*, I'm no burner of the good earth. And in Melkathi, when she saw we wouldn't obey her order, she fired the first arrows herself. Some of the Orhlandis did, also, but none of us. And if we'd known it would end so, we'd not have left the city.'

'It is late in the day to make excuses,' Suthafiori said. Turning her attention to Kurick bel-Olinyi, she added, 'Something you would be wise to bear in mind, ambassador.'

The Harantish woman stood. 'She forced control of my ship!'

'That I don't doubt, Witchbreed are noticeably careless of their tools when they have no further use for them. No, I do not think you would have helped her willingly.'

'There's been much said of conspiracy,' bel-Olinyi put her bleached mane back out of her eyes. 'Consider: where has the tale come from? From the Brown Tower and the Citadel, both no friend to the Emperor-in-Exile. You offer me no recompense for the loss of my ship to Orh-landis—'

'I'll offer you this,' Suthafiori said, 'the rest of this day to leave Southland waters, and my own ships to pursue you to Kel Harantish if you're tardy.'

The Harantish party left then, and there was some consultation between Suthafiori and the priests before she spoke again.

'I've heard all,' she said, 'and now I'll give judgement.'

Ruric's head lifted. 'For Witchbreed gold—or Melkathi land?'

'Hear me!' Suthafiori's voice cut through the noise. 'This is my word: there is no Orhlandis *telestre.*'

Sound rose in confusion, perhaps protest.

'No Orhlandis,' she repeated. 'For the land, let it lie until it heals, and then be divided between the *telestres* that border on it. For the people . . . such as are *ashiren,* if they have no other *telestre* they prefer, I will take *n'ri n'suth* into Kerys-Andrethe. No blame lies with the *ashiren.*'

A baby cried and was quieted, two women bent weeping over another child.

'For the soldiers, and those Orhlandis who are of age, this: you shall be exiled outside the Southland for the space of a year, and then return to such *telestres* as will take you *n'ri n'suth,* or to the church.' Her eyes flicked across the seats. 'For Hana Oreyn Orhlandis, who was co-conspirator, the lesser penalty of death.'

Beside me, Blaize n'ri n'suth Meduenin stood. His scarred profile was toward me, I couldn't decipher his expression. *'T'An Suthai-Teles-tre,* you have one there who is blameless.'

With her gaze still on Orhlandis, Suthafiori said, 'They are adult. She is their *s'an.* It was their responsibility, all of them, to see that she did nothing to harm the *telestre.*'

'What about the unborn?' Passionately convincing, he pointed to Rodion. 'Will you have them, blameless, born outside the land? *T'An,* what will you say to the *ashiren?*'

'This, then: let them be born in the land and taken *n'ri n'suth* into *telestre* or church, and after that let the mother serve her term of exile.

And,' she said softly, 'I did not say, hired-sword, that she should go into exile alone.'

He sat down heavily beside me. The small fairmaned woman rose and crossed the floor, with all the Orthean grace, to stand looking up at the place where Ruric Orhlandis sat. The dark Orthean female stood, the chain between her bare feet striking sharply on the stone.

'Well, Dalzielle?' she said quietly.

'And so it comes to this . . .' she shook her gilt head slowly, Dalzielle Kerys-Andrethe, Suthafiori, *T'An Suthai-Telestre.* 'What did it ever matter that you were *amari* and golden-blooded? You were the best with a blade, the truest friend—'

'Has that changed?' Ruric demanded. 'I played the game with a little outside help. Melkathi's a poor province, and what did the *T'An Suthai-Telestre* ever do for it? Less than I. And I was *T'An* Commander, and *T'An* Melkathi . . . but you'll throw away the help I could give you, just for a few *seri* of earth. The day will come when you'll be sorry for that, *t'ans.*'

'Hear me,' Suthafiori said. 'You will not die, you will be exiled from the Southland for as long as you live, and you will have the exile's brand on your face—I will put it there myself! Ruric-*amari* you will be called, and if you set foot in any of the Hundred Thousand, then the rest of your life will be spent in the dark cells under the Citadel.'

The yellow eyes watched her steadily. 'I think you'll regret this.'

'Take her,' the *T'An Suthai-Telestre* ordered, 'or I may kill her myself.'

I didn't watch her go.

'You have no business going off to god-knows-where,' David Meredith said irritably. 'We must leave here by Fourthweek Sevenday at the latest, and it's Fiveday now—'

'I was acting as observer, that's all.'

'Observing what, for Christ's sake?'

'I've been asking myself that.' I suspected two reasons for his lousy temper: Huxton would have been getting at him in my absence, and, now I had finally got back, I wasn't telling the full story. 'How I'm going to make a report on this, God only knows. It's just one of those things, David, you know how it is.'

He stared absently at the map of the Southland that was tacked to the office door: the mosaic pattern of the Hundred Thousand, the wilderness beyond the Wall of the World—and is the barbarian woman still

in Kirriach? I wondered—and the enigmatic symbols marking that vast
area of fused rock, the Glittering Plain.

'I do know how it is,' he said at last. 'Difficult to explain in the
department, those bastards who've never been offworld.'

His tone was bitter. I looked at him curiously. I'd tended to forget,
seeing him only as an unwelcome arrival, that anyone in the department
has their own offworld-caused eccentricity. What's Meredith's? I wondered.

'There's some points I have to clear up with the Eliots, I'll be down
there most of the afternoon.' He dropped a crumpled paper on my desk.
'As far as I'm concerned, no report's needed; I've been standing in for
you while you were sick. But don't pull one like this again.'

After he'd gone, I uncrumpled the paper. It was my pre-dated resignation. I sat staring at it for a long time before I finally tore it up.

'Christie?' Maric put her head round the office door. 'What's the matter
—are you sick?'

'Sick to death of something. I'm not sure what.' I left off picking the
bandages on my blistered hand, and stood up. I ached. 'Let's have some
tea. No, sit still, I'll make it.'

She followed me back into Easthill Malk'ys's kitchen, where a low
fire burned in the old iron stove. She was still the same youngster, I
thought; seeing this plump brown-skinned Orthean female, and in my
mind's eye the sullen scared kid that Haltern brought to be my *l'ri-an.*
Hill-Damarie, Corbek, and the Wall . . . and now she wore Theluk's
harur blades, and behaved with that frightening confidence that young
Southlanders have.

'What will you do?' I asked. 'Go back to Salathiel?'

'Not yet.' She reached over and set out the tea-bowls. 'I've been
talking to Haltern n'ri n'suth Beth'ru-elen. He might keep me at court,
he says, in the Crown Messengers.'

Her dark eyes whitened with membrane: was that amusement or
disquiet? One spidery hand slid to a blade-hilt. 'He says I've had experience.'

My hand shook, pouring tea; I laughed outright. 'Now that's a man
you should listen to. Yes. If it's what you want?'

'I think so.' Her manner was hesitant. 'But I'm not part of the
takshiriye yet . . . I don't know if I should tell you, Christie.'

'Tell me what?'

'In the Wellhouse today.' A supple shrug. 'I'm no friend of the
Orhlandis, why I should carry her messages . . . she asked if you

would come to her. I think she'll be in the Citadel now. I didn't know whether to tell you or not.'

'Always tell me these things.' The midafternoon bell sounded then, thin and clear over the sunlit city.

'Will you go?'

'In a while you can saddle Oru,' I said, 'I'll ride up and speak to them at the Citadel. I suppose I owe her that.'

'She's made some petition for you to visit her, I understand.' Evalen folded her arms. Light from the slit windows silvered her mane, shone in her eyes like glass. The Citadel's stone struck chill. *'S'aranth,* it wouldn't be permitted to a Southlander, and perhaps no Outlander, but my mother and the Orhlandis . . . if you wish, you can speak to Ruric-*amari* for a short time.'

'It's her wish, not mine; but yes, I'll speak to her.'

'Romare will take you,' she said, calling the scribe. 'Take care you do no more than speak with the traitor.'

The young scribe led me down stone steps and passages, where the polished grey rock ran with condensation, and breath smoked on the chill air. We passed barred doors, going down spiral steps cut into the rock of the Citadel crag, and small chambers where guards warmed themselves round braziers and played *ochmir.* I was searched, politely but thoroughly, before being taken to another guardroom on the lower levels. Ruric sat there at a table, and rose when she saw me.

Five Orthean guards were there, Romare stood by the door, it was a small room with no privacy. Veiled, curious eyes watched us.

'I didn't think you'd come.' Ruric was as I'd seen her in the Wellhouse, except for a bandage that covered her high forehead. She hesitated, then pushed one stool at me, and reseated herself.

I remained standing, at a loss for words.

'What the hell do you expect me to say to you?'

She eased back against the wall, breaking into the familiar smile. I wanted to hit her. She made me realize how much affection I still had for her.

'I've a fair idea—Dalzielle's said most of it, and what she didn't say, her daughter and mine more than made up for.' She brushed the black mane away from the bandage, looking at me self-consciously. What Suthafiori said came back to me: branded exile.

It was awkward to stand. I sat down opposite her.

'I'm leaving tonight,' she said. 'There's a ship that'll take me to the Desert Coast. And you're going to the Eastern Isles?'

'Sevenday. Hopefully to coincide with the shuttle.'

' "Shuttle".' She echoed the word, strange in an Orthean accent. 'That's a further exile than mine.'

'I've done nothing to prevent my coming back. All right, that's unfair, I know. No,' I said, 'Why am *I* apologizing?'

She chuckled briefly. There was a restlessness about her, her eyes moving round the windowless cell. Almost to herself she said, 'I wish I could see the city.'

'I don't believe it,' I said. 'All that time we were going to Corbek, and then in Shiriya-Shenin, and now—I mean, I can't take it in.'

The nictitating membrane slid over her whiteless eyes and she was animal, alien, unfathomable.

'Why did you come to Melkathi?' she asked.

'I wanted to . . . I don't know.'

'My errors aren't your concern.' Her single hand, corded and dark, strayed to her empty belt. She shook her head. 'I'd have found it easier with Huxton for an envoy, or Carrie, or that physician Adair.'

'Tell me something,' I said. 'Did you order Kanta Andrethe killed, or was Brodin telling the truth?'

'That poor Charain man . . .' She lifted her head. 'Don't they say chance is the last player in any game? Well, it's true.'

The silence was broken by Romare's dry cough, and the click of counters where two guards squatted by the brazier.

'Why did you ask to see me?'

'I wanted to know if you'd come. You understand me, Christie, better than my own people. Did the goddess birth us on the wrong worlds, do you think?' She smiled wryly. 'Worlds—and this a small one among many, yes. But all the same . . . I'm going away now, and even if they send you back, we won't meet again. So goodbye is what I wanted to say.'

'What will you do?'

She looked startled. 'I've lived by my wits since I was *ashiren-amari*, I won't starve now.'

Romare signalled that time was up. I stood. A thought came to me. 'Have you considered Kasabaarde?'

'The city of the Brown Tower? I wouldn't be welcome, I think.'

'The Hexenmeister doesn't concern himself with the internal affairs of the Southland. Or so he told me.'

'Envoy,' Romare said from the doorway.

'I'll consider it. There are many cities on the Desert Coast,' Ruric said with a thoughtful smile. I remembered she had been willing to go with bel-Olinyi. 'Goddess give you a safe journey, Christie.'

I couldn't tell how genuine the Orthean woman was. And so I was escorted back out, and searched again, and left the Citadel for air and sunlight; and it was the last time I saw *amari* Ruric Orhlandis.

And on Sixday:

'I'm not sorry to go,' Rodion said. 'Meduenin's a good *telestre,* and Ryloth will be milk-mother . . . Feel.'

She placed my hand high up under her breasts, and I felt the skin shiver; a movement wholly unlike a human baby kicking. She smiled. Her mane was not braided, the wind blew it about her veiled eyes. Golden eyes. Leaving Tathcaer, she took obstinate care to look as much a Witchbreed as she could.

The *marhaz* cropped the mossgrass a little way off. Here in the dell where we'd eaten lunch, thousandflower grew azure under stunted crimson *ziku.* The day was hot. Maric and Blaize were talking quietly, and I saw the young woman touch her *harur* blades, and heard Theluk's name.

'I never thanked you,' Rodion said. 'For the Ai river *telestre.*'

'There's nothing to—'

'That was my life. And in Kasabaarde . . .' her golden eyes cleared. 'I don't know, Christie. When you left Shiriya-Shenin, I wanted more than anything else to go with you. I wanted to travel. Now, after Riardh, I won't have a choice. And I don't know if I want to leave the Southland at all.'

'It's only for a year.'

'And in good company, I know. Travelling's uncertain,' she said, 'but I think I'll return, and you will, I know. We'll meet in Tathcaer.'

'I hope we do.'

The young Earthspeaker who travelled with them to Meduenin came and sat by us. He had the same serenity that I remembered with Theluk.

'Ruric-*amari,* also, will return.' Rodion said deliberately.

'She will return,' the Earthspeaker agreed mildly. 'Let the Goddess's fire heal her, burning that other fire out of her spirit; she'll live on earth again, *t'an* Rodion.'

'That's not what I meant.' The woman was sullen. A cloud shadowed us, going over the Rimon Downs on a west wind, and when the sunlight returned, she spoke. 'I've heard people say your Earthspeaker past-dreams are nothing more than memory, memories of people that once lived, passed down to us as Ruric-*amari* passed her golden blood to me. Nothing more.'

'Do they seem like that to you?'

'I don't know. You,' she rolled over on the thousandflower moss, facing me again. 'You don't past-dream, *S'aranth,* you have no *telestre,* no links with the earth—what's the Goddess to you?'

'I don't know, Rodion.'

The Earthspeaker linked his thin fingers, digging his claw-nailed feet into the moss. 'You were marked for the Goddess, *S'aranth.'*

'You heard about that?'

He shook his head. Shadow darkened his shaven mane: clouds passing. 'It's obvious.'

I said, 'I still don't know what it means.'

'Nor me,' Rodion said, 'and you live like this, you Outworlders, but I'm not used to it.'

'As for having no *telestre*—they call us the Landless,' the Earthspeaker said, 'because we leave the *telestre,* and we're the only ones who do. In the church there are no *telestres.* Having no land, we have all of it. It's only holding a small area of it that means the rest is lost to you. That's to be remembered in exile: owning nothing, you have all.'

Oru was straying, I saw, and Maric too deep in her own talk to notice. I excused myself and went to catch the *marhaz.* It was a relief to be out of a conversation I didn't understand. That Orthean certainty . . . not afraid of death because they know they'll return, not afraid of pain or disease because suicide is no sin. Living history and dead technology, the paradox of Carrick V.

I looped Oru's reins over a *ziku* branch. The *marhaz* lowered its head and butted me gently, hissing, and I scratched it behind the cropped horns.

Blaize and Maric, as well as talking, were engaged in playing *ochmir.* I watched them, lying under the stunted *ziku* with the board between them, and thought of Kirriach. That wilderness of snow and stone . . . and now the heat-haze shimmering on the Rimon Downs, and the wind-borne scent of wild *sidimaat.*

Blaize glanced up, his mottled red and white face twisting into a smile. He stared open-eyed at the sun.

'Time we were moving.' His broad hands swept the *ochmir* counters into their case, the game forever unfinished. 'You'll ride on further with us, Christie? You can still get back before sunset-bell.'

And Kirriach might have been the best time, I thought, when there was only the land and the cold to fight, and no Orthean or human malice.

'Yes,' I said, 'I'll ride with you.'

'I don't know what I've forgotten,' Carrie Thomas whispered, 'but you can bet your life it's something vital.'

'Everything all right, then?' Sam Huxton eased past us, not waiting for an answer. The long gallery was crowded now, at this farewell audience.

Carrie shifted uncomfortably, adjusting her uniform jacket. 'Lord, but I do hate the formal side of this job!'

'I could do without it myself.'

'I don't trust Ortheans to pack my data-tapes anyway . . .' she subsided, as Huxton struggled through a farewell address in badly-accented formal Ymirian.

Sevenday was proving so busy, I'd hardly time to realize we were leaving. Easthill Malk'ys had been packed and emptied by the midmorning bell—due to help from David Meredith, who I now saw in conversation with Evalen Kerys-Andrethe—and then we had no time for anything except hurrying to the Citadel.

'They could've brought the shuttle down on one of these offshore islands easily enough,' Carrie added. 'God help us if the boat sinks.'

'It's a ship, and—barring typhoons—we'll be OK.'

'That's a comforting thought.' She was sardonic.

A *jath* ship would take us to the Eastern Isles, the *Lyadine-Southwind* on its long journey down to Saberon and Cuthanc. And where was the *Hanathra* now, I wondered, and Geren? Still sailing west towards (if the satellite surveys could be believed) the shattered island-remnants of a great continent?

I put the memories aside and went forward to speak with Suthafiori, taking her final messages for the Dominion authorities. These were formal leave-takings, conducted with that style and sly humour that are the mark of the Orthean mentality. Dalzielle Kerys-Andrethe: complex simplicity.

'This, I hope, is not the last we shall see of you,' she said at last.

'I hope not, *T'An.*'

She wore *chirith-goyen* summer robes, her mane caught up in Dadeni braids; thin *harur* blades slung from her belt. Nothing marked her as *T'An Suthai-Telestre,* unless it was the shadow in her eyes.

'*S'aranth,*' she said, 'if your people accept our terms, bring the news to us yourself. The Goddess give you a safe journey.'

We went down from the Citadel to the *skurrai-jasin* in the square, Huxton and David Meredith, the Eliots, Carrie and Adair, John Lalkaka and the others. The light glowed on the dome of the Wellhouse, on the blank-walled *telestre*-houses, on the white paving stones of Crown Way. Pausing for Maric to catch up, I saw Haltern waiting in the last carriage, and joined him.

We passed through the crowded alien city, under a blazing starridden sky, the heat reflecting back from the high walls.

'It's a strange time we live in.' Haltern watched the scurry and bustle as we approached the harbour. 'Outworlders in the Southland . . . you realize, I suppose, it's the largest single change we've had to face since Kerys founded the *telestres*—since the Golden Empire fell?'

'Ah, but you take change slowly.' I knew stories of Earth were going out towards the Rainbow Cities and the Desert Coast, to the unknown lands beyond the Barrens. What would it be like on Carrick V, twenty years from now? 'You take us, we've had the star-drive less than a generation and it's tearing us apart, it's too much, too soon. But we'll adapt. We're good at that.'

'Oh yes.' Amusement flickered in his eyes. 'We're *n'ri n'suth* cousins at least, Earth and this world. Christie, will your people accept our terms?'

'Limited contact? I think so.'

But would they? There's Orthe's technology to be considered, I thought: the dead ruins, and the live remnants in Kasabaarde and Kel Harantish. How will they classify Carrick V, knowing that?

'There's Kel Harantish,' I said, not mentioning Kasabaarde. I know just how ambiguous a reputation that city has in the Southland.

'The Witchbreed, yes.'

The *skurrai-jasin* came over the brow of the hill and headed down towards the quay. Haltern brushed his sparse mane out of his eyes, blinking in the sea-wind. I followed his gaze: the *Lyadine-Southwind* lay where bel-Olinyi's ship had had its moorings.

He said, 'Whoever it is that holds the throne of the Emperor-in-Exile, it means trouble for us—perhaps for your people too, being so closely allied in their minds with the Hundred Thousand. That's part of the game. But if the Witchbreed sully us in your eyes—'

'You know I can't say what their decision will be. But that won't affect it.'

He nodded slowly. The *skurrai-jasin* were pulling up now beyond the office of the Harbourmaster, where the double-masted vessel was docked, lateen sails furled: the *Lyadine-Southwind*. Waiting on the noon tide.

'You know Suthafiori is giving you the opportunity to return.'

'They may not choose to send me.'

He stepped down out of the carriage beside me. 'More sensible, though, to send someone who's known and trusted; someone who knows their business.'

'Meaning that, having got me nicely trained, you don't want to go through it again with anyone else?'

'You know that's not—' he broke off, laughing, pale eyes as clear as glass. Shabby, ordinary, passed over in the crowd; and yet he can add recruits to the Crown Messengers, accompany the *T'An* Commander on military expeditions, keep a watching brief on an Outworld envoy. I wonder if Haltern n'ri n'suth Beth'ru-elen isn't the most remarkable Orthean I've met.

Maric leaned over the side of the *skurrai-jasin*. 'Christie, I'll miss you. Will you be back?'

'I think—'

But what I'm thinking about are the Eastern Isles, and how the shuttlecraft towers against the dusty sky, there where the warm tideless seas wash over the rock. Ninety days travelling between here and Earth, here and home. Time to get used to the Dominion, after close on eighteen standard months away. I adapt back at frightening speed, I know: to headaches, industrial stink, racketting noise, and blank, empty skies; and to warm homes, good food, soft beds, all the benefits of technology. Time to get over that first desire to be home. And time to realize *amari* Ruric Orhlandis, see her in perspective. After that, I can make a decision.

'I think,' I said, 'sometimes you have to go away to come back.'

Huxton called something from the dock steps, where the team were going aboard; I saw David Meredith waiting with him.

I embraced Haltern and Maric, and went aboard the *Lyadine-Southwind* with the other Outworlders. Sunlight flashed off the dirty harbour water. The shouts and smells of Tathcaer came clearly to me, and the city shone white under Carrick's Star.

The noon bells rang.

APPENDICES

Glossary

Ai-Telestre – literally the Hundred Thousand, traditionally all the *telestres* existing between the Wall of the World in the north, the Inner Sea to the south, the Eastern Sea, and the Glittering Plain to the west. Unified by Kerys Founder after the fall of the Golden Empire. Sometimes called the Southland, a translation of the Golden term applied to their province occupying the southernmost part of the northern continent.

arniac – a small shrub that grows in the infertile soil of the Desert Coast. Broad red leaves, black berries, growing to a height of eighteen inches. The leaf when dried is used to make herb-tea, and the berries are a cure for headaches and fevers.

ashiren – a child, nominally under fourteen; literally one who has not yet attained adult gender. Diminutive: *ashiren-te.*

ashirenin – one permanently *ashiren,* one who does not change to adult gender at age 13–15 but remains neuter. Change then occurs between the ages of 30 and 35, and invariably results in death. The *ashirenin* are rare, said to have strange qualities for good or ill. Most famous of the *ashirenin* is Beth'ru-elen.

ataile – tough-leafed herb growing mostly in Melkathi and the Rimon and Ymirian hills. When chewed, the leaves produce a mildly narcotic effect, and are addictive.

becamil – the webweaver-beetle, giving its name to the tough multi-coloured waterproof fabric spun from its web. Hives are kept commercially all over the Southland.

Beth'ru-elen – called Beth'ru-elen *Ashirenin,* a latent Orthean who died at 35 during late change to female. Reformer and revolutionary. During exile from Morvren Freeport spent time in Kasabaarde's inner city, formulated the philosophical and religious insights that led to the reformation of the church of the Goddess. Later became *s'an* of one of the six founding *telestres* of Peir-Dadeni: the *n'ri n'suth* line is still in existence.

bird's-wing – bush with broad, wing-shaped leaves and edible yellow fruit, common to Roehmonde and border Fen-country; striations of white on green-yellow leaves give 'feather' effect.

brennior – large quadruped used as draught-beast in the Desert regions. Sand-coloured, thick hide, tri-padded foot, tailless. Short flexible snout. Poor sight, good hearing. Omnivore.

Brown Tower – home of the Hexenmeister in Kasabaarde's inner city. Founded some ten thousand years ago on the ruins of an Eldest Empire settlement, for the preservation of knowledge. Most of the underground installations are defunct, though it is still said to have connections with the Rasrhe-y-Meluur and the ruins under the Elansiir. One of the two sole remaining instances of viable Golden technology.

chirith-goyen – or clothworm, the fibre-spinning larvae of the *chirith-goyen* fly. The fibre is woven into a light fabric throughout the Southland, and is easily dyed.

del'ri – staple crop of the Desert Coast, a bamboo-like plant with edible seeds in the knobbed stems. Pale green, growing to a height of six to eight feet. Harvested twice a year.

Desert Coast – general name given to that part of the southern continent that borders on the Inner Sea, and to the various ports and city-states there. Cut off from the wastelands of the interior by the Elansiir mountain range.

Earthspeaker – sometimes called the Landless. An office held by the members of the church of the Goddess after their training at the theocratic houses. They travel the Hundred Thousand, giving up their own *telestres,* and acting in a multitude of roles which may include priest, agrarian advisor, psychologist, healer, etc. The extent of their authority is impossible to define.

Emperor-in-Exile – hereditary ruler of Kel Harantish, chosen from the lineal half-breed descendants of Santhendor'lin-sandru's imperial dynasty. A tyrant with absolute authority in Harantish's highly-structured society. Claims the ancient right of ruling both northern and southern continents as the Golden Empire did.

fenborn – aboriginal race of Carrick V, now reduced in number and confined mainly to settlements in the Greater and Lesser Fens. Oviparous night-hunters living in a stone-age culture. In the past carried out raids of considerable ferocity on north Rimon and

Roehmonde, but have remained within the fenborders since Galen Honeymouth's treaty with them some two hundred years ago.

Fens – the Greater and Lesser Fens: marsh and fenland covering some two thousand square miles, paralleling the Wall of the World and separating the provinces of Roehmonde (to which it is comparable in size) and Peir-Dadeni. Not least among the dangerous fauna are the fenborn.

ferrorn – see *ochmir* appendix.

Goddess – sometimes referred to as the Mother or the Sunmother, or occasionally the Wellmother. A sun and earth deity. The church was designed and set up by Kerys Founder as an anti-technology device after the fall of the Witchbreed. It was later transformed by Beth'ruelen *Ashirenin* into a genuine religious movement. Now more of a philosophical discipline including a reverence for all life, and a recognition of reincarnation. They hold that their spirits pass through many bodies, reuniting in death with the fire of the Goddess ('fire' and 'spirit' have the same root-word in most Orthean languages); the main heresy holds that this is merely genetically inherited memory—possibly why the Hexenmeister is regarded with such deep distrust.

Golden Empire – the five-thousand-year rule of the Witchbreed race, under whose autocratic rule the two continents enjoyed peace, prosperity, and total slavery. Ended by Thel Siawn's infertility virus, which gave rise to a war that devastated most of the southern continent, left the cities and land north of the Wall of the World in ruins, and is still visible in the transformation of Eriel to the Glittering Plain.

hanelys – commonly called tanglebush, a plant propagating itself by runners; six to ten feet high, stems very hard black fibre with long thorns, yellow leaves during Hanys and Merrum, and small orange fruit in Stathern.

harur-nilgiri, harur-nazari – traditional paired blades, the former a kind of short rapier, the latter a kind of long knife. Used ambidextrously. Common throughout the Southland.

Hexenmeister – ruler of Kasabaarde, guardian of stored knowledge, and a sequentially immortal personality. Head of an information-gathering network that spans two continents.

hura – species of hard-shelled water clam found in rivers throughout the Southland.

jath – double masted, ocean-going vessel, usually with lateen sails; design originating in Morvren Freeport.

jath-rai – single masted small coaster or fishing boat.

jayante – short weighted weapon similar to quarterstaff, used mainly to immobilize or disable. Originally from the Rainbow Cities, especially Cuthanc.

Kasabaarde – a Desert Coast city with curious philosophies and influences. Sited at the point between the southern continent and the Kasabaarde Archipelago, gaining wealth from trade and tolls. Divided into trade-quarter and inner city, the latter run by the Order houses; both under the authority of the Hexenmeister.

kazsis – usually called *kazsis* nightflower, a vine native to Ymir and Rimon. Bronze leaves, dark red blooms, the scent is particularly noticeable after dark.

kazza – carnivorous reptilian quadruped, often trained in the Southland as a hunting animal. Short white pelt with blue-grey markings.

ke, kir – neutral pronoun used for the young of the Orthean species, and sometimes for the Goddess.

kekri-fly – an insect with a short segmented body and triple paired wings; coloured blue, green, or black, with reflecting wing-surfaces. Fond of sewage.

Kel Harantish – once a garrison outpost of the Golden Empire, now one of the smaller Desert Coast city-states. Dependent on imports for survival. Home of the last surviving descendants of the Golden Witchbreed, and the Emperor-in-Exile.

Kerys Founder – credited with spreading the *telestre* system that arose after the fall of the Golden Empire, of unifying the Hundred Thousand and founding the Kerys *telestre* at Tathcaer. Led the first crusade against Kel Harantish, and began the Southland's long association with the Brown Tower. Set up the church of the Goddess to prevent the rise of another industrial society.

Kirriach – ruined city over the Wall of the World, once known as aKirrik. Part of the Golden Empire's middle province, now called the Barrens, along with Simmerath, Hinkuumiel, Mirane, etc.

kuru – pig-like reptilian beasts sometimes domesticated in Roehmonde and north Ymir. Smooth dark red hides, small eyes and ears, tailless; cleft feet have traces of webs. Omnivores.

lahamu – riderbeast of the Barrens tribes. Long-necked quadruped with tough grey hide, solid hooves. Round cup-like ears, hooded eyes, and long muzzles with pointed upper lips; no manes, and flaplike tails. Very skittish and speedy; slender legs and sloping barrel-bodies, with a belling cry.

lapuur – the feathery-leaved tree of south Ymir, Rimon, and Melkathi;

pale green trailing foliage, main trunk growing to a height of ten to twelve feet.

leremoc – see *ochmir* appendix.

l'ri-an – one who is learning a trade or performing a paid service; usually a young adult or *ashiren*. Literally: apprentice.

marhaz – the common Southland riderbeast, referred to as *marhaz*-mare, *marhaz*-stallion, *marhaz*-gelding; of reptilian ancestry like the *skurrai*. Cleft hooves, and a double pair of horns. The thick shaggy pelt is composed of feather-structured fibres. Enduring rather than speedy.

marshflower – skin blemish: a dappled pattern sometimes said to resemble the marshfern, and to be more common in those *telestres* that border the Great Fens.

Melkathi – that Southland province distinguished by the Melkath language, comprising the Melkathi peninsula and the Kadareth Islands, the *T'An* Melkathi being resident in Ales-Kadareth. The most infertile *telestres* of all the Hundred Thousand, the most reluctant to accept Crown rule. Mostly comprised of heathland, bog, marshes, and sandflats. Ales-Kadareth has the name of being an old Witchbreed city, pirate port, and home of strange sciences. Famous for atheists, malcontents, heresy, and rebellion.

Morvren – small cluster of *telestres* holding land round the mouth of the Ai river; the Seamarshal is resident in the Freeport itself. Freeport has links with the Rasrhe-y-Meluur, Kasabaarde, and the Desert Coast; its language is a south-Dadeni dialect. A great maritime trading centre famous for voyages to strange places, river-craft, false coins, sharp practice, odd visitors, bureaucracy, and general moral irresponsibility. Rumoured to trade with Kel Harantish.

moss-eye – preying lizardbird found on the Dadeni Heath, with eyelike markings on wings.

mossgrass – staple vegetation of the Southland, a stringy-fronded species of lichen that roots shallowly in topsoil. Seasonal changes in colour.

muroc – shaggy white-pelted beast of the Barrens, tremendously strong but slow; stands five to six feet at shoulder. Short single pair of black horns. Carnivorous quadruped. Sense of smell excellent.

n'ri n'suth – 'adopted into the *telestre* of': literally translates as brother-sister. A Southland child bears its mother's name, its own name, and the *telestre's* name.

ochmir – see Appendix 2.

Peir-Dadeni – the newest province, founded five hundred years ago by a group of rebels from Morvren Freeport. Follows the Ai River, bounded on the west by the Glittering Plain, and on the east stretches from Morvren and Rimon up past Dadeni Heath to the Fens, and the Wall of the World. Keeps the pass at Broken Stair guarded. One founder was the reformer Beth'ru-elen, another the assassin Lori L'Ku, and another was Andrethe, from whom the ruling *telestre* takes its name. Famous for river-craft, trade, dubious frontiers, legends of Berani and the Eriel Frostdrakes; for the Heath's *skurrai*, the riverport of Shiriya-Shenin, and for mad riders. Swears alliance with, rather than allegiance to, the *T'An Suthai-Telestre.*

Rainbow Cities – general name given to the settlements in the tropical regions of the southern continent, of which only Saberon and Cuthanc are large enough to be properly called cities.

rashaku – generic term for the lizardbird having the appearance of a small archeopteryx. Feathered wings, scaled breast and body. Four clawed feet, the front pair greatly atrophied; gold eyes with nictitating membrane. Distinctive metallic call. Size and plumage colour vary according to habitat: from the white of the *rashaku-bazur* (sea) to the black and brown of the *rashaku-dya* (hill country). Other varieties include the *rashaku-nai* (fens) and *kur-rashaku* (mountains).

Rasrhe-y-Meluur – commonly called Bridge Alley, a remnant of Golden Empire engineering; being a suspended tunnel-structure built on pylons from Morvren Freeport down the Kasabaarde Archipelago to Kasabaarde itself. Still passable, though inhabited.

Rimon – central province, bordering the Inner Sea between Morvren and Tathcaer, sharing the Oranon River border with Ymir. Downland country, lightly wooded, having one main river, the Meduin. Famous for *marhaz*, grain, vines, wine, and border-river disputes with Ymir. The *T'An* Rimon is resident in Medued.

Roehmonde – northern province bounded by Ymir, the Lesser Fens, the Wall of the World, and the Eastern Sea. Hilly frosted country, famous for mining, metal-working, charcoal-burning and hunting. The *T'An* Roehmonde is resident in Corbek, a city that never wholly accepted Beth'ru-elen's reformation of the church. There are few large ports on the inhospitable eastern coast. Roehmonde is one of the largest and most sparsely inhabited provinces, a country of insular *telestres.* They guard one of the great passes down from the Barrens, the Path of Skulls.

rukshi – land arthropods, small and segmented with patterned shells and two pairs of claws. Now rare.

s'an telestre – landholder, elected to office by the adult members of the *telestre*, and having unspecified authority. More of an administrator than ruler, having more responsibility than power. The *telestre* is held in trust for the Goddess.

saryl-kabriz – an organic poison, fatal to Orthean life, distilled from the bark of the *saryl-kabriz* bush. Has a characteristic sharp scent, difficult to mask. Not to be confused with

saryl-kiez – a similar shrub, brown with blue berries, non-poisonous.

seri – unit of distance, equal to one and one-fifth miles on the standard Earth scale.

sidimaat – commonly called 'fire-rose', a large-blossomed bush that flowers once in Merrum and once in Torvern; favours the hot climates of Melkathi and south Ymir.

siriye – the starmoth, a triple-winged insect with poison sting. The wing-surfaces are luminous. Web-weaver. Common on heathland, and at the edge of forests.

skurrai – the Southland packbeast, referred to as *skurrai*-mare, *skurrai*-stallion, *skurrai*-gelding; double-horned and reptilian; basically a smaller stockier version of the *marhaz*.

skurrai-jasin – the *skurrai*-drawn carriages common in Tathcaer.

Southland – *Suthai-Telestre:* literally the south hundred thousand *telestres*. See: *Ai-Telestre*.

sweet mosseye – plant from which a sour wine is distilled, using the roots; a fern with eye-like markings on the fronds. Rare except in the Kyre.

takshiriye – the court or government attached to the *T'An Suthai-Telestre*, resident in Tathcaer (and Shiriya-Shenin during the winter season).

T'An – the administrator of a province: *t'an*, general polite term for strangers and visitors. Derives from 'guest'.

T'An Suthai-Telestre – in the informal inflection, the Crown of the Southland; translates as the *T'An* of the Hundred Thousand. Self-chosen from the *T'Ans* of all the provinces, re-elected on every tenth midsummer solstice. The unifier of church and *telestres*.

Tathcaer – capital of the Southland, an island-city solely under Crown law, sometimes called the eighth province. Home of every *T'An Suthai-Telestre* since Kerys Founder. The Hundred Thousand have each a *telestre*-house in the city; also there are the Guild-*telestres*.

telestre – the basic unit of Southland society, a community of any number between fifty and five hundred Ortheans living on an area of land. This unit is self-supporting, including agriculture, arts, and crafts. The *telestre* system rose spontaneously out of the chaos that followed the fall of the Golden Empire. Given the natural Orthean tendency to form groups, and their talent for making the earth yield, the *telestre* is their natural habitat.

tha'adur – a Peir-Dadeni term for the Andrethe's court and governing officials resident in the city Shiriya-Shenin.

The Kyre – a province of remote *telestres* in the mountains that lie south of the Wall of the World and north of the Glittering Plain. Very insular in character, occasionally trading with Peir-Dadeni. Mostly they subsist on hunting. The province is very sparsely populated; the *T'An* Kyre is resident in Ivris, a market *telestre*. Famous for milk, cheese, wood-carving, mountain-craft, and lack of humour, popularly supposed to be a result of the appalling weather.

thousandflower – mosslike plant growing in woodlands over most of the Southland, forms a thick carpet four to six inches deep, and varies in colour from light to dark blue.

thurin – see *ochmir* appendix.

tukinna – evergreen tree, thin-boled with black bark, twisted limbs, growing to a height of thirty feet. Foliage concentrated at the crown: scroll-like leaves, small black inedible seeds. Prefers northern climates (like Roehmonde forests).

Wall of the World – gigantic geological slip-fault that has split the northern continent in a northeast-southwest division; being now a range of mountains in which there are only two known passes from the Barrens to the Hundred Thousand: Broken Stair and the Path of Skulls. The barren land north of the Wall is occupied by barbarian tribes living in the ruined cities of the Golden Witchbreed.

Wellkeeper – title given to those members of the church who give up their own *telestre* to run the Wellhouses, sometimes called theocratic houses. These may be places of worship, of philosophy and refuge; working communes for adults or *ashiren;* universities or other places of learning, weapons training houses, or craft workshops.

wirazu – semi-biped semi-quadruped lizardbeasts found in wooded country; brown pelts, thin horns, run in herds of eight or ten. Herbivores.

Witchbreed – sometimes known as the Golden. Originally the humanoid race brought to Carrick V as servitors to the Eldest Empire—this being an apocryphal name given to the alien settlers who first landed some twenty thousand years ago, but died out soon after that. Nothing is known of the 'Eldest Empire,' but it left its mark in the genetic structure of both the Witchbreed and the native race of Orthe. The Witchbreed had great talent for using and developing the technology that was left to them, and made use of both the physical and sociological sciences. They fell to a sterility virus. Sporadic instances of interbreeding took place between Witchbreed and Ortheans, but in general the two species are not inter-fertile.

Ymir – the oldest province, with the most archaic form of language; occupying the land east of the Oranon that lies between Melkathi and Roehmonde. Good grazing on the Downs, good soil in the lowlands, and the many tributaries of the Oranon make this one of the richest provinces, famous for good harvests. The *T'An* Ymir is resident in Tathcaer. The *telestres* close to the city are famed for ship-building. Ymir is known for its theocratic houses, traders and merchants, beast-tamers, eccentricities of all kinds, and the most convoluted argumentative minds outside of Kasabaarde.

ziku – broad-leaved deciduous tree with edible fruit, grows to a height of twenty-three feet. Bronze-red foliage, dusty-blue fruit. Common in Ymir and Peir-Dadeni, preferring to grow near water. Hybrid form grown in Rimon with larger and more plentiful fruit, harvested in Stathern.

zilmei – found in north Roehmonde and Peir-Dadeni forests. Black and grey pelts, wedge-shaped skulls, and retractable claws. A bad-tempered carnivore. Distinctive hooting cry.

2

Ochmir

A game played in the Southland, originating in the cities but popular everywhere. It is played on a hexagonal board divided into 216 triangular grid-spaces. The 216 counters are double-sided, the ideogram-characters traditionally blue-on-white and white-on-blue; and are divided into *ferrorn,* which must remain stationary when placed on the board; *thurin,* which may move one space (across a line, not an angle); and *leremoc,* which have complete freedom of movement. The object of the game is to have all the pieces on the board showing one's chosen colour.

This is accomplished by forcing a reversal of the opposition's counters, by gaining a majority of colour in a minor hexagon. The 6-triangle minor hexagons form a shifting, overlapping framework.

The distribution of characters means that a counter may or may not have a duplicate value on its reverse side; it is thus necessary to remember when placing a counter what is on the obverse.

A 'hand' of counters is drawn, sight-unseen, from the *ochmir* bag on every sixth turn (a hand on Orthe is six). Only one move or placement can be made per turn, unless this results in a majority in a minor hexagon, in which case all the counter reversals are carried out. Since majorities are retrospective, the turning of one hexagon to one colour will affect the hexagon-frames overlapping it.

There are no restrictions on where on the board a game may begin, and it is usual for two or three separate pattern-conflicts to be set up. It is the *ferrorn* that determines the area of conflict.

Ochmir can also be played with three players (blue-white-brown), in which case the number of spaces that need be occupied for a majority in the minor hexagons decreases from 5 or 4 to 3. In this case there is also the shifting balance of alliances between players; and the game ends when one player gains the 144-counter majority of one colour.

A player may not turn own-colour counters to reverse. In the case of a 3-3 split in a minor hexagon it is left until the shifting framework divides it up among other hexagons. The game can be played with retrospective reversals even when all 216 counters are on the board. *Ochmir* is not only about gaining control, but about keeping it afterwards.

The game is based on manipulation, not territory; and on mobility rather than on rank. The values of the counters shift with the game; a player's own counters are also those of the opposition. These themes of interdependence, mobility, manipulation, and control have led some authorities to see a connection between *ochmir* and *Ai-Telestre*, and even to equate *ferrorn, thurin,* and *leremoc* with *s'an telestre, T'An,* and *T'An Suthai-Telestre.*

3

The Calendar of the Hundred Thousand

WINTER SOLSTICE: New year festival.

ORVENTA: the longest season, 11 weeks. Winter. Favourite season for the custom of keeping *telezu*. No trade, travel, planting etc due to bad weather. One of the two main periods of activity for *takshiriye* and *tha'adur* in residence in Shiriya-Shenin. Practice of arts, music, sciences, etc. Usually the First Thaw festival occurs around Tenthweek.

SPRING SOLSTICE: festival of the Wells.

HANYS: 3 weeks. Spring ploughing and planting: busy time for the *telestres*. Prevailing westerly winds. Floods. Inner Sea liable to sudden storms.

DURESTHA: Early summer, 8 weeks. Long spells of hot weather. Travel possible, roads repaired. Guild ships leave for Desert Coast and Rainbow Cities.

SUMMER SOLSTICE: Naming day and midyear festival.

MERRUM: 9 weeks, high summer. Period of great administrative activity in the *takshiriye*, resident in Tathcaer. Favourite season for travel, trade, sea voyages, etc.

STATHERN: 2 weeks. Everything stops for the harvest. Culminates in

AUTUMN SOLSTICE: harvest festivals.

TORVERN: 4 weeks, early autumn hunting season; also the time for fairs and markets. The last season for travel before winter weather makes the Inner Sea impassable.

RIARDH: 7 weeks. Hunting season. The beginning of winter, preparation of provisions, storing food, weaving, etc. Some late autumn sowing. Usually includes First Snow Festival.

Note:–the week consists of nine days, of which every Firstday is a feast-day, every Fiveday a holiday, and every Nineday a fast-day. The day has a length of 27 standard hours. With a 400-day year, this means that in practice the Orthean year is 85 days (12 weeks) longer than the Earth standard year.

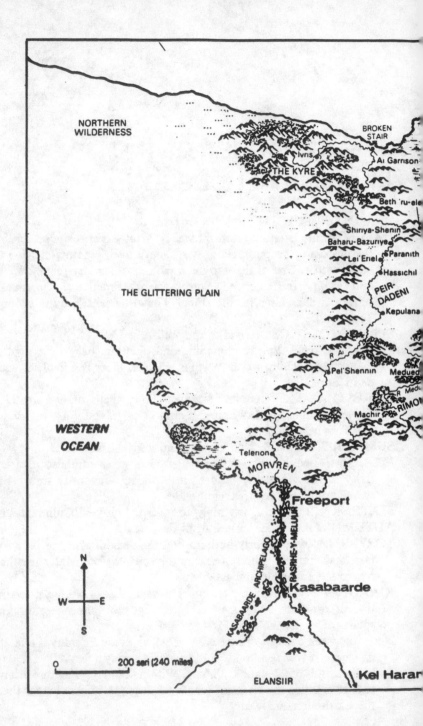

Kirriach

GREAT
FENS

WALL OF THE WORLD

PATH OF SKULLS

Skulls Garrison

ROEHMONDE

LESSER FENS

Oetha

R Berufal

DADENI
HEATH

Corbek   Temethu
Ereval   Remoth

R Berufi

ROEHMONDE FOREST

Salmar

R Turi

Afrual

R Orrin

Charain

YMIR

R Tumor

Toreth Sheratha   Terison

EASTERN
SEA

Gabrile   Hanathra

Damory   Elyre   Orhlandis
        Beriah
    Tathcaer   Rimnith
        Kumiel Vincor
Valerah   Rynnal
    Ahrentine Methemna

YMIRIAN HILLS

MELKATHI

MELKATHI
FLATS

Perniesse

THE SISTERS ISLANDS

LONE ISLE

INNER
SEA

Ales-Kadareth   KADARETH
                ISLANDS

sh

THE SOUTHLAND

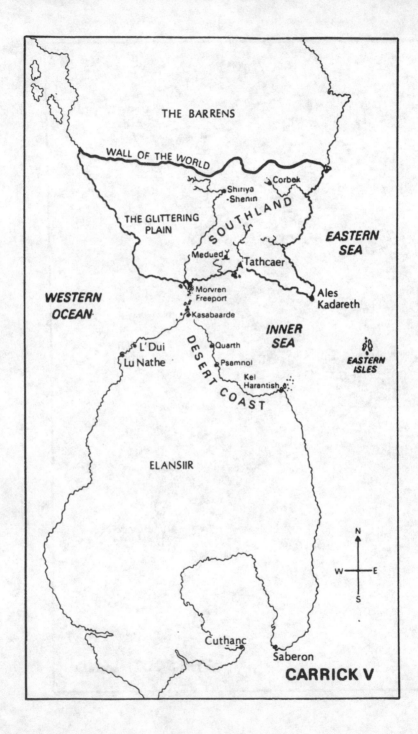

THE BARRENS

WALL OF THE WORLD

THE GLITTERING
PLAIN

Corbek

Shiriya
·Shenin

SOUTHLAND

EASTERN
SEA

Meduedꞏ

Tathcaer

WESTERN
OCEAN·

Morvren
Freeport

Ales
Kadareth

·Kasabaarde

INNER
SEA

·Quarth

EASTERN
ISLES

·L'Dui

Psamnol

Lu Nathe

DESERT COAST

Kel
Harantish·

ELANSIIR

N

W━━━E

S

·Cuthanc

Saberon

CARRICK V